Trapped

To Netta,
(at long last)
for always being a friend
Love

Mhairi Kay

Mhairi Kay

This book is dedicated to Bobby
(For his love, encouragement and endless cups of tea)

With grateful thanks to my mentor Sheila Martin M.A.

This story is fictitious, and does not relate in any way to any place or person

Chapter 1

1924.

*T*he atmosphere was electric; you could practically taste the girl's excitement and pleasure.

"Me Miss Black?"

"Yes Sarah, You."

Sarah stood in front of the Headmistress's desk, her face beaming, and she could not help herself. Miss Black held out a letter for her to take home to her parents.

"Sarah, this letter is to ask your parents to come and see me. You have done extremely well and the school has decided to put you forward for a Bursary. We feel that you would do very well in higher education. The Bursary would allow you to have any expenses paid. Who knows? You could even go to College or University. Do you understand what this could mean for you?"

"Yes Miss, thank you Miss."

"You are top of all the School and we cannot take you any further. The High School could. If you do as well there as you have done here, you could have a good future. I will meet your parents whenever it suits them. Let me know what their decision is and I hope everything works out for you."

"Yes Miss, thank you Miss, I will take the letter straight home now."

She flew out of the room. Miss Black was left smiling. The girl was well above average,

Miss Black seldom referred to anyone as brilliant in case she was proved wrong. Sarah Shaw was an exception, it never ceased to amaze the headmistress how out of a poor family, every now and again, one of the family would shine academically. She was sure that Sarah Shaw was one of these pupils. Whether her parents would allow it was another matter, only time would tell.

Sarah ran excitedly all the way home, a tall girl for her thirteen years, with her very dark brown hair and beautiful brown eyes. Sarah took the street and stairs to her home quickly.

Sarah lived in a poorer district of the town, where inhabitants were supported mainly by shipbuilding and its related industries. She lived in a Tenement on the top flat with her parents, one younger sister and three younger brothers. There were two houses in each storey containing two apartments with toilet, better known in Scotland as a room and kitchen and closet.

She burst through the door, which was never locked in the daytime.

"Mammy, Mammy, I have a letter for you and Daddy from Miss Black."

Her mother turned from the sink, which was piled with washing. She was a hardworking woman who never seemed to stop; she had no option with five children and a husband who never lifted a hand to help. Not many men did help at home, this was the age of the "master of the house" and women did what they were told, or even sometimes got knocked about for having an opinion

"Calm down Sarah, what's it all about?"

"I have to get to High School and, maybe College; I am top of the school."

Her mother dried her hands on her apron and moved to sit down at the table. She was old before her time and tired. In her eighteen years of married life, she had had ten pregnancies. Five of the babies lived and five had died, if not at birth then before they were two years old. All these births, shortage of money, poor diet and a taskmaster for a husband had taken their toll. A woman just turned forty years on her last birthday.

Sarah still excited was pleading, "Open the letter Mammy, open the letter."

"I can't Sarah, it says Mr. and Mrs. Shaw he'll kill me if I open it before him. Now you know that, tell me about it."

"Miss Black says I can go to the High School, I can get a Bursary, and I can stay on at the High School and learn everything I can, then get a better job. She wants to see you and Daddy." Sarah burst the words out in her excitement.

"No Sarah, you can't stay on. We need you working."

"I want to stay on and go to the High School, I want," she trailed off the conversation at this point. Her mother had banged the table.

"Well you can't, you will have to work and help us with the rest of them."

The rest of the family charged in the door, four voices all shouting at once; they suddenly stopped when they saw Sarah was crying. The other children knew from experience, young as they were, keep your head down and your mouth shut or the anger would come your way.

They all stood at the table, Mary ten years old, Jimmy eight years old, Andrew seven years old and then the youngest Archie just five years old.

"Why are you crying Sarah?" asked Mary

"For wanting something she canny have. Now straighten your face Sarah, before you father comes in. He has a job lined up for you, and it will be worse for all of us if you fight this."

"Miss Black says I'm clever, I want to go to the High School, Sarah was now shouting at her mother.

In desperation, frustration and tiredness her mother slapped Sarah hard across the face.

"If you are as clever Miss Black says, you will shut your mouth now. Don't you make this bad for me and there is an end to it. You get this washing down to the green and hang it up to dry. There is a good wind and it should dry.

Sarah's mother ordered the rest of her family, "you lot get out to play and don't get filthy."

Sarah did as she was told and stayed in the washing green as long as she could. As Sarah came back up the stairs with the empty washing basket she met Davie Russell who lived next door to them, with his mother and father. Davie was a year older than Sarah and was now working with the Carter in the town, delivering goods by horse and cart. Davie Russell was learning all about being a carter, and someday he had promised himself, he would have his own horse and cart. Sarah and Davie had always been friends and often told each other their problems. Davie saw that Sarah was upset.

"What's wrong, you been crying?"

Sarah told him about the letter and how she was not to get to the High School.

"Listen Sarah, don't cross your Daddy, but try and talk to him on your own. Wait till the rest are in bed. You know how he is; you will end up getting hammered if you cross him. I'll hear how you get on." They were now on the landing at their doors.

Her mother threw the door open, "What kept you, get in!" The door was slammed shut.

"Get that table set and butter the bread."

Sarah set the table for two; her parents ate first, when they were finished, the family was fed. Her mother placed the letter on her husband's place and she turned to Sarah.

"Now I'm warning you, keep your mouth shut." She stopped speaking as they heard the door open.

Archie Shaw handed Sarah his cap and jacket to hang up in the lobby, and went to the sink to wash his face and hands. A very tall man, six foot three inches, a strong man, whose work at the shipyard had made him strong. A man who worked hard for himself and his family but he came first in every-thing, his beer money, his cigarette Woodbine money, all came before his family. He was master of his house and family and woe betide anyone who crossed him. His wife stood by with the towel, "Hard day Archie?" she asked.

"They're all hard Missus and they get harder every day." When he dried his face and hands he sat down at the table." What's this Sadie?" he asked pointing to the letter.

"It's from the school about Sarah," she spoke as she placed his dinner in front of him.

He threw it on to the one fireside chair that sat in the corner by the fire. A working kitchen, also the main living room, sparsely furnished with a white wooden table and four wooden chairs. There were two recessed beds in the kitchen; the floor was covered with plain linoleum. The fireplace was a black cast iron grate, which also served for cooking food. One side of the grate was a coal fire which had a hanging hook, onto which a kettle or pot could be hung. The other side of the grate held a small oven. Food could be cooked very slowly if a fire was burning. The room was lit by a gas mantle which was only burned when darkness came. A Penny Meter paid for the gas, if the penny ran out; they would sit by the firelight. More than a penny a day was considered an extravagance, and often there would not be a penny a day.

They ate in silence because he liked peace and quiet for his meal. Only when he was finished he shouted for Sarah, who came through from the other room.

"What's this about? You been up to anything?"

"No Daddy, I'm top of the school and I can go to the High school." Sarah ignored her mother's warning look. "I can get a Bursary, it won't cost anything. Miss Black says that I could get a good job." She stopped when she saw the anger in his face, and then continued quickly ignoring her mother's warning look." Miss Black said I would get a better job and I want to go." Her voice rose and she spoke defiantly.

"Did you know about this Missus?"

"No, I only heard when she came home. I told her to leave it alone, but no, she'll no listen to anybody."

"Well she'll listen tae me, and don't you ever raise your voice to me girl, ever again"

He stood up and took his razor strap from the wall. The first crack came across Sarah's legs.

With the thought of not being able to get to the High School, Sarah screamed out at him.

"Miss Black said it would be better," Sarah never finished speaking because the second blow came from the strap came with all the force he could muster, for her daring to question him.

"Miss Black will no run this house, I will," and he continued with the beating.

"I've got you a good job; the sooner you start the better."

"Archie," his wife pleaded.

"I'll deal wi you later,"

He took out his temper on the girl, now cowering in the corner, Sarah had no escape and she was now screaming as the leather strap bit into her legs, bringing up red weals.

"Where's my tea, get me a drink of tea. Canny get peace in your own home." He dragged Sarah out of the kitchen and into the room. "No food for you," the room door banged shut.

Davie Russell, his mother and father sat and listened to the screaming, the banging and shouting. Davie stood up, "I'm going in there; this is all because she's clever."

"Leave it, Davie, you'll only make things worse. Listen it's over now. "

The three of them sat and listened. Davie went to the door and opened it. Mary and the three boys were all sitting on the landing. They looked at Davie, four pairs of eyes brimming with tears. "In you lot go and be quiet that will help Sarah and your Mammy."

What else could anybody do?

In the morning Sarah was told not to go to school, her mother could not look at her.

"Get the tin bath out and get a good wash, do your hair as well. You've to be ready for three o'clock. Your father will be home to take you to your job, I told you to leave it but you wouldn't. Time will pass and you will be back at the end of the summer."

"Where have I to go? Mammy please, don't let him do this." Sarah pleaded.

"Don't let him do it. You know better than anyone I can't do a thing. I wish it was me going away for the summer. We need the money and you have to help."

Sarah cried all morning but her mother never heard as she got on with her housework, as she knew there was nothing she could do. Sarah was ready and waiting for him when he came. Her mother gave her a parcel tied up in brown paper.

He changed himself quickly and they left before the others were back from school. He never spoke to her as he hurried down the street. A tall man striding out his entire six feet three inches frame, and with a scowl on his face, with no consideration for the girl hurrying to keep up with him. When they got to the corner they took a tram to Princess Pier, then a boat to Dunoon. It was a pleasant early summer afternoon, but Sarah was unaware of this.

It was a fine day for a sail as the steamer made its way down the River Clyde. She was crushed by the beating of the night before and that she was being sent away for being clever. Neither father nor daughter spoke to each other. He could not bring himself to even ask her to help him, why should he? She was his daughter, she belonged to him, and she would do as she was told.

Sarah was frightened, what was going to happen to her? She hated him for this, and she would never forgive him. She never even got a chance to say good-bye to her sister and brothers. She silently vowed that till the day she died, she would hate him.

They arrived in Dunoon early evening; he strode off the boat with Sarah still hurrying to keep up with him. The walked along the Promenade and crossed over into a big house. He rang the doorbell and a girl answered it.

"Tell Mrs Barr that Archie Shaw has brought his girl. A woman came out and told them to come in; she led the way into a small office. There was a desk and chair, with a chair facing the desk. The woman sat at the desk and said, "Please sit down."

"I'm fine Mrs Bar, I don't need a seat. This is my girl Sarah that needs a job. The Domestic Agency told me that you needed someone; Sarah's a good worker and she's strong."

"Hello Sarah," Mrs Barr spoke with a soft voice.

"Mind your manners, say hello."

"Hello."

"Would you like to work here Sarah?"

"Yes she would, do you want her? I've got to get back; I can't afford to miss the boat." Her father scowled as he spoke.

Mrs Barr looked at him and at the terrified girl in front of her.

"I will give Sarah a trial, and we will see how it works out. The wages are one pound and ten shillings a month. Food and board are part of the wages. Sarah will be paid at the end of every month."

"No, the money has to be sent to me, she's no to get it, she'll agree. Sarah nodded.

"What about stockings, she will need stockings, two pairs, black artificial silk. I provide the uniform but I do not provide stockings." Mrs Barr looked defiantly at the man. Mrs Barr had faced up to a bully before and there was no way, she would allow this man to dictate to her, raising her voice slightly higher, "Take it or leave it Mr Shaw, Sarah will need money for stockings and at one shilling and sixpence a pair, I think you will have to leave Sarah at least five shillings a month."

"The Missus and I were counting on one pound ten shillings."

Mrs Barr stood up. "Well I am sorry, if you do not want the job."

"Yes she does, right then, one pound and five shillings sent every month to me."

"Do you agree Sarah?" Mrs Barr asked. Again Sarah nodded.

"Well that it settled then. I'll get for the boat. You behave yourself; just let me know if you have any trouble, I'll sort her out," to emphasise this, her father pushed Sarah as he spoke. He never even said goodbye to his daughter as he left.

" I'll show you out Mr Shaw, you wait here Sarah."

Sarah was trembling; she could not stop the tears. How could her Mammy let this happen?

Mrs Barr came back into the room and sat down at the desk." Sit down Sarah." Mrs Barr watched the girl practically collapse in the chair, she was crying and gasping.

"Sarah take big deep breaths, come on now, and breathe deeply, that's fine now. Here dry your eyes," she handed Sarah a handkerchief. "Sarah, look at me," Mrs Barr commanded. "Nothing bad is going to happen to you here. You are going to help me run this Boarding House do you understand that? Look at me Sarah, look at me."

Sarah lifted her head, "Yes Mrs Barr, I'm sorry Mrs Barr."

For the first time Sarah really looked at Mrs Barr. Sarah saw a woman with a kindly face, smiling eyes, a bit like Miss Black, looked as old as her Mammy.

"You have nothing to be sorry for. Is this your first time away from home?"

Sarah nodded.

"You will be hungry?"

Again Sarah nodded. Sarah had very little to eat since yesterday.

"The dinner is over Sarah, but Mrs Malcolm, who is the cook, will find you something.

You sit here a minute and I will sort something out for you."

Mrs Barr left the office and went into the kitchen.

Mrs Malcolm and Lizzie Bradley were sitting together at the table. The kitchen was a large room with a white scrubbed large table which dominated the room; six chairs were placed round the table, against the wall stood a dresser which held all the crockery and cutlery. Two ovens stood beside the fireplace, one on each side of the large black fireplace. A door led out into a scullery which housed two large sinks and shelves where all the cooking pots were stored.

"I have just started a new girl and I want you Lizzie, to take her to your room. She has to share with you. Show her where everything is and then bring her back here for her supper."

Lizzie immediately jumped to her feet. "Right Mrs Barr."

When she had left the kitchen Mrs Barr explained to the cook. "We have our hands full tonight. This poor lassie has been brought here and did not know anything about it, I'm sure. Her father brought her and a right bully he is, left word that she has not to be paid. Her wages have to be sent to him. She has been crying for ages by the look of her and she is terrified. I am sure she is hungry; will you get her something Isa? There is nothing worse than a bully who thinks they own you," sighing heavily," If we don't get her settled she will be not be of any use here and we will get busy next week."

"Don't worry I'll see to her Jenny."

The door was knocked and Lizzie came in with Sarah.

"Mrs Malcolm this is Sarah who has come to work with us. Sarah needs some supper and then I think we could all do with our cup of tea and maybe a cake."

"Hello Sarah, you sit here beside Lizzie and Mrs Barr and I will sit here." Mrs Malcolm spoke kindly.

The two older women never referred to each other by their Christian names in front of any of the other workers who came in to help from time to time.

The cook busied herself and brought out a plate of cold cooked ham, cheese, tomatoes and a crusty loaf. A jug of milk was put on the table and Lizzie brought out plates, cups and saucers.

They were all watching Sarah; she was shaking so badly that when the cook poured her a glass of milk it was rattling against her teeth as she tried to drink it.

"I think a hot cup of tea would be better Sarah, you are a wee bit cold. Lizzie, make the tea."

Again Lizzie jumped up and made a big pot of tea, brought it over to the table. Mrs Malcolm piled ham, cheese and tomato onto a plate and handed it to Sarah.

"Tuck in, you'll feel warmer with something inside you," said Mrs Barr as she sliced the bread and spread the butter on it. "Would you like something Lizzie, this is not your supper just a bite extra to keep Sarah company." She nodded to Lizzie as she spoke.

"Yes please Mrs Barr." Lizzie could always eat. Lizzie was a thin slip of a girl, barely five feet tall, and a cheery cheeky girl, who had just turned sixteen, and had worked for Mrs Barr over two years.

Mrs Malcolm had poured the four cups of tea and brought a plate of cakes from the pantry. Lizzie had made a big ham sandwich for herself and was tucking in.

Sarah started to drink the warm tea and started to eat, she was so hungry and the food was so good she quickly finished what was on her plate. The cook immediately put more ham and cheese on the plate and Mrs Barr cut more bread. They all had a cake and more tea and talked amongst themselves, Sarah never uttered a word.

"Do you feel warmer now Sarah?" asked Mrs Malcolm."

Sarah nodded her head and then said, "Yes thank you, very much."

Mrs Barr noticed how well spoken and mannerly Sarah was and the girl now seemed a bit more settled.

"Now tomorrow Sarah, Lizzie will show you what to do. Just follow Lizzie and you will soon learn," then turning to Lizzie. "You take Sarah a walk along the Prom and let her see a bit of the place. No later than ten o'clock, mind Lizzie and no talking to any boys Lizzie. Do you hear me?"

"Yes Mrs Barr, loud and clear, I won't talk to any boys, but I can't stop them talking to me!"

"Lizzie Bradley!"

"Yes Mrs Barr, No boys."

"Off the pair of you go and back for ten o'clock or you'll miss your Cocoa."

"Right Sarah, come on."

The two girls left the house and crossed over onto the Promenade. They walked a good five minutes and neither spoke. Then Sarah asked, "Have you been here long, Lizzie?"

"Heavens above, she speaks, I thought you were never gonnie speak. Whits wrong wi you that you cried so much?"

Sarah told Lizzie all about how she had wanted to go to the High school and her father would not have it. He's very strict Lizzie. I miss my wee sister and brothers, I didn't want to leave home, and now I am trapped here."

Lizzie looked at Sarah, shaking her head, with all the wisdom of her sixteen years.

"Weel I couldnie get away quick enough,"Lizzie stated

"Naw, I like being away, and so will you. I don't go back at the end of the season, only for a visit. Mrs Barr lets me sleep in one of the attic rooms in winter and I get work from time to time that keeps me goin. I get a bed to myself here. There's eight of us at home and I share a bed wi my sister and two wee brothers, an one a bed wetter, no I like working here. Mrs Barr and Mrs Malcolm are no bad. You can see the meals are good. Mind ye have tae work hard but ye get paid end of every month an then there's the tips."

"What do you mean Lizzie, tips?"

"Do you no know whit tips are?" exclaimed Lizzie, thinking to herself, this one's right soft.

"I have not to get paid, my wages are to go home, but Mrs Barr has asked for five shillings to be left for stockings, every month."

"Well, wouldnie have that, your right soft, you work and they get your pay."

"But, Lizzie, I've to help my sister and wee brothers."

"The waens are theirs, don't be so saft. Anyway listen, the tips are good. When we get busy an we will. Folk on holiday like a lot done for them, carrying their bags, tea in their room at night, we have to make it an your running frae room tae room and up an doon tae the kitchen, extra toast in the morning. Well when they leave they usually, but no always, leave something for us.

Threepenny bit, maybe a sixpence, there's one man comes an he leaves a shillin. That money is ours, so it's extra, an don't be tellin about that. Keep it tae yerself."

"Do you not send anything home Lizzie?"

"We get a day aff once a month, I go hame then. I take sweeties for the waens an a leave ma mither something towards the rent, The old boy get five woodbine. Mrs Malcolm gives me something tae take hame. I think it's on the quiet right enough, maybe a jar of jam, eggs an sometimes ham. They think it's Christmas when I gae hame. We had better turn an go back, don't want tae miss the cocoa."

"What's cocoa Lizzie?"

"It's magic, a chocolate drink, Mrs Malcolm makes it wi hot milk and I take it up tae bed wi me, she slips me biscuits as well. Ye can be sure o this, I'll never cry tae gae hame. Another thing, you can have a hot bath on a Friday night, I love it, I lie back in that big bath an it's magic an all. Mind you have tae wait tae the guests are all in their beds, you'll love that an all. Mrs Barr lets me use bath salts, just about a tablespoon, magic, I feel great lying in that bath." Lizzie paused for a moment, savouring the memory.

"What are bath salts, Lizzie? Sarah asked, puzzled.

Lizzie thought for a moment, how could she describe bath salts, well one thing for sure, her brain was gonna get well tested with this one, fur she new nuthin, "Well, bath salts are like big sand, ye know, when ye let sand run thro yer hands, well it's bigger than sand

An it smells lovely, kinda flowery. You'll get it as well, mind now, no using their towels, take your own an clean the bath, or ye'll hear aboot it, are ye listening?"

"Sarah was dreaming about the bath salts, "yes Lizzie, I hear you."

They walked back along the Prom and Lizzie pointed out different boarding houses and small hotels. There were a few people out walking and Lizzie pointed out the holidaymakers and the local people.

"Dae ye fancy a paddle afore we go in."

"In the sea at this time of night." exclaimed Sarah.

"Aye in the sea, where dae ye think, come on."

Lizzie led the way down steps leading of the Prom and they sat on the steps and took off their shoes and stockings. The water splashed round their toes and they had to lift their skirt higher.

"My God, who done that tae you?"

Lizzie could clearly see the weals and bruising on Sarah's legs. One of the weals had been bleeding and looked worse than the rest.

"My daddy, because I wanted to go to the High school." Sarah said dejectedly.

"You're crying because of a swine like that, yer nuts. Am gonnie have ma work cut out educatin you girl, come on, cocoa time." They returned to the house and went into the kitchen, sure enough there was hot milk being mixed with cocoa powder and sugar, poured into two mugs.

"Right girls on you go to bed, the pair of you."

"Sarah let Mrs Malcolm see thae legs."

"What do you mean Lizzie? Asked the cook

"She's got right sore legs, one looks real bad." Lizzie looked at Sarah and the tears had started again. "Stop greetin. Let Mrs Malcolm see thae legs."

So Sarah took off her shoes and stockings and lifted her skirt. Mrs Malcolm never said a word; she left the room and came back with Mrs Barr. The two women looked at each other. Mrs Malcolm went and out of the kitchen and came back with ointment and a bandage, both women smeared the ointment on Sarah's legs. On the one that was bleeding they wrapped a bandage.

Mrs Barr spoke softly, "I'll see that first thing in the morning Sarah, I will check it every day till it is better, the pair of you off to bed now."

Once the girls had left the kitchen, Mrs Malcolm said.

"That's some legs she's got, all those bruises, did you see the how many there was Jenny?"

"Oh yes, I counted them, all in all, back and front she has over twenty bruises on her. I think she had been beaten with a belt that has wound round her legs and two are broken, one looks bad. I will need to watch that it heals. I knew looking at him and listening to him he was a bully, but he's worse than that. Men like him should never marry and have a family. He is a sadistic brute doing that to a slip of a girl and she's that cowed she's frightened to look anybody in the face. Let's you and I have a wee sherry and get the bad taste out of our mouths."

Lizzie led Sarah to their bedroom; it was a room that led off from a passage through from the kitchen. It had been a washhouse that had been changed into a bedroom. White washed walls and a stone floor. A rag rug was on the floor between the two beds. There was a wardrobe and a chest of drawers, with a mirror on the wall, against the opposite wall, below the window stood a large wooden sink. Lizzie told Sarah to use the two bottom drawers of the chest and we have to share the wardrobe, for the clothes that her mother had wrapped in the paper parcel, a few items of underwear and a blouse. Sarah had never had a place of her own before to put her clothes so she was mesmerised by it all.

Sarah followed Lizzie in everything that she done.

Lizzie put her mug down on the floor at her bed, then turned the bed right back down to the sheets, and pulled the bed back from the wall a little. Then she tucked in the sheets and blankets at the bottom and sides of the bed.

"Why are you doing that Lizzie?"

"Cos sometimes ye can get a creepy crawlie in the sheets an am no sharing my bed wi any spider and having anything crawlin up ma legs. This way am checking the beds fine an tuckin it in at the bottom keeps me safe. Am no losing ma virginity tae a spider." Lizzie laughed as she spoke.

Sarah looked puzzled, "What do you mean virginity?"

"Am a virgin an am staying a virgin tae a pick the lad that's going to despoil poor me."

Lizzie laughed as she said this. She realised as she looked at Sarah in the fading light that she did not know what she meant.

"Do ye no know anything about being a virgin?"

Sarah shook her head, "Tell me about it Lizzie."

"I'll tell you all about it, am educatin you an your gonnie be hard tae educate. Ye tell me something first, how come ye speak posh?"

"Miss Black told me always to speak a little slower and to pronounce each word. Not to have an accent, just to speak proper. Miss Black says that proper speech will take you into good company and good jobs. You should read as much as you can. Do you like to read Lizzie?"

"Naw, am no good at it, an you've been reading the wrong books if you don't know whit a virgin is. Right, get in the bed, lift your mug carefull like, they don't like you spilling anything on the sheets. Catch, here's a biscuit. Now here's the deal. You teach me tae speak proper an read an I'll teach you all about being a virgin an about boys, agreed."

"Right Lizzie, agreed."

The education of Sarah began, which took many weeks, with nights of talking in bed. Sarah read to Lizzie from a newspaper and made her repeat the words after her. Later on they bought a "Penny Dreadful", this was a women's magazine frowned on by decent women, but also the first paper to dare to refer to sex. This way Sarah learned things she could hardly believe and Lizzie learned to read.

Chapter 2

$\mathscr{S}$arah wakened with Lizzie shaking her, an alarm clock was ringing. It was six o'clock in the morning. Lizzie put off the alarm." Come on Sarah, we have got to move."

They both washed themselves quickly in the sink; the water was so cold that it soon wakened them up. They dressed quickly and Sarah followed Lizzie into the kitchen.

Watch everything that I do and then you can help do it tomorrow. They filled two very large kettles and put them on the stove to boil. Then they cleaned out the fires in the kitchen, dining room, sitting room and office. They relit the fires, using paper, wooden sticks and coal that was kept inside the large brass box that sat on the Hearths, except the office fire, which Mrs Barr lit if she used the office. They went back into the kitchen and the kettles were boiling.

"Now we can get a cup of tea and we take one to Mrs Malcolm at seven o'clock every morning and knock her door to waken her.

The two girls sat with their cup of tea and at seven o'clock they knocked Mrs Malcolm's door and handed in her tea.

They went into the dining room and set the tables that were required. Mrs Barr had left a note of how many tables and how many breakfasts were needed. When they went back into the kitchen, Mrs Malcolm had started the breakfast. The appetising smell of ham and eggs was more than Sarah could bear. Lizzie set the table for four and Mrs Barr joined them at eight o'clock. The two women and two girls sat down to their breakfast. Sarah could not believe how lucky she was, slices of ham and an egg was put on a plate and placed in front of her, two large slices of toast each and a cup of tea each. Once the breakfast was finished Mrs Barr told them what she wanted for that day.

Sarah and Lizzie washed the dishes and dried them. Then they went and put on a black skirt and white blouse with a lace apron over the skirt. As guests came down to breakfast, the girls served out as Mrs Malcolm cooked. Then they cleared the dining room when everyone was finished and washed and dried the dishes. Mrs Barr inspected every dish and every piece of cutlery before it was put away, ready for the next meal.

The girls changed out of the skirt and blouse back into their own clothes. They then went round every bedroom, making the beds and dusting. Again Mrs Barr inspected everything. When she was satisfied and not before, they all went into the kitchen, for a cup of tea, and one of Mrs Malcolm's pancakes. Sarah had never tasted such good food before. Mrs Barr then looked at Sarah's legs again, Mrs Barr changed the bandage and put more ointment on the open wound, and then they started work again.

The pattern was more or less repeated for lunch. A woman called Jeanie came into help with cleaning every afternoon. The girls were allowed one hour off in the afternoon but they could not leave the house. They were back into their black skirt, white blouse and apron for serving dinner at six o'clock. Mrs Malcolm gave the girls their lunch and dinner after the guests. The evenings were free when all work was done for the day. It was then time for them to wash their own clothes, as was necessary. They could go out but had to be in by ten o'clock and could not leave the house without letting Mrs Barr or Mrs Malcolm know.

Sarah settled down into the routine of the house and by the end of the first month she had learned everything well. It was noticed that Lizzie speech was greatly improving and she was following Sarah in greeting each guest with a "Good morning" or "Good evening."

Mrs Barr had commented on how well the girls were working when they were sitting having a break one-day. "I have to go out for a while Mrs Malcolm, I have had a letter from France and I know a lady who could translate it for me."

"Sarah could do that," exclaimed Lizzie.

"Can you speak French Sarah? Mrs Barr asked.

"A little, Miss Black used to take me some days for French and Latin, mostly phrases and lots of nouns. She wanted me to be able to cope if I got to the High school but I never got."

"What can you make of that letter?"

Sarah read the letter over, "I can't be sure but I think this gentleman is looking for accommodation for the month in August and he wants to paint, I think, he must be an artist."

Mrs Barr and Mrs Malcolm were clearly impressed with Sarah, and Lizzie had that look on her face, "I told you so."

"Could you reply to that letter Sarah?"

"I could if I had a dictionary, I could get one at the Library."

"Right then, later on we will go to the Library. A full month's accommodation is not to be turned down in August, just when things are slackening off. I wonder how he heard about this house."

"I think it says here that a Mr. Moffat told him."

"Mr Moffat comes here every year, must be a friend of his."

"I am learning to speak La Di Dah, Sarah is teaching me, Mrs Barr."

"Yes Lizzie I noticed and very well you are doing. Now down to more serious matters.

I notice that you are putting all your tips into a jar, are you splitting them between you."

Both girls nodded. "Well as you know it is pay day, so each of you come into the office when you finish, one at a time and I will pay you."

"Mine has to go to my Daddy Mrs Barr."

"I want to talk to you about that Sarah, so at three o'clock I will see you both. Now back to work."

Sarah had never worked so hard and never been so happy. As much as she missed her sister and brothers she did now not want to go home, she would speak to Mrs Barr about staying on in the winter if that was possible. She vowed she would never live in her father's house again. Three o'clock found both girls outside the office, Lizzie went in first and when she came out she was smiling. "See you in our room." Sarah nodded.

Mrs Barr called for Sarah to come in.

"Sit down Sarah and I will explain your wages to you."

"They must go to my father or he'll come and take me back."

"You do not want to go back then?"

"I will never live in his house again; he can't make me, can he?" Sarah asked anxiously.

"How old are you Sarah?"

"I will be fourteen in July next month."

"No I do not think he can but only if you are cautious. You see he abused you Sarah and you could have charged him. Not that I think the police would listen to you.

The day may come when children may have rights; women have now got rights but not yet children. I do not think it is fair the way that you have not to get share of your wages; however Sarah it is up to you to say what I have to send to your father. This is your wages, one pound and ten shillings. There is two shillings extra for all the hard work that you and Lizzie have done. There is ten shillings and threepence in your tip money, so I have divided it in two, five shillings each and I have put the threepence back in the jar to start of next month."

"Thank you very much Mrs Barr. I do not want to go home, I miss my sister and my brothers but I do not want to go back, please Mrs Barr."

"I am not sending you back Sarah. We must find a way to satisfy your father until you can please yourself. Are you going home on your day off?"

"I don't know what to do, send them the money and maybe they will forget about me. If they get the money, they will want me to stay here."

Very well, I will send the one pound and five shillings in a letter and inform them that you are satisfactory, and that I have decided to offer you the job for the summer. You take the five shillings that you may need for stockings, remember Sarah I will not have girls with holes in their stockings working in the dining room. There is your five shillings tip money and the two shillings extra. You should keep that for yourself."

"Mrs Barr can I ask you something?"

"What is it?"

"Can I stay here like Lizzie does in the winter?"

19

"Sarah I cannot pay you in the winter and your father will want you working."

"If I could get some kind of work to pay for my keep and to pay him, could I stay, please?"

"Well let me see what could be arranged, I can make no promises you understand."

"Yes Mrs Barr, thank you Mrs Barr."

Mrs Malcolm knocked the door at that moment and came in with tea for Mrs Barr and herself. "Off you go Sarah and we will go to the library next week sometime."

"Is she alright now Jenny?" asked the cook.

"She's fine, Isa. Her legs are all healed now, Sarah does not want to go back home, and has asked to stay the winter. I can't turn her away, nobody knows better than you that I see myself in that girl; I was terrified of my father. It is terrible when you are not wanted at home; it stays with you all your life. If she stays we will have to put on our thinking caps. I can't afford to keep them through the winter if they don't work."

"Here Jenny, drink your tea and I have made some cakes. It will be alright, between us we will come up with something."

Sarah raced into their bedroom, "Lizzie, Lizzie look." She held out the twelve shillings in her hand

"I know I got two shillings as well and the tips are good, what did I tell you."

"I know you did."

Both girls sat on their beds and counted their money. Lizzie separated hers out between her mother and herself. Wrapped it up in a handkerchief and put it under her pillow.

"Now your old man no tae get any of that, mind. Are you listening to me Sarah Shaw, Lizzie commanded?

"No Lizzie my father has not to get any of this money, old swine that he is."

Sarah spoke more polite than was usual. Both girls burst out laughing.

"Come on, Mrs Malcolm has left us tea and cakes in the kitchen, roll on Saturday night."

"What happens on Saturday night Lizzie?"

"Another part of your education and you will definitely enjoy learning."

Saturday night eventually arrived and the two girls went out for the night with a strict warning that they were to be in by half past ten, and not a minute later.

Lizzie tried hard to get an extra half-hour, because it was Saturday. Mrs Barr would have none of it. When Mrs Barr called you by your full name you knew she meant it.

"Lizzie Bradley and Sarah Shaw, no later than ten thirty, mind

Lizzie and Sarah set out after eight o'clock, Lizzie had put lipstick and powder on and had shown Sarah how to use it. The Prom was very busy and it was a sunny night.

"Where are we going Lizzie?"

"To live it up at the Dunoon Pavilion, after the show there is always dancing."

"I can't dance Lizzie."

"Well you will be learning tonight, did I not inform you that you would be more educated after this evening.

" Lizzie spoke so politely, they both started to laugh.

They paid their sixpence to get in and went into the dance hall. When the music started a boy approached Lizzie and asked her to dance. When the dance was over Lizzie came back, she brought the boy and another boy with her. She introduced Sarah and the four of them stayed together and danced with each other. Lizzie and the two boys showed Sarah different steps. She was just getting used to it when Lizzie said they would have to go. It was quarter past ten and they had to be in for half past ten. They left the dancing and ran all the back to the house. Mrs Barr was waiting for them at the door,

"You two were nearly locked out, go and get your cocoa and off to bed."

"Would she have locked us out Lizzie?"

"No she wouldn't, but I don't want to find out and the two of them went to bed laughing.

Sarah had never been happier; they were very hard worked as the summer season approached. There were times when they were too tired to talk to each other and fell into their beds at night. Nevertheless it was the happiest of times, money in your pocket, well fed and although Mrs Barr had strict rules about everything, she looked after her workers.

It was now another payday and both girls were waiting at the office for Mrs Barr. Again there was extra this month, there was twelve shillings in tip money and one shilling and sixpence extra from Mrs Barr.

"Your father now knows you have a day off Sarah, what will you do?"

"I don't know what to do, what should I do Mrs Barr?"

"Go home and see your family for the day, you must be back on the six o'clock steamer, so you must leave Greenock around four o'clock. Go in the late morning and spend a couple of hours with your family. Sarah, do not take all your money home; take enough for your fare and what you want to buy. Do not let your father know about the extra."

So it was decided that Sarah would go the next day. She left in the eleven o'clock steamer from Dunoon to Greenock and took the tram from Princess Pier to the corner of her street in Greenock.

Mrs Malcolm had given her a pot of jam and an apple tart to take home. She had bought her mother a pair of stockings, which had cost her one shilling. She bought sweets for her sister and brothers. She had a return ticket for the tram and steamer and had nine pence left in her pocket.

She was nervous when she went up the street, Jimmy saw her first, and he came running down the street. Sarah, Sarah, where you've been?

"I've been working, didn't Mammy tell you?"

"No, she said you were bad and they sent you away."

They were now at the door and Sarah thought, why did I bother coming home?

"Mammy, Mammy here's our Sarah", Jimmy shouted.

Her mother was sitting at the table combing Mary's hair; she could hardly look at Sarah.

"What brought you back then? You still got your job?"

"Yes, I got a day off and I thought I would come and see you, the cook sent this to you."

Sarah placed the jam and tart on the table and then gave her mother the stockings. She gave her sister and brothers the sweets and there were shouts of excitement.

"Jimmy you divide them out. How are you Mary?" Her sister turned to look at her, she had a black eye."

How did that happen," Sarah demanded.

"Don't you use that tone with me, Miss high and mighty, bringing your presents when we haven't got anything. Wasting money on a steamer and tram fare, oh great for you, but my cupboards empty", cried her mother.

"What happened to Mary? I want to know, please tell me Mammy."

"Well stay and ask your Daddy. Did you bring your pay?"

"No, it is his instructions that it has to be sent to him by Mrs Barr."

"Where did you get the money for this then?" Her mother demanded, pointing to the presents on the table.

"Mrs Barr gave me the money."

Her mother put her head in her hands, "Oh Sarah, It's not easy for me, I felt bad about the leathering you got. I'm tired and I can't get through all the work"

"Let Mary help you, sure you'll help Mary." Sarah looked at her sister and for the first time she realised that there was something wrong with her." What's wrong with Mary?"

"I don't know," her mother looked really tired, "I'll make some tea."

They sat with the tea and Sarah cut up the tart and gave her mother tea and cake.

Again Sarah Asked," What happened to Mary?"

"He leathered her and threw in the room, she struck her head on the door, and she seems dull since, he didn't mean it. He had a drink in him."

"Mammy she's only ten, he could have killed her. I hate him, I hate him."

"Sarah don't say that."

Sarah spoke vehemently, "I really hate him. Take Mary to the doctor."

"Your father will not give me the money; I'll get leathered if I take Mary to the infirmary, if he found out." He is a proud man and he wouldn't want anyone to know he canny pay the doctor.

"If I can get you the money would you take Mary to the doctor?"

"How will you get the money Sarah, and how would you get it to me?

"Listen Mammy, "I'll get the money to you, give me a week."

"Thanks for the stockings Sarah." Her mother put her hand on hers and they looked at each other. "

I don't know what to do for the best, Sarah. If I go against him he'll leather me."

"Things will get better, stand up for yourself Mammy, he's a bully."

"Will you come back for the winter?"

"I'll work as long as Mrs Barr keeps me then we will see, I'm going back on the six o'clock steamer."

"You look so well Sarah and bonnie." Her mother started to cry.

"Don't cry Mammy, we will look back on this and laugh. God forgive me for telling a lie, thought Sarah, I hated my father before and I hate him even more. I will never come back.

They had another cup of tea and her mother walked her to the tram.

"I'll get you the money, take Mary to the doctor, and let the doctor see Mary's face maybe that will shame him."

Sarah waved good-bye to her mother, wishing she had never come home.

As soon as Sarah returned to the house Mrs Barr was waiting to see how she got on.

Sarah told her what had happened and how she wished she had not gone.

"At least you and your mother are fine now, how will you get the money to her."

"The boy next door and I are friends, I will send Davie the money, and Davie will give it to my mother on the quiet. My father does not need to know about it. I hate him, for what he has done to Mary, and she's only ten. They have no food but he can get a drink."

Sarah sobbed her heart out on the kitchen table. As ever Mrs Malcolm was there with a comforting cup of tea,

"Come on now Sarah, I have kept you something to eat. If you cry much more you'll wash us all away. I have never known a girl with so many tears."

Lizzie came in with dishes for washing. "Awe no, yer no greetin again."

Mrs Barr, Mrs Malcolm and Sarah all together shouted.

"Lizzie, speak properly." All four of them started to laugh.

"That's better now, eat up Sarah; you're home where you belong."

Sarah wrote to Davie and enclosed a ten-shilling note that she had been saving for the winter. She told him that Mary needed to see a doctor. Would he please give this money to her mother on the quiet? Her father must not know. How she was sorry that she could not say good bye to him before she left and how she hoped everything was fine with him and his family. I miss my sister and brothers and I miss you Davie, you were the only friend I had. I am happy in my job and Mrs Barr is very good to me. This is something else my father should not know. If he thought I was happy he'd drag me back, I felt when I came here to work I was trapped into work I did not want but I love it here.

She signed her letter and Mrs Barr gave Sarah a stamp and Sarah went and posted it the same night. There was not much more Sarah could do.

The house was very busy over the next weeks and everyone was working longer than normal. Lizzie explained that as the July Trade holidays started they would even get busier. After work most nights if it was nice the girls went for a walk and then a paddle in the sea. Sarah was still teaching Lizzie reading and now spelling and Lizzie was telling Sarah all about boys and how she had to look after herself. Mrs Barr had spoken to Lizzie about Sarah being too young to go dancing and not to take her again before her birthday. Mrs Barr had taken Sarah to the Library to borrow a French Dictionary and the letter was sent to Monsieur Pierre Renaud, that accommodation was available for him with Mrs Barr for the month of August. Sarah suggested that Mrs Barr write a letter also, in English.

The Library fascinated Sarah and Mrs Barr allowed her and Lizzie to borrow books occasionally and Sarah would read to Lizzie at night.

August came and brought with it Monsieur Pierre Renaud. A very quiet unobtrusive Frenchman, who was friendly with another of Mrs Barr's summer guests, both men were artists and went out most days to paint. Sarah had taught Lizzie how to say a few phrases in French and they had such laughs and a good time that August. When August was over and the house became quiet Mrs Barr told them that there would be no more guests after September. She had spoken to a few people about looking for work for the girls in the winter and she was hopeful of getting them part time waitress's jobs. There were a lot of

Business dinners in the large hotels in the winter and there could be something in the kitchens.

Sarah went home for a day at the end of August and as before Mrs Malcolm had given her something for her mother. Sarah did not buy anything this time but took some money for her mother and threepenny pieces for her sister and brothers.

When Sarah arrived at the house she was dismayed to find her father there. A boat from the local shipyard was going out on trials and her father had the day off as he was going out with the boat. Trials could last a week or two and it meant he would be away for days.

Her mother was busy getting his clothes ready and when Sarah went in he said,

"Just in time to help, have you brought your wages?"

"You know Mrs Barr sends them to you, I don't get them." Her mother threw Sarah a warning look. Sarah did not care." You will not be getting wages after September, Mrs Barr is keeping me on for the winter but I only get food and lodgings. She cleans the whole house top to bottom in the winter and I have to help her."

"Well find another job." Her father demanded.

"I will not and you will not make me." Sarah spoke defiantly.

As her father rose from the chair Sarah said, "You touch me and I'll split you open. I could have had you charged the last time you beat me. I spoke to the police and they told me the next time it happened you could go down for it."

"He lifted his hand to strike her and frightened as Sarah was, she stood in front of him.

"Go on try it, you're nothing but a big bully. If I hear of you hitting any of them again I'll report you to the police."

Her father hand fell to his side and he walked out of the kitchen.

"Sarah, what's got into you, we'll all suffer," her mother cried

"No you will not if you stand up to him. Look I'm not waiting. How did you get on with the doctor for Mary?"

"He thinks she's deaf. He is going to have some kind of test done to see how bad it is. I told him she fell and he said it could be temporary. Your money was a godsend," her mother whispered incase he would hear.

"Mrs Malcolm gave me a dozen eggs for you and here take this; she put five shillings in her mother's apron pocket and give these three penny pieces to the rest of them.

I'll ask Mrs Barr to send my money to you tomorrow and anyway he won't be here. Stand up for yourself; at least you'll get peace when he's working away. Remember the good time we had when he went on trials before."

"Remember how he came back drunk," her mother answered.

"I am away Mammy; if I had known he was here I would not have come. Try and let me know how Mary gets on, Davie would write a letter for you."

As Sarah left the house and was going down the Close Stairs she met her father coming up, she ignored him and as she turned to go down the next flight of stairs she shouted.

"I am warning you, don't look for any more money from me and don't touch my mother or my sister or my brothers. You're the one who made Mary the way she is. I will go for the police, I'm warning you, you swine."

Her father went back into the house and lifted a chair from the table and threw it back down on the floor. Her mother lifted the other chair and threw it back down on the floor as hard as she could. He sat down at the fireside with his head in his hands.

"From now on Archie things are different in here. I won't need Sarah to go for the police, I will." She returned to her washing.

When Sarah returned to Dunoon she related what had taken place with her father.

Mrs Barr, Mrs Malcolm and Lizzie were listening spellbound," Good for you girl, see you have learned something from me," Lizzie said.

"All very well for you but it was me who wet my knickers with fright," Sarah explained.

They all started laughing.

"Tried sitting on a tram and a boat with wet knickers, if you lift your skirt the seats wet, so I had to stand all the way back and folk wondering what was wrong with me."

They were all helpless laughing. "Mrs Malcolm I'm desperate for your tea."

"You shall have it and two cakes for being brave."

"Mrs Barr please, do not send any more money to my father, I would like my mother to get half of my wages and I will just have to see how the winter works out."

"Well Sarah I am delighted to see you asserting yourself, you have come a long way this summer from the frightened girl you were. Mrs Malcolm bring out the cakes and we'll all have two each."

The holiday towns on the Clyde River always made a big effort with lights on the promenade and special concerts and bands in the parks. September holiday weekends lasted most of the month, with each town taking a different weekend, for this trade was the last till the early summer of the following year. Dunoon like the rest of the holiday resorts became very quiet and all the Boarding Houses closed down for the winter months and Mrs Barr made a list of everything that had to be done, before closing the house down for the winter.

Lizzie and Sarah washed all dishes and cutlery and they were all put into cupboards that would not be used till the following Spring. All the silver trays, milk jugs, sugar bowls and the condiment sets were all cleaned and wrapped in newspaper, not to be used till the next Spring.

All beds were stripped and all linen and blankets were washed, all linen ironed and again all put away in the linen cupboard.

All rooms thoroughly cleaned and mattresses up-ended for airing. Everyone worked hard and helped each other. Jeanie came in to clean all floors, carpets, and windows and polish anything that stood still. Lizzie said they were all to keep moving or Jeanie would polish them as well.

After all the work was finished Mrs Malcolm made a lovely tea and Mrs Barr paid them all a bonus of two pounds each for the end of the season.

The end of September wages was the first that Sarah kept to herself.

Mrs Barr moved Lizzie and Sarah into the two attic bedrooms, but both girls still wanted to share the one bedroom and Mrs Barr agreed. It was a long narrow room with Cam Ceiling and the window looked out onto the sea front. Mrs Barr gave them extra blankets; she said that it would be much colder as the winter progressed. The girls were to share the kitchen fire through the day and sit with Mrs Malcolm and Mrs Barr at night. This way it would be warmer and would help to keep costs down

Once Lizzie and Sarah were in their bedroom, they sorted out their money.

"I can't believe I have all this money Lizzie," Sarah exclaimed. One pound ten shillings in wages and six shillings in tips, add the two-pound bonus and I have three pounds, sixteen shillings

"Sort it out; it has to do a long time. We might not get a lot of work and we must pay Mrs Barr for our food, or we will have to go home."

"I am not going home to stay, I'll go for the day but that's all. Mrs Barr said that we should go home for a day at the beginning of October as the weather will change and there will not be as many boats sailing in the winter. Will you go for a day Lizzie?"

"Yes but I will not go back again until the Spring, you should do the same because if a storm or bad weather comes the steamers will not sail and you could be stuck at home. Now you wouldn't want that, would you?" Lizzie asked

"No I would not, remember how I cried Lizzie?"

"I'll never forget you nearly washed us all away." Sarah was quiet for a while and Lizzie said," Don't you be going sad on me? Come on you, it is time to go for our tea."

They both went downstairs and joined Mrs Malcolm and Mrs Barr in the kitchen. Mrs Barr told them that she had a few cleaning jobs lined up for them both and they were to be taken on as waitresses nearer the Christmas season. Mrs Malcolm was knitting and Sarah asked her if she would teach them to knit.

"Speak for yourself Sarah, my free time is just that, free." Lizzie laughed.

"I will teach you both to knit and bake if you like," Mrs Malcolm replied.

"I would like to be able to bake and cook properly. I will learn to knit as well."

"Then so you shall," Mrs Malcolm said.

"All this education is not good for me," Lizzie replied, as they all laughed.

Sarah went home at the beginning of October to see her family. She went mid-morning and arrived to find her mother at home alone.

"Where's Mary, Mother?"

"Mrs Russell has taken her out for a while; Mrs Russell has been so kind since the accident. They won't have Mary at school at all, I still have not heard from the hospital."

It had not escaped her Mother that Sarah had not called her Mammy as usual. There was no doubt about it; Sarah had blossomed since working in Dunoon.

"You look real nice and bonnie Sarah, one thing for sure Dunoon seems to suit you."

"I love it there, Mrs Barr is keeping me on but I will not make much money in the winter. If I can help I will. The steamers are often off in the bad weather and I may not be back till the Spring but I will send you something if I can. Are the boys fine?"

"Yes they are getting bigger; Jimmy is sprouting and getting tall. They'll no be pleased if they don't see you Sarah."

"I have got to go back on the four o'clock steamer at the latest. Now this is for you."

Sarah left one-pound note on the table, a pair of stockings and sweeties for Mary and the boys.

"I'm grateful Sarah, your Daddy is working full time at the moment and getting some overtime, but I don't get any of that. Things are much better; mind how you told me to stand up to him. Well I did."

She related how she nearly hit him with a chair and they both started laughing.

"I miss you more than I ever thought I would, would you no come back, Sarah?"

"No it is better this way, maybe someday but not just now." Sarah hoped God would forgive her for the lie.

"I'll make a cup of tea and thanks for the money; you know I'll not waste it. I went to the Church Guild and they were asking me where I bought my nice stockings. I was so proud to tell them you bought them for me."

Sarah was choked up, it was the first time her mother had ever really said anything nice to her to make her feel good.

"I'll get away for the Tram, I must not miss the steamer, Mrs Barr is good but she's strict and I want this job."

"I am sorry you couldn't stay on at the school Sarah, what could I do against him?"

Her mother spread out her hands in a useless gesture, "I am sorry."

"It does not matter now, don't worry about it, but I will never forgive him. Not because he would not let me go to the High School, more because he would not even try, he would not even talk with Miss Black, and also for the beating he gave me. Do not worry anymore, everything will be fine, stand up to him, do you hear me? Sarah pleaded."

Her mother nodded her head, "I'll try, and I'll try."

"Good, now I will need to get on my way."

They walked down to the tram together, mother and daughter, arm in arm.

"I will send more money when I can; there are no extras when they are closed. Take care of yourself, and if you need me get Davie to write."

The waved goodbye to each other, understanding each other better not so much as mother and daughter, more like two women who were friends.

Sarah returned to Dunoon and as usual they were waiting for her, when Sarah told them how she felt that she understood her mother better this time. And how she did not feel so angry with her mother any more.

"Mrs Barr said, "Maybe you just understand a bit better, that there was nothing she could do against you father."

"I hate him and I always will."

"Don't hate so much Sarah, hate can eat you up and the only one harmed is you.

The weeks passed and as promised Mrs Barr got work for Lizzie and Sarah. They went out on cleaning work together and they were waitressing at the weekends. Sometimes there was a lot of work, and sometimes a little. At Christmas they were rushed of their feet and were often tired, but the money was good and they were able to pay their way with Mrs Barr.

Mrs Malcolm taught Sarah to knit and before Christmas she had knit knee-high socks for the boys and a cardigan for Mary and her mother. She sent a parcel home for Christmas and Mrs Barr had talked Sarah round to knitting a pair of socks for her father.

"Sarah it will make things better for the rest of them if he gets a present as well," Mrs Barr reasoned with her

Christmas spent with Mrs Barr, Mrs Malcolm and Lizzie, was one of the best Sarah had ever had. Mrs Malcolm made a lovely Christmas dinner and they all exchanged presents.

Lizzie and Sarah had bought the two older women a box of handkerchiefs each. Mrs Malcolm had knitted them all gloves and matching scarves. Mrs Barr gave them all a lovely box of writing paper and envelopes. Then Mrs Barr produced another surprise for everyone. She had bought a Wireless, which worked by battery, rechargeable at one of the local shops. The all listened to the King's Christmas Day Message. Then they listened to Christmas music and Mrs Malcolm had them all singing. Lizzie was dancing round the kitchen pretending she had a dancing partner. They were all so happy that Christmas, although it did make Sarah wonder about her family's Christmas and she hoped all was well for them.

Mrs Barr produced a bottle of sherry and the girls tasted their first drink, which Mrs Malcolm watered down for them. The following week was Hogmanay, which brought the New Year. The girls were busy at work with various functions that were on, over the festive period. The months flew past and before they knew it the house was being opened up for another season. All the rooms were again cleaned and aired; everything unwrapped and brought back out ready for use. From April Lizzie and Sarah were once again working for Mrs Barr.

Chapter 3

1926

Sarah had come along way under the care of Mrs Barr and Mrs Malcolm. In her spare time she was still learning her French lessons, teaching herself with books from the library. Monsieur Pierre Renaud once again booked for the full month of August and he helped Sarah with her pronunciation. She continued to see her family once a month and continued to help her mother. Sarah visits were always when her father was at work. On her visit in April her mother told her that they had all been delighted with the Christmas parcel and that her father showed everyone the socks she had knitted for him. It meant nothing to Sarah. Her mother thanked her for the money she sent and told her that things were now better for all of them and she was sure it was all Sarah's doing. Mary was deaf; the tests at the hospital had proved this. There was not much they could do and Mary had withdrawn into herself and rarely tried to speak. When Sarah saw her brothers and sister they always clung to her and did not want her to go.

Sarah had now spent over two years with Mrs Barr and her sixteenth birthday was now only a few weeks away in July, which was the busiest time of summer with Glasgow Fair holidays being the busiest.

Lizzie and Sarah had very little time off, most nights they tried to go for a walk and have a paddle in the sea. They usually sat on the same steps depending on the tide and of late a young man would come and speak to them. He was very interested in Lizzie and Lizzie in him. He was a local lad and worked with the fishing boats. His name was John Duncan.

"Do you girls never get a night off?" he asked one night.

"At the end of the month," Lizzie was quick to reply.

"Maybe we could go for a walk?"

"All three of us?" Sarah laughed, and hurried on in front of them.

Lizzie caught up with her as they were hurrying back to the house.

"John Duncan has asked me to go out with him."

"Do you like him?"

"I'll not know till I go out with him."

They were laughing as they went up the front path. Mrs Barr came out to meet them.

"Lizzie, go straight into the kitchen. Sarah you come with me."

"What's wrong Mrs Barr? Sarah asked anxiously.

"Remember Sarah, I am your friend and you are not alone. There are two people to see you."

Mrs Barr led Sarah into her office where Sarah was surprised to see Davie Russell and a police officer.

"Sit down Sarah, "Mrs Barr spoke quietly.

Sarah looked at Davie asking, "Davie why are you here? What's wrong?"

"I came so I could be here for you, the policeman needs to speak to you Sarah."

Sarah looked at the policeman.

"What's wrong, it is my family?"

"I am Sergeant Murdoch. Are you Sarah Shaw?"

"Yes," whispered Sarah.

"I am very sorry to inform you that there has been a terrible accident, your parents Archibald Shaw and his wife Sarah are dead."

Mrs Barr came and put her arms round Sarah.

"What happened? How? Why?"

"A crowd of them all went out in a boat two nights ago, they were drinking, and the weather was nice. They only went for a wee sail on one of the boats from the rowing club. Someone must have stood up or something, they all ended up in the water. The boat was apparently upside down. Your father saved them all except himself and your mother."

Davie held Sarah's hand as Sergeant Murdoch explained everything to her.

"From what we know, we think you mother was trapped under the boat and your father, trying to find your mother saved everyone else. He went back looking for your mother. That was the last time anyone seen him."

Sergeant Murdoch stopped speaking for a moment. She was only a young girl, sometimes he hated his work and this was one of these times.

There was silence for a minute and then Sarah stood up and walked round the small room, she was like a caged animal, she walked back and forward, she folded her arms across her chest.

"My poor mother, my poor mother," the tears started then.

Mrs Barr led her back to a chair and sat her down. Mrs Barr held Sarah for a while.

"What will I have to do now? Mrs Barr."

"Take each day as it comes Sarah, everything will work out, it will take time but you will be alright."

Sarah looked at the policeman, "what happens now?"

"I am sorry but you are the next of kin and the bodies must be identified by you. You must come back to Greenock as soon as possible."

"Davie, what will I do?"

"We will sort it out, that is why I came, and I am here to help you. You must come back with me." Davie knelt down in front of Sarah." We always helped each other haven't we?"

She nodded. The policeman and Mrs Barr looked at each other; it was a pitiful sight that was before them, a young man about eighteen and a young girl nearly sixteen, having to deal with such a terrible tragedy.

Mrs Barr left the room and came back with a tray with tea and biscuits.

"Drink some tea Sarah, I have sent Lizzie to get your things. You have to go back tonight on the late steamer. Don't worry about things here. Let Mr Russell help you. Please have tea before you all go."

Lizzie came into the room with a small case and Sarah's handbag.

"Oh Sarah, Oh Sarah," the tears were running down Lizzie's face. The two girls clung to each other. Mrs Barr separated them.

"Come on now, you have to be strong, both of you."

She led Lizzie away from Sarah and out of the room.

Sarah, Davie and Sergeant Murdoch all left for Greenock on the ten o'clock Steamer.

It was only when they were on the Steamer that Sarah asked,

"Is Mary and the boys with your mother Davie?"

This was a question he had hoped Sarah would not ask until they were home. He had to be careful how he answered this.

"They only found your father today; your mother was found yesterday. It took time to sort things out. My mother could not cope Sarah with the four of them and I had to come for you. The Minister took charge of the boys and Mary. You will see them soon. They do not know yet what has happened. You have to understand that everybody is upset. The Minister did what he thought was best."

"Our Minister, the East Shore Church Minister."

"Yes, he came and helped. He did what he thought was best meantime."

"Are they with the Minister's wife?"

"No they are in care." Davie answered Sarah hesitantly.

"What do you mean, in care, in care of what?" She was staring at him and she started to shake.

" Oh no Davie not, Ravenston, not the Poor House, tell me he did not put them in the Poor House."

"It's only till we sort things out. You will have to see to a funeral for your mother and father first."

"No Davie, I'll see to my brothers and sister first, they are still living and they need me more."

"Wait till we get back and then we will sort it all out as I promised you, what was I supposed to do Sarah? I done what I thought was best."

"It's alright Davie, I should have stayed at home, this might never have happened. If anyone is to blame it's me."

"Don't blame yourself; we all know who's to blame here. It is too late to start blaming anyone. We have to get you through this and then we will get the boys and Mary, right."

She nodded; nobody spoke until they were at Princess Pier. The police met them from the boat and took them to the police mortuary. Davie stood with her as she identified her mother and father, it was as if they were both sleeping, she stood looking at them. Davie turned her away and took her home.

Mr and Mrs Russell were waiting for them, there was nobody about as they went up the close entrance?

"You'll stay here tonight Sarah, it is all sorted." Mrs Russell spoke as she put her arms round the girl; Sarah sobbed her heart out in Mrs Russell's arms."

She drank the hot tea and choked on it. Mr Russell had laced it with brandy.

The next day Davie and Mrs Russell took her to the Undertaker and a funeral was arranged for two days later. Then they went back home. Sarah was hesitant as she opened the door of the house. It was all so quiet. Her mother's apron was on a chair, it seemed unreal, and her father's socks were hanging on the brass rail over the fireplace, the one's she had knitted. Sarah sat at the table she did not know what to do. The door knocked and Mrs Russell came in.

"You should stay with us Sarah till the funeral is over; it is too much to take in all at once. Leave things for a few days till you get over the shock. You will be able to decide better then."

"I don't know what to do, but I can't leave Mary and the boys at Ravenston. They should be at the funeral."

Mrs Russell pleaded with Sarah, "They are so young, and will it really hurt them leaving them a few more days. Sarah how would you cope if you bring them home? All these questions have to be answered. Leave it a few days."

"No, they should be here, I can't leave them there."

"Let me get Davie in, he might know what to do." Mrs Russell went for her son.

"You try and talk some sense into her. She wants to bring the rest of them home, if she does, they will only have to go back to the Poor House, how can she keep them?"

"I'll go and talk to her, you make something to eat and I'll bring her in."

Davie found Sarah as his mother had left her; he sat opposite her at the table.

"If you bring them home Sarah you will maybe have to take them back, that will be worse for them."

"You don't think for a minute that I'll let them stay at Ravenston?"

"What about your work? You like it. You could maybe help more if you were working for them. You could always visit them."

Sarah put up her hand.

"I'm the eldest; I'll have to get on with it. They need me; I'll have to give up the job in Dunoon. Mrs Barr will understand. How could I go back and leave them in the Poor House, for that's where they'll be."

"How will you manage? Sarah think about it, this will not be for a week or a month, this is for always, until they are all grown and looking after themselves." Quietly Davie spoke, "please think about it, will Mary ever be able to look after herself?"

Sarah looked at Davie, shaking her head. "I will do it; at least I will have to try and, try I will, as best as I can, I'll have to get work here somehow. Do you know Davie, I'm angry with them for leaving me with this. My mother asked me to come home and I refused. Surely I am entitled to a life of my own. She wanted me here, and now here I'll have to stay, trapped in their life."

"At least leave it till after the funeral, give yourself some time." Davie again pleaded.

"No, I'm going for them now. Would you come with me?"

"If that's what you want. I hate to mention this Sarah, but how are you placed for the funeral, for paying for it?"

"My mother has some kind of Penny Insurance's for her and him. The man collects it every month. I have heard her say often that she is worth more dead than alive."

"Find them Sarah, you'll need them, and then we will go out the road. Come and eat something first with us."

"No Davie."

"If you don't eat something I'm not going, so there you have it."

At that point Mrs Russell came in,

"Right you two I have ham and eggs ready now." She emphasised the word, now.

Sarah rose from the chair and followed Davie into their house.

As soon as they had eaten they left for Ravenston. They took a tram into the town and from there they walked out to Ravenston. They had a good two miles to walk. Sarah told Davie all about her job in Dunoon and about the good people she had met.

"I have learned a lot since I've been away. I can knit and cook. I have even tried baking at the Boarding House."

As they walked up the driveway at Ravenston they had to stop at the gate-house to tell them where they were going. The man directed them round to the front of the big house.

Ravenston was divided into three large homes. There was the Poor House, the Lunatic Asylum and the Administration dept. The buildings were opened in May of eighteen seventy-nine. It was built to replace the Poor House that was situated in a street, which was near the town centre and had long been an eyesore to the Town Council as the Town was now spreading. The grounds of the new Poor House belonged to Ravenston Farm, which was owned by a Mr Dunstan, and there was plenty of ground on this site. The Town built a chalet to house Consumption patients, which was a very infectious disease, later to be known as Tuberculosis, and at the back of the grounds was another building for other infectious diseases. The complete buildings were a big improvement for the town. The Poor House was the biggest building where people who were destitute lived.

Men and Women were separated, as were children, who again were separated from their parents and babies were taken to a nursery, also in the Poor House lived men and women of bad repute, who again were separated. All who were able, had to work either on the land or in the Administrative building. This building consisted of a reception office, bakery, meal and flour house, kitchens, straw house, mattress making room and a room for oakum picking. Oakum picking was a method of loosening fibres of old rope by picking them by hand. The straw and the oakum were used to fill the mattresses. Everyone worked very hard under a strict regime, controlled by a Governor, a matron and a medical officer. Everyone worked in the house or in the grounds, children as well as adults.

As Sarah walked up the driveway, the large building with an imposing entrance frightened her, she had never been here before, the stories she had heard, frightened her. She had to get the boys and Mary home.

They went up and into the Administrative House and a girl told them where to wait; she would go for the Matron.

A very large lady came hurrying down a very long corridor, and as she walked the large bundle of keys that hung round her waist, jangled as she walked, it was the only noise until the woman spoke.

"What do you want?" she demanded.

"I have come for my brothers and sister, Jimmy, Andrew, Archie and Mary Shaw; they have to come home with me."

"You just can't come here and demand to take them out; The Minister brought them here,"

Sarah cut her off.

"You look here, the Minister had no business bringing them here, I am their next of kin. I should have been consulted. If you do not let me have them now Madam, I will leave here and go to the police and then I shall consult my legal adviser. Do you understand me? Then I shall go to the Gazette and let them know what you have done to the children of a man who saved people from drowning and lost his own life while doing so. Have I made myself clear?"

Davie was dumfounded, he had never known Sarah to be so sure of herself, and this was a new Sarah. He did not know who was most surprised, himself or the Matron.

"Wait here." She walked quickly down the long corridor and went in a door at the end.

"That was great Sarah where did all that come from."

"I told you Davie I had learned a lot in Dunoon."

They waited about fifteen minutes and then the door at the end of the corridor opened. The Matron came pushing the three boys in front of her, when they saw Sarah they ran as fast as they could. They threw themselves at Sarah. They had no boots on.

"Where are their socks and boots? Get them now."

At this Davie moved forward,

"Look Missus, you get the boots and socks now or replace them with new ones," he shouted the word, now.

"Where is my sister?" Sarah demanded.

"Your sister had to go into the hospital, I have sent for her. We had to restrain her."

"What do you mean?" Demanded Sarah

"She was violent."

"You liar, she would be terrified not violent." Sarah moved right up to her, till they were face to face.

"Madam, my sister now, boots and socks now, and do not take another fifteen minutes, or you will find yourself and this establishment charged with theft."

The boys were hanging round Sarah's waist, the three of them crying.

"It's alright now, I'm here, it's alright, and we are going home." Sarah looked over their heads at Davie. The tears were running down her face. She pointed to the three shaven heads. The boys looked terrible which one was the worse Davie did not know.

"Don't let her see you crying Sarah."

She pushed the boys over to Davie.

"Stand beside Davie. Once we get Mary we are going home." She wiped her face.

The door behind them opened and they turned to see Mary being led in, Sarah gasped when she saw her. Another shaven head, a course dress covered her to below the knees. Her head hung down as if it was unable to stay straight up, again no shoes.

"Mary, look at me, look at me," Sarah pleaded. There was no response. Sarah lifted her head and looked into her eyes. They appeared glazed.

"What's happened here," she asked the nurse who had brought Mary in.

"You will have to speak to the Matron. I am not allowed to talk to anyone, here she comes," the nurse pointed back down the corridor.

The matron came hurrying along the corridor carrying boots.

"Nurse put these boots on these children," then turning to Sarah. "Can I ask you what age you are?"

"Yes you can, I am an adult, over sixteen years of age, not that I consider it any of your business. Now Madam, please explain the state my sister is in, look at her."

41

"We had to restrain her; she is not of sound mind."

"You fool; she is deaf, not stupid. What have you done to her?"

"She has had her medicine to control her; it will wear off in about four hours' time. We cannot find her clothes so you can leave her till we find them or take her as she is."

"Sarah stepped forward, looked right into her face, and she said,

"My name is Sarah Shaw, remember it well. I will not rest till you have answered for the state my family are in."

"The Matron stepped back.

"I have to keep them all clean, the only way I can do that is by shaving all heads. No one informed me that your sister was deaf. The Church Minister brought them in; he said they were in for long term. I am only doing my duty."

"Well here is something else you can do for your duty, arrange some kind of transport for us. We cannot take them through the town as they are."

"I do not have that authority."

"Well if I were you Madam, I would find us transport. If I have to take my family through the town in this condition, my first stop will be the local paper. The choice is yours."

"I'll see what I can do." The matron was confused, what had happened she did not know but this young woman was well spoken, which meant that she was well educated. In turn this meant that there was some money behind her, she had to be careful who she was dealing with and more to the point, who she was upsetting.

While they waited, Sarah took her coat of and put it on Mary, It hung down to her ankles.

Davie told the boys to sit on the floor and the nurse sorted out the boots. They were all new boots but no socks. When the nurse was finished she turned to Sarah and Davie,

"Good for you, she been needing this for a long time."

She left before the Matron came back.

"The only thing I can get just now would be our ambulance, will that do?"

"Yes, the sooner the better."

Another five minute wait and then they were taken outside and into the ambulance. Davie went in with the driver and Sarah went in the back with her family.

It seemed an age before they were home. The whole close had turned out to see who the ambulance was for. Sarah stepped out and ushered the boys into the close, told them to hurry upstairs, she had to help Mary. All the time her neighbours were clapping their hands. Someone shouted, good for you, girl. Davie helped Sarah with Mary.

Mrs Russell was at the top of the stairs, she led the boys into their own house and the table was set for a meal. Mrs Russell brought freshly cooked food from her home.

Sarah put Mary to her bed and when she joined Davie and his mother in the kitchen, they were feeding the boys.

Only then did Sarah start to cry and nobody could stop her, Davie sat with his arm round her while she wept. He tried to stop her but his mother said,

"Let her cry, let her get it out, she will be the better of a good cry."

So they waited till Sarah stopped.

"Drink this tea just now, I will keep your meal hot, you will enjoy it later when you feel better. You'll have to let them know what's happened Sarah."

Sarah nodded, so Mrs Russell and Davie left, as he left Davie asked her,

"When were you sixteen Sarah?"

"Next week Davie, but to everyone else I will be seventeen on my next birthday."

"Right, see you later."

"Thank you Davie."

Sarah sat the boys down on the floor and she sat in her father's chair,

"There's been an accident and Mammy and Daddy will not be coming home again."

"Where are they Sarah?" Jimmy asked.

"They have both died in a drowning accident. Your Daddy was very brave and saved a lot of people, but Mammy got lost and he went back into the water for her. Nobody knows what really happened. They think the boat capsized and they were trapped under the boat. You must always remember how brave they were."

The three boys had got up from the floor and they were all lying across Sarah crying.

"What will happen to us?" Jimmy asked.

"Nothing is going to happen to you. I am here to take care of you all. We will all stay here together and we will help each other."

"How will we get money?" Jimmy asked.

"We will work for it. For the time being we are all right for money. I have my pay and a bit that I have saved. The funeral is tomorrow and I think we should all go together."

The three boys nodded their heads.

"Now I need you all to help me, Mary is not well, so you will have to help me look after her for a while." Again three heads nodded, Andrew and Archie had never spoken a word since the came back from Ravenston.

"Now we need to find papers that Mammy had, so we will look through every drawer and cupboard for papers, any that you find put on the table and we will go through them together. We will do it now." Again they nodded.

"I want to hear each of you say yes, will you do that for me."

"Yes," they all spoke through their tears.

Every cupboard was turned out and all papers were put on the table. When Sarah started to go through the papers she found three Insurance Policies. Two insurance policies in her father's name and one insurance policy in her mother's name, now Mrs Russell would no doubt know how to deal with this.

Her mother had a small case, so she put all other papers into the case and she would deal with these later.

Sarah had to get the clothes ready for tomorrow for all of them. What was she going to do about their heads? The four of them looked so odd with no hair. Where will I start? Do what Mrs Barr does make a list; so Sarah made a list, she was busy writing when Mary came into the kitchen. Mary looked such a poor soul, how could I leave any of them, she asked herself. No I couldn't, so get on with it.

"Right boys go and get your boots and see if you can find socks for tomorrow, do it in the other room. I will need to see to Mary, I will need to wash her."

She took Mary to the sink and filled the basin with some hot water from the kettle at the fire and added some cold. Sarah stripped her sister and washed her well, as she looked at her she made a sign with her hand drawing a circle and Mary turned round. Sarah was so pleased she hugged her tight and Mary smiled. I could teach her some signs Sarah thought. Leave it just now, too much to be done. All this was going on in her head as she finished washing her sister. She sat her in the chair and went to find clean clothes for her. Her mother did not have much but she was a clean woman and there was fresh underwear ready, for all of them. She found a skirt and the cardigan that she had knitted for Mary.

She dressed her sister and then called the boys and they shared the meal that Mrs Russell had left. When they had eaten Sarah told them she was going next door to see Mrs Russell and to keep their eye on Mary.

Mrs Russell went through the policies that Sarah had and read them all, then went through them with Sarah.

"You are fine for the funeral, you will have enough to pay for everything but you must inform the City of Glasgow Insurance Co., as soon as possible. Write a letter tonight and post it away as soon as possible. The Insurance man will call on you after they know that you are claiming. Let the Funeral Undertaker know you have a little insurance but you need time for the Insurance Company to pay. They will be fine about it. Are you ready for tomorrow? Can I help you?"

"I am worried about their heads, they look awful. I can put a scarf on Mary but what about the boys."

"Don't you worry about that, anybody that's there knows what happened? I have made a pile of sandwiches and Davie going to bring in some drink to help with the funeral tea. You'll want it right, won't you?"

"I never thought about that, thank you Mrs Russell."

"Get the funeral over and then you and I will have a talk, I'll help you all I can."

Sarah left and went back into her own house. Between them all they got their clothes ready for the morning. Jimmy polished all the boots; Andrew tucked socks into each pair of boots. Sarah ironed their shirts again to make everything fine, Mary and Sarah would wear dresses. Archie started to cry again and that set the rest of them crying.

"Now be brave, all of you, I need you all to be good."

"Everybody will laugh at us with no hair."

"Well everybody can see how clean you are and your hair will soon grow. Let's all have tea and toast. Then we will all have an early night."

There was a knock at the door and Sarah answered it. It was the Minister, Mr Brown.

"Hello Sarah, I have come about the funeral tomorrow at ten o'clock. I have just heard from the undertaker, I thought you would have contacted me." he said sourly.

Sarah stared at him, how dare he reprimand her, he was a dour man, and she remembered her mother saying his sermons were as dull as he was. He narrowed his eyes at her for he was not used to anyone staring at him and he felt that Sarah was defying him.

Sarah brought him into the kitchen and he was surprised to see the children. Before he could speak Sarah demanded.

"Why did you put them in the Poor House?"

"I did what I felt was right to keep them safe, as you were not here."

"I wonder if you would have done that with your own children." Sarah demanded.

"That does not come into it. Was I to leave them in the house alone? Do not even think of reprimanding me." Mr Brown was flustered by this girl in front of him.

"Look at what they have done to them. Would you look at them?" Cried Sarah.

The minister was annoyed at being questioned by a slip of a girl.

"I am here about the funeral Sarah. Do you want me to officiate?"

"Yes you do that, you are good at organising. Ten o'clock tomorrow morning. Will you come to the house? The hearse is coming to the close and we are to follow."

"Very good, if that is what you want," The Minister's reply was very curt.

"Thank you very much Mr Brown, I'll show you out."

They all had an early night and Sarah wakened them all early. They had their tea and toast and then all got ready. Sarah had the family organised by nine o'clock.

She then dressed herself and tried her hair many ways to make herself look older. She did not want anyone else questioning her about how old she was. She decided to roll her hair into a tight bun at the nape of her neck. It did make her look older. She wore her dress and her mother's black cardigan.

Mrs Russell came in with black armbands for the boys and Mary. She stayed with them until the Minister came. Davie and his father joined them.

The minister said a prayer and then they all went downstairs at ten o'clock

Sarah was so surprised at the number of people that were waiting and they all joined them in walking behind the hearse

Mrs Russell kept Mary beside her and the boys walked with Sarah.

Davie walked with his mother and father. The neighbours all walked with them.

It was a sad sight, two coffins side by side. People lined the streets here and there. By half past ten, they had reached the cemetery.

When they were all by the graveside Archie started to cry and Sarah lifted him in her arms, the two older boys hung onto her waist. Mrs Russell brought Mary over and they all stood together. When the service was over Davie took Archie from Sarah. They all walked back to the house. Most of the neighbours came back for a cup of tea and the men had a drink. Mrs Russell had done very well.

Everyone except the Russell's had left by one 'clock. There was the silence that only comes at a time of mourning, where no one speaks and then everyone speaking at once.

"You done well Sarah," Mrs Russell said.

"Thank you, I could not have done it without you all helping. When I sort out things I will settle with you Mrs Russell."

"No Lass, no need for that. No doubt in time to come you will be doing a favour for us. We will leave it like that. We will go in home, now we are only through the wall, knock for anything you need or just for a chat. We will see you later."

Davie stayed a while longer. "Sarah, are you going to be fine?"

"I'll have to be Davie, I will need to go over to Dunoon and let them know that I will not be coming back. I have to see the man from the Insurance, but I won't see him till next week because I'll be sixteen then. I don't know if it matters or not, best not to chance anything. Then I will settle with the Undertaker. I will have to go and see the Factor about the house; I'll ask your mother to come with me so that she could speak for me to get the rent book in my name. After that I will have to find work. Do you think I can pass for older than I am Davie?"

"Yes, nobody would know you are so young, but will you cope, you are taking a lot on. What will you do about Mary?"

"She's not as bad as you think. Watch this." She touched Mary on the shoulder and signed for her to turn round. Then she signed with her hands over the table and walked to the sink and turned the water on. Mary immediately started to clear the table and started to wash the dishes.

"That's only two days of showing her signs, she's now only twelve, Jimmy will soon be eleven, Andrew will soon be ten and then there's Archie just seven. The baby of the family aren't you?"

"No I am a big boy now." They were all smiling, as Archie was small for his years.

"I'll take the boys out for a while if you like, Sarah. I'll just change my clothes and come back in. What do you think?"

"That would lift them a bit, thank you Davie."

Once they had all left Sarah sat alone her head in her hands thinking, her father had her well and truly trapped now, she would have to live her parents life now what else could she do

Chapter 4

*I*t was now over two weeks since the funeral and they were settling down in the house together. Sarah had cleaned the house and sorted out their clothes. She had sorted linen and towels and had arranged them all neatly, she only now realised how hard her mother had worked. She had explained to her brothers that she was in charge of them all. If they got into trouble, she would be in trouble. Everybody must behave themselves. People would be watching to see if she could manage, they had to prove that she could. Nobody would get the belt and to prove it she threw her father's razor strap on the fire. Mary clapped her hands and they all laughed.

"I have a treat for us all tomorrow. We are going on the Steamer to Dunoon. I have written to the lady that I worked for and I am going to collect my things. You will all see where I worked and I will take you with me. I am not leaving any of you with anyone. I want you all to speak properly," Jimmy cut in here.

"I don't want to be a sissy; they'll make fun of us."

"No one will, I am asking you to speak properly not swanky, it will help you all as you get older. It helped me and it will help you, right."

She placed her hand, palm down on the table and they all placed theirs one on top of the other. This had been something they had done with their mother when she was trying to get then to behave, showing that they all agreed.

The funeral had been paid and there was money left over, enough to see them through a few weeks. The only problem was a letter from the Town Council asking her to an appointment at the end of August. Sarah wondered if this was about the Poor House. Mrs Russell had agreed to go with her. She was now sixteen so it could not be about her age. Mrs Russell had gone with her to the Factor and her name was now on the rent book.

"As long as the rent is paid the house is yours," was the cold comment.

So it was up to Sarah to keep them all together and she did worry about how she would manage. To everyone else she appeared very confident

Ten o'clock the next morning saw them all ready and going for the Tram. Archie could not get on the Steamer quick enough and his excitement rubbed off on his two older brothers. By half past eleven they were walking along Dunoon Promenade. Sarah left them sitting on a seat opposite Mrs Barr's house, now stay here and I will be back in a minute, remember I am depending on you.

As she walked up the path and knocked on the door she felt nervous and yet she was really desperate to see them all. A young girl opened the door; Sarah did not know her,

"Would you please tell Mrs Barr that Sarah Shaw is here."

Mrs Barr came hurrying out. "Sarah, Sarah, how are you? Come away through to the kitchen."

Mrs Malcolm was there and she put her arms round Sarah. "Let me look at you, are you alright?

Lizzie came hurrying in. "Oh Sarah I've missed you so much, are you coming back?"

"That's what I have come to see Mrs Barr about," her eyes all filled up and tears started down her face again.

"No you don't, we will have no crying in this establishment."

The two girls had their arms wrapped round each other.

"Lizzie get a pot of tea made, and I will get out a cake." Mrs Malcolm said.

"I can't wait; I have my brothers and sister with me. I have left them across the street. I knew you would be busy."

"Yes we are busy, but not too busy for you. Away and bring your family in here and we will all have something to eat."

Mrs Barr ordered. "Off you go and get them."

Sarah went and came back with them all. As they went in the door she said.

"Mind your manners and speak properly."

"Well, well well, what a fine bunch you are, and all a bit like each other. Now sit down here."

Mrs Malcolm pulled chairs over to the table as she spoke.

"We will all have a cup of tea and sandwich now. Then we will serve the lunch in the dining room. After that the children can play in the garden and we will have a talk.

I see you've changed your hairstyle, it makes you look older Sarah."

"Yes that was the idea; there could have been a problem with my age."

"I see, well we will talk later, come on now eat up, stretch or starve, that's what my mother used to tell me. Now who likes milk rather than tea?"

The three boys all said, "Yes please," all together and "Thank you very much," when they were handed their glass of milk.

Sarah signed to Mary, pointing to milk or the teapot. Mary cupped one hand and with the other put it under her hand like a saucer, and said very quietly, "thank you."

Sarah went round to Mary and clapped her gently on the back.

Mrs Barr, Mrs Malcolm and Lizzie were all taken aback with the children's hair or lack of it. Their hair had started to grow in again but all heads were covered with a very short growth. The children were all very clean and neat, their boots all shone.

Mrs Barr was so choked up when she looked at them all, that she could hardly speak.

"How are you managing Sarah?

"As best as I can, they are all very good, but we are all still a bit frightened."

The three boys were hanging onto every word and Sarah laughed at them.

"Big ears, the lot of you, eat your sandwiches."

Sarah signed to Mary to take the boys outside into the back garden, to Jimmy she said,

"Keep an eye on things for me." The boy nodded.

It was due time for the lunches to go into the Dining room and Sarah helped Lizzie and the young girl, whose name was Betty to carry through the meals, as Mrs Malcolm put them out.

After the Dining room was cleared and all the dishes washed, Mrs Malcolm put out lunches for them all. Sarah brought the boys and Mary back in for the meal and then back out to the garden again. She needed to talk to Mrs Barr.

"Come through into the office Sarah, you can see them in the garden from the window.

Mrs Malcolm you and Lizzie come through shortly and we can all have a talk and hear Sarah's news."

They went into the office together and Sarah stood at the window looking out at her brothers and sister. Mrs Barr came and stood beside her.

"What will you do Sarah? It a right handful you have there."

"Yes I know but what else can I do? The Minister put the boys in the Poor House and Mary into the Insane Asylum. I am sorry but I cannot come back, how I wish I could. I loved being here with you all. I had a life of my own but now I am trapped, I have to lead my mother's life and bring up her family. It is not fair, you know they were all drinking, a crowd of them and the boat capsized. My mother and father were the only two who lost their lives. My father saved them all but could not find my mother and went back for her. Nobody really knows what happened. I am now trapped because I could not leave them in the Poor House, how could I?"

"Come and sit down Sarah. Will you be able to manage? You will need to work to support you all. It will not be easy. Is there no relative that could help you?"

"No but I have excellent neighbours, you know Davie that came here, his mother and father have been great. Davie came with me, and he helped me to get them home, he has been great. We were always friends. I am just sorry that I am letting you down at the busy season, but there is nothing else I can do."

"It is alright, I will give you an excellent reference and I do not want to lose touch with you. Promise me you will come often."

"I will, I will." Sarah started to cry then, at that moment the door knocked and Lizzie and Mrs Malcolm came in carrying a tray with tea and cakes.

"Are you crying again Sarah Shaw"? She put the tray down and went and put her arms round Sarah.

"I will come and see you, we will keep in touch. I take it you are going to look after them."

"What else can I do, Lizzie? I want to be here but I cannot leave them, what else can I do?"

Mrs Malcolm put out the tea and they all sat while Sarah told them all that had happened, all about her parents death, the Poor house, the children's shaved heads, their lost clothes, how good the neighbours were and all about the funeral. How she would try for some work and that she thought her sister was improving, she finished by saying again,

"What else can I do?" Sarah was wringing her hands as she spoke.

Mrs Barr covered Sarah's hands with her own as she spoke.

"You will manage Sarah, you mark my words, and you will manage because it is a brave and good thing you are doing. They will grow up and then you can have your own life back again. Do they behave for you?"

"Yes Mrs Malcolm they are good. The first night none of us slept and we all went into the one bed. I had that many legs round me I thought I was sleeping with an octopus."

They all laughed at this.

"I must get back for the boat and you will be busy soon with dinners."

"Lizzie you walk Sarah to the boat and stay and see her off. Go and get the children will you. When Lizzie left the room Mrs Barr gave Sarah an envelope.

"This is for you; it is your wages that you are due and a bit extra to help. Mrs Malcolm has a basket ready for you and the next time you come you can return the basket. Now you take care of yourself, these children need you. You must look after yourself or you cannot look after them."

Mrs Barr and Mrs Malcolm gave her a hug. Sarah promised to come back and she left with Lizzie for the Steamer home.

As they left the two older women stood at the door.

"How will she manage Jenny?"

"She'll manage fine, she is very strong to be so young, as you say they will grow up, but it will take years."

The boys and Mary ran along the Prom in front of Sarah and Lizzie, "I miss you something awful Sarah."

"I miss you and the life I had, we had a great time, didn't we?"

"You know that fellow that spoke to us, that John."

"Yes, I know who you mean; he wanted you to go a walk."

"Well I have been out with him a few times."

"Is he nice?"

"Yes but a bit too staid for me I think, anyway I go a walk with him some nights. Mrs Barr said I have to be careful." She giggled as she said this,"you know what she means, always ready to spoil my fun."

"Lizzie you are terrible, she only means well and is looking out for you. You be careful, you know what I mean," she nudged Lizzie as she spoke."

They both started laughing, heads together as they went on to the pier. Lizzie waited until the Steamer had left the pier and they were all waving at each other and shouting "See you soon."

Sarah had enjoyed seeing them all again and felt sad at leaving which made her quiet on the journey home.

"You all right Sarah," Jimmy asked her with a worried look on his face.

"I'm fine, don't worry so much. I need to talk to you later on. When they all go to bed you stay up a while longer and we will set out a sort of routine for us all. We have got to appear to manage you and me."

Jimmy was pleased, he felt grown up. He would help his sister all he could, after all as Mrs Russell had told him, "you are the man of the house now, Jimmy." He sat close to Sarah and held her hand.

Once they were home Sarah emptied the basket that Mrs Malcolm had given her. She took out a steak pie; mince round, sausage rolls, slices of ham and a dozen eggs, all covered with a small tea cloth. Underneath the cloth were pancakes and scones.

She sent Jimmy into Mrs Russell with some scones, pancakes and sausage rolls.

She made the supper for them all and told them to get ready for bed.

Their kitchen had two recess beds and there was also a recess bed in the room, these beds were common in tenement properties. Her mother and father had used one of the kitchen beds and the boys had the other. Sarah and Mary had the room bed.

Sarah changed this round so that the two older boys had the room bed and Sarah and Mary shared one of the kitchen beds, with Archie the youngest boy in the other, as it was smaller. He sometimes had nightmares, and he was nearer Sarah if he needed her.

Sarah hurried them all to their beds accept Jimmy and they sat at the fire till the rest were asleep.

"I need you to help me Jimmy. I will have to find work to keep us all soon. It means that you will be in charge if I am out through the day. If you needed any help Mrs Russell or Davie could help you but not unless it is necessary. The sooner we can look after ourselves the better. You would have to be in for Andrew and Archie; Mary could maybe stay with Mrs Russell while I am out. Do you think you could do this for us all?"

"Yes Sarah, I will look after them till you come in."

"We must all look out for each other; I have to be able to depend on you as you are the oldest boy. You would have to come straight home from school; it means you cannot go out with your pals till I come in."

"I'll do it, don't worry Sarah and I think it's time we went to our bed. That was a grand day wasn't it? Can we go again?"

"Yes, you go to bed and I will follow soon."

Sarah took out the envelope that Mrs Barr had given her. There was her Month's wages and two five-pound notes inside with a letter. The letter read,' this is just a present from me to you; take care of yourself, Mrs Barr'. She put the money with the rest that she had put away safely and went to her bed.

She lay and thought about how she would organise them all and how she would work hard to keep them all together, sleep soon took over and she slept soundly for the first night since it had all happened.

Life had settled down for them all and Sarah decided to wait till the school re-opened at the end of August before she would look for work

When the school had re-opened Sarah sent a letter with Jimmy asking to see Miss Black. Jimmy brought back a note to say that Miss Black would see Sarah next morning after eleven o'clock.

As Sarah went up the wide staircase of the school it seemed as if she had been away for years and at the same time as if she had been there yesterday. The same smell of the disinfectant Lysol, permeated everywhere. The tiles on the walls, the railings with the polished banister, that ran down each staircase and the smell of polish. As she made her way to the Headmistresses office, Sarah remembered how she had loved this school as she knocked the door.

Miss Black was waiting for Sarah," How are you Sarah? I believe you have had a very bad time. I am so sorry. I understand that you are taking over the care of the boys and Mary."

"Yes, I just thought that I should put you in the picture. I will look after them very well; I will try very hard Miss Black."

"I do not doubt that at all Sarah. You were always a very competent girl and older than your years Sarah"

"Well I have had to grow up in a hurry. I will try to see that you have no problems. The boys are well behaved with me but I don't know how they are outside. I hope they behave."

"The boys are fine, any problems I will let you know. Do not worry about that. I did notice that they are well turned out, that is credit to you. If I can help you at any time let me know. Tell me what happened to you when you did not come back to school."

Sarah went over most of what had happened to her and the good job that she had in Dunoon.

"There was no chance of you continuing your education then?"

"No, but I learned other things, how to knit, cook and bake which is very handy now.

I wanted to ask about Mary. Is there no place here for her at all?"

"What made you think there was no place here for her." Miss Black asked surprised.

"My mother told me that she could not come any more."

"No, that is not the case, Mary can come but she is very restricted because she is deaf. What happened to her Sarah?"

"My father leathered her and threw her into the room. She struck her head on the door. I was not here so I only know what my mother told me. I can believe it, because that was what happened to me because I wanted to learn. Mary has seen a doctor at the Glasgow Hospital and he does not know why, but the tests prove that she is deaf. If I could get her back into school what would she learn?"

"Well as I explained to your mother it would be mostly Housewifery, the drawing class. She could help with the very young ones and I was prepared to see if I could find out anything about her learning to lip read."

"Lip read?"

"Yes, in the mills and factories where there is a lot of machine noise, the workers lip read because they cannot hear what they are saying to one another. I believe that a doctor is trying to use this method to help the deaf.

"She understands a lot of signs, and I am teaching her to knit. She is better at that than I am, and if I drop stitches she picks them up for me. She washes all the dishes and gets annoyed if we try to help her."

"Does she ever speak?"

"Yes she can, but it is a whisper and she does not seem to want to speak."

"Well we could try and help her there. Bring her in at the beginning of next week and we will take it from there."

Sarah rose to leave, "thank you very much Miss Black. If they were all at school I could look for some kind of work. I will need to work soon."

"Do not do anything about that at the moment Sarah, give me a week I might know of something. I will see you on Monday morning and we can have another chat."

Miss Black showed Sarah out and watching the girl leave the school Miss Black could not help but feel, that the children would now have a better future, but what a waste of an extremely intelligent young woman.

The following week Sarah went to keep her appointment at the Town building, Mrs Russell came with her. Sarah was to be at the main office for three o'clock in the afternoon and to ask for Baillie Robertson.

While Mrs Russell and Sarah waited, they talked about why a Bailie would want to see Sarah. They agreed that if it were over her being too young to look after the family, they would say that Mrs Russell was looking after them all.

"Miss Shaw, Bailie Robertson is ready to see you, will you come this way."

An older woman showed them into a large office. They were given seats and then a middle-aged man joined them.

He sat behind a large desk facing them, "Good afternoon Miss Shaw, I am Bailie Robertson."

"This is my friend Mrs Russell, I wanted someone with me."

"Very well, that's fine. I will start by saying that I am very sorry for your sad loss. It must be a very bad time for you and your family. Your father was a very brave man and there are many people very thankful that Mr Shaw saved them. The boat involved in the accident belonged to the East Shore Rowing Club. The club ran a benefit social and tea last month. People in the town have also contributed and the Town Council has made a donation as well. The fund at present totals one hundred and two pounds and this will be for the benefit of your family, including yourself."

Sarah looked at Mrs Russell and then again at the Baillie.

"I don't know what to say, I wondered why you wanted to see me, I was worried," she stopped speaking then because Mrs Russell had pressed her foot against Sarah's, warning her not to say too much.

"There is no need for you to worry; you have to decide how this money will be handled.

I understand there are five beneficiaries. Mr Shaw left five children, am I right."

"Yes I am the eldest; I have three brothers and one sister."

"Well then the fund is between the five of you. I would advise you not to take it all at once. You could have some of it and leave some until you require it. As a fund has been set up the Town's Cashier will administrate it. Do you follow me?"

"Yes very clearly. I can have some money now and take the rest as required."

"Yes that is correct. You will write to the cashier when you require anything from the fund. You will require signing a form when you need the money. We also need permission from your brothers and sister that you act for them. If you like I will make another appointment for you all to come and sign."

Mrs Russell spoke for the first time.

"Could I ask if this is necessary when Sarah is the guardian of her brothers and sister? They are all under the age of sixteen. Sarah is the only adult."

"I assume that they would all understand what they are signing and they can sign their name."

"Yes, they can all read and write," replied Sarah.

"It would be better and correct that they all sign. Will I make it the same day next week at three o'clock?"

"Yes that will be fine, thank you very much Mr Robertson." She held out her hand to him, and they shook hands.

Mr Robertson was confused, this young woman was educated and well spoken, and he had been led to understand that the family was in dire need of help. Well it was his job to see to the administration of the fund and not to go beyond that. After next week it would be the duty of the Town Cashier.

Sarah and Mrs Russell left the Town building. It was only when they were outside Sarah asked Mrs Russell," What do you think of that?"

"Davie had heard that there was something being done at the boat club but he did not know what. That is a nice windfall Sarah that will help you. There is so much that you could do with it. Think about it, you could sit rent-free for nearly two years. It could clothe you all. I am glad for you, you deserve it."

"Can I ask you something Mrs Russell, something personal?"

"Yes, you use such big words at times Sarah, I've got to put my thinking cap on. You want to ask me something about myself."

Yes, do you have a bank book?"

"Lord no Sarah, my money's kept in the house. I have a wee bit, but I borrow from it and sometimes I don't know what's mine, and what's the hurdy. I am forever paying myself back. We call my wee stash the "Hurdy."

"Well I think I'll open bank books in all their names and only spend the interest."

"What do you mean, spend the interest"?

"Well if you leave money in a bank you get a percentage of interest every year and that's how money grows."

"How do you know this?"

"I read in a daily paper once. I couldn't understand it. So I went to the library and the Librarian got me a book to explain it to me. Mind you these books talk about hundreds. If I did this nobody could say any of them were poor again."

"You're too clever for me Sarah Shaw. Come on, Davie gave me money for a treat. You and I are going to Crawford's Restaurant for tea and a cake."

"Davie is really very kind isn't he? Mary is knitting him socks as a thank you for all the help he has been. I don't know what I would have done without you Mrs Russell. Sometimes I get an awful feeling and get frightened, and then I remember that you say I can come in anytime. I don't feel so alone then."

"I don't think I could have done what you are doing Sarah bringing up four children. I only had the one child, why I'll never know, but it's a blessing the one that I have. Better to me than his father is."

They had arrived at the restaurant and Mrs Russell said, "Come on, let's celebrate. Your big words are rubbing of on me." They both laughed at that.

Next Monday morning Sarah took Mary to the school. Mary was very nervous; Sarah had tried to reassure her that she would be fine.

Miss Black was waiting for them and one of the older girls in the school was there to take Mary into her class.

"She is very nervous and has been crying, I don't really know how it will go. I think she's frightened."

"She will be fine; it must be strange for her. We will take our time, an older girl is keeping her with her at all times for a few days till she gets used to school. I have spoken to Jimmy and he will come to my office every day this week where Mary will be waiting for him and they can go home together. Now, my neighbour is a doctor and has two surgeries. One he operates from his home and he needs someone to help him, to make appointments for patients and bring patients into the surgery. You would answer the door, bring the patients in and see the patients out. This surgery is held on four afternoons a week. If you are suitable he would want you to keep records for him and there could be more work as you learned. This is a good job that could grow but the pay is only seven shillings and sixpence a week to start with. Would you be interested?"

"Yes I would but I would need to get something else."

"I may have something else. The caretaker of the school is being allowed to take on help for the cleaning of the school; again it is only a few hours a week but it will pay five shillings. I have spoken with the caretaker and he said that you could come in early evening to help him. He usually does the cleaning around six o'clock in the evening. Would this be of any help to you?"

"Yes, thank you very much. I did not know what to do. Mrs Russell could get me into the Woollen Mill, but it is far away and it is full time. I need to be handy especially for Archie. Yes thank you. I will not let you down. I could manage on twelve shillings and sixpence."

"Right you leave it with me and I will let the doctor know. Now if Mary comes back and tells you that she is not happy, you have to ignore it, till she settles. Will you do that?"

"Yes, we will try it out; I will see that Mary is here. Thank you very much.

There is one other matter I wanted to discuss with you, one afternoon next week I have to take the family to the Town Office for three o'clock in the afternoon. I would like to keep them from school that afternoon. Would that be all right? We have to sign a document to receive money that has been gifted to us from the Rowing Club."

"Yes that will be fine."

Sarah left the school and went into Mrs Russell to let her know what had happened.

"Somebody up there is looking out for you, mark my words. You will manage fine."

"I had better go and get the washing started and get into some kind of routine if I am to start work. I'll see you later."

The following week Sarah told the family about the money that had been gifted to them and how she thought they should keep it as an emergency fund."

"What do you mean Sarah," Jimmy asked.

"Well in case we run out of money. I am going to work but there could be times when I may not earn enough to keep us. We must stay together, agreed." She slapped her hand palm down on the table and one by one they placed their hand. Palms down, one on top of the other.

"We have to sign a paper saying that I will take care of the money for us all and we will go to a bank and put the money in all of our names. So you will not go back to school today. Miss Black has allowed you all half a day off from school."

The faces of the boys were beaming and Sarah wrote down the words for Mary. She started to clap her hands.

Three o'clock in the afternoon found them back in the Town office with Mr Robertson.

Sarah sat in the chair offered and the rest stood round her. Mr Robertson explained the situation again and asked if they all understood. They all nodded.

"Could I please ask something about the money?"

"Yes certainly."

"This one hundred and two pounds, which we are to receive, if we leave the money in the trust will it gather interest, which we in turn would receive."

"Well no, Trust Monies are all held in the one account and the interest is used by the town."

"What for?" asked Sarah

"For other charities or good causes, "Mr. Robertson replied gruffly.

Sarah paused a moment before she asked, "In that case then, can we have all the one hundred and two pounds today?"

Mr Robertson studied Sarah" Well it is most unusual. I would advise you to take some and leave some for future use."

"Is there any rule that says we cannot have it all, Mr Robertson?"

"No, there is no rule against you having it all, but I would advise you to leave it."

"In that case then Mr Robertson, we have all agreed to take the money and put it in a bank account."

Sarah could see that he was not pleased, but she felt it would be better for them all, in their own accounts.

Mr Robertson went out and spoke to his Secretary and then returned some five minutes later with the money.

Sarah then took them all went to the bank. Where five accounts was opened and twenty pounds put in each account. The two pounds left Sarah asked for four ten shilling notes. When they got home she gave each of them ten shillings for themselves.

"You can spend it how you like but remember, it is a nice feeling always to have some money for yourselves. Spend it quickly and you will not know the benefit of it."

She hoped to teach them to look after money by doing this.

Sarah started work the next Monday at the Doctors. Sarah was to work in the afternoons with the exception of Wednesday. The following week Sarah started as a cleaner in the school from six o'clock till seven thirty each evening, five days a week.

There were days that she was very tired, with working at housework in the mornings and then going out to the different jobs.

The children settled at school but not Mary. She discussed this with Miss Black and it was decided that as she was now nearly thirteen years old, maybe it would be better if some work could be found for her.

Sarah decided to keep her at home and she could help her in the house. Mary had become a very keen knitter and was very good at it. Sarah was hard pushed to find enough wool to keep her going They went to the Woollen Mills where you could buy good wool cheaply, for three penny an ounce, and often less than three pennies. Neighbours would buy her socks and cardigans and she made some money this way.

They were coping well but there was many a time when there was not much food on the table, nevertheless there was always some food.

That Christmas the boys were ten, nine and seven years of age. Remembering the lovely Christmas's that Sarah had spent at Dunoon; Sarah decided to do the same for them all. A dinner they all liked, as turkey was out of the question on their money. She bought Jimmy a set of games, Andrew two books and Archie coloured pencils and a colouring book. She bought Mary matching combs and brush for her hair. She decided to ask the Russell's to come and share their dinner on Christmas Day. As it was not a holiday they had the meal at night. She also bought a pair of stockings for Mrs Russell and a tie each for Davie and Mr Russell. Sarah had worked hard and had baked; she made a mince pie with vegetables and then an apple tart.

They all enjoyed themselves and when the night was over Mrs Russell said,

"That was lovely Sarah, we enjoyed ourselves."

"I wanted to thank you for all the help you have all given us.

Sarah had set the pattern for many years to come for often Mrs Russell would help especially with Mary, and Sarah would invite them for Christmas dinner.

Chapter 5

1928

It was a very cold winter and keeping warm was a problem, particularly at night. They would all go down to the beach and pick up any driftwood that the tide had washed in. At these times Sarah found life very hard and often there would not be much wood, however it was rarely that Sarah came from the beach without some of them finding wood.

This helped Sarah to save a bit of coal from time to time. Her father had built a coal box on the landing just outside their door, to save her mother from having to carry coal up to the top flat. It was Jimmy and Andrew's job to see that the coal box was filled. Coal was normally kept in the cellar in the basement, normally called the 'Dunny' in Scotland. Every house had a cellar for coal. If the cellar were not in the 'Dunny' it would be at the back of the common drying green. There was many times that winter when they had very little food in the house, Sarah was learning just how much food three hungry boys could eat, they could eat at any time and all the time. Very often a decision would have to be made as to whether to buy food or coal. It was very difficult for Sarah to decide; usually buying coal would be more important because, it heated the house, cooked their food and dried the washing that was hung on the pulley in the kitchen. The pulley was made of three or four long thin strips of wood. These strips of wood were joined together and knotted with strong rope that was threaded through them and the rope was left long enough to allow the raising or lowering of the pulley. When the pulley was raised it went right up to the roof of the kitchen. Many a washing was dried this way particularly in the winter. At these times Sarah would fry any left-over bread that she kept, with any scraps. Sarah never withdrew any money from their savings for either food or coal; Sarah never considered this an emergency. This had to be kept for what emergency that may arise, that was considered more urgent.

The Gas Man came to empty the Penny Meter. The gaslight for the house was paid at a penny a time in the meter. When the Gas Man came to empty the meter there was usually a rebate of money. On this occasion Sarah had a rebate of one shilling and sixpence. She always gave each of them a penny when she got the rebate and they went into the town to spend their money.

Woolworth's was a great attraction for the children with many Penny items for sale. Sarah would leave them to look to see what they could spend their penny on while she would go and see where she could get some extra food, with her share of the rebate. They had to wait till she came back before they could spend their penny.

As she went from shop to shop she eventually came to a shop that showed a gas cooker sitting in the window. Notices were all round the cooker explaining that if you had a cooker fitted; the town council would supply the cooker and install it free of charge. There was a display of cookery recipes and a book, which was also free.

Sarah thought if we had that, I could cook at night when I am in and surely that would help to heat us as well. I could bake and cook the things that Mrs Malcolm had taught her, Sarah went into the shop. The man explained that you left your name and address and an employee of the Council would come and see if your house was suitable. A date was arranged for a morning, and she went back to meet the family, feeling excited about maybe getting a cooker.

They were all waiting for her at Woolworth's Store, desperate to spend their penny. When she had approved of what they wanted to buy, she let them go ahead.

"What are you buying Sarah," Jimmy wanted to know. He was always keen to see that Sarah got her share. He knew that she often went without.

"I have been to see about getting us a gas cooker, so I am keeping my money for that."

They wandered back home and Sarah made a hot meal. Sarah switched two eggs with a little milk, dipped slices of bread into the mixture and fried them quickly in fat. This was a meal that would fill empty stomachs when money was short, till Sarah got paid the next day.

The school janitor paid her every Friday and the Doctor paid her every month, the next day was a good day because apart from being Friday it was also the end of the month.

Sarah never complained about how hard she worked outside and inside. She enjoyed the Doctor's house and she was learning all the time. The school cleaning Sarah did not like but it was near home and more and more the Janitor was giving Sarah extra chores. Sarah questioned him about it once." I am supposed to do all this work in one and a half hours?"

"If you want the job, you'll do the work. Just because the Headmistress has a soft spot for you, doesn't mean you can be lazy, he smirked at her."

"I am not lazy," Sarah said indignantly.

The Janitor came and put his arm round her and whispered in her ear,

"It is better if you and I are good to each other Sarah, we can help each other."

She moved away quickly from him and stood and faced him,

"Just as you say," Sarah snapped back at him, because she had to keep the job, because she needed the money.

From then on she took Mary with her every night to help her. And asked Jimmy to come and meet them, as she did not like the janitor.

The Council Official came the next week and went over everything with Sarah.

"Yes the cooker comes free of charge, the Council will install it."

"Why are they doing that? Sarah wanted to know.

"You will use the gas for the cooker, the council own the gas for the town and in time the Council gets its money back"

So it was arranged that a gas fitter would come and install the cooker on Friday morning.

Friday came and they were all excited. Sarah chased the boys to school and she waited for the cooker. She was so excited, that Mrs Russell remarked,

"If this is as good as you say it is Sarah, I think I will have one as well."

The gas fitter arrived with the cooker and it was decided that it should sit near the kitchen sink. It was a black cast iron cooker with a large oven, with a gas burner running down on the inside, on either side. Above the oven was a hot plate, which was slightly broader than the oven. There were two large rings and in the centre a grill burner. Between the oven and the hot plate was a space for the grill pan. Shiny brass taps controlled all the burners. The entire cooker sat on high legs which made it approximately waist high, which made it easier for handling pots and allowed you to keep the floor clean underneath the cooker. Once the gas fitter had gone, leaving her with instructions, Sarah, Mary and Mrs Russell examined everything more carefully. Sarah lit the gas in the hot plates, grill and oven, it was similar to the oven that Mrs Malcolm used but not so large.

The boys came home from school and Sarah made toast on the grill for them. Sarah was the only one allowed to use the cooker until they were more used to it.

The oven in the black range fire could now be used to store the wood that they brought up from the beach, which allowed it to dry for burning.

Sarah was soon turning out meat pies, scones, tarts and cakes from the recipes that Mrs Malcolm had given her.

Mrs Russell came and helped her when she baked and they shared the cost as well as the baking.

Life had settled down for Sarah and her family. Sarah never complained although sometimes seeing a group of girls going out for an evening or maybe just for a walk, she used to wish that she could go. Sarah would never leave them because she was frightened that someone would say she was not capable. After the Church Minister putting them in the Poor House Sarah felt she had to be so careful, and she never went back to church. When the minister questioned her about this one day when Sarah met him in the street. She told him that if that was what he called Christianity, putting children into the Poor House and not checking up on them, she would do without it.

He was appalled that a girl so young would question him and he told her to watch her step.

It was the early Spring when Sarah received a letter from Lizzie, to let her know that she was to be married in April just before Easter. Lizzie wanted Sarah to be her Bridesmaid. It was to be a quiet wedding and John wanted married in Dunoon. Mrs Barr had agreed to have a small wedding for Lizzie. The boys and Mary were also invited, and they were to stay the weekend with Mrs Barr.

Sarah was delighted and wrote back accepting the invitation. It was also the first time that the boys and Mary had a holiday.

Whenever Sarah looked back on her time in Dunoon, she felt the two years she had spent there was like one long holiday

Sarah wrote to say that they would come over for the day on Saturday to see them all. Sarah made cakes and packed them in the basket that Mrs Malcolm had given her on her last visit.

They were all excited as they went for the tram and then the steamer to Dunoon.

They were all waiting for them, there were hugs and tears all round. Mrs Barr saw a big difference in all of them, although Sarah visited them every three or four months, she went alone. Mrs Russell watched them so that Sarah could have a day to herself with her friends. It had been two years since the family had last visited.

The boys had all grown and Mary had turned out a very pretty girl.

"They are a credit to you Sarah, now let's all have some lunch and then the boys can go out for a while and we can all have a talk."

They all sat round the table as if they had never been separated. Lizzie was so happy.

"Tell me all about your young man, Lizzie."

"He is John Duncan, you remember him."

"Yes I do, I am happy for you Lizzie."

"Are you going to stay in Dunoon?"

"Yes we have managed to get a small house, but I will continue to work for Mrs Barr. We are having the wedding before the summer season starts."

"Will there be room for everyone here. What about your family?"

"They don't think that I should marry John, and they will not be at my wedding. There was a disagreement and John won't let me see them. It will just be all of us here and John's friend who will be the best man."

"I am sorry Lizzie, could you not sort it out. You must want your own family to be there?"

"No, John has told me to leave things as they are."

Sarah realised that Mrs Barr was trying to warn her in some way so she did not pursue the conversation any further.

"Tell us all about yourself, Sarah. I see you are baking."

"Our Sarah is the best cook in the country," Archie said proudly, while the rest all nodded.

"I can see that by how well you all look. Now if you boys are finished eating, you can go for a walk and see the place."

They were out of the door very quickly.

"Boys," Sarah shouted.

"Yes we know, behave ourselves," they all spoke in unison, and laughed as they left.

"They are all excited about coming to the wedding, they have never been on a holiday before, and we are all excited" Sarah explained

"You three sit and blether and I will wash up and make a pot of tea after I have washed the dishes. Come and help me Mary?" Lizzie signed to Mary and she followed her through to the kitchen.

"She is turning into a bonny girl, isn't she Mrs Barr." Mrs Malcolm said.

"How are you coping Sarah, tell us all about yourself, we miss you so much."

"Well we are fine; I am working at the doctor's surgery four afternoons a week. I really like that. I work five afternoons at the school as a cleaner from six o'clock till seven thirty, and I do not like that. I do not like the janitor but it is near the house. The doctor is talking about taking me on full time but not for some time yet.

I manage fine, some days I am so tired and other days I manage well."

"Do you ever get out to enjoy yourself?"

"Only when Mrs Russell lets me come here to visit you, I am worried about the Church Minister. He was angry because I went against him and brought them out of the Poor House. I told him what I thought of him then and he told me to mind myself. I am older now, I will be eighteen soon and I do not think that they would take them from me now. I was afraid of that at first so I will not leave them other than for work. Mary is also in the house with me and that is help. Is everything fine for Lizzie? It is a shame about her family not coming to see her married."

"I think she is making a mistake Sarah, and Mrs Malcolm agrees with me. He bosses her about and he collects her wages because he has a bankbook and is saving for them getting married. Lizzie thinks he is wonderful and after all she will be twenty soon. We heard he had another girlfriend for a while and was seeing both of them. If she wants to do anything, she has to check with him and he objected to the money that she gave her family. They went for a visit but he feels that she should put him first. Everything is all about him, anyway they are getting married and we are giving them a tea here."

"I don't suppose you have time for a boyfriend Sarah?"

"No, who would want me anyway with my lot." Sarah laughed.

"What about Davie?"

"Oh Davie is great, and so is his mother. They have been a great help to me and I can go to them at any time, but Davie is just a friend. Lizzie told me once that when you meet the right person you will know because the earth moves, so that is what I will wait for."

They were all laughing when Lizzie and Mary came in with the tea. They sat and discussed the wedding. Lizzie had a new dress, which Mrs Barr had bought her and Mrs Malcolm had treated Lizzie to new shoes and a handbag."

"That's lovely, I have a new dress which I bought myself last Christmas and I thought I could wear that for being bridesmaid so I will not let you down Lizzie."

"The pair of you will look lovely, I am sure. Now you come with the family and stay with us for the wedding, we could do with your help as well Sarah for that weekend."

"I will love that and so will the boys and Mary

It was soon time to go and Lizzie walked them to the steamer.

"I miss you so much Sarah, we had a grand time didn't we?"

"Yes, the best and you will always be my best friend. Does John agree about me being bridesmaid?"

"Yes John wanted you for bridesmaid, I wanted you as well, and he thinks that you will get on well with his friend."

"What is his name?"

"He is called John as well. He is John Black. A bit stuck up Sarah. I think he tried to put John off me."

"Well he did not manage it when you are getting married. Are you happy Lizzie?"

"Yes I am, but I do not want to let him down. John wants me to speak better than I do and I am trying. Remember how you used to teach me. If he could have heard me then he would have something to complain about. Those were great days Sarah."

"Yes they were, but you are going to have better days when you are married."

"I hope so, I really love him but when he gets angry he frightens me."

"Are you sure about this, I mean getting married Lizzie if you feel frightened at times."

"I want to marry him. He says that everything will be fine as long as I improve myself."

Sarah looked anxiously at Lizzie, "Is that what you argued with your mother and father about?"

"Yes it is, my father says that there is nothing wrong with me. It all started so simple, John said that he was hoping I would realise that I could do better than be a maid in a boarding house. Mt father lost it and said that it had served me well and that Mrs Barr was good to me. John said that she was exploiting me, letting me stay in the winter when I really was working without wages. It got out of hand and they were shouting at each other.

My father told me to get rid of him and John said that if we married I was to have nothing to do with them. It makes me sad Sarah, because none of them are thinking of me."

"You do what you want. Just be sure that you love him before you marry him. Remember what you told me 'the earth must move'"

"That's only in books Sarah."

"Well that is what I will wait for and if I remain an old maid, it is your fault. You educated me on men, so the earth must move."

They were laughing now as they approached the pier. Mary and the boys were waiting for her.

"See you in two weeks' time Lizzie."

They waved to each other as the steamer left the pier.

They were later than usual getting home and were still excited. Sarah made them cocoa with hot milk for their supper. They all sat at the fire toasting their toes and then she chased them all to bed. She sat by the fire thinking of Lizzie and her wedding, thinking on how nice it would be to have someone love you. You would never be lonely; sometimes Sarah felt lonely even when she was at her busiest with the family and her work. Every now and again, like tonight, she felt lonely.

Lizzie was married on the Saturday at the end of April. The wedding was a great success and all the guests went back to Mrs Barr's house for the wedding tea. Mrs Malcolm had made a wedding cake as well as the usual sandwiches. Everybody enjoyed themselves and Sarah was sure that Mrs Barr and Mrs Malcolm were wrong when they thought that Lizzie had made a mistake.

Lizzie and John asked Sarah and John, the best man to walk with them back to their house after the wedding was over. Mrs Barr said that she would see to the boys and Mary till she came back.

They went back with Lizzie and John to see their home. It was very nice and Lizzie had made it very homely. John poured a drink of whisky for them all. It was the first time that Sarah had tasted whisky and it caught her throat and she choked as the hot fiery liquid scorched the back of her throat. They were all laughing at her and Sarah laughed with them. When John poured a second drink Sarah refused.

"I think we should say goodnight and leave Mr and Mrs Duncan on their own."

"Don't worry Sarah, it is not as if it was our first night," John said.

It took Sarah a moment to understand what he meant; she was embarrassed and lost for words. The two men were laughing and Sarah did not like the way the conversation was going.

"I think it is time I went anyway."

"I will walk you back then," John Black said.

They said their goodnights and the two of them walked back along the Promenade to Mrs Barr's house. As they went along John Black put his arm round Sarah's waist. She moved his arm and he grabbed her and pulled her towards him.

"I would rather you did not do that, thank you."

"Prim aren't we or just pretending we are."

He had both arms tightly round Sarah and was pressing himself against her.

Sarah stamped hard on his foot with the heel of her shoe. He released her and she ran.

All she heard was him shouting, "You bitch."

When she arrived back at the house she was breathless and charged in and sat down at the kitchen table.

"What happened to you Sarah?" Mrs Barr wanted to know.

"The best man thought he would get fresh with me and he is nursing a sore foot. I ran as fast as I could."

"Good for you, the boys are away to bed and Mary is helping Mrs Malcolm clear away the dishes."

"I will help them."

"You sit where you are and we can have a blether."

They talked for ages on everything, and then Mrs Barr asked her,

"Do you remember Monsieur Pierre Renaud?"

"Yes, I used to practice my French on him, do you hear from him?"

"Yes we write to each other and he is visiting again this August. He has asked me to marry him and return to France with him."

"Mrs Barr," exclaimed Sarah, "that is a surprise, what will your answer be."

"I would like to say yes but Mrs Malcolm has been a good friend to me and I would feel that I was letting her down. This is her home."

"How does she feel about it?"

"That is the problem; I have not discussed it with her. What should I do Sarah? You are always so good at weighing things up. I know she would tell me to go ahead but how can I leave her."

"Wait until Monsieur Renaud comes in August, see how you feel then. I take it that you would sell up here and move to France permanently. You would get a lot of money selling a house like this. Could you not buy a small house for Mrs Malcolm or could she go with you. Do you love him?"

"At my age Sarah companionship is what I am looking for. I am very fond of him and I look forward to his letters. We have a lot in common and I cannot go on working here forever. I will have to make a decision about retiring someday, but I must consider Mrs Malcolm.

"I go to Mrs Russell when I am not sure what to do. I had a problem with the school janitor, he told me that I should be nice to him and he could help me. Well Mrs Russell said, as you need the money, do nothing, take Mary with you and get Jimmy to come and meet you every night, which should cool the janitor down. Do nothing till you are sure. Sometimes when we leave things they can sort themselves out. That is what I think you should do, say nothing just now, wait till August and then discuss it with Monsieur Renaud."

"Yes that is what I will do; I do not want to upset Mrs Malcolm when I myself am not really sure. If I go Sarah you will be able to visit me and then you can really practise your French."

"I sometimes wonder if I will ever be free to please myself, but if you go to France I will visit you somehow."

Mary and Mrs Malcolm came back with hot cocoa and they all had a cup. Sarah enjoyed herself and it was like old times.

The summer was coming as was the school holidays. This was a time that made things more difficult for Sarah. Mary was now nearly fifteen, Jimmy would be thirteen on his next birthday, Andrew twelve and Archie was now ten years old. She would have nearly two month's holiday from her cleaning job at the school. The Doctor was now ready to offer her full time work at the Surgery, which she wanted. She was sure that Mary would cope with the boys, as Jimmy was very sensible. Andrew was a very quiet boy who was always reading. Archie was a problem, if there were any fights or arguments amongst the children in the street; he was in the middle of them all. Always ready to sort somebody out.

Sarah went to see Mrs Russell to ask if she would mind keeping her eye on Archie for her, so that she could take the full time work at the Surgery, which was to start at the beginning of August. Davie was in from his work early, when he heard about Sarah's job he said,

"I could take Archie out with me, he would like that. I will be going to the farms to collect vegetables. It is a contract that the boss has got and I have to deal with it."

"That would be great Davie; I will tell him that you need a hand."

"Don't worry, you take the work at the Surgery and get out of that cleaning job at the school."

"I don't like the Janitor Davie."

"I know Jimmy told me that he goes to meet you to see that you get home. I knew there must be something else at the back of it."

"Well thanks once again Davie, I am always thanking you and your mother. Now how are you? We have not seen you lately, still walking out that nice girl."

"No Sarah, I am waiting for you, he laughed at her."

"Get away with you, stop kidding me on. You will meet somebody else at that dancing you go to."

Mrs Russell went out of the kitchen, as Davie leaned forward,

"Let me take you to the dancing Sarah? You would like it. We have a good laugh and we are all learning the new dances."

"I have never been to a dance Davie, well I went once with Lizzie but Mrs Barr put her foot down and said I was too young."

"Come with me on Saturday, let Mary sit for you."

Sarah smiled at Davie, "Yes I would like that Davie, thanks, yes I will come."

Mrs Russell had come back into the kitchen,

"Mother if Sarah comes with me to the dancing on Saturday, she will leave Mary in charge of the boys, would you look in on them now and again."

"Yes, no problem, it is about time Sarah had a night out."

So it was settled and Sarah was excited about going out with Davie.

She never got dancing because on Friday morning a letter came from Lizzie, to let Sarah know that Mrs Malcolm had died suddenly and could she come, as Mrs Barr was so upset. The funeral was to be Saturday morning at ten o'clock, if you have to bring the family, there is a room they could all sleep in. Everything here is all upset at the moment.

Sarah never hesitated, on Friday evening they all left for Dunoon. She had to be there for Mrs Barr, and poor Mrs Malcolm, they would all miss her. She had asked for a few days off from the doctor, and sent a message to the Janitor that she would be away for a few days.

They arrived in Dunoon at seven o'clock and hurried over to the house. Lizzie opened the door to them.

"Sarah I am so glad you could come, Mrs Barr is in an awful state. I am managing as best as I can. The boys can have our old room out the back of the kitchen. If they put the two beds together, do you think they could do that? You and Mary can have my room in the attic because I have to go home and that's another problem."

"Look don't worry, you show the boys where to go and I will go and see Mrs Barr."

"She is in the kitchen, just sitting there."

Sarah went through with Mary. The sink was piled with dishes to be washed and pots and pans everywhere. Sarah told Mary to start the dishes and she would help.

Mrs Barr was sitting in a chair crying,

"I have lost my best friend, it was so sudden, Isa felt tired and sat down and that was it. The doctor said a massive heart attack. I should have known something was wrong but I didn't."

"You could not tell, nobody could," Sarah tried to reassure Mrs Barr.

"I cannot cope without out Isa, Sarah what will I do and Lizzie is in bother with him for staying here."

"I am here to help and Mary will help as well. What about guests, is there any here."

"There are a few, people that I could not get in touch with and I could not turn them away."

"Have they had their evening meal?"

"They are all eating out for a few nights and I will take it off their bill at the end of the holiday."

"Why don't you go and have a nice bath and get into bed and I will bring you up something to eat later. We can have a talk then. Is everything organised for tomorrow for the funeral."

"Yes, I was all she had, so everybody is here and the minister has been."

Sarah took over and let Lizzie get home.

"How are you, enjoying married life Lizzie?"

"No I am not enjoying it at the moment Sarah; I do not know what to do. I must get back, John is furious because I stayed here the past two nights. He came over this morning and has ordered me back home, and in front of Mrs Barr, and it was terrible. Will you manage? There is a girl coming in at seven o'clock to help with the breakfast. Mrs Barr has not been taking so many visitors this year so that has been a blessing now." Sarah could see that Lizzie was very agitated.

"You go home and I will see you for the funeral. We will have a talk tomorrow. ."

Sarah went to see how the boys were and they were sitting on the beds waiting for her.

"Come and get something to eat, you can go out but get back here by nine o'clock.

Sarah found a cooked ham in the larder and started to make sandwiches, the boys and Mary ate them heartily and had a glass of milk to drink.

"I will make you all a supper later once I have seen to Mrs Barr."

Mary had washed all the dishes and Sarah started to tidy the kitchen and put everything in its place.

Sarah started in the dining room and set tables for the morning breakfast. Mary helped her and learned quickly. They made scones and pancakes, which, would help with the funeral tea. They dusted and tidied the sitting room ready for tomorrow.

Sarah made some scrambled eggs, toast and a pot of tea and took it up the Mrs Barr, who was sitting by the window.

"All I could worry about was how I was going to tell Isa that I had decided to go with Pierre to France. I was only worried about myself, and all the time she could not have been well."

"You do not know that, maybe she was well and this came out of the blue. If you can think of it this way, she did not suffer; she did not lie in a bed and fade away. If this had to be, is this not the best way for her."

"Sarah, how did you get so wise and you so young."

"I am not wise but I read a lot, this happens to a lot of people. I read once in a book a verse of poetry, which said,

'If I die suddenly, let me in your memory remain,

Healthy and happy because I had no pain,

If I leave quickly, then I cannot say goodbye,

Be glad for me, do not sit and cry.'

This is what you must do for Mrs Malcolm; now let you and I eat something. The boys have gone for a walk and Mary is making some sandwiches for tomorrow. I can stay for a few days and then I must go home but I will come back again soon."

They ate their supper and Sarah left Mrs Barr in bed and went to see Mary.

Mary had made a very large pile of different sandwiches and they wrapped them up in a fresh supper cloth ready for tomorrow.

The boys came back and had their supper and Sarah settled them for the night. Then she waited up for any guests that may come in late.

Sarah was wakened very early next morning and had everything under control when the girl came at seven o'clock to help with the breakfast. Sarah asked Mary and the boys to clear up as quickly as possible. Mrs Barr came into the kitchen and she was now more composed.

Lizzie arrived in time for the funeral, not looking very well.

"Are you well Lizzie? "

"I am fine, how did you get on? I am sorry but I could not come any earlier."

"I was wakened and could not get back to sleep so I just got dressed and started to get things moving," Sarah explained.

Mary helped to make the breakfasts and the boys have helped as well. I have sent them into the town until the funeral is over.

They were all waiting in the sitting room when the Minister arrived to take a short service. The hearse arrived at the door and they all walked behind it to the cemetery. It was not a long walk. A few of Mrs Barr's friends from the church were there and also some neighbours. They all came back for the tea, nobody waited very long and by one o'clock Mrs Barr, Lizzie, Sarah and Mary were sitting round the kitchen table.

"We had better start and prepare a dinner for the guests that are here and get the tables set, what do you think Mrs Barr? Sarah asked.

"Yes we will, I can't seem to think straight, but I have decided to close the house. I will write to everyone and cancel their booking. I will try and get alternative accommodation for everyone. Lizzie you will not lose your job because I will need you."

"Would you like me to leave Mary with you, to help you out in the kitchen, she would like that I'm sure? "

"Would she stay with me, would she not be unhappy without you Sarah?"

"I can come back at the weekends, but I must bring the boys. I also have two weeks holiday due to me from the Doctor, which I could use and come here to help out."

"That would be great Sarah, it would be like old times," Lizzie smiled as she spoke.

Sarah spoke and signed to Mary,

"Would you help Mrs Barr and stay with her for a few weeks. Lizzie will take care of you. I will come at weekends to help out, I will bring the boys."

Mrs Barr was amazed at how Sarah and Mary could speak to each other by signing.

"I do not know what I would have done without Lizzie and you," as she said this she touched Lizzie's arm and Lizzie winced with pain.

"What has happened to you Lizzie, have you hurt yourself?" Mrs Barr wanted to know.

"Yes I fell on the stairs, I will be fine, it's nothing," and she rose from the table and started to clear the dishes. Mary immediately started to help her.

The boys came back and had their lunch of yet more sandwiches and soon cleared all the plates. They wanted to go down to the beach in the afternoon and Jimmy said," I will be in charge of you lot, sure I will Sarah?"

"Yes you can go but be careful and no arguing."

So it was decided that Mary would stay with Mrs Barr and Lizzie. Sarah would come at the weekends with the boys and also for two weeks during the school holidays.

They were busy all that weekend and Mrs Barr was starting to feel better.

"I will pay you and also the boy's fares Sarah and I will pay Mary."

"No we want to help you and I will have my job at the Surgery, we will be fine for money."

"No, Sarah I must do right by you."

Lizzie and Sarah went for a walk before dinner, there was only to be six guests staying so they would manage fine.

"Right Lizzie, tell me all about married life, is it great?" Sarah wanted to know if Lizzie was happy, because she realised something was wrong.

"No it is not Sarah."

When Sarah looked at Lizzie there were tears in her eyes.

"What's wrong Lizzie?"

"I cannot decide anything for myself. I have to do exactly what John says. He was not pleased at me staying with Mrs Barr for the two nights but I could not leave her. I have no money of my own now. John takes charge of all my money and, look."

Lizzie rolled up her cardigan sleeve and showed Sarah her arm; it was bruised from the shoulder to the elbow.

"I thought you said you fell."

"No I did not," declared Lizzie sadly.

There was a silence between them before Sarah spoke "Did you get that for staying with Mrs Barr, John has no right to hit you like that."

"He gets so mad Sarah, he gets so mad for nothing and I don't know what to do. Then he is very sorry and says that it won't happen again."

"So this is not the first time he has hit you?"

"No, but I love him Sarah, if I could have a baby, it would maybe be better. John desperately wants a child."

Sarah turned Lizzie round to face her. "Now you listen to me. It may get worse and with a child you are tied to him. No, you get this sorted out before you have any children. My mother put up with getting knocked about for years and it did not stop until she stood up for herself, you stand up to him. You also need money, how are you supposed to pay for your groceries."

"John leaves so much out and he decides what we need. When he is kind to me Sarah it is great and I try not to make him angry with me." Lizzie spoke so dejectedly.

Sarah could not believe the difference in Lizzie. This was the girl with all the cheeky answers and Lizzie was now so subdued. Sarah thought to herself, it is just as well that I will never marry, for I could not put up with a man like that.

They went back to the house and started serving out the meals.

It was a good summer for all of them, the boys enjoyed going to Dunoon at the weekends and Mary loved her work with Mrs Barr. By the time August had arrived both Lizzie and Mrs Barr were using signs to talk to Mary, and Mary was so good at understanding them, that Mrs Barr was sure that Mary must be able to hear something. Mrs Barr had become very fond of Mary and would take her out for walks. She had also become a very pretty girl and many admiring glances came their way.

Sarah was now fully employed at the Surgery and working for two Doctors. Doctor Small had taken on a young doctor at the Surgery, a Doctor Hendry, and was planning to have another doctor by the beginning of winter. Sarah was to have a young girl to help her in the office. Sarah had left the school cleaning job and was very glad not to have to go there anymore.

By September Mrs Barr had sold the boarding house and preparations were underway for her going to France with Monsieur Renaud.

Lizzie had a job with Mrs Barr's friend in another boarding house. They all had a day together before Mrs Barr left for France. Mrs Barr gave Lizzie and Sarah an envelope from Mrs Malcolm. Mrs Malcolm had left a letter leaving anything she had to Mrs Barr with the exception of two hundred pounds. Lizzie and Sarah were to receive one hundred pounds each.

"Now keep it safe so that you will always have that money. Your own money is your best friend, especially when you have trouble. I also want to give each of you a present for all your help. You two have been like the daughters I never had. Promise me that you will both write to me and I will write to you. Mrs Barr gave each of them an envelope with instructions not to open them until they were home. Mrs Barr and Monsieur Renaud were to be married in France in October.

Lizzie and Mrs Barr saw Sarah back on the steamer for the last time; they were all crying and hugging each other, promising to keep in touch.

When Sarah returned home, Mary had a meal ready for them all. Sarah opened the envelope that Mrs Barr had given her and there was another one hundred pounds in her envelope.

Sarah banked her money as soon as she could. She had plans to educate the boys and this money would enable her to do so.

Chapter 6

1930

*C*hristmas had come and gone, as usual Sarah had Mr and Mrs Russell and
Davie in for Christmas dinner. Once again it had been a great success.
Dr Small had organised a New Year dinner for the Surgery, which his wife had
organised for the 2ⁿᵈ January. Sarah was to bring a friend with her and she had
asked Davie if he would like to go. He was pleased to accept as he had been trying once again to get Sarah to go out with him.

It was a great night; Dr Henry had brought his sister along. Elsie, the new
girl that Sarah had taken on as her assistant was also there. Another doctor
was joining the Practice, a Doctor Young and he also joined the party. He was
interested in Sarah and was talking to her a lot. He was new to Greenock and
thought that he might need some help in finding his way around.

"When I start next month Sarah, would you show me round the town, I
would not want to get lost."

"Somehow I do not think you will get lost," Sarah laughed at him.

"Come on, say yes, just to make me feel welcome. Is that your boyfriend
that is with you?"

"No Davie and I are just good friends."

"Well then."

"Behave yourself and I will think about it."

"I will take that as a yes then."

"You are very persuasive Dr Young."

"Please call me Colin, you and I are really going to be good friends, so we
should skip the formalities."

"Did you graduate in medicine or glib tongue?"

He laughed out loud at her answer, which made everyone look at them. Sarah looked at him and said to everyone.

"I will leave Dr Young and his silver tongue to explain."

"I just want Sarah to show me around; now nobody would want me to get lost, would they?"

Dr Small came to her rescue,

"Yes Sarah will help you; get him a good map of the district. That way you will not get lost."

Sarah noticed that everyone laughed at this except Davie.

The evening was soon over and it was time to go home. Sarah and Davie walked home, it was a lovely night, crisp but not too cold. Sarah tucked her arm through Davie's arm as they wandered home.

"Did you enjoy yourself tonight?"

"Yes I did. I see you made a conquest with the new doctor."

"He was just having a bit of fun Davie, when he knows about my family that will cool him down."

"Do you think that because you look after your family that would put boyfriends off you. You have to be admired for what you have done."

He stopped walking and turned to face her.

"Let's face it Davie who would want me with my responsibilities

"Sarah I want you, I will take on your family. Sure I have helped you, do you think that I would not want the boys or Mary?"

"I know you have helped me, where would I be without you and your mother. I would never have managed. It would not be fair to anyone and especially to you, to expect anyone to take us all. Jimmy is only fourteen, Andrew is thirteen and Archie is just eleven. It is going to be years before I am free, and then there's Mary, who needs me, will I ever be free?"

"I love you Sarah, you must know that."

"Yes and I love you but like a brother. I love you the same way that I love the boys. You should have someone who really loves you more than that. I am trapped Davie and I am not trapping you.

"I will settle for that, surely that is my decision."

"My friend Lizzie says that when you meet the right person, you really know because the earth moves."

Davie laughed at that explanation.

Sarah laughed," Yes she swears blind that is the truth. If she is right, that is what we both want for ourselves. She has a lot of experience."

"What with, the earth moving or boys, I think your friend Lizzie is a nutcase."

They were both laughing now.

"Seriously Davie you would love Lizzie, she was such good fun."

"Why do you say, was such good fun?"

"Well Lizzie has married now and he is a bully, Lizzie is not the bubbly, happy girl she was."

Davie shook his head, "So much for the earth moving then, will you think about marrying me Sarah? I have a good job now and I am hoping someday soon to have my own lorry. Lorry transport is going to be the modern way; cart and horses are on their way out. When I have my own lorry I can work for myself and build a business. Think about it Sarah, we could do well for us all, you, me, the boys and Mary. We know each other so well; think about it, will you?"

"Yes Davie I will, and nobody Davie has ever been as good to me as you have. You have always been there for me. I want you to know that I have never taken our friendship for granted and I value it very much. You should go out with other girls and enjoy yourself. I am tied to the family, what else can I do?"

"Think about it for me, will you. It would make me so happy Sarah"

"I will think about it and thank you Davie."

He put his arm round her and they continued walking. Sarah felt safe with Davie and she also felt comfortable in his company. Yes she would think about it.

They reached home and as he left her at the door he kissed her goodnight. It was a gentle kiss of a friend to a friend. Sarah knew this, because hadn't Lizzie told her all about kissing.

The time passed quickly for Sarah, between her new hours at the Surgery and being busy with the family. Mary helped a lot now; she had turned into a very pretty girl and was becoming more confident. With Mary's help, Sarah was managing her working hours. Colin Young, the new doctor was also now working at the Surgery. Sarah had shown him round the town a few times and she did enjoy his company. She was now able to go out occasionally with Davie. Life for all of them was getting better.

Jimmy was now pleading to leave school and get work of some kind. He was now over fourteen years old and Sarah made an appointment with Miss Black to see what they should do. She wanted him in further education of some kind and Jimmy wanted to work in the shipyard.

Miss Black saw Sarah one afternoon by herself, at first to discuss Jimmy.

"What do you want Jimmy to work at Sarah?"

"I would like him to have a good education, I can afford to send him to college but he wants to work in the shipyard like his father."

"There are good trades in the shipyard Sarah. It is my experience that if a boy or girl does not want to go to college it could be a waste of time and money. Let me send for Jimmy and we will discuss it together."

Jimmy was sent for and when he came into Miss Black's office he was quite pale.

"Everything is fine Jimmy, you have not to worry. Your sister and I are discussing what you would like to work at."

"I want to go to work to help Sarah out."

"Sarah pleaded with Jimmy; we are managing fine just now. You want to think ahead not just for the present but for the future."

"Sarah is right Jimmy, not many boys get this opportunity. You could go onto the High School and then onto a College."

"I don't want that Miss Black; I would like to work in the shipyard."

"What do you want to do in the shipyard, do you want a trade? You cannot start a trade until you are sixteen and you are not yet fifteen years old."

"I would like to be an engineer, I want to see how things work, how engines are put together."

"In that case then you will have to go to night school as well as serving an apprenticeship. So you would still have to learn." Miss Black spoke firmly,

"I will learn, please Sarah let me go to be an engineer."

"What should we do Miss Black?"

"Leave it with me and I will see if I can get Jimmy into the yard as a message boy. They use boys in the yards to run from one shop to the other, make tea and generally help. These are the boys who get offered a trade first. If you want to be an engineer, you will need to show you are reliable and that you will go to the Watt College as well as serving an apprenticeship. I will be in touch when I have some news. Jimmy you must realise that if it was not for Sarah you would not get this chance. Sarah has raised you well, now it is your turn to show that you appreciate it."

Sarah Looked at Miss Black, shaking her head, "All I wanted was an education and I was not allowed to have it, I would have liked them all to go to college, but they must have the choice that I was not allowed. Thank you very much Miss Black, we will wait till we hear from you."

As they went back home Jimmy could not hide his excitement,

"Thanks Sarah. When can I leave school?"

"When Miss Black gets you a job in the yard and not before it. It might be a good while away but I would think it would have to be before the summer. Time will tell, I can hardly believe you are going out to work. It will be Andrew next wanting to leave."

"No Sarah he wants to be an architect, he will stay in school."

Sarah was surprised," Where did he get that idea from?"

"I suppose out of one of these books he is always reading."

"Well things are looking much better for us all now and we are not just so short of money now."

Sarah and Jimmy went out to buy overalls and boots for him to start work. Jimmy was so excited that his excitement rubbed off on them all and Sarah had her hands full calming then all down. They were sitting at their dinner when Archie came in dressed in the overalls, which drowned him and the boots which were far too large for him. He tap-danced his way round the kitchen till they were all laughing. Jimmy made a dive at him and Andrew separated them. Mary and Sarah were sore laughing.

Sarah looked at them all so happy and she thought that maybe now life would be kinder to them all

Chapter 7

The summer had not long started when Mary developed a bad cough, and somehow seemed to be more withdrawn than she had been recently. When Sarah asked her if anything was wrong she would turn her head away. Sarah would come home from work and find that she had not done any housework and seemed to be sitting staring into space. When Sarah questioned her about what was wrong, Mary broke down and started to cry.

Mrs Russell could not make anything of her behaviour either and Davie said he would try and find out what was wrong. Davie told Sarah that she would not even look at him and pushed him away.

Sarah spoke to Dr. Small and he suggested that she brought Mary to the Surgery with her and he would check her cough and make sure she was well.

Sarah waited outside while Dr Small examined Mary. He seemed to be taking a long time, when he opened the door and beckoned for Sarah to come into his room.

Sarah realised that something was far wrong.

"Is it the cough Dr Small?"

"Yes Sarah, Mary has a bad cough, were you worried about Tuberculosis?"

"Yes I was, there is so much of it in the town at the moment."

"No, she has just got a slight chest infection at the moment but there is another problem."

Dr. Small looked at Sarah and hesitated, "Sarah, Mary is expecting a baby, she is pregnant."

"Mary can't be Dr. Small, she can't be."

"She is Sarah, or I am in the wrong profession. I would make a guess and say at least three months."

Sarah looked at Mary, who was just sitting looking at her hands.

Sarah signed to Mary, "Do you know what the Doctor has said."

Mary coughed and clapped her chest.

"No, you are having a baby." Sarah signed by holding her arms together and gently swaying her arms from side to side.

Dr Small sat and looked at Sarah, looking at Mary in disbelief and then Mary understood, and then she started screaming.

Dr Hendry came rushing in and between him and Dr Small they held Mary tight till she stopped.

Sarah could not take it in, and she sat in disbelief. Dr Small sat with Sarah letting his words sink in, Sarah looked round the Surgery walls, at the bookcase, at the desk and even looked at the roof, taking in every part of the Surgery and yet not seeing anything, for all Sarah could hear was the word baby. She pleaded with Dr.Small.

"Are you sure Dr Small, Mary is always with me."

"I want Dr Hendry to examine Mary; I need a second opinion on this. We will examine Mary again but I need you to stay with her now. Try to calm her down and try to stay calm yourself."

The examination was difficult for them all, while Mary was dressing behind the screen.

The two doctors spoke with each other, and then turned to Sarah.

"Sarah we are of the opinion that Mary has been raped. She is fully three months pregnant; we are of the opinion that the baby will be due around the end of November or the beginning of December."

Mary joined them and when Sarah tried to question her she started screaming again. Sarah had never seen Mary like this before,

"What will I do Dr Small? How will I find out who has done this?"

Dr Small leaned forward, listen Sarah," This is a crime, but what will you gain by reporting this, if you have no idea who has done this to your sister. Is Mary alone often? Have you any regular visitors that could do such a thing."

"I have to work to keep us all; she stays at home and helps in the house. She only goes out with me because of the deafness. The boys are always around."

"What age are your brothers?"

"Oh no, no, this has nothing to do with my brothers," Sarah broke down then. Mary came and put her arms round Sarah and the two of them clung to each other.

Dr Small sat at his desk and Dr Hendry perched on the edge of the desk and both doctors looked at each other. It was a pitiful sight before them.

"We will help you all we can Sarah, you will have to help Mary through this and we will help you. I think you should take a few days off. I will get in touch with the District Nurse and ask her to come and speak to you. As Mary blood pressure seems high and as she has a chest infection I think we should try and get her into the maternity home until you can see what you want to do."

"What about, what do you mean?"

"You will need to decide if you should report this to the police or would you rather not.

Mary is an adult; does she want to report this?"

"You think that one of my brothers is responsible? They are not, they are not," Sarah cried?"

"No we are making no accusations, you say that it could not be any of them, but someone has done this. It may be that you will never know who is responsible. Even if you could find out who has done this, they could say she was a willing partner. How can she defend herself, how can you help her, this must be your priority, and in time to come you will have to decide about the baby."

"How do you mean? I cannot take this all in. how could this happen and I did not know?"

"Will you keep the baby or will you have the baby adopted. These are the questions that you will have to answer; it is early days yet. Mary could not look after the baby without your help."

"What will I do first?" Sarah was now distraught, wringing her hands together.

"Right I will try and get Mary into the Maternity home for the present. I will send the Nurse to speak to you or you could see her here when you are at work. We have to see that Mary does not try to harm herself, she is screaming because she is distressed. If I can get her in even for a few weeks it would give you a chance to sort things out at home. I do not think that Mary should be left alone at all now until her confinement is over. The maternity home does not have a large number of beds and they can only take a few patients at a time. I will see what I can do."

"Thank you Dr Small. I will take Mary home now and we will try and sort this out."

When Sarah had left both doctors discussed her situation.

"I wonder just how much Sarah will take before she has a breakdown, that girl has had more than her share of trouble and none of it caused by her."

Dr. Small filled in Dr Hendry on her background.

"Sarah has been great for me; she set up our filing system. She knows where everything is; she has even started a child clinic here for young mothers, and bullied a nurse into giving the mothers talks about how to care for their babies. Looks after our finances, I will have to help her or we could lose her, for she will look after her sister and see her through this."

"Will we manage to get her into Toga House, I have never been there yet, all of my patients have been able to have home confinements." Dr.Hendry asked.

Dr Small explained," Toga House was a family home, and it was gifted to the people of Greenock by Ex-Baillie Daniel Orr as a maternity home and child welfare clinic. This is the first maternity hospital we have ever had in Greenock. It was gifted to Greenock in March nineteen hundred and nineteen. It takes the more difficult cases. We will need to help Sarah; she could have done without this."

Sarah took Mary home; she could not believe what she had just learned. She would need to find out who was responsible. How would she tell the boys about this? How would she cope with a baby? No, she could not and would not. This baby would have to go for adoption. Dr. Small would see that the baby got a good home. What was she going to do about Mary?

As she went into the house Mrs Russell came out to speak to them. On seeing Sarah's worried look she asked,

"Everything fine Sarah?"

"No, anything but fine, could you come in?

Mrs Russell came in and sat at the table, Sarah made some tea and set out the three cups and saucers, she never spoke till she sat down with Mrs Russell.

"What's wrong lass"? Mrs Russell asked concerned.

"Mary is going to have a baby, she has a chest infection and I took her to the doctor and he discovered this. She is about three months," Sarah broke down at this, "what am I going to do now? I was just congratulating myself on how well we were getting on and now this."

"Are you sure?"

"Yes, two doctors have examined her and they are of the opinion that she has been raped."

"Sarah I can't believe this. Who would do this, have you tried asking her?"

"She just starts screaming, it is terrible. I have to keep her calm because they say her blood pressure is high. How am I going to tell the boys? Dr Small wants her to go into Toga house for a few weeks. How am I going to tell her that? Who is responsible for this, how will I find out, will I ever find out? I have to decide whether we will keep the baby or have it adopted. If I ever find out who has done this I will have them charged. The boys will go crazy over this."

Sarah broke down again and Mrs Russell held her while she sobbed. Mary sat and picked up her knitting, but the tears were running down her face.

The next few days were very difficult days. Sarah explained to the boys what had happened and how Mary would maybe go into hospital for a while.

"What do you mean Sarah," Archie wanted to know.

"I will explain it to you later." Jimmy told him.

"Who has done this Sarah, where has she been?"

"I don't know who is responsible and when I question her she just starts screaming. Dr Small said that I must keep her quiet and calm. I certainly do not feel calm, nor can I look after a baby. I need to work you all know that. I have to go back to work and I now cannot leave her alone at any time. I really don't know what to do."

The door was knocked as they all sat staring at each other, the boys could not take it in and Jimmy was angry, how could someone do this to Mary?

Archie answered the door and came back to tell Sarah that a nurse was at the door wanting to speak to her.

"Bring her in Archie and you boys leave me with the nurse on my own for a while."

Archie brought in the nurse,

"How do you do Sarah, I am Nurse Baxter. Dr Small has asked me to come and speak to you about your sister Mary."

"Please sit down, Mary is sitting at the room fire, I am trying to keep her quiet and calm, did you know that she was deaf?"

"Yes, Dr Small has filled me in. We have to do what is best for Mary and also for you. I have spoken with the Matron at the maternity home and we have discussed your problem."

"How do you mean?"

"Well you have a lot of responsibility looking after the family and working, so maybe it would be better all round for everyone if Mary went to stay at the maternity home till the baby was born."

"She would never go, she needs us all."

"Do you not think that maybe we could persuade her to go? She needs to get her chest infection cleared and get that cough cured. She would not need to be in bed all the time but she would get rest. You could visit her at any time. Will you let me speak to her?"

Sarah hesitated, "Yes but it will be difficult, I will bring her through."

Sarah brought Mary through from the room, where she had been sitting at the fire.

Sarah explained that she had a bad cough and the doctor wanted her to get well. The nurse watched how Sarah had signed to Mary.

"What about the baby," Mary asked.

Sarah was surprised that she did not get as upset this time.

"It would be better for the baby if you did not have a cough."

The nurse noted that Sarah cradled her arms when she spoke about the baby. She herself followed Sarah method of signing.

"I will help you look after the baby, is this your knitting? You are a lovely knitter, I wish I could do that." the nurse smiled at Mary as she spoke.

Mary was all smiles at the nurse and went to show her the things that she knitted.

"These are lovely, you are a good knitter, isn't she Sarah? You could knit for your baby.

Would you like to come with me to get better?"

Mary looked at Sarah and she started to get upset,

"Mary I would come and visit you and bring you anything you needed. I would see you often. When you are better you will come home."

"With the baby?" Mary stated.

Sarah looked at the nurse; she could not look Mary in the face and lie to her. The nurse took over.

"When you are better you will decide."

She held Mary's face gently in her hands and smiled at her.

"I could do with your help with my knitting, could you show me please?"

"I will come back each day for a few days till Mary gets used to me. You have not to worry about your work this week Sarah, Dr Small has instructed me to help you."

"I can't let her go, she needs me." Sarah pleaded.

"Listen Sarah, listen to me, they all need you and if you do not look after yourself you could be ill and where would the family be then. You have to be brave for all of you, not just for Mary. The time will pass and she will be home with you soon. Have you thought about the baby?"

"Mary go and see if the boys are fine."

When Mary had left the room Sarah looked at the nurse and said,

"How can I bring up a baby as well look after the family and work? I could not leave Mary alone. I will have to find out who is responsible for this. I had to leave her so that I could go to work and Mrs Russell next door kept her eye on her. She cannot understand this either."

"You are not to blame for this Sarah; do not take this blame on yourself. The baby could go to a good home, Dr Small would see to that and you do not need to decide right now."

"I have decided I cannot keep the baby and neither can Mary. If I do not find an answer to this, could it happen again? Somebody has been in this house when we have all been out and Mary in alone."

"I am here to help you Sarah, I will come back tomorrow evening at the same time, and once Mary has got used to me we will try and get her into the maternity home. We have a room for her at the moment so the sooner she comes in the better. That will give you time for the rest of the family and yourself."

"Thank you Nurse Baxter that is what we will do, stay and have a cup of tea, Mary likes to make tea for us all."

"Thank you I will."

Sarah brought Mary back into the kitchen and the three of them sat and had a cup of tea together. When Nurse Baxter rose to leave Sarah said," show Nurse Baxter out Mary."

Mary and the nurse went out to the door together.

"I'll see you tomorrow Mary, you keep warm and watch that cough." Nurse Baxter left with many thoughts in her head. How clever Sarah was to make her sister understand her between signing with her hands and speaking slowly, you could hardly tell that Mary was so deaf. Her work in this district was hard, for many of her patients lived in poverty, but Sarah Shaw was lifting her family out of poverty, it was hard to watch her being so sad,

After the nurse had gone the boys came back into the kitchen,

"What are we going to do Sarah," Jimmy was very upset as he spoke.

"We are all going to help each other through this and that way we will help Mary. She has to go into hospital till the baby is born. I cannot look after her and work. We will all go and visit her and she will be back with us soon. Help me to make something to eat, I am really tired today."

"We will make scrambled eggs and toast, would like that wouldn't you?" Archie said.

The tears were running down Sarah's face, she could not help herself; this latest trouble for the family was more than she could take. Sarah wondered to herself why they had all the trouble, why all the bad things were happening to them.

The three boys all put their arms round her and they all clung together.

Later on when everyone was in bed and Sarah was sitting alone, Davie came into see her.

"Your mother fill you in Davie?"

"I can hardly believe this, who could have done this? Have you any idea?"

"None at all and when I question her all hell breaks out, she starts scream-ing. I noticed that the janitor of the school used to keep looking at her, I wonder if it was him. I took Mary there to keep me safe because I did not want to be left alone with him. It could be him and he met her through me. What a mess, I can-not question her. Dr Small says that I must keep her quiet and calm. Mary has to go into hospital to get her chest infection cleared up and they have suggested that she goes into the maternity home until the baby is born."

"Let her go Sarah, what about the baby?"

"I cannot possibly keep the baby; I will have enough problems without the baby, Davie will I ever get out of trouble? Is this my life, living other people's lives, will I ever have a life of my own, Am I always going to be trapped?"

"Let Mary go to the maternity home and let the baby be adopted. They will find a good home for the baby. Please do not get so down, I hate to see you like this. My mother said to tell you that she would help you all she can and you know I will. You must change the lock on your door Sarah."

"Do you think someone has a key, they would not need one? We all leave our doors unlocked throughout the day. Do you think that someone must have come in? She must have been terrified. I have not slept or eaten right since this started and I have a long way to go and through it all I am more concerned about how this will affect me, I have been selfish I should be more concerned about how Mary must be feeling."

"That's you isn't it, why must you take all the worry? Things are getting better for you now, leave it that way. Take the help that has been offered, it will be better for Mary and in the long run better for you all. Have you thought anymore about us getting married?"

"How can I Davie, no it cannot be, not now."

"Were you considering it? We know each other so well and I will take care of you all."

Sarah looked at him, shaking her head slowly," You should get yourself someone who is free Davie, any girl would be glad to have you."

"No I will wait for you, the boys will grow up and they will soon all be working."

"Sarah did not tell him that she wanted them all educated, if she could do this, it would be their chance of a better life.

"Please Davie do not waste time waiting for happiness, if it comes along you grab it, according to Lizzie!"

"I will personally brain that Lizzie some of these days. You make me a cup of tea and some of your apple tarts please, to make up for me being disappointed again."

They were both laughing now and Sarah was feeling better, there was no doubt about it, Davie was good for her.

Two days later Sarah took Mary to the maternity home to have a look round. It was rather like a large family home. You entered through a wrought iron gate and went up a slight hill; the path took you right up to the door. The garden was neat and tidy and when Sarah turned to look back, you could see over the houses right across to Helensburgh. It was a nice day but Sarah heart was heavy and she sighed as she rang the doorbell.

Nurse Baxter was waiting for them and showed them round and took Mary into a small bedroom that would be hers until the baby was due. Nurse Baxter had brought her knitting in and there were a few dropped stitches, she showed the knitting to Mary to see if she could help her. Mary laughed at the state the knitting was in and sorted it out.

"Why don't you stay here and help us, we need clothes for babies, you could knit for us and for your own baby."

Sarah signed and explained to Mary,

"Would you like to help out here with some knitting and light work. You will have a bedroom to yourself and I will visit often. Will you try it Mary?" Sarah pleaded.

Mary shrugged her shoulders," Well mind, if I don't like it I will come home."

"Yes, I promise you that you will come home."

So it was agreed and Sarah went home without Mary, promising to bring wool and her clothes the next day.

Sarah walked all the way home through as many back streets as she could find, she did not want to meet anybody. She had never felt so bad, she was sure about this. Things could not get any worse and once again she felt alone, so very alone.

When she arrived home the boys were all waiting for her. The house seemed so empty without Mary and Archie was inconsolable, they could not stop him crying and none of them wanted anything to eat. Jimmy and Andrew swore that they would get who had done this to their sister. Archie was going to bash his brains in, whoever he was.

The boys made tea and toast for Sarah and themselves.

"How did you all get on today at school."

"Miss Black wants to see you Sarah," Andrew said.

"What about, do you know?"

"No, she just said would I ask you to come and speak to her."

"I will go tomorrow before I go to see Mary. Tell Miss Black that I will come to see her after two o'clock tomorrow. You will all have to visit Mary to keep her calm. If we can keep her happy and calm while she is in the home it will be better for her and us. Do not worry about her, she is well looked after and it will not be long before she is home."

Sarah went to see Miss Black before she visited Mary; she knocked the headmistress's door.

"Come in, Sarah how nice to see you again. I have some good news for you.

I have had word that Jimmy has to start work on Monday at the Shipyard, He has to ask for a Mr Armstrong and be at the main office for eight o'clock. He will need working boots and overalls or dungarees, can you arrange that?"

"Yes we have them ready and thank you very much."

"There is something else; Andrew can go to the High School for higher education. How do you feel about that?"

"That is wonderful, does he know?"

"Miss Black shook her head, not yet; he will need a uniform, blazer, grey flannel trousers, tie, white shirt and a pullover, and maybe some sports equipment. I could maybe manage to help with this, through a Bursary, it is not easy and might not be much, what do you think?"

"I can manage; each of them has a bankbook to help with education. It is not a lot but will certainly cover what he needs."

Sarah explained about the money that came to them in a benefit from the rowing club and the town. How she had saved the money for just such a purpose.

"I had hoped to educate the boys but Jimmy is set against it as you know."

"He will do well in an apprenticeship and I am hopeful that he will go into engineering. Now how are you and Mary?"

Sarah sat and looked at Miss Black, she could not speak.

"What is wrong Sarah?"

"Mary is expecting a baby and is in the maternity home. According to the doctor she has been raped, I had no idea about this. It has been a dreadful shock."

"Who has done this, do you know?"

"No but I used to bring her here to keep me company because I did not like the way the Janitor spoke to me and Jimmy would come and meet me."

"Did he do anything to you?"

"No, but did say that we should be good to each other, it was the way he said it."

"You cannot make accusations Sarah, be careful."

"I know but he is the only person who has ever made me feel uneasy. I wonder about him that's all, because she sometimes came to the school to meet the boys. And if I was busy, I left her sitting in a classroom, maybe then; I think that she was lonely with me working. I have tried to question her but she starts screaming and the doctor said I was to leave well alone."

"What will you do Sarah?" Miss Black shook her head slowly, how much more could Sarah Shaw take?

"I don't know, Miss Black."

"Listen to me Sarah, you have had worse than this put upon you and you have survived. You will survive this and so will Mary."

"We are just getting on our feet and things were picking up for us, the boys are devastated. This news you have for us will cheer us all up. Andrew I am sure will want to go to the High School and hopefully on to college. Jimmy cannot wait to start work."

As Sarah rose to go, Miss Black came round and put her arm around Sarah and gave her a hug, Sarah broke down then, and Miss Black held her until she stopped crying. "You sit there and I will get you a cup of tea."

"I have not the time Miss Black, thank you

Miss Black nodded for she understood only too well,"Now you take care of yourself, you cannot help your family if you are not well, and I will speak to the boys today and you tell Mary that I was asking for her."

"Thank you Miss Black, I am on my way to see her now."

As Sarah left the school she felt much better for her talk with Miss Black. She went shopping for wool for Mary and bought her a few other things that she might need.

When she arrived at the maternity home she found Mary busy making afternoon tea for everyone. She hugged Sarah and they went round together with the tea for everyone.

The nurse on duty told Sarah that Mary seemed very settled and was getting on well with everyone. When Sarah left she waved to her as she left and Sarah promised to see her soon.

That night Jimmy and Andrew were both excited with their news. Andrew was to start at the High School after the summer holidays and Jimmy was not to go back to school again.

"You will go to the Technical Night School, you promised."

"Oh Sarah, don't spoil it for me."

"You promised, what's wrong Archie, are you feeling left out?"

Archie was sitting looking glum, he was not happy with the changes that were coming; he did not want to be on his own in school." I don't want to go to school on my own."

"You will not be on your own and you know that, come on, before we know where we are you will be going on to the High School."

"No, not me I want to be a painter."

Andrew and Jimmy started laughing, "You will never make a living being an artist."

"Don't be daft, you two are daft, I am going to be a painter, that paints houses and I am not going to work for anyone else but myself." Archie looked at them all defiantly.

"When did you decide this?"

Sarah was surprised at Archie; she wondered when he had thought this out and why.

"I listen to all the men worried about work; well I will not be, for any jobs that come will only be for me."

"You will have to get an apprenticeship for a painter; you just don't get a pot of paint and a brush and start work. You have to learn. It would be better if you went to the High School, Archie."

"No, Sarah, No."

His brothers were still laughing at him and Archie made a dive at them and they all landed on the floor. Archie managed to get on top of Andrew and he was shouting,

"I give in, I give in." They were all laughing, as Andrew was the tallest of them now, nearly fourteen and over six feet in height.

"You lot stop this, listen stop it. I have something I want to talk to you about."

Thy all looked at her waiting for more bad news.

"Nothing to worry about, now how would you like it if we bought a wireless."

"A wireless for us, could we Sarah?" Archie had forgotten all about being a painter now.

Sarah continued "I was in the town and they are in most of the shops. They work with a battery, which gets recharged. I think we all need a treat. Right what do you all think?"

The excitement of them getting a wireless lifted all their spirits and Sarah felt that somehow they would get through this and it would not be long till Mary came home.

It was agreed that on Saturday they would all go out and buy a wireless. The boys were to find out before then what would be the best kind to buy

The weekend was a great success. After they visited Mary they went into the town and bought a Marconi wireless and Battery, which was rechargeable. It was to be Archie's job to see that the battery was replaced when it was needed. After tea they all sat round the wircless listening to the news being read, then music and a play. The boys were tuning in to different stations. Davie came in to hear it and then brought in his mother and father.

Sarah had baked apple tarts and they made tea and made a party out of it. They all had a great night and they were all more settled.

Davie waited after his mother and father had gone back home,

"How about going for a walk Sarah, it is a nice night."

"Yes I would like that, you lot clear up the dishes for me."

"I am the working man now I don't need to do dishes," was the quick reply from Jimmy.

"I did them at dinner time," from Andrew," I dried them, I helped you," shouted Archie.

Sarah and Davie left them all arguing and walked down the street to the waterfront and walked along by the harbour.

"Are you feeling better about Mary now?"

"Yes Davie I am. I have decided that if possible the baby will be adopted. Dr Small will find a good home for the baby with someone who does not have any children. The thing is how Mary will take it. You know Davie I am tired worrying about things."

"You have the baby adopted and don't listen to Mary, you think on yourself for a change. We have a right to be happy." Davie spoke with bitterness in his voice.

"What's wrong Davie, that's not like you?"

"Well you know I want to marry you and all you get is one problem after the other. I have to look after my mother because my father does not seem to care one way or the other about her. We are entitled to our own life, the boys will soon all be working it will be easier for us. It is time for us."

"The boys will not be working Davie, I want them educated. I will have to work for a long time. I did not want Jimmy in the shipyard, and you know that. Archie is not even twelve yet. I cannot think about marrying just now."

"You are using this as an excuse."

"Please Davie, I have told you to find another girl."

He turned and shouted at her," I don't want another girl, I want you."

They walked on in silence, this was a new Davie, and Sarah did not know how to handle him. They were at the far end of the harbour and there was no one about. He turned and grabbed her and kissed her hard, she did not respond.

"That's how I feel about you; I see that you really do not feel the same way."

"I do love you Davie but as I have told you before, you are like one of my brothers to me. You know what my friend Lizzie said,"

"Damn your friend Lizzie and you Sarah, I won't waste any more time on you."

He turned and walked away from her. She stood and watched him till she could see him no longer then, she made her way home and again. She felt the loneliness wash over her.

Well, thought Sarah, that must be our first row, she was sorry but she could not help it. When she reached the top flat to go in home, Davie was sitting on the stairs. She sat down beside him.

"I am sorry Davie, if I could make myself different I would. I appreciate you asking me to marry you, I do really."

"Don't you want a family of your own, your own things, and your own home? You are living your mother's life."

"What else can I do, but see to them all. Do you think I never want time to myself? Do you think I never want to go out with the girls? Have a laugh just for fun. Go dancing. I did not want to be an old maid I had it thrust on me. I will bring up my brothers and look after Mary; I could not live with myself if I did not. I will educate the boys as best as I can so that they can have a future. A better life is what I want for them, I am trapped Davie, now you know that."

"They will walk away and not look back, what future will you have?"

"We all care for each other, that's a nasty thing to say. I do not want to argue with you but you are making me very angry, I am going in, goodnight."

"Promise me one thing Sarah."

"What is it?"

"Have the baby adopted, don't bring it home, if you do you will never have a chance."

She left him sitting on the stairs, and she never answered him. She went in and closed the door, wishing she had never gone for a walk with him. That was not the first time he had practically demanded that she did not bring the baby home. She did not want to bring the baby home but Mary had to be considered.

Jimmy was getting ready to go out with his pals, Andrew and Archie were listening to the wireless. They all looked at her realising that she was upset.

"What's wrong Sarah, "Archie wanted to know?

"Nothing I am just tired."

"I will make you tea," Andrew offered.

"Thanks that would be fine."

She sat down at the window and stared out at nothing, she was trying hard not to cry.

Things were now going to be different with Davie, she felt as though she had lost a friend.

The summer passed and Andrew was getting ready to go to the High School. One other girl from the class was going also. Andrew and her had become friendly. She lived with her mother in the next close to theirs. Her mother, Mrs Bell was a widow and she had raised her daughter Jean, by herself, as her husband had died young. Jean was becoming a constant visitor. When Sarah came home from work she found Andrew upset because Jean would not be going to the High School.

"What happened? Why is Jean not going?"

"Her mother has tried to get the uniform, there was supposed to be a Bursary, but it does not cover the uniform. Jean cannot go without the uniform. She is very upset and so is her mother."

"Andrew go up and ask Mrs Bell to come and see me, I might be able to help Jean."

"Could we Sarah, could we help her."

"I will try but you have not to tell anybody."

Andrew was not long before he came back, Mrs Bell is just in from her work at the Mill, and she will come up after tea time."

Sarah was busy preparing their meal ready for Jimmy coming in from the shipyard. Jimmy had settled into his work well and seemed to like it. There was still no word of an apprenticeship as yet but they were hoping that he might hear soon.

After they had eaten and Sarah had washed up, she was telling the boys how Mary had been. Sarah went to see Mary at her dinner break.

"Mary is very well and likes the maternity home, she does light housework and she is still knitting. I told her you would all be up to see her on Saturday."

She saw by their faces that they had other plans for Saturday.

"We have to keep her calm and contented. We must support her through this. We must be here for each other until we are all a lot older." Sarah slapped her hand on the table, palm down, and one by one they followed putting their hands one on top of each other. This was Sarah's way of allowing them some say in what was happening in the family.

Mrs Bell knocked the door just after seven o'clock that night. She had chased the boys out for a while till she spoke with Mrs Bell.

"You wanted to see me Sarah, something wrong?"

"No, I wanted to ask you about Jean going to the High School. Did you get a list of what they need?"

"Jean can't go Sarah, she is right upset but she understands, it is the money. I was depending on overtime and I have not been getting any."

"Will you be getting overtime later?"

"We usually do. A month's overtime would have paid for what she needed."

"I could help you, I could let you have the month's overtime and you could pay me back when you can."

"It would not be right Sarah. You have five mouths to feed and I only have two."

"Look I never got the chance; it is Andrew and Jean's chance now. This is their chance of a better future, a better job. Let her go if she wants to."

"Do you know what it costs?"

"I paid twenty five shillings for the blazer, and twenty shilling for the trousers, the tie was five shillings and the boys wear a white shirt. I think that about three pounds would be enough. I have knitted the pullover and socks; you could do the same with the cardigan."

"Sarah I would pay you back, you can be sure I will."

"I will not need this money for a few months and nobody will ever know. You think about it. What will Jean do if she does not go? The mill, the Rope works or like me in service. This is a chance for them if they want it. Jimmy would not go, and he is in the shipyard. He is hoping for an apprenticeship."

"I will speak to Jean and thanks a lot Sarah. Is it true about Mary?"

"You heard then, yes it's true."

"How will you cope? If I can help you I will, it is not fair what happens to us. I'll let you know what Jean thinks and thanks again. I did not mean to be nosy."

"No it's alright Mrs Bell, it is true and it is terrible and I am worried sick about the whole thing. We will just have to wait and see what happens."

"Don't worry so much, this happened in our family, sometimes things work out for themselves and we have worried needlessly. Thanks again Sarah, you have done a great job with your family and you be proud of what you're doing."

Sarah showed Mrs Bell out, she would be glad to get some sleep tonight she felt tired and depressed and busy as Sarah was, she felt very lonely.

Andrew and his friend Jean started the High School at the end of August and Sarah was so proud of him. He had grown taller over the summer holidays and was now fourteen years old. Jimmy had been promised an engineering apprenticeship when he was sixteen. He was now fifteen years and Archie was twelve years old now. They were all tall, Archie being the smallest. Mary had been home for a day lately and was keeping well. She seemed pleased to go back to the maternity home that night. The Matron spoke to Sarah about possible work for Mary after the baby was born. She had apparently taken on keeping the kitchen in running order and helping the cook.

"I have always kept her at home because of her deafness. I work and if Mary brings the baby home she would need to look after the baby."

"I thought it was decided that the baby would be adopted?"

"Yes, that is what I want but will Mary agree?"

"I think you will have to convince her that the baby should go to a good home and she could have work here if that was what she decided. It is up to you and me to convince her that she is too young. She likes being here and I think that may sway her. Leave it just now but I take it we are both of the same mind."

"Yes, I have to work and I now have a good job and I want to keep it."

Sarah was busy at the Surgery and she now had two younger girls helping her. She enjoyed her work and Jimmy's wages were also helping, once again she was feeling that life was getting kinder to them.

Sarah was missing Davie, as she was not seeing him so much and he had stopped coming in to see how they all were. When they met he was friendly but there was now a difference. Mrs Russell and Sarah still baked one day a week but at night after tea. They would have long talks about everything but never about her and Davie.

Sarah wrote regularly to Mrs Barr in France, or as Sarah would remind herself Madame Renaud was her name now. Monsieur Renaud and Mrs Barr had married shortly after Mrs Barr had arrived in Paris. They were living in the outskirts of Paris in a country house. Plenty of room for you and the family to visit someday, she had written in her last letter. She had asked Sarah to find out if all was well with Lizzie, as she was not having her letters answered. Sarah had not heard from Lizzie for some time. She had written to tell her about Mary and was surprised that she had not received an answer. Sarah made up her mind to visit her soon in Dunoon.

The weeks and months passed, as they were all busy. It was December again and Mary's baby was due any day now. On her visit yesterday to the maternity home Mary seemed to be very tired and Nurse Baxter had explained that this happened just before a baby was due. They wanted Mary to have as much rest as possible, as soon as Mary went into labour they would send for Sarah straight away.

Doctor Small was to be at the confinement and he had discussed with Sarah that he had in mind an excellent married couple that would like to adopt a baby. They could not have any children and this could be a blessing to both families. It was now a question of waiting for the baby to be born but Sarah was still concerned about how Mary would react. Mary did not talk about the baby and some days Sarah would wonder if she were really aware of the situation. She seemed to have blanked everything out of her mind. Sarah had only once more tried to find out who the father was and Mary started screaming again and Nurse Baxter said that it was better to leave it alone. Mary was in very good health and all should go well at the confinement.

All Sarah decided she could do was to wait, and it would not be long now

Chapter 8

$\mathcal{I}$t was the second week in December when the local policeman, wakened Sarah in the early hours of the morning asking her to go as soon as possible to the maternity home.

She wakened Jimmy and told him that Mary had started and to see to the boys till she got back.

She dressed as quickly as she could and the policeman walked her most of the way. She hurried the last street on her own. It was a clear cold morning, still dark, the sky was bright with stars and the moon shone its eerie light over the streets.

She hurried in the entrance of the maternity home to be met by Nurse Baxter and Dr. Small.

"I came as quickly as I could," she stopped there because she knew that something was wrong.

"Come into the office Sarah," Dr Small put his arm round her and Nurse Baxter led the way.

"Sit down Sarah we have to talk to you, there has been a problem with Mary's confinement. She went into labour very quickly and the baby was born quickly. Mary has haemorrhaged and we could not stop the bleeding. She became unconscious and died very suddenly, she died very peacefully, and I did not have time to get you sooner."

Sarah looked from Nurse Baxter to Dr Small,

"No, tell me no, it is not true, no, she was well, she was only tired."

"I am so sorry, we done everything that we could; Mary could not have been in a better place to get help quickly. She did not suffer Sarah, and she slept away quietly. I will take you to see her if you would like to."

"Yes, she was to come home soon, how will I tell the boys? I should have kept her at home; she must have thought I deserted her."

"No Sarah, she did not, she liked it here, and we asked her if she wanted to work here and she said she would. None of this is your fault; do not take this on your shoulders. You have been a good sister to Mary; you did what was best for her."

Dr Small took Sarah to see Mary in her small bedroom, she lay peacefully as if she was sleeping, and there was a hint of a smile on her face.

"Did she know she had a baby?"

"Yes she did, it is a little girl, and would you like me to get the boys?"

"Could you please? I don't want to leave her alone just now."

Nurse Baxter sat with Sarah for nearly an hour before Dr Small came back with the boys.

He had explained everything to them and they came into the room, they threw themselves at Sarah and they all clung together and cried. Archie was so distraught that Nurse Baxter took him out of the room. Dr Small took them through to his office and hot cups of tea were handed round them all. He spoke directly to Jimmy,

"You have to be strong for the rest of them, you have to help Sarah. Drink the tea it will help you all. Nurse Baxter brought Archie back and Sarah held him tight."

"Would you all like to see the baby, you do not need to, but it would help you all to see the lovely baby that your sister had and she lives on in the baby."

Dr Small said softly, Sarah nodded.

Nurse Baxter brought they baby for them to see and Sarah cradled her in her arms. She was beautiful and she pushed her hand out of the blanket and Sarah caught her hand. The baby held tightly on to Sarah's finger. Jimmy was on his knees beside Sarah. Andrew and Archie bent over Sarah's back, they all stared at the baby. Sarah looked at them all.

"What will we do? Jimmy asked them all.

"We will take her home and bring her up for Mary; she is one of us and should be with us." Sarah put her hand palm down on her knee and one by one they followed.

"I thought it was agreed that the baby should be adopted," Nurse Baxter spoke quietly.

"Not anymore, we will take her home with us."

"How will you work with a baby?"

"I don't know but I will work it out."

The nurse left and came back with Dr Small,

"I hear you have changed you mind over the adoption. Why don't you all think it over, it does not have to be decided today."

"We have decided Dr Small, she now belongs with us, and I will work something out."

Dr Small nodded his head.

"I will take you all home in the car. Try to get some sleep, you all have a busy few days ahead and you all need your rest. The nurse will give you the necessary bottle and food for the baby to start you. You will need nappies."

Nurse Baxter brought through everything for the baby and also clothes that Mary had knitted including a shawl to wrap the baby in.

Dr Small managed to get them all into his car and took them home. As they left the car he spoke to Jimmy,

"You will need to attend to the funeral for your sister. If I can help you do not hesitate to come for me. Tell Sarah not to worry about her work for a while."

"Thank you Dr Small, I will see the Undertaker tomorrow."

They all went upstairs and into the house, Jimmy went next door for Davie. He hoped he had not left for work yet, as it was now nearly eight o'clock in the morning.

"What's wrong Jimmy?"

"Mary died having the baby."

"Dear God, no, I'll come right now."

Davie went into the kitchen with Jimmy and found Sarah sitting in the chair with the baby in her arms, Andrew was sitting with his head in his hands and Archie was sitting at Sarah's feet crying. As long as he lived Davie was never to forget the sadness that early morning.

He went over to Sarah and knelt at the side of her chair, they looked at each other, and the tears were running down her face,

"I had to bring the baby home, what else could I do?"

"I know, I know, we will manage between us all, Archie go for my mother."

Mrs Russell came in at that moment,

"What's happened, Sarah have you brought the baby home?"

"Mother leave it, Mary has died giving birth."

"Oh no, oh no, not Mary," Mrs Russell was distraught.

The door knocked and Archie went to answer it, he brought back in Dr Small with a nurse.

"This is Nurse Allison, she is going to help you today Sarah."

Sarah never lifted her head, she just held the baby.

They doctor, nurse and Davie all looked at each other. Then Davie said sharply,

"Sarah, pull yourself together, you have a lot to do. The baby has to be looked after and you have to see to things for Mary."

"I can do that," Jimmy replied.

"Yes I know you can and I will come with you. Sarah give the baby to the nurse."

"Right I will go in next door and make a breakfast for everyone; you will all need something inside you for what's ahead." Mrs Russell left then.

The nurse took the baby from Sarah and told Archie to get her a kettle of hot water and a basin of warm water and help her. She showed Archie how to make up the baby's bottle from powdered milk.

"Now you watch me and then you will be able to tell Sarah later."

The nurse settled Archie in a chair and he held the baby and fed her.

"Andrew you come with Jimmy and me to see the undertaker, come on now," Davie insisted.

They went into Davie's house and left the doctor speaking to Sarah.

"Listen to me Sarah, you do not need to keep the baby, and I know of a good home where the baby will be wanted."

"No, we will take care of her, I just do not know at the moment how I will manage everything, but I must keep my job. You must be tired of all my problems interfering with my work"

"You will keep your job I promise you, take some time to sort things out. I am leaving Nurse Allison with you for today. She will have a talk with you about what the baby needs and when to feed the baby. I will look in at some time tomorrow. Let the boys see to the funeral."

Sarah just nodded, the nurse went to the door with the doctor and they spoke for a while and then the nurse returned.

"You are good at feeding the baby Archie, now you show me how to get a fire started for the baby needs heat and we will have to make up a crib for the baby. Have you a washing basket."

"Yes."

"Good you bring it to me and a sheet and some towels."

Archie came back with everything and they made up a bed for the baby in the clothesbasket. When the baby was fed, she showed Archie how to hold the baby and lay her down in the crib. Archie sat down on the floor beside the baby. Sarah was still sitting in the chair.

Mrs Russell came into to tell them all to come for something to eat. Sarah never moved.

"Get yourself out of that chair now Sarah, you are needed. You can cry all you like after but I need help right now."

Sarah rose and the nurse led her into Mrs Russell's home. Archie would not leave the baby.

"You stay Archie and I will bring you something in and bring a cup for myself, now I am depending on you Archie, Nurse Allison spoke kindly.

They all sat round Mrs Russell's table and tried to eat; they all drank the hot tea. Sarah remembered later that there was no sign of Mr Russell.

Davie came back with Jimmy and Andrew later on in the morning to tell Sarah that the funeral was arranged for Saturday morning at ten o'clock, two days away.

The nurse and Archie were still attending to the baby; as yet Sarah had shown little interest.

Mrs Russell made the food for all of them all day; nobody had an appetite to eat much except the baby, who started to whimper. Sarah lifter her out of the make-do crib, and held her close. Archie handed Sarah the baby's bottle and the baby sucked away contentedly.

Archie and Sarah smiled at each other and the nurse then knew that they would be fine.

Mrs Russell came back into see Sarah and found her with the baby in her arms.

"I will help you to look after the baby Sarah; we will work it out between us."

"What would I do without you and Davie, where's Mr Russell?"

"I told him to stay out of the way, there is too much to do without having to bother about men."

"He must be fed up with us, you are always helping us, does he really not mind?"

The door knocked and Mrs Russell answered the door, she shouted back to Sarah, "Mrs Bell here to see you Sarah."

Mrs Russell brought Mrs Bell into the kitchen where Sarah was sitting still with the baby in her arms.

"Is it true Sarah, I have just come in from an early shift, I can't believe it, Mary was such a bonny girl. Is there anything I can do?"

"Yes there is Mrs Bell, could you look after the baby on Saturday morning, the funeral is at ten o'clock and I need someone to look after the baby. Mrs Russell will you help me with the tea after the funeral."

"Yes, you know I will, don't you bother your head with that at the moment, you see to the baby. What will you call her Sarah?"

"I don't know, I will see what the boys think about a name later. I cannot believe that she has gone, I only saw her yesterday and she was just tired. I should have kept her at home but I was frightened for her."

"Listen to me Sarah, you did what was right, and you tried to protect her. You should let the baby be adopted; it would be better for the baby and better for you. Would you not agree Mrs Bell?"

Sarah was to remember later just how adamant Mrs Russell was. "No, the baby stays with me. I will bring up Mary's baby. I know you are only thinking of me, please don't ask me again."

Mrs Bell and Mrs Russell looked at each other shaking their heads.

"I'll get away Sarah, if you need help meantime let me know, and I will see you early on Saturday morning. Mrs Russell if I can help you let me know."

"Thanks Mrs Bell, I see you out." The two women went out onto the landing, reasoning with each other how sad it all was and how best to help.

The Funeral Undertaker brought the Hearse with Mary, back to outside the Close at ten o'clock prompt. The minister had arrived at the house half an hour earlier. Sarah had not met him before, as she had not attended church since her parents had died. He was a young man not much older than Davie and newly ordained.

He conducted a short service for Mary and then they all went downstairs and once again walked behind the Hearse to the cemetery. Jimmy, Andrew, Archie and Sarah together, with Mr Russell and Davie behind, then the neighbours, the street was lined with neighbours.

Later Sarah tried to remember who everyone was at the graveside. There had been so many people there, the three doctors from the Surgery, the nurses from the maternity home and more neighbours.

They returned to the house and Mrs Russell with the help of Mrs Bell and Jean, attended to the tea.

Later when everyone had gone, Davie stayed with Nurse Allison and they spoke to Sarah and the boys once again about adoption for the baby.

"I know you don't want to hear this again Sarah but please consider what will be best for the baby, and best for all of you," Davie pleaded with them all.

"I don't know why you are so insistent that the baby is adopted, I told you that I had made up my mind, I told your mother as well," Sarah stated angrily.

"Now Sarah, have you discussed it with your brothers. A baby will change all of your lives and maybe not for the better. You have all managed well but a baby will bring extra responsibility and expense. Davie is only thinking of you all," Nurse Allison explained.

"Don't send the baby away Sarah," Archie pleaded.

"We all agreed in the maternity home that we would keep her, am I right?" The three boys all nodded their agreement.

"Are you still all of the same mind, I need to know now."

"We will keep her Sarah, we will all help, won't we," Jimmy asked Andrew and Archie.

It was agreed that the baby would stay with them.

"Well that is it and I will not be questioned about this again. We need to think on a name for the baby. I think we should call her Alison, after Nurse Allison."

"Sarah, would you not call her after her mother?" Nurse Allison wanted to know.

"I like the name of Alison and you have been so kind to us all, I think we will call her after you. We can call her Alison Mary Shaw, what do you think boys?"

So it was agreed between them all that would be the baby's name. Davie agreed that it was a nice name.

"There won't be many called Alison when she grows up and somehow it suits her well."

Nurse Allison thanked them all for the compliment,

"I am thrilled that you would call the baby after me and can I come and see her often?"

"Come anytime you like, I will ask that young minister to christen the baby and you must come as well as Davie when she is christened.

Mrs Bell had brought the baby back and she started to whimper.

"Here we go again," said Archie. "Leave it to me, I will feed her."

They all smiled at each other, Davie and Nurse Allison left then saying that they would see them all soon.

Later that night Mrs Russell came back in with Davie to say that she was willing to look after the baby to let Sarah work.

"I feel that I am depending on you too much Mrs Russell and that it is not fair."

"I would like to help you with Mary's baby and Davie agrees. You will have all the work and I will have all the pleasure. Please let me help you. Think on how handy I am just next-door. You can trust me with her Sarah."

"I know I can, I would rather leave her with you than with a stranger, but I am worried that it will be too much for you."

"Let my mother do it for you Sarah, please," Davie took her hand as he said this.

"It would solve a problem for me but I must pay something for this. We cannot continually be leaning on you."

"Are we not friends Sarah, you know you can pay me back in other ways," Mrs Russell pleaded.

So it was agreed that once Sarah started work she would hand the baby into Mrs Russell until Archie and Andrew came home from school, then they would watch the baby under Mrs Russell's supervision.

Sarah did not sleep that night; she could not believe that in a matter of a few days the changes that had come into their lives. She cried bitterly for her sister and for the crime that someone had committed against Mary, and the boys could not comfort her.

Life became much more difficult for Sarah, balancing her work at the Surgery and coping with the family, the baby and the household chores. The boys helped as much as they could. There were many days when Sarah was exhausted.

The baby blossomed, and Davie had bought Sarah a second hand pram for the baby and Nurse Allison had bought her a second hand cot.

The new Minister had christened the baby, Alison Mary Shaw. Davie with his mother and Nurse Allison had been present at the christening, which Sarah held in the house. The boys and Sarah stood as parents and Mrs Bell was there with Jean. They had a small party that day and when Sarah asked where Mr

Russell was. Davie answered that his father was not so well. Afterwards Sarah was to remember that once more Mr Russell was not present.

The new Minister, the Reverend Robert Young, became a regular visitor to the house and would play Snakes and Ladders or Ludo with the boys. Sarah would tease him,

"Are you trying to get us back into church or do you just like my scones?"

"You will all come back to church when you are ready, yes I do like your scones but there are other reasons."

"You like Sarah, don't you?" Archie laughed at him.

"You behave yourself and remember you are talking to a minister."

She busied herself at the sink but she could feel the Minister's eyes on her, she thought to herself, that this was a problem she could do without right now and decided to ignore the remark.

Chapter 9

1932

*T*he New Year once again found life better for them all and as they sat down to tea at Hogmanay, Sarah was pleased with what she saw.

Jimmy was well into his apprenticeship at the shipyard, Andrew was doing well at the High School and was preparing this year to sit his higher examinations, all being well he would soon be seventeen and ready for college. Archie wanted to leave school when he was fourteen in a few months' time and Sarah was arguing with him all the time about it. Alison was now two years old and followed Archie everywhere. The boys had her playing football and Sarah was forever telling them that they would make her wild. Alison was a lovely child, and Mrs Russell had been as good as her word and watched her to let Sarah work. Mr Russell seldom spoke to Sarah and she questioned Davie about this one day.

"What have I done to your father, is he not pleased that your mother watches Alison?"

"Pay no attention to him, he is becoming very moody and we have a bother with him at home. If he ever bothers you, you let me know right away and I will sort him out."

Sarah was surprised at the bitterness of Davie but did not pursue it any further.

Sarah and Mrs Russell still baked on a Thursday night and now they had Alison in the middle of it. Sarah always tried to get her into bed and sleeping before they started.

"Is this Thursday Sarah." She would ask.

Sarah would shake her head and smile at her,

"You are too smart for your own good madam."

The little girl was showing promise of being very smart for her two years. Knew everyone that came to the house and was forever asking 'why', if Sarah asked her or the boys to do something.

Sarah was writing to Mrs Barr regularly and keeping her up to date with Alison's progress. Mrs Barr had invited Sarah to have a holiday with her and to bring the family. It was impossible because of money and the different stages that the boys were at. Sarah often thought of her happy days in Dunoon with Mrs Barr, Mrs Malcolm and Lizzie. She often wondered why Lizzie never answered her letters. Every now and again she would write but never received an answer.

She had promised Mrs Barr, Sarah could not get used to calling her Madame Renaud that someday she would go for a holiday. It was a promise that she intended to keep, but there were too many other priorities.

Summer arrived and with it the school holidays. Andrew was ready for University at Glasgow if his Higher Exams result were good. Miss Black and Sarah had tried to keep Archie at school but he was determined to be a painter. As he had just turned fourteen years, he would have to wait for a while to start an apprenticeship. Miss Black once again came to their help and had Archie apprenticed to a local house painter and was to start as a helper with the trades-men until he reached the correct age. He was to start after the school summer holidays and Sarah had agreed only if he kept up some night school education.

"I want to leave school completely," he would argue.

"You never can agree to anything without an argument. You will go to night school or stay in school. Jimmy goes to night school and so will you," she would argue.

Andrew's results duly came and he had excelled himself and was accepted into the University. His friend Jean Bell had also gained a place at University, Jean planned to be a doctor and her mother was thrilled. She would often come to Sarah for advice or just for blether.

The summer was soon over and Andrew travelled daily to Glasgow to study, Archie had started work and his wages also helped the family.

The winter was severe and there was the problem of them all keeping warm. The stove proved an asset and Sarah was forever making soup and baking. There was a lot of unemployment with the shipyard laying off men but there was talk of a big ship being built in the Clyde but not yet.

Sarah had become well known in the street for helping out people, sometimes with food, or with advice, never money. Mrs Barr used to tell her and Lizzie the quickest way to lose friends was to lend them money. She helped out Mrs Bell from time to time but with food only. Sarah made the excuse that she had made too many pies or too much soup, because she knew that Mrs Bell was struggling to keep Jean going at the University. Jean had managed to get a bursary award but it was needed for travel, books and fees.

Alison was now approaching her third birthday and Christmas would soon be upon them.

Sarah once again had her Christmas dinner and as usual she prepared a dinner for all of them. Davie came with his mother and father and Mrs Bell and Jean were also invited.

After the meal was over the boys started to play snakes and ladders with Alison shaking the dice for them all. Mr Russell had taken the little girl on his knee to read a book that Davie had bought her for a present. Davie took the child from his father and said,

"You shake the dice for us all Alison, father you look tired, do you want to go in home?"

"Yes maybe I should," he rose and left.

"That was a bit mean Davie; your Dad was only reading to Alison." Mrs Russell said quietly.

Davie never replied or explained.

After everyone had gone home Jimmy asked Sarah,

"What's wrong with Davie and his father?"

"I don't know, he told me that he was giving them bother, but that was a while ago. Davie is annoyed that he has to see to his mother so much when his father should be looking after her more. That was also a while ago, I really don't know. Davie is not as friendly with me as he used to be, since I would not get married to him."

"Will you never marry him Sarah?"

"No, I like Davie but only as a friend."

"What about the Reverend Mr Young," Andrew laughed as he said this.

Sarah threw a dishtowel at him,

"Do you see me as a minister's wife, or better still, you lot living in a manse, no I don't think so."

"What about the doctor Sarah, would you marry him? Archie asked.

"Are you lot wanting me married? You lot would frighten anybody away. No I will have to be an old maid till you lot are married."

"If you wanted to marry Sarah we could look after ourselves now, I mean you are getting old and you would not want to be a burden to us, now would you. I think you should go for the minister, you would not have to pay rent." Archie was walking round the room with both hands clasped together and speaking very slowly and loudly, as if it was a sermon. Andrew and Jimmy were laughing at him.

Sarah made a dive for a wooden spoon and went after them all,

"Cheeky monkeys, the lot of you. I will get you lot married off as soon as I can, I'm warning you."

They were enjoying the joke between them when Jimmy said,

"Seriously Sarah, do not let us stop you, we could manage."

"No, I will not marry and I have to bring up Alison, I am happy doing what I do. I like my work and you all keep me busy. Do not make so much noise or we will waken Alison and then she will not settle."

They listened to the wireless before they all went to bed. Later Sarah thought over what Jimmy had said. She never expected to marry, who would take her with a family and when they boys were independent, who would take her with a child. She was busy and her days were filled but in the evening she would feel lonely, she never spoke of this to anyone.

It was in the Spring of the year that Sarah had washed blankets and had them drying in the common drying green. She had left them out all day and went down to the green to bring them upstairs. The boys were all out and Alison was asleep in her small bed, which was at the side of Sarah's bed in the room.

Sarah went into the kitchen with the blankets when she heard a noise in the room. She went through to check on Alison and found Mr Russell standing at the bed looking at Alison sleeping.

Sarah watched him as he put his hand out to touch the child and she felt such a frightening feeling wash over her.

"Don't you touch her, what are you doing in here anyway?"

"I don't mean any harm, I just wanted to see her, don't tell Davie."

"Get out of here and don't come in here without knocking the door."

At that the door knocked, Sarah had left it opened.

"Sarah, are you there?"

Mr Russell pushed past Sarah and rushed out to be met at the door by Davie. He caught his father by the front of his shirt and pushed him against the wall on the landing.

"I warned you, I warned you, get in the house."

Sarah watched this as if in slow motion and then she realised what was wrong, she sprung forward in one quick movement and threw herself at them both.

"Did you touch Mary, was it you, was it you?"

Davie swung round to catch Sarah and his father stepped back quickly and fell down the stairs. He never shouted or screamed, all they heard was the bang of his head as he hit the landing below. Davie ran down the stairs to where his father lay, Mr Russell tried to speak but could not. Blood oozed out from the back of his head onto the stair landing.

Sarah watched the scene in complete and utter rage. Mrs Russell came out to see what was going on and looked at Sarah, then at Davie and his father, then back at Sarah.

"Send someone for the doctor mother, quickly. Sarah help me lift him please."

Sarah ran down the stairs and helped Davie lift his father, up into the house. They laid him on the bed.

"Did you know Davie?"

"Not now Sarah, please, he is in a bad way."

Mrs Russell came back in,

"I have sent your Archie for the doctor Sarah."

"Did you know?" she spat the words out at Mrs Russell.

"Leave it, I told you to leave it just now." Davie spat the words out.

"You don't tell me anything, you both knew it was that filthy old man, you protected him, while my sister died, and you kept your mouth shut, both of you. Have her adopted, don't bring the baby home, marry me, I could not understand why you were so persistent. It was not for me, it was for you and your family, all to protect that swine of a man.

The three of them stared at each other, not a word was said.

Dr Small came into the room at that moment,

"What has happened here?"

"My father has fallen down the stairs Doctor, he looks bad."

They all stood back while the Doctor examined Mr Russell, Mrs Russell was quietly crying.

The Doctor looked at them, and then spoke to Davie,

"He is bad, it looks like a brain injury, I will need to get him into the infirmary but I do not think I should move him at present. I will bring in the surgeon from the infirmary as soon as I can. Do not move him or undress him at the moment, I will be back as soon as I can."

He left and Sarah went with him,

"Are you all right, you are so pale."

"Yes I am fine Doctor; His head hit the stair with such a bang."

"I will not waste any time, I will get the surgeon but I doubt he will last the next twenty four hours."

Fine thought Sarah, he has no right living when Mary died. What were his intentions with Alison? How could Davie not have said something? No wonder they bought the pram and been so good to the baby. How stupid she had been. When had Mr Russell been in the house and how often? More to the point how long had Davie and his mother known.

Sarah sat at the table and tried to work it out, she had been an utter fool. Davie had wanted to marry her to keep her mouth shut. Alison was his half-sister. She sat numb, she could not take it in, she sat there for a long time, she could not cry, she was so angry.

She started to be sick then, she was shivering and shaking when Archie came in.

"Sarah what's wrong, are you ill?" he turned and went out again, and came back with Dr. Small.

"Sarah let me look at you, have you any pain?"

"No, just sick, it must be the fright I got."

"Let me examine you, you are shaking." The doctor examined Sarah and told Archie to put a hot water bottle in the bed and get her into bed. Make Sarah a cup of tea later on. I will leave medicine for you to take if the sickness does not stop."

"Dr Small, it was him."

"What do you mean Sarah?"

"I am sure it was him that raped Mary, there was a row."

"Was there a fight Sarah, I have to know?"

"No, it happened so quickly, he fell. He stepped back when I went for him. I did not push him. I found him over the cot about to touch Alison. I came back from the drying green with washing, that's when I found him."

"What happened then?"

"Davie came in and pulled him out onto the landing, he said to him, I warned you. That was when I realised that it could have been him, I threw myself at both of them and he stepped back and went down the stairs."

"Now you stay here and do not speak to anyone until I come back, Archie you get your brothers home at once. Do not talk to anyone, all of you stay in and wait for me. Do not go outside. I will be back as soon as I can."

Sarah sat at the table with her head in her hands until Archie came back with Andrew and Jimmy.

Sarah looked at them both,

" Mr Russell is in a bad way, I think he may be Alison father. I flew at him and he stepped back, I never pushed him but I think Dr Small thinks that I may have. I did not push him, I never touched him."

"Tell us what happened Sarah," Jimmy asked as he put his arms round her.

Sarah recalled the events that had led up to the fall.

"They knew it was him, they covered up for him and all the time pretending to be so nice to us all."

"Wait a minute Sarah; they have been helping us long before all this happened to Mary. Are you sure it was him?"

"It was him, if you had seen their faces you would have known."

"I am going in then to see them," Jimmy turned and left.

As he walked across the landing to the Russell's door, the door opened and Dr Small came out with another man. Davie came out onto the landing.

"Thank you for your quick attention."

"I am sorry, but there is nothing that we could have done."

Davie shook hands with both men, who went downstairs.

"Are you coming in Jimmy?"

"Yes, I would like to, how is your father?"

"He died about ten minutes ago."

"I will come back later."

"No come in now, we need to talk."

They both went into the kitchen; Mrs Russell sat at the table crying.

"Oh Jimmy, where's Sarah?"

"She is in a state, leave her just now. I am sorry that Mr Russell has died; this is terrible for you both. Is there any truth in what Sarah is saying, we must get this cleared up."

"We think there may be, but we do not know and my father has always denied it. I even asked Mary but she would not answer me."

"What made you think it was him?"

"I found him coming out of your house one day and I wondered why he was there. It was not until later that I thought it might have been him. We warned Sarah to change the lock on the door in case it was him. We will never know for sure, it might not have been him. He was very fond of Alison, I blamed him myself but it might not have been him."

"Could you not have spoken to us about this, could you not have warned us?"

"What good would it have done, Sarah would have went for him anyway."

"She did not push him."

"No nobody said that she did, he stepped back and fell. There may be an inquiry because of the sudden death."

"What do you mean?"

"We have been told to get the undertaker but he has to clear it with the Doctor in case there is an inquiry. We have not to arrange the funeral until he knows. The police have to be informed."

"Sarah found him over Alison's cot about to touch her; she had been down at the green for the washing."

"I do not think he would have harmed her."

"No but he harmed her mother, didn't he. Sarah said that she saw it in both of your faces. I am sorry for you loss, but you should have warned us."

"I will come and speak to Sarah."

"No, leave this to me; I will handle this from now on."

"Let me speak to her."

"No, not tonight, if I can be of any help, let me know. Andrew and I will help you; leave Sarah and Archie alone at the moment. If the police become involved, all we have to do is tell the truth."

"We would rather this did not come out, we don't know for sure Jimmy, I have my mother to think about. He fell down the stairs, it was an accident."

"Yes and I have my sister and my niece to think about and for all we know now, your half-sister and you mother's step daughter. Have you any idea how it feels to know that someone raped your sister and you done nothing about it. I am sorry Mrs Russell I really am that it has come to this, but you both must realise that we are the losers here and Sarah feels betrayed by Davie. I will speak to you later."

Jimmy left and went back into his own home.

"Well Davie, what will we do now?"

"We will have to wait mother until the Doctor tells us what to do. I will go and let the undertaker know. You know that it was him, don't you?

"Will we ever know the truth now, but one thing for sure Sarah will be bitter about this and she is now convinced it was him. Maybe it is all my fault; if I had been a wife to him he might not have looked elsewhere."

"It is all too late now; he caused the problem all those years ago. I hope when I die that someone is really sad for me. It has to be an empty life when you are not mourned."

Sarah was still sitting at the table when Jimmy came back. Andrew was sitting with her. Archie was making more tea for them all.

"What did he say?"

"He said that they never really knew, they have no proof, he always denied it. Davie caught him coming out of here once, when Mary was in alone. He even asked Mary if it was his father but she would not answer him. They are devastated Sarah and it could get worse."

"Why?"

"They have not to arrange a funeral until they are told to as there could be a police investigation because of the sudden death. They are not bad people Sarah; they just did not know what to do and it might not be him."

"They think it is him, I saw it in their faces. They did not want me to bring Alison home, they told me that they were concerned about me, but all they were concerned about was themselves. Davie tried to get me to promise that I would have her adopted. When I would not, he then thought we should get married. Think on it, they bought the pram. They helped when we decided to keep Alison, but both of them tried to persuade me to have her adopted. They were trying to hide it. Where was the truth when we buried Mary? He could have told us what he suspected. I will never trust them again and I am suspected of pushing him down the stairs by Dr Small."

"No you are not, Davie said it was an accident and if Davie had not hid this, his father would be alive today, so you are not to blame."

The door knocked at this moment, Archie ran to open the door and showed in Dr Small.

"This is a sad business, now listen to me all of you," he pulled out a chair and sat down at the table with them.

"This was an accident but because it was a sudden death there has to be an inquiry. The police will come and take a statement from you Sarah and you could be called as a witness. When questioned, tell it as it happened and there will be no problem. Do not say that there was an argument unless you are asked. Do not say why you made for him unless you are asked. It was an accident, his son and wife can testify to that."

"There was no argument, I did not even speak to him but as soon as I realised what they were trying to hide, I rushed at him and Davie. Davie tried to keep me back from him and that's when he stepped back and fell."

"It would be better all round for everyone if it comes across that he stumbled and fell back down the stairs."

"Why is everyone protecting Mr Russell, my sister died because of him?"

"There is no proof of that Sarah only a suspicion, and if it comes out it gives you a motive for pushing him downstairs."

"I did not push him down, he deserves what he got."

"Sarah, do not say that," Andrew shouted at her.

"I know you did not push him nor did his son push him, it was an accident of his own making. Keep it as simple as possible for the sake of Alison. Otherwise you could label her for life."

"We will Dr Small; I have told Davie that he has to deal with me and Andrew from now on and to leave Sarah alone."

"Good, then we all know where we stand. You will probably hear from the police tomorrow or the next day. Get in touch with me if you need me and you had better take a few days off Sarah till the dust settles. I must go, I have other calls to make and it is late."

After the doctor had gone they all went to bed, Sarah never slept. It went over and over in her mind of just how unfair it all was. Everything was to be hushed up and Mary would never get justice. She would have to leave her work now; she had no one to leave Alison with. She would never speak to them again, well she would at least once, and to tell them exactly what she thought of them. Life was going to be very difficult again but she would have to leave things until after the funeral. It was may be as well that the boys were all working now, when things had started to pick up she was slapped back down, no it was not fair. She would never live her own life, that was not for her, she tossed and turned all night and was glad when morning came.

As usual Alison was first wakened and had them all up one after the other. They sat round the table to discuss what they would now do.

"Who will watch Alison now?" Archie wanted to know.

"I will have to leave work and take care of her, what else can I do?"

"I will leave University and get a job, that will help." Andrew offered.

"No you will not, Jimmy and Sarah said in the one voice," they all laughed at that.

"Well I will work at the weekends, I could pick up some kind of work," Andrew stated.

"If it comes to that, yes, but not for the moment, we will sit tight and see this through, we have been in worse pickles than this before."

"Yes Sarah but Davie always helped us out, we have to give him credit for that, him and his mother. I will get dressed and go with Davie this morning, you Archie see if they need any messages and Andrew you stay here in case Mrs Russell needs you while we are out, agreed."

They all nodded.

"I will do a baking for Mrs Russell to help her out but I don't want to speak to Davie just now. Archie when you have time you can take Alison out for a while and I will stay in and wait for the police. This will stir up the street and here we are in the middle of it again and it is not our fault. Sarah started crying then and the boys tried to stop her.

"What have you lot been up to making Sarah cry, you are bad boys."

They all started laughing at Alison, she was wagging her little finger at them all with one hand on her hip."

"Right madam, you come and give Sarah a hug and tell her we are all sorry and we will not be bad again," Archie lifted her onto Sarah's knee as he spoke.

"Sarah I love you," the child kissed Sarah as she spoke and two small arms came round her neck, "they are not really bad boys."

Sarah smiled at them all through her tears.

Jimmy left and went next door with Archie and Andrew; Sarah heard them all going downstairs later. When she had started her baking she heard a knock at the door.

Mrs Russell stood there,

"Sarah, Sarah what are we to do?"

Sarah brought her inside and sat her down at her fire; she poured them both a cup of tea.

"I don't know what to do or say, we should leave it for now till after the funeral."

"It is all my fault Sarah; I have not been a wife to him for years. There was an incident when Davie was a young teenager; he was accused of trying to be friendly with a young girl. Her father nearly killed him and I moved into a bed of my own from then on. I tolerated him and so did Davie. I never tried to help him, he was a lonely man, and it is all my fault."

"No you cannot blame yourself, but you should have warned me. I never suspected him I thought it could have been the school Janitor and Davie knew that. I have walked past that man now for the last three years near enough. Jimmy said that we should leave things alone until after the funeral, you were here for us and we will be here for you."

"Will you speak to Davie?"

"No."

The two of them sat at the fireside with tears running down their faces, the older woman because of what she should have done and the younger for what had been done to her sister and she could not forgive. Alison climbed on Mrs Russell's knee and Sarah lifted her off her knee.

"Please Sarah, it is not the bairn's fault and I am so fond of her, not because of who she might be but because she is your niece and just because she is a lovely wee girl, please Sarah."

Sarah lifted Alison back onto Mrs Russell's knee.

"I am going to do a baking for you to help with things, you will accept it."

"Yes thanks, I can't manage without you Sarah."

"You will never have to; I will be here for you."

Sarah busied herself about the house and thought to herself, Mrs Russell was not to blame but she should have confided in her and then again, she thought, what would I have done. I pride myself on being honest but where has it got me, nowhere.

"Can I still watch Alison for you Sarah? Davie thinks that you might not let me have her anymore."

"Yes if you still want to, I don't want to be unfair to you and Alison loves you so. It is a great help to me. I had considered giving up my work and the boys want me to. Then if the police charge me I will not be working anyway, God knows where I will be."

"It was an accident Sarah, Davie swears by that. What will we do Sarah?"

"We will tell the truth, we will not go into details unless we are pushed, try not to worry."

Mrs Russell played with Alison until the boys came back.

Jimmy raised his eyebrows at Sarah.

"I will get away in, I take it Davie is back."

"Yes, he will fill you in."

"Thanks to all of you for helping, and thanks again Sarah."

Sarah walked to the door with Mrs Russell,

"I'll send in the baking with Archie and I'll see you tomorrow."

Davie was standing with the door open, Sarah never looked at him.

When she went back into the kitchen the boys were all waiting for her,

"I take it you have changed your mind then when Mrs Russell was here," Jimmy asked.

"Just about Mrs Russell not about Davie, when this is over I will let him know exactly what I think of him. What is to happen, tell me?"

"The undertaker has to wait for word from the police, there has to be an inquiry because of the sudden death. As far as we know the Procurator Fiscals office will hold the inquiry and possibly Davie, Mrs Russell, the Doctor, the police and you could be called. They may also call Archie."

"Why Archie, he was not there?"

"No, but he went for the Doctor, and they will have to hear from him, how quickly the Doctor was called. No one is sure yet, but that could happen. The police will be in touch with us. One thing anyway, I would say that Davie was not put out at losing his father. What did Mrs Russell want?"

"She does not want to lose any of us; she is frightened that I may not let her have Alison any more. I told her not to worry; unfortunately we need Mrs Russell more than she needs us. Davie though, that's another matter."

"Don't be so bitter Sarah, it was not him."

"No but he asked me to marry him, he tried to make me promise to have Alison adopted and all the time he was trying to make sure that he kept my mouth shut. He was supposed to be my best friend. Telling me that he was only concerned about me, well we all know now what he was concerned about and it was none of us."

The door knocked again and Archie brought in two policemen, a constable and a sergeant.

They introduced themselves and told them that they required statements from Miss Sarah Shaw and Mr Archibald Shaw.

They sat down and took notes in their notebook from them both, read them back to them and asked if they were correct and would they please sign the statements. They then went next door to the Russell's house.

The Procurator Fiscal's enquiry was held the following week in the local Courthouse. Sarah and Archie were called as witnesses into the sudden death of Mr Russell. When they arrived at the Courthouse it was to find Doctor Small, Mrs Russell and Davie also there.

They were kept in a separate room with a police officer with them, to make sure that they did not speak to one another. The Doctor was called first, then Mrs Russell, Davie, Sarah then Archie. They were allowed to sit in the Court after they had spoken. Sarah was very nervous when she was called. She spoke only to answer the questions she was asked.

"Please state your name."

"Sarah Shaw."

"Where do you live?"

"10 East Shore Street, Greenock."

"Were you present when the late Mr Russell had his accident?"

"Yes."

"Please tell what happened."

"I stepped out of my door to speak to Mr Russell and his son Davie; Mr Russell stepped back and fell down the stairs. It happened so quickly, he did not shout or scream. He just fell and his head made an awful noise when it hit the landing."

"Was he at the edge of the stairs when he fell?"

"He must have been closer than he realised."

"Why did you go out to speak to Mr Russell and his son?"

"We have been very close neighbours for years. I was left with my brothers and sister to bring up and Mr and Mrs Russell helped me over the years. Davie their son, we have always been very close friends, he also helps me with my brothers, takes them out to give me some time to myself."

"Was there something special that night that you wanted to speak to them about?"

"Yes."

"What was that?"

"Mrs Russell watches my niece to let me work. My sister died giving birth and I am bringing up her child. I worry that it is too much for Mrs Russell. I always check with her son that she is not tired."

"Did you ask that question that day?"

"No, I did not get a chance to, Mr Russell fell."

"What happened after Mr Russell fell?"

"Davie rushed down after his father and I went down to help. My brother went for the Doctor."

"Can you tell us anything else of the accident?"

"No, only what I have told you."

"You may sit down."

Sarah practically collapsed on the seat, she did not look at anyone else, and she was still shaking when Archie was called.

Archie spoke clearly and answered all the questions he was asked. Mrs Russell had asked him to run for the Doctor. He ran as fast as he could. There was not anything else he could tell. He had not been there at the time of the fall.

The Procurator Fiscal summed up all the witnesses' reports and concluded that Mr Russell had died from an unfortunate accident. Expressed his condolences to the family and ordered Mr Russell's body could now be released for burial.

As they all left the Courthouse Sarah was so relieved to see Jimmy and Andrew waiting for them outside. She grabbed Archie and hurried away without looking back.

Mr Russell's funeral took place on the Saturday morning following the Inquiry. Sarah and her brothers were there. Mrs Bell took care of Alison and brought her home later in the day.

Sarah helped Mrs Russell with the Funeral Tea and avoided Davie as best as she could.

Once everyone had gone home and Sarah was back in their own home, she asked Jimmy to go for Davie and for them all to go out so she could speak to him on his own.

"It is not a good idea just now Sarah."

"If you think for one minute that I am not going to tell him exactly what I think of him, you are wrong. I have to do this for Mary. I want questions answered. I feel betrayed by him. He has made me a liar."

"Sarah you did not lie, you answered the questions you were asked."

"I hid the truth."

"Yes to protect Alison. Let it go."

"No, if you will not ask him I will."

"Very well then, but you know Sarah, you are not always right. Why should you be judge and jury? Davie and his mother don't really know the truth."

"They hid what they did know."

Jimmy went next door and asked Davie if he would come in and speak to Sarah later on. He agreed to do this.

Sarah was sitting at the table waiting for him, when he knocked the door. He opened the door and shouted.

"Sarah."

"Come in Davie."

He came in and sat opposite her at the table.

"Did your father rape Mary?"

"I don't know, he denied having touched her. I found him coming out of your house and asked him why he had been in to see you. He told me that he had taken back baking trays. He had done this before but there was something that bothered me. I warned him to stay away from you. I did not know that you had not been in and that Mary could have been alone, I just don't know, please believe me, I just do not know."

"You could have warned me."

"You are not the only one that this affects Sarah"

"Don't I know it, my sister lies dead. It affects her and it affects Alison. I saw the look on your face when you grabbed your father. You said' I warned you, I warned you'. It is a pity you did not warn me. All this talk of how you loved me and wanted to marry me. You were making sure that you kept my mouth shut."

"I wanted to marry you long before this happened and let's face it Sarah, it is a brave man that would try to shut your mouth. You are always so right. Did you never hide anything? What about hiding your age to keep the family together?"

"I did that to protect my family."

"Yes Sarah and that is all I have done. So don't tell me that it is all right for you and not for me. You know me and know me well, long before this happened. We were friends Sarah and could have been more, that is all water under the bridge now isn't it?"

Sarah paused for a moment," Davie, have you any idea how bad I feel? I rushed at your father, if I had not done that he would be alive."

"No Sarah, I grabbed my father by the shirt, if I had not done that he would be alive. He tried to get away from me. My mother blames herself for not forgiving him one mistake that he made years ago."

"Do you think that Alison is your father's child?"

"It looks that way, but will we ever know? No I do not think we will. Please let's put this behind us, we can go on being friends."

"I will not make any difference with your mother and I will not try to stop the boys still being friends with you. I thank you for all the times that you have been there for me and I hope that I have in some way been there for you all. I am sorry that your father is dead but if he did rape Mary."

Sarah could not continue, the tears were running down her cheeks and she started to sob uncontrollably.

"Please Sarah, please don't get so upset."

"You should have warned me Davie, just go home, just go home."

He stood up and turned to go,

"You may not want me as a friend anymore but I will always be there for you, try to see it from my point of view. I was only protecting my family."

Sarah never lifted her head as he left the room and the boys found her still crying when they came home. It would be years before Sarah and Davie made up their difference.

In the days, weeks and months to follow Sarah was to regret her argument with Davie. She still felt that he could have warned her but she missed his company so much, much more than she could believe. She questioned herself on the fact that maybe did she love him and not realise it? She was sure she did not love him, then again what experience did she have, how would she know. The only thing that she knew was what Lizzie had told her, how when you fell in love, you just knew. It was hard to forgive him the remark about, ' it would be a brave man that would shut her mouth.'

Did he think that she was too loud? Did he think that she was too self-opinionated? Did he find her overbearing? One thing for sure he had stripped some of her self-confidence, no, a lot of her self-confidence. Why had he never said anything before about her not being able to 'shut her mouth? When you were friends and good friends as they had been they had talked about everything, why not that?

Then there was the remark that Jimmy had made, 'why should you be judge and jury'

Her days were busy with working, looking after them all and she seemed to everyone else to be quiet and withdrawn. She worked well at the Surgery but some of her enthusiasm had gone and it was the same at home.

Dr. Small had noticed that something was wrong and asked her one day to come through and bring your tea with his coffee and we can have a talk.

"Something wrong Doctor?"

"No, everything is fine; I just feel that we have not spoken much since the death of your neighbour. Are you still worried about it?"

"Yes, very much so, if I had not gone for him he may still be living. It is hard on my conscience."

"You must not take all the blame. His son blames himself and I understand the mother feels she is to blame. Then again the man himself is really to blame."

"What if he is Alison's father, I feel sick thinking about Mary? Davie and I do not speak any longer."

Sarah broke down and the tears started.

"I blame Davie for not warning me and I will not forgive him. It is terrible when we pass each other."

"Do you not even say hello."

"No, it is just, if I meet him, I say 'Davie' and he replies 'Sarah', we are like strangers and I miss his friendship."

"Do you love him?"

"No, I am sure that I love him like a brother, but nothing more, anyway what do I know about loving a man but I don't think I love him, well not like that. He told me," she hesitated here.

"Yes, he told you what?"

"He said that he only protected his family, he did ask me to marry him, and I said that he did that to shut my mouth. He said that it was a brave man that would try to shut my mouth, and that hurts. I never knew that he thought I was a loud-mouthed person. Am I Dr. Small, am I loud-mouthed?"

"No Sarah you are not. You have strong opinions, you are confident. All the trouble you have had has made you the person you are. You have had to be strong to survive and to raise that family of yours. Would you not make up with your friend Davie, you would maybe feel better."

"No, I cannot, he can say what he likes but nothing can ever take away that Mary died. If I had known that his father was going into our house, when Mary was alone, I could maybe have prevented him. Davie knew that I blamed the janitor of the school for Mary getting pregnant and he allowed me to think that. He stills says that we will never really know and that there is no proof that it was his father. How he can say that when he found him coming out of the house I will never understand. I am exhausted with the whole situation. I think Jimmy blames me as well because he told me I had to be 'judge and jury,' and that hurts."

"Listen to me Sarah, you are still all very upset, and it will take time for this to pass. Jimmy did not say that to hurt you, he was maybe trying to get you to forgive Davie. You know Sarah; you have had to make decisions on many issues regarding the boys, Mary and now Alison. It is very easy for other people to find fault when things maybe go wrong. These are the people that are not strong enough to make the decisions because they are frightened that they fail. I find this in my work all the time."

"Do you Dr Small?"

"Oh yes, if I cure someone I am the best doctor going, but if I cannot cure them, and I quote. 'You are hopeless as a doctor' and if they die, well it is my fault. I did not try the proper treatment. If I cure a patient, I feel wonderful and I feel terrible when someone dies."

"You are a fine doctor."

Dr. Small leaned forward in his chair and took Sarah's hand in his own and then continued.

"You are a fine person Sarah, a good sister to them all and Alison could not have a better aunt or a better mother and do not forget that, where would she be without you. You had to be strong to care for them all. Now I think that you could do with a tonic. This has taken more out of you than you realise, a tonic would do you good, are you sleeping?"

Sarah shook her head," No, not very well."

"That will pull your health down. You must look after yourself for you have many responsibilities. Take this prescription down to Cockburn's the chemist, it is a blood tonic and buy some malt extract. They will help build you up for the winter anyway. Now promise me that you will do this."

"I will, I will go tonight on my road home."

"I do not know what you should do about your friend Davie, but my mother used to tell me to 'let the world turn' when I did not know what to do."

"You mean I should let time take care of it."

"Yes and Dr Young will be pleased to know that you have no boyfriend at the moment."

They both laughed at this.

"He is only joking with me you know."

"Well Sarah, I do not think so, given any encouragement, you never know."

"With my lot, I don't think so."

Sarah was now smiling and seemed to be more relaxed. The Doctor was pleased to see this.

"Are you feeling a bit better now since we have a talk? Do not pick faults in yourself Sarah. The boys are growing up and Alison will as well. You mark my words; you and Davie will get over this."

"Thank you Dr Small, I do feel much better now."

When Sarah left for home that night, she felt better than she had in a long time. She hurried into the town and bought the tonic and the malt extract, maybe they would all take it.

As she left the Chemist shop, she saw Davie talking to a young woman and they seemed very friendly. He looked over at Sarah, their eyes met. He turned his back and putting his arm across the young woman's shoulders, they walked in the other direction.

Sarah felt bad and then thought, no; it is nice for him if he has met someone else. Maybe in time to come they could be friends again. Not at the moment though but I do wish him well. She then realised that she did not love Davie and somehow that seemed to lift a burden from her. She should pay more attention to what she was going to make for their meal, for she had been extravagant buying herself tonics.

She made her way to MacSymons, the grocer and decided to treat them all tonight. She bought one pound of their finest cooked ham at two shillings for the pound, twelve oranges and a two-pound, pot of jam. When the assistant asked her for five shillings, she thought to herself, I must be mad today.

She hurried home, the boys had set the table and when she went into the house, the three of them looked at her.

"What's wrong? Oh no, she thought, what's wrong now?"

"Where have you been Sarah, we were worried. You are always in."

Jimmy asked her anxiously.

"The doctor gave me a prescription for some medicine and I went for it before coming home

"You not well?" Archie wanted to know.

"A bit run down, the doctor thinks, nothing much. Look I bought us all a treat for our tea."

She emptied her shopping on the table and as she did, she realised that they were all still looking worried.

"Did you think I had run away or something?"

"Well you have not been yourself lately and we wondered what we had done wrong."

Archie threw himself at her as he said this.

"It is not anything that any of you have done. We are all upset about what happened and about my argument with Davie. I am fine now and it will be fine given time. You must tell me if you do not agree with decisions that I make for us all. If you want to change things you must say so. I do not mean to be 'judge and jury'"

"Sarah I am sorry I said that. It has been bothering me and Davie gave me a row and reminded me where we would be if you had not made decisions for us."

"Jimmy forget about it, and maybe I needed it anyway. Come on you lot, cut the bread, I'm starving."

As she looked round them all at the table they were all smiling again. Yes, Sarah decided, things were getting better.

Chapter 10

1936

*S*ara was busy preparing the evening meal for them all. The boys would be in anytime now, they are all men now, I must stop calling them the boys, she reproached herself over this many times, but still she called them 'the boys'.

Jimmy was in his last year of his engineering apprenticeship; his twenty first birthday would be soon. Andrew was more than half way through his degree course at University, he would soon be twenty and Archie was in his second year's apprenticeship as a house painter. Alison had started school and was in the second class, having moved out of the baby class.

Sarah smiled to herself, a clever child, who found her lessons easy. Sarah had to help each of the boys with their lessons from time to time, when they were in school, but never Alison, not so far anyway. A proper lippy little miss, always ready with an answer. She reminded Sarah very much of Lizzie.

I wonder why I have never heard from Lizzie. She asked herself. We were good friends, more than good friends.

Mrs Barr was always asking in her letters about what had happened to Lizzie. Sarah had promised to find out. Her letters were never answered and one Saturday in the summer, Sarah had taken Alison and had gone to Dunoon for the day. She had gone to Lizzie's address, but the name on the door was not Duncan. She had knocked and asked the occupant of the house, if they knew where Mr & Mrs Duncan were now living.

The lady who answered the door told Sarah that she had never met them so she did not know. Sarah had tried some more of the neighbours but nobody

141

knew. One neighbour had told her that they did not mix with other people and Mrs Duncan was seldom seen, they had moved out suddenly and there was talk that he had gone north for the fishing.

Sarah decided that she would someday go to Largs and perhaps try to trace Lizzie's family. It was now nearly nine years since Lizzie married and perhaps they had healed their difference.

Her thoughts were changed as she heard the boys and Alison coming in. Alison always waited on the front stairs for the boys coming home at night.

The house was really too small for them all now but Sarah was frightened to make a move, remembering the really bad days. They had all discussed whether they could try for a bigger house. The council had plans to build a housing estate, high up on the Greenock Hill, It was to be called Strone housing Development. There was so many families overcrowded and the doctors were blaming the overcrowding for the bad cases of Tuberculosis that was in the town. There were many families with more than six living in one and two roomed houses. The neediest would qualify for a house first but anyone could put their name down. The rumours were that you would have to pay about twelve shillings to fifteen shillings a week for rent and that would put many families unable to pay the big rent from moving. If they tried for another private factored house, they would have to move out of the street, as all the houses were the same size or smaller. Alison had settled at school and it was very handy being at the corner. Jimmy and Archie could walk to work and the train station was nearby for Andrew. Sarah had discussed it one night when they were having their meal and they decided to wait till Jimmy's apprenticeship was finished, Andrew had finished at University, so that there would be no shortage of money. Sarah was also frightened of making a move; she never wanted to be as poor again as they had been in their poorest years.

Sarah, Jimmy and Archie were all contributing their wages and they were now one of the more well off families in the street.

The three boys now shared the two beds in the kitchen and Sarah shared the room with Alison, who had her own small bed that the boys had made.

They were all sitting having their meal at the table when the door was knocked very loudly; Sarah rose and answered the door.

John Duncan stood on the doorstep.

"Well where is she?"

At first Sarah did not recognise him, so it took a minute for her to realise that it was John Duncan.

"Where is she?" he shouted.

"Who do you mean? Lizzie, she is not here."

"Well where is she, she is not making a fool of me."

The boys came to the door.

"What's going on Sarah?"

"This is John Duncan, my friend Lizzie's husband; he does not believe me that she is not here."

He leaned forward menacingly.

"If anybody knows where she is, you do. I have had you rammed down my throat for years."

"Listen pal, you change your attitude and you get down these stairs and don't come back here, threatening our sister." Archie was now shouting.

Andrew moved out onto the landing all six foot three inches of him, towering over John Duncan.

"If I were you I would walk down the stairs before I throw you down."

"Let's just throw him down anyway, you scram and don't think of coming back here." Jimmy said menacingly.

"She knows where my wife is, I just want my wife."

John Duncan moved backwards as he spoke. The three men moved forward and he turned and hurried down the stairs.

They closed the door and all returned to the table.

Alison was still sitting tucking into her meal; they all looked at each other and laughed.

"You know I was thinking about Lizzie today. I wonder where she is. She must have left him. Mrs Barr wrote asking me to find out about her."

"Sarah you have enough to do, leave it, if your friend wants you she knows where you are." Jimmy advised.

"Jean was telling me."

"Ooooooh, came a chorus from Jimmy and Archie, don't believe all Jean tells you."

"Give over you two, she is only a friend. Sarah, her mother helps out at the Salvation Army and they trace missing people."

"I would not want to do that, she has not been in touch for years with me."

"They would know how best to find someone, that's all."

Later when Sarah was sitting by herself she thought about Lizzie. What if she had nowhere to go? Maybe she had gone to her family. I could try Largs at the weekend, if I could manage the time. So Sarah decided that she would try and find Lizzie's family, as it happened Sarah did not have to look for Lizzie.

Sarah as usual on a Friday afternoon finished work at three o'clock. The doctors allowed her these hours because one night a week she went back for a late surgery. Sarah used this time on a Friday to shop for herself and Mrs Russell. She would go in with Mrs Russell's shopping first before she would go into her own house. Alison would be waiting there for her. Mrs Russell always had a cup of tea ready for Sarah, and they would sit and just talk. Mrs Russell did not go out very often and Sarah would bring her news of neighbours if she met them on the street. Sarah would tell her a little about her work, what she would be knitting, just small talk, normally she would sit till Davie came home. The boys also came in later on a Friday night and Sarah made their meal later than usual. They all more or less wound down on a Friday night so that they could enjoy their weekend away from work.

Sarah knocked the door and shouted in.

"It's me."

This brought Alison running to the door, only this time shouting.

"You have a visitor."

Sarah went into Mrs Russell's kitchen to find Lizzie sitting at the table with Mrs Russell.

"Lizzie, oh! Lizzie, I was going to try to find you this weekend."

Lizzie came and put her arms round Sarah, she did not speak for a moment, and then asked.

"Sarah is it all right that I have come? I did not know where to go."

"Yes it is fine, John Duncan has been here looking for you."

Lizzie started to cry and Sarah held her tight.

Mrs Russell put three cups of tea on the table and sent Alison to look out of the room window for Davie coming home.

"Your pair, drink your tea now, while it is hot. I found Lizzie waiting at your door and asked her in to wait for you. Sarah has spoken so often about you Lizzie I feel as if I know you."

They drank their tea in silence; Sarah could not believe the difference in Lizzie. She was obviously very frightened.

"Have you left him Lizzie?"

"Yes I will never go back to him. He told me once that if I left him, he would never give me a divorce that I am his for life and that he can do what he likes but I do not care. I am away now and I will not go back."

"What happened, I wrote to you every now and again and Mrs Barr has been worried about you. I tried to find you at your address but neighbours did not know where you went. They thought you had gone north for the fishing."

"No, he moved us to a run-down cottage up at the Glen, it was very desolate, he had a bike and he would cycle up and down to Dunoon and the boat. If he were in a good mood and only if, we would walk down into the town. I was sent into the bank to put the money in. Everyone was told at the bank how he was saving to buy a house, he had the best wife in the town He was very fly, and he let everyone think we were so happy. He would buy me some sweets or chocolates only if anyone was about. He brought in the food. I tell you I ate that much fish I must be a great swimmer. If I did not please him, he brought no food in, at these times he never seemed to be hungry, he must have eaten outside."

"Oh Lizzie!" Sarah gasped.

"He controlled me in every way. He took my wages from me and I was allowed only what he bought me. He made me go to the bank every week and put my wages in. I could only get money out if he allowed it. He made a mistake though because people stopped giving me cleaning work because I lived so far out. When he went out he would lock me in the house. He had both our names on the bankbook and would send me for money from time to time. I once spent money on a few things for myself and he went crazy, he punched me stupid and then told me he was sorry but it was really my fault. I never took anything for myself again until this week."

"What happened?"

"He sent me for ten pounds and I took two hundred out, we had four hundred pounds in the bank, one hundred was the money that Mrs Malcolm left me. Every penny had to be saved for when we had a child and it was all my fault because I could not get pregnant."

Lizzie was crying now,

"I only took what was mine but I could not go back after that or he would have gone for me. No decent food, look at my shoes."

Lizzie took of her shoes; both had holes in the sole of them

"He came here at the beginning of the week looking for you; I don't think he will come again for the boys were going to throw him down the stairs, and Lizzie why did you stay with him so long?"

"I know, I know, my mother said he could not be that bad, when I stayed with him so long. I am frightened to be alone. I went back to see my family but my father said I had made my bed so I could lie on it. They would not let me stay. I cannot blame them when you think on the way I put him first. I have been a fool for nearly ten years now. I am worried that he will put the police on me."

"Why would he do that? He can't make you go back to him."

"What about the money, he will say I stole it."

"If your name is on the book as well as his, he cannot do a thing. You cannot steal your own money."

"What will I do Sarah, he'll find me."

"You will stay with me until we sort this out."

"I have got the money on me." Lizzie lifted her blouse to show Sarah and Mrs Russell a stocking tied round her waist, with the money stuffed into the foot of the stocking.

"We will not bother about money just now; we had better get in and see to the tea for the boys."

Alison came running through to the kitchen.

"Here comes Davie, here comes Davie."

She flew out of the door to meet him.

Davie came into the kitchen with the little girl on his shoulders. He was surprised to see Sarah still sitting there.

"Sarah."

"Davie, this is my friend Lizzie."

"Oh! So you are the Lizzie that we hear so much about."

His voice was heavy with sarcasm.

"Your mother will fill you in, come on Alison and thanks again Mrs Russell for taking care of my friend Lizzie." Sarah had emphasised 'my friend'.

They left and went into Sarah's home. "I will fill you in on Davie later, " Sarah explained.

"What's wrong, he didn't seem pleased. Have you any room for me Sarah, could we maybe find me somewhere to stay?"

"Stop worrying Lizzie, you will sleep in the room with Alison and me."

"Is the little girl yours Sarah?"

"No, she is Mary's child. Mary died giving birth."

"Oh Sarah, no," Lizzie cried.

"We will talk later, I am so glad to see you. You are very thin Lizzie, have you lost weight."

"Yes a lot but I will put it back on now."

The boys came in later and they remembered Lizzie from Dunoon. They all sat round the table and after they had eaten, Sarah told Alison to take Lizzie and show her the bed the boys had made for her. Alison took Lizzie by the hand and took her into the room.

"I wanted to ask if Lizzie could stay with us for a time, she has left her husband and she is worried he will find her."

The boys agreed that she would be better with them. If he was to come back they could deal with him.

"Lizzie can share with Alison and me. She is so small that she could have Alison's bed and Alison can sleep with me. I have to help her because she helped me years ago. I don't know what I would have done without Lizzie. She taught me so much. She is a worker and she will help. She will find work given time."

It was agreed that Lizzie should stay.

Sarah went and brought Lizzie out of the room.

"Can I stay Sarah, just for a while?"

"We have all agreed you will stay with us."

Lizzie started to cry, she could not speak, Alison climbed on her knee and they held each other tight.

They all smiled at each other. Archie tried to cheer her up by saying,

"Come on Lizzie, we have enough to put up with these two without you getting upset."

Friday night's routine was different from any other night. They all sat round the table and sorted out money for them all for the week. Sarah took housekeeping money and set it aside, part of Sarah's money went to Andrew's expenses, and then they all had pocket money including Alison. The boys gave her pennies; every one of them had a little money to spend as they wished. Lizzie wanted to pay her share as well and Sarah told her she could but not until she found work

Once they boys had gone out for the night and Alison was tucked up in bed Sarah and Lizzie talked all night, catching up on what had happened to them both.

Sarah explained all about Mary, about Davie and his father. How he had wanted to marry her, how she had refused. All about the row and how he was angry with her and they seldom spoke. How she could not have managed without Mrs Russell and how she would always help her.

Lizzie told Sarah all about her marriage and how she had made a bad mistake. She did not think that John Duncan would allow a divorce, which was the reason she wanted the money and that was why she took it. How he constantly complained because she could not have a child. How she had hoped for a child but it had never happened. She had tried to please him and in everything he made her feel that she was to blame. When he really got angry he would lock her in and often she had been frightened. She was the guilty party in the marriage and if she was right in the way she thought, he could refuse a divorce and there would be nothing she could do about it. She would, given time find out from a solicitor. It could be that she would be tied to him for life but she would never live with him again.

They spoke of everything, about Dunoon and how some day they would visit Mrs Barr. Lizzie said she would look for work as soon as she could. She knew that it would be difficult because once a woman was married; there were very few employers who would take on married women.

"I read in one of the papers recently that women doctors and teachers were trying to stop this treatment of married women. They were going to hold a meeting to start a protest about how married women more or less became the chattels of their husbands, whether they wanted to or not."

"Do you still read as much Sarah?"

"More so now than ever before, if I am not knitting or darning, I like to read. I get very lonely Lizzie from time to time. The loneliness washes over me. I know that I have the boys and Alison, but you know what I mean. Reading helps me when I feel so lonely."

"Yes I know what you mean but there is a lot worse than loneliness, believe me. I am nearly twenty-eight years old; I hope I remain lonely for a very long time. I want to please myself, and work for myself, and answer to no man. Marriage is not all it's cracked up to be. I know that you had a family thrust upon you but you answer to no one. When they all grow up and get married, what would you like to do, I mean for yourself?"

"Study, I would like to study at a college or the University, that's why I am so pleased that Andrew has managed to get to University."

"Trust you, you always wanted to learn, remember when we used to."

She was stopped there as the boys came back in.

"You two still sitting there, talking," Archie said loudly.

"Have you had a drink Archie?"

"No Sarah not me, I have taken care of my brothers at the dancing, and made sure that they did not go for a drink."

"I am not having it, I warned you all against drinking, and you are only seventeen, you two should have watched him"

They all sat round the table and Lizzie made tea for them all, as she poured the tea out, she asked them all about the dancing and what was new in dancing steps.

"We will take you and Sarah to the dancing some night. It would do Sarah good to get out and then she will see that we behave ourselves."

"Get to bed the lot of you."

"If you would get out of our bedroom we would go to bed." Andrew laughed.

"Oh I must get away, I must not be found in three men's bedrooms," Lizzie quipped back at them.

They all laughed.

Sarah watching this exchange and saw a semblance of the old Lizzie. Sarah was sorry her marriage did not work out but she was so glad to see her again.

Lizzie coming to stay made Sarah's life a lot easier. They shared the housework and shopping. Sarah was still left with all the cooking.

"If you want proper food, don't look at me. I can only cook with a frying pan but I will help with everything else.

Often after their meal at night they would all sit round the table and discuss the latest news on the wireless, the daily newspaper or local gossip.

Lizzie was finding it difficult to get work. Mrs Bell had managed to get the foreman at the Woollen Mill to see if there was any place that Lizzie could get. He had sent for her but when he realised that she was married he would not take her on. Lizzie explained that she had left her husband, it made no difference. As he explained, the Mill only takes on single women or widows, sorry. She decided that she would try for housework.

Jimmy was reading the newspaper and shouted to them.

"Come and hear this. There might be some work here for Lizzie.

The Torpedo Factory will be taking 600 extra workers. The government has decided that because of the Italo- Abysinian war and the unrest in Europe, that the Experiment work in England should be moved to the Greenock Torpedo Factory and more munitions would be made ready for protection should the unrest spread.

You could maybe get into the munitions factory Lizzie."

"I don't know anything about munitions but I would give it a try if they would have me."

"You could find out at the Labour Exchange, will I put more coal on the fire Sarah?"

"No don't, we should all go to bed. The miners are to get nine pence extra for every shift and that will put the price of coal up again. We need to be careful for a while longer."

"Sarah let me give you some money to help."

"No Lizzie, when you get work you can, don't worry we will manage fine. Things are much better for us now and in a few years we will be able to buy new furniture. I watch the prices of furniture and we will soon be able to buy a three-piece suite. They are asking around nine pounds for a new suite, when we get that we can then save for a dining room suite and just think how posh we will all be then."

"Oh yes, lah-di dah, I think I should retire for the night, so if you ladies will get out of our bedroom, or you can just stay there but shut your eyes."

"Archie," shouted Sarah. They were all laughing as all of them went to bed.

It had been a severe winter with the worst blizzards that anyone could remember. Fishing boats and steamers had been driven into the harbours. The cold was so bad that everyone was wearing as many clothes as they could and the river had started to ice up in some parts.

Everyone was depressed with the national news. The Corinthia had sailed from Greenock bound for New York, it was the largest working ship to operate out of Greenock and it had been sunk. Many lives had been lost. King George V had been very ill and had died. Edward, Prince of Wales was soon to be crowned King. There was much talk everywhere of Hitler and his hatred of the Jewish people.

Sarah's home had become a Sunday night meeting place for the boys and their friends, Jean came with Andrew and sometimes her mother would come for an hour. Jimmy had brought Davie in one night and he came most Sunday nights now. They would all squeeze in round the table and as there were not chairs for everyone, the boys would sit on the floor. Sarah would bake scones or apple tarts and Lizzie would make tea or cocoa for everyone.

The world was put to right by them all, they discussed the political situation, work in general. Who was working and who was not? The latest film shows, and whether talking films were here to stay or not. The latest dances that were sweeping the country. More and more there was talk of what would happen if war came, they would listen to the newsreader on the wireless and often they would listen to the Sunday night play. Everyone would leave for their own home after the play, Mrs Bell would help Sarah and Lizzie to clean up the supper dishes before she left for home, she waited behind one night to speak to Lizzie.

"I know someone who could maybe get you into the Torpedo factory, if you would like I could ask for you?"

"I will work anywhere, but will they take me when they know I am married."

"Leave it with me, I will find out first. I will get away home now and thanks again Sarah for having me."

Mrs Bell was back to see Lizzie before the week was over. Lizzie was to have an interview the following week at the Torpedo Factory.

"You have to go for an interview to see one of the factory foremen. Do not bring up that you are married unless you are asked. Make sure that they know you can work shifts. Take anything that you are offered and see how it goes. The money is very good, I am thinking of trying myself but I have been in the Woollen Mill for so long now I am frightened to move. I cannot chance changing work in case it did not work out or I did not suit them. I have to be sure of a wage till Jean gets through the University. You wonder if we women will ever be free of worry, if it's not one thing it's another. At least Sarah your job is secure."

"Yes but I am like you, tied to it because I want to be sure of a wage. I just could not go back to being that poor again. Lizzie can get into the factory and let us know all about it."

"I will go for the interview Mrs Bell; if I can't get in I will start looking for cleaning work. I must start paying my way; it is not fair on Sarah."

Sarah started to speak but Lizzie cut her off.

"No Sarah, not any longer, I am paying my keep, I am lucky you took me in and it is time I found a room for myself."

"Are you looking for a room Lizzie?" Mrs Bell asked.

"I must look soon, do you know of any rooms."

"No, but if you would share my kitchen with me, you could have one of the beds. I have the same house as Sarah and we have the same two beds in the kitchen. Jean has to have the room because she has to have peace to study."

"Are you sure?" Both Lizzie and Sarah spoke at once.

"I need the money, I am struggling and I don't want Jean to know."

"Well, you keep that bed for me for a while to see if I get work. Would that be fine with you Sarah?"

"Yes, that would be fine, we would still be near each other, I am getting used to your company again and I don't want to lose our friendship again."

"I will go for that interview and I will come back with a job."

A week later that is exactly what Lizzie had done. She came back from the interview in high spirits.

They were all back from their work and Lizzie was last in.

"I start on Monday; I have to go on the early shift. There are three shifts, early starts at six in the morning till two o'clock in the afternoon. Late shift starts at two o'clock till ten o'clock at night and then there is nightshift, ten till six o'clock the next morning."

Lizzie's face was aglow, she was so happy. They all wanted to know what she would work at.

"Don't know, there has to be a training period but the foreman said that they make Torpedoes. He took another man and me round the factory and the noise of machinery made it hard to hear him speak at times. There are Turners and fitters and some kind of machines, small ones that women were working called Dolls-eyes. There was a Tool store, an examination of parts, was going on in another part of the factory. There was also a drawing store. It is huge; according to the foreman he came from Woolwich in England and has been given a house in Gourock. Houses were built for factory workers coming here; I could hardly take it all in."

They were all saying 'Well done, Lizzie'

Later when Sarah and Lizzie was by themselves Sarah asked,

"Did they ask you about being married?"

"No he never mentioned it, but I told him anyway. He told me that there were a good few married women working there. If you learn the work and can keep good time, which was all he was interested in. I walked back with the fellow who is starting with me."

"Did you not have money for the bus from Princess Pier Lizzie?"

"Yes I had, but the he did not have the money and we walked all the way back. Anyway we did not care for we were both so pleased. He is married and has a small family, and he could not get home quick enough to let his wife know. I am so pleased Sarah, where would I have been without you. I will now pay my way and when it suits Mrs Bell I will move in with her. I would like to stay a while longer with you; I don't want to move just yet. I love it here Sarah, you have made a happy home for them all."

"Stay till you are ready to move and Mrs Bell will be glad of the help with her rent, but I will miss you even though you are just up the street. I have not been so lonely since you have come."

"You are so busy Sarah why do you feel so lonely, what would you really like for yourself?"

"A handsome husband, but who would take me? I am destined to be an old maid."

"Davie would take you."

"No I do not think so, not anymore and I do not want Davie because I do not love Davie. You told me that I would know, remember how you told me 'the earth would move'"

"Ach Sarah, I was a daft lassie, look what happened to me. Seriously though, how do you feel about Davie coming in on a Sunday night?"

"It doesn't bother me, he is here with Jimmy but I notice that he never looks at me or speaks directly to me."

"You do the same for I have watched you both. Could you not get back to where you were with each other?"

"I really don't want to. I still think he was so very wrong but he has been so good to me and so has his mother. I want to learn and to read everything that I can, so I want someone like that. Who, that is educated, would want me with a child? I will be responsible for Alison for years and I hope to educate her as well. The boys will move on and will marry. I feel sometimes as if I watch other people living. When I see the girls I was at school with settling down or maybe going out for the night I wish I were with them. They have stopped asking me to go out now because when I was with them I was bored. I was not interested in what they talked about and I suppose it showed. Do you never feel really lonely Lizzie?"

"No not me, not anymore. I know what you mean, it must be great to marry someone and feel as if he was just meant for you. When I feel lonely now I thank God for my loneliness and long may it continue. We will just be a pair of old maids together and when we are free and in the money we will go and see Mrs Barr."

"Yes we will do that someday, how I loved Dunoon. It all seems so far away now."

"Here you get to your bed or you will be 'greetin again'. You are getting all melancholy on me, now there is a big word for Lizzie, is it not?"

They went to bed laughing with each other.

Chapter 11

1939

*S*arah was sitting at the table reading a letter to Lizzie.

"When did it come Sarah?"

"Yesterday's post, I sent Alison to let you know as soon as I had read it, I knew you were on night shift. It is a strange letter.

Dear Sarah,

I am writing this in a hurry, we are leaving France as soon as we can. We are hoping to come back to Dunoon, do not write here anymore. I will need a place to stay. Could you please try to get us some accommodation in Dunoon? We hope to be back in about four weeks. I will contact you as soon as we arrive in England.

Hope you and Lizzie are both well.

Love Jenny.

I don't know what to make of it. It could be that if war comes they want back to Scotland."

"Do you think war will come Sarah?"

"I hope not because the boys would be called up to fight, surely I have not brought them up to lose them in a war."

"Davie says that if war comes he will enlist."

"Do you like Davie, Lizzie?"

"Yes I do but how do you feel about that?"

"It is up to you, have you been out with him?"

"No, he is just very friendly and he dances me from time to time if we go to the same dances. The factory is holding a dance, why don't we go together, you would enjoy it."

"It is not for me, I don't really like hanging about to see if I get danced. That last time we went, you were up for all the dances."

"You were asked up for dances as well."

"Yes with my brothers and even Davie gave me a dance, that was about it and as you well know I would rather read a book. I worry leaving Alison; Mrs Russell is not as well as she makes out. I have been helping her with a few things in the house lately."

"Sarah you should have told me and I would help her as well, we could do that house between us in a couple of hours, does Davie know?"

"Davie and I don't talk much as you know so don't you go telling him. Now what are we going to do about Jenny."

"Let's you and I go to Dunoon together and we will see if we can find her a place."

"What if you meet John Duncan?"

"He doesn't bother me now and anyway I have applied for a divorce but I have to wait seven years, so three down four to go. Sarah if Davie does ask me out are you sure that it would not upset you?"

"No I will not be upset, I do not think Davie likes me very much now."

"No Sarah that's not true, he speaks very well of you. We walked up the road home one night; I met him coming from the Picture Hall. He asked where you were and I told him I did not know but I supposed you were at home."

"What did he say?"

"Aye she has her hands full." That was all he said.

"I miss his friendship but that's all, you do what you want about Davie. If we can why don't we go to Dunoon at the weekend and see if we can arrange a place for them. We might have to think about bed linen, towels and things for them."

So it was arranged that they would go on Saturday.

Lizzie had been living now with Mrs Bell for close on two years and was established in the Torpedo Factory. Mrs Bell also now worked at the Torpedo Factory.

Sarah and Lizzie met up on the street on Saturday morning, with Alison between them they made for Dunoon.

It was easier than they thought to find a place. They found a small cottage nearer to Kirn, just outside Dunoon, and they rented it on a month-to-month basis. It had been lying empty for some time and needed aired and dusted. It also smelled of dampness but as the woman had said, it had not had fires on for some time. As it was the month of March they agreed to take it from the beginning of April. Sarah and Lizzie agreed to come back at the weekends to air and to give the cottage a good clean. They explained that the cottage was for their friend who was coming from France with her husband.

As they left they decided to go back and see where they had worked and take a walk round Dunoon.

"It is still my happiest of places to live Sarah."

"Me too, look Alison this is where Lizzie and I met. We used to paddle here."

"Can I go for a paddle Sarah?"

"No it is too cold."

"Oh I don't know though," laughed Lizzie as she took of her shoes and stockings.

The three of them sat on the steps and bathed their feet, the water was so cold but they were all laughing.

They bought fish and chips and ate them on the pier as they waited for the steamer.

"You know Lizzie it is great to think that we will be back here from time to time now."

There was no reply as Lizzie and Alison were hungrily eating their fish and chips.

"You will never change Lizzie."

"I hope not," was Lizzie's garbled reply.

The day had been a success and although it was very cold the three of them had colour on their cheeks.

The newspapers and the wireless reports were all full of war talk and what would happen if war came. Sarah worried very much about the boys. She was also worried about Mrs Barr and her husband. Where were they? Were they well?

One day the letter came to say that they had arrived in Liverpool and would make to Dunoon for the end of the week. They would meet them on Saturday at the pier by the kiosk. It was now the middle of April and the house was now ready for them.

Sarah and Lizzie made their way to Dunoon on mid-morning steamer and when they came off the steamer there was Mrs Barr waiting by herself.

"Sarah, Lizzie."

They hugged and kissed each other.

"Are you by yourself?" Sarah wanted to know.

"We arrived yesterday, Pierre is not so well I left him in the hotel waiting for me, I knew you would not let me down. Let me look at you both, are you well?"

"Yes we are fine; we have so much to tell you. We have managed to get you a small cottage and we have it ready for you. The rent is paid till the end of May so that will give you time if you want to move elsewhere. Where is your luggage?"

"We have very little luggage, we left in a hurry I will explain it to you later. Could we get Pierre first and I would like to get him settled."

They all walked over to the hotel and collected Pierre. Sarah and Lizzie exchanged glances; it was obvious that he was far from well. They collected what little luggage they had and all went on the bus to Kirn. Soon they were all settled in the small cottage.

Sarah lit the fire and Lizzie made tea for them all. Sarah wanted to know what had happened to them.

"Mrs Barr what's happened to make you leave France, you loved it there."

"Just call us by our first names now, Jenny and Pierre."

"Oh I'm sorry, it is just a habit."

"First we must thank you for your help and we will pay you back soon. We have money but we will need to change our money at the bank."

"Do not worry we are not looking for repayment. You would have done this for us, but what happened?"

Pierre spoke for the first time, and his voice was weak.

"We had to get back here; I feel that there will be a war soon. Hitler is determined to control Europe. My father was a Consulate in the First World War, if Hitler takes France, and I am sure that he will. Jenny would be in danger because of me. I am sure that at the best I would be a prisoner. I am not well as you can see and I had to get her home. We have sold everything that we had, as money is easier to carry if you are careful."

"Do you really think there will be a war," Sarah asked anxiously.

"Yes I am sure that it will not be many months before war starts. We are safe now thanks to you and Lizzie, I will never be able to repay you both."

"Get away with you we are so pleased that we can come back to Dunoon now. We had a great day finding this house and we will be to see you often, won't we Sarah."

"You will be tired of us before you are much older, you wait and see."

Sarah and Jenny were watching this exchange between Lizzie and Pierre.

"A way with the men I see Lizzie. What about your husband."

"That's a bad word, I am trying for a divorce but I might never get it. I am the guilty party, I left him for beating me, but I will tell you all about that later."

"What about you Sarah, never married Davie then?"

"No I am an old maid, the family are well though and Alison is lovely. We did not bring her today because we thought we might have to wait around for you. I have three very handsome brothers, haven't I Lizzie."

"Oh yes Sarah has done very well and she took me in and looked after me when I made my break. She also runs a doctor's surgery. You will see us all again soon. I am working in the munitions factory in Greenock. We have so much to tell you."

"I think we should leave you to get settled. We have brought in some groceries and things to keep you going and Lizzie has left some money to start you off. If you need us, you can phone me at the surgery, I have left the Surgery number with the money. If I am not at the Surgery leave a message I will get it. We will go for the steamer, you both looked tired."

Jenny saw them both to the front door,

"I cannot thank you enough for your help, you will come back."

"Lizzie works shifts and we will come back on her next weekend off which will be in a few weeks' time, you take care. I will bring Alison to see you."

They all send their goodbyes and Lizzie and Sarah walked back along the promenade to the pier for the steamer.

"He looks ill Sarah, what do you think?"

"Yes I would say you are right but maybe a rest will do them both good, she had so much and now she seems to have lost it all. You wonder if she would have been better off not married. Men! Are they any good for women?"

"Yes Sarah lead me to them, they are the spice of life."

"You behave yourself Lizzie."

They walked arm in arm along the promenade laughing.

Jenny and Pierre settled down very quickly and Lizzie, Sarah and Alison were regular visitors. Now it was Sarah who brought the baskets of home baking to Jenny. Lizzie would always do some cleaning for them. They moved to another cottage that they had bought and sometimes their girls would stay the weekend with them. They now looked on Sarah and Lizzie as their girls.

Sarah and Pierre always discussed 'would there be war or not' situation and Jenny would chastise them for always talking about war. Where ever Lizzie was there was always laughter and that summer was good to them all.

Jimmy had finished his apprenticeship and he had continued at the Night school in Engineering and was very keen to take the advanced engineering exams. He would be twenty-four years old on his next birthday.

Andrew had graduated from the University and had been placed for two years with a firm of Architects; this experience was necessary if he wished to establish himself as an Architect. He would be twenty-two on his next birthday.

Archie was just finishing his apprenticeship as a house painter and was the first of the boys to have a regular girlfriend. He would be twenty on his next birthday.

Alison was now nine years old, a very clever child, ready to go to the High School in another year's time.

Sarah was proud of them all, they were also in a better position financially and last year they had bought new furniture for both rooms. Sarah was still frightened to move to a bigger house and the boys seemed content to stay where they were. Maybe later they would move.

Jean bell was now working in a Glasgow hospital in the final two years of study. Her mother was so proud of her.

Davie now had his own carrier business and had his own lorry. When Sarah thought about them all she was that pleased all of them were now in a better position. No more poverty, hopefully that was behind them all.

On the third of September 1939 war was declared at eleven fifteen am. It was a Sunday and as usual everyone had gathered at Sarah's after seven o'clock at night.

The talk was all about war, Sarah felt a fear that she had never known before, she was afraid for the boys, her own brothers and every other young man that would be conscripted. They listened to the wireless, there was to be gas masks issued for everyone. There was to be a blackout at night. Everyone was to observe the rule; every window was to be covered with blackout material so no light would show at night. There was to be food rationing so that everyone would get a fair share in case there would be shortages. No hooters or sirens were to be heard any more from factories or places of work. The only sirens allowed were to be air raid sirens. The Government had already called up Army and Royal Air Force Reservists. Men between eighteen years and forty-one, years were to be conscripted. Every story told made Sarah feel sicker by the minute, she was settling Alison down for the night and she was now nine years old and had caught on to what everyone was talking about.

"Will we all die Sarah?" she asked innocently.

"No we will not, we will chase the Germans away, do not worry and you lot stop this at once, you are frightening Alison."

There was silence in the room as Sarah ushered Alison off to bed. When Sarah returned it was Davie who spoke first.

"Sorry Sarah, is she frightened?"

"Not as much as me, this is not an adventure, don't you realise that all you boys could be called up."

"I will enlist, I will not wait to be called up," Archie stated.

"That's just you isn't it, can't wait to get into a fight. None of you will enlist, if you have to go you will, "she could not go on, she broke down then.

"Come on Sarah, we will all be fine and it might not last long anyway, it could be over before anyone is called up." Archie said trying to reassure Sarah.

"Please don't enlist at least wait till you are called up."

"We are men and we have to fight for our country, I will enlist." Davie tried to reason but was cut off by Lizzie.

"You will not enlist, you will not." She stormed out of the room as she spoke. The outburst took them all by surprise.

"Ooooooh Davie," the boys shouted at him.

Davie looked at Sarah and she shrugged her shoulders.

He rose slowly from the floor where he had been sitting; no one spoke as he made his way into the other room

Lizzie was standing looking out of the window in the dark.

"Would it bother you if I was not around?"

"I don't want any of you to enlist"

"Oh I thought maybe it was just me." He was standing directly behind her. He leaned closer and spoke quietly into her ear. "Look at me Lizzie."

She did not turn so he put his hands on her shoulders and turned her round to face him. They stared at each other in the darkened room.

"Do you still care for Sarah?"

"Yes I will always care for Sarah but she is right we are just friends, I care for Sarah as friends care about each other. There is nothing between Sarah and me, not like there is between you and me."

"How do you mean?"

"You know what I mean; I never made a move because of you being married. I did not want to put you in a difficult position, but you know there is something between us." He slipped his arm round her waist and drew her to him.

"Oh Davie, I might never be free. I thought it did not matter but it does."

"We will take it one step at a time."

"But."

He silenced her as he kissed her, Lizzie responded in a way that Sarah never had. She kissed him back and they clung to each other.

"I think we had better go back to the others Davie."

"Why, they will have drawn their own conclusions by now, let's go back to my house. My mother will have gone to bed and we can have the kitchen to ourselves."

They quietly left the house and went in next door, Mrs Russell had left the fire on and Davie pushed a poker into the fire and the flames burst the kitchen into a warm glowing, flickering light. Lizzie sat down on the floor in front of the fire.

"I love to sit at a burning fire with no lights on; it is so peaceful and safe somehow, although I don't suppose anything will be safe from now on."

Davie sat down beside her and handed her a small glass of Port.

"I keep this for my mother, will you take a drink?"

"Thanks Davie I am partial to a little drink now and again, but don't tell Sarah, she frowns on me at times. I only take a small glass now and again."

"You are not frightened of Sarah, are you?"

"No, no, Sarah and I are best friends, but you must know what I mean."

"Only too well, I tried with Sarah but she shut me out. If Sarah ever marries and I doubt if she ever will, he will have to be well educated and speak properly. Sarah does not realise that people like that are looking for similar or better. I am convinced that she will be an old maid."

"Sarah is my best friend and she taught me to speak properly, but I slip up at times. Where would I have been without Sarah? I hope that Sarah meets her prince. She is very lonely at times."

"I don't think so. Let's face it, Sarah will need someone who will be very romantic and sweep her off her feet. Write poetry for her, promise undying love, and come on! Do you know any working man that can reach up to Sarah's standards?

"Well a Doctor fancied her and then there was the Minister."

"Yes but she would not have either of them. She sees it as her duty to bring up Alison as she did the boys. They will all leave her and where will she be then."

"You are bitter and you have not really spoken to Sarah properly for a long time, now have you?"

"I can't get near her to really speak to her anymore. She freezes me out and I am not bitter. I don't believe she is lonely either, this is how she wants her life."

"Yes Davie she is and I don't want her to be lonely."

Lizzie was sitting cross-legged in front of the fire. The heat from the fire had given her rosy cheeks with maybe help from the Port she was sipping. Davie was sitting with his back to a chair watching her, sitting very quietly as if she was miles away.

"What are you thinking about?"

"The war, I'm like Sarah, I am frightened about what it will mean to us all."

"Do not worry Lizzie; we will look back on this. Who knows we could tell our children about it in years to come. It may not last long anyway."

"I can't have children, so I will never tell mine."

"Well we can just tell each other."

"John Duncan does not have to divorce me Davie. I am free off him but I may never be free from him. He beat me up, he locked me in the house, he took my money from me but I have no witnesses and I stayed with him. All this is in his favour but I can try after seven years of living apart. Sarah took me to see a lawyer so I will have to wait and see."

He pulled her over beside him and they sat looking at the flames in the fire. They turned to each other at the same time, they were kissing each other, he stroked her neck and his hand travelled down to her breast, and she did not pull away from him. She was very loving and encouraged him.

They lay on the floor in front of the fire, oblivious to everything else. He was so considerate and loving, something she had never experienced. She was so happy to please him. He was ecstatic at the loving way she received him

Later as they talked they made a promise to each other, come what may, they were going to be together.

Lizzie left the house quietly and went straight back to Mrs Bell.

Next day everyone was talking about war, at the surgery, in the shops and on the streets. Sarah was becoming more depressed by the hour. She was glad to see Lizzie when she came in after her work. Alison was fast asleep and Sarah was sitting alone. The boys were all out.

"Well how are you tonight?" Sarah asked with a laugh.

"Just great, really great, are you sure you don't mind."

"No Lizzie, we have been through all this before, if you like each other I am happy for you both. Where did you go anyway?"

"Next door."

"You will have to be very careful, the pair of you."

"Don't worry, we will be fine. I am going to be working all the hours of the day; I will not have much of a chance to see anyone. We have to go on extra shifts; we have been told that applies to the whole factory. They are bringing in people from non-essential work, to work in the munitions. There will be plenty of work, and lots of overtime so if you want a change now is the time."

"No I will stay at the Surgery, I am really frightened Lizzie. Promise me that you will see to Alison if I am not here."

"Come on Sarah, this is not like you. We are all here for each other more so now than before.

"Yes I know, but promise me Lizzie."

"You are now frightening me, I will help you with Alison, and I promise you."

Lizzie did not have to worry about people knowing about her and Davie. Davie enlisted and was away within the week. He came in to see Sarah.

"Could you help me with my mother Sarah please?"

"What's happened?"

"I have enlisted," he saw the look on Sarah face. "Now listen if we all wait to be called it will be worse for everyone. The sooner this is over the better. My mother knew I would enlist and so did Lizzie. They are both very upset; could you try and talk to them?"

"What about your lorry and all your work?"

"I have a fellow that will not be called up taking over for me, I was just about to take someone on anyway and he will report every week to Lizzie and she will write me. I don't know where I will be stationed but I will be away before the weekend."

"I will help your mother, Lizzie and I between us will see that she is fine. No doubt the boys will go soon. You take care and see and get back here safely."

The day that Davie left Sarah's head was sore trying to stop the boys enlisting. It did not take long; Archie was conscripted first into the Army and a few weeks later Andrew followed into the Royal Navy. Jimmy enlisted, as he explained to Sarah, I do not have to go because I would be doing 'War Work' at the shipyard. I cannot let my brothers go while I stay at home. Within two months Sarah and Alison were alone at home. Lizzie decided that she should move in with Mrs Russell so that she could be there at nights with her. Mrs Bell was sorry to see Lizzie leave but understood that Mrs Russell now needed help.

Like all other women left behind, letter writing became a weekend pastime for Sarah and Lizzie. Another pastime was going out and joining any queue you could find at the shops. Sarah, Lizzie and Alison joined any queue, no matter what it was for, and if you could not use it, a neighbour could. Everywhere throughout the town, all communities became very close. Women were on their own a lot, whether their men were away fighting and those unable to go were working at two jobs. One being their paid work and the other being voluntary work. Firemen, Air Raid Wardens, some schools were taken over to act as Warden Posts and boys volunteered to be message boys for the Wardens, those who had cycles were used in delivering messages between Warden Posts, and volunteer workers of every kind were called on. People turned out in their hundreds to fill sand bags. Greenock saw a huge increase in shipping and many men left for all parts of the world from Greenock in the Troop ships that came into the Clyde for food supplies and repairs. The town had set up Forces Canteens where any men from the Armed Forces could get a meal and have company. Women worked on volunteer shift to cook and serve the food. Every church in the town was open for anybody that needed help. The churches prepared their halls so that they could be used for civilians to stay, should there be a bombing raid at any time

Food rationing had started for meat, butter, margarine, sugar, cooking fats, bacon and ham. A food office had been set up in the town, where you collected your coupon books.

Sarah and Lizzie were busy all the time between looking after Mrs Russell and Alison, writing letters and helping out at the Forces Canteens.

Davie came home on Embarkation Leave, he was allowed home for five days before being shipped out. Lizzie spent all her time with Davie and Mrs Russell; Sarah did not see much of any of them during that week. The morning that Davie left he came to see Sarah.

"I just wanted to say cheerio for now and thanks for looking after my mother, Sarah if anything." Sarah cut him off at these words.

"Davie nothing is going to happen, you get back here and marry Lizzie. Do not worry about us; we will all look after each other."

They gave each other a hug and Sarah pushed him out of the door because the tears were spilling down her face.

Sarah never knew where Andrew was; all his letters were sent to a clearing office and forwarded from there. He had been sent to join the H. M. Hood and had then been transferred to another ship, which she did not know the name off. These details were withheld for security reasons.

In the months that followed Davie leaving, Archie and Jimmy also came home on Embarkation Leave. Jimmy arrived first and then two months later Archie came home. Sarah was so pleased to see them and yet so frightened for them both. They had a great time being together, when it was time to leave, Sarah and Alison went to the railway station to see them away. On each occasion it was a sad send off, trying to be cheerful and brave for each other.

Sarah and Lizzie wrote every week; sometimes they would not get a letter back for months and then two or three together.

Life settled down for them as best as it could. Mrs Russell was not keeping well now. Sarah and Lizzie were sure she was fretting for Davie. The doctor assured them that she would be fine as long as she took things very easy. Her heart condition had deteriorated; medication would help, the doctor explained as he left the house after a visit.

"Our job is to keep her going until her son hopefully returns; this is all we can do."

Lizzie broke down and was crying, which was most unusual.

"Come on let's have a good strong cup of tea, I managed to get some extra tea, and I always said I would never buy anything on the 'Black Market'."

"Not you Sarah, I can't believe you bought something unlawful," Lizzie smiled through her tears. "If anything happens to Mrs Russell I will feel that I have let Davie down."

"No, we cannot be held responsible for that and Davie would not feel that you or I were to blame, anyway we will not let it happen. You must cheer up, are you feeling well, you look a bit pale?"

Lizzie stared at Sarah as she spoke.

"What is it Lizzie, what is it?"

"Dear God Sarah I don't feel too well. I am sick most mornings and I am late."

Sarah stared at her, "you can't be, and I thought you could not have any children."

"John Duncan said it had to be me, it was not him."

They stared at each other, "Dear God Lizzie what are you going to do?"

Lizzie could not control her tears, she was sobbing so much that she could not get her breath.

"Take deep breaths come on Lizzie, come on, you could be wrong."

"Sarah what will I do if I am right?"

"The first thing we will do is see about getting you an appointment to see Dr Small. I will make it first thing in the morning and then we will take it from there. Does Mrs Russell suspect anything, have you let Davie know?"

"No I am always away before she gets up in the morning and I will not worry Davie with this."

"Do not go into work in the morning, come to the Surgery with me and I will slot you in somewhere. The doctor will need to do a test to be sure. Let's get some tea so we can get or head round this."

They drank their tea in silence, Lizzie worrying what she would do and Sarah wondering how she could have been so silly.

Next morning found them both at the Surgery after Alison had gone to school. Sarah managed to get Lizzie in to see Doctor Small as soon as she could. She explained that she was her friend and she thought she was in trouble.

Lizzie came into Sarah's office to see her before she left to go to work.

"How did you get on?" Sarah really did not need to ask she could see by her face that her news was not good.

"Doctor Small thinks yes I could be, we have to wait for the test results, he thinks I am further on than I think I am. If it is the case, I am terrified Sarah."

"Do not go to work, go home."

"I would need to tell Mrs Russell, she would wonder why I was not at work" Lizzie was wringing her hands.

"Take my keys and go into my place and we will sort this out later." She handed Lizzie her keys, the telephone rang at that moment and when she was finished answering the call, Lizzie had left.

Sarah could not get home quick enough, but Lizzie was not there. She went into Mrs Russell to pick up a spare key that she left for Alison.

It was obvious that Mrs Russell had found nothing unusual that day.

"Alison is away to the library and I let her go as long as she hurries back. She is right clever Sarah. My how proud Mary would be, she is so like you it is uncanny."

The door knocked at that moment, Sarah turned to answer the door. When she opened the door, she could not speak.

A Telegram Delivery boy was standing with a buff coloured envelope in his hand. He was holding it out to Sarah.

"A telegram for Mrs Russell."

"Who is it Sarah?" Mrs Russell asked as she came to the door.

"OH my God no, no not my Davie?"

They both stood looking at the boy as he tried to get one of them to take the envelope.

Sarah put her hand out for the envelope. She was numb, she could not speak, and she nodded to the boy and led Mrs Russell back inside the house.

She sat Mrs Russell down in the chair and handed the envelope to her but she would not take it. Sarah then opened the envelope and the telegram read,

'The war office regrets to inform you, that Sergeant David Russell is reported missing in action. Any further news will be forwarded to you.'

"Look at it, it does not say that Davie is dead, look at it, it says that he is missing."

Mrs Russell was distraught; Sarah gave her a small glass of Port and took her into her house. "I will try and get Dr Small to phone the Provost tomorrow, because the town gets a list of war casualties. We will try and get more information."

Alison came back from the library at that moment,

"Alison, run as quick as you can to the chemist and ask them to phone for a doctor for Mrs Russell."

"Are you not well Granny Russell, don't cry."

"Run quick Alison before the chemist closes." Sarah did not like the way that Mrs Russell was breathing. "You sit quietly till the doctor comes."

All the old woman could do was say repeatedly, "Davie, oh Davie" over and over again.

Alison came back quickly, she had managed to get the Chemist before he closed and the Doctor would be as soon as possible.

The Doctor came within the hour and Alison was waiting to tell him Mrs Russell was in their house.

Sarah showed the doctor the telegram and then pointed to Mrs Russell, now just sitting staring at the fire.

"She won't eat or drink anything and she was gasping for breath. I gave her a small glass of Port, she has one occasionally."

The doctor nodded, after he examined Mrs Russell he gave her a tablet to take.

"Get her into bed as soon as you can, she will sleep well into the morning. If she would take a drink, milk, tea or water. Do not worry about her not eating, it is the shock, this is my third call today for people receiving telegrams. This telegram does not say that he has been killed, so there is a good chance that he is still alive. How are you?"

"I am just sick, how will I tell Lizzie now, it is Davie that Lizzie is friendly with. How could she have been so stupid?"

"Now Sarah, love makes fools of us all and we are living in very uncertain times. Does Lizzie stay with you?"

"Yes but she sleeps in Mrs Russell's house so that she will not be alone at night."

"Well that's maybe a good thing now and good that you are here for each other. I will leave you some tablets that will calm Mrs Russell for a few days, do not give any to Lizzie."

Sarah nodded, she could not ask and the doctor would not tell her anyway but Sarah knew then that Lizzie was expecting Davie's baby.

"Could we ask you if you can telephone the Provost to see if we can get any more information?"

"Yes, we will attend to that tomorrow, goodnight."

Sarah took Mrs Russell into her own house and put her to bed, Alison and Sarah stayed with her.

"Will Davie come back Sarah?"

"Yes, we will pray that he does."

It was years since Sarah had been to church and though the Minister called on Sarah from time to time, she had never gone back to church. She prayed that night for Davie and her brothers.

When Mrs Russell was in a sound sleep Sarah took Alison to get washed and ready for bed, once Alison was asleep, she sat at the room window and watched for Lizzie coming home. The moon was full that night and it lit up the streets. Sarah felt sadness all around her that night; she felt a loneliness that she had never experienced before. In a way she envied Lizzie that someone had loved her so much and that she had loved someone in return. She hoped and prayed for Davie to return safely; at least Lizzie would have his baby. She knew she was destined never to have anyone and yes she had Alison as a baby and she brought her up like her own daughter. Sarah was all the mother that Alison would ever have, and they loved each other like mother and daughter. She did wish though that she could love a man the way Lizzie did.

It was the click of Lizzie's heels on the pavement that made Sarah realise that she was coming up the stairs; Sarah flew out to the landing and caught her at the top of the stairs.

"Come in here first Lizzie."

"What's wrong, does Mrs Russell know?"

"No, come in and sit down."

Once Lizzie was seated Sarah took the telegram from behind her clock on the mantelpiece. She sat at Lizzie's feet and handed her the telegram.

Once Lizzie had read the telegram she clung to Sarah. They hung on to each other and then Lizzie started to cry.

"Listen to me; it says that Davie is missing, not dead. You must hang on to that. I had to get the doctor for Mrs Russell and he is going to make a couple of phone calls to try and find out more, listen to me, are you listening?"

Lizzie nodded.

"We will cope with the baby, you and me; tell Mrs Russell it will give her something to hang on to."

"What if he is injured Sarah what if he never knows. Sarah I love him, I really do."

"I know, I know come and try and eat something and then we should go to bed."

"I will never sleep Sarah."

"Yes you will at least you must rest, it could be months before we get anymore news. Dr Small is going to try to get some more news for us."

Sarah went through with Lizzie to Mrs Russell, who was sound asleep.

"How can she sleep?" Lizzie stared at her.

"The doctor gave me some pills for her. That is why she is sleeping so soundly."

"Could I have one then?"

"No, the doctor left instructions that you were not to have any."

"He knows doesn't he?"

"Looks like it, but he did not say. Look we will manage fine; you have got to manage for Davie. Pull yourself together Lizzie, you must think about the baby."

Lizzie was crying again, Sarah felt so sorry for her. What had happened to the cheeky, cheery girl, she once knew. As she went back to her own house she was angry, not with Lizzie, with life. They were all doing well and along came this bloody war. She could not sleep that night, and she tortured herself all night. What if anything happened to the boys? She felt guilty because when she realised that the telegram was for Mrs Russell, she was so glad it was not for her, so sorry that it was about Davie. She started to cry because she felt so mean and bad, this bloody war, this bloody war. She was then angrier with herself for swearing, even in her thoughts. She always maintained that anyone who swore did so because they did not have command of the English language, and swore because they could not express themselves any other way. She looked at Alison sleeping peacefully, she was a lovely child, now ten years old, she remembered how she used to wonder how she would manage to bring her up and here they were ten years later. What will the future hold for Alison she wondered? She prayed that night harder than she had ever prayed before, for the boys, for Davie, for his mother and Lizzie and the child she was expecting. Then she cried herself to sleep because she was so lonely.

Chapter 12

1941

*T*he weeks and months passed, and as Dr. Small suspected Lizzie was expecting a child. There had still been no more news of Davie. Lizzie and Sarah still continued to write, only now Lizzie wrote care of the Red Cross and kept hoping that Davie was somehow still alive. Every day started with waiting for the Postman and ended with the hope that there may be a letter the next day.

Greenock was now experiencing Air Raids and they came around midnight. Sarah would get Alison out of bed and they would go next door for Lizzie and Mrs Russell. They would then join the rest of the neighbours in the Shelter, downstairs in the dungeon of the property. Often the All-clear would sound within in the hour; the Wardens would tell them that the German planes were flying over the Clyde on their way elsewhere. In early May of 1941, the Siren sounded most nights. Clydebank was targeted with very heavy damage and casualties. At 12.15pm on the 6th May Greenock was Bombed. Bombing devastated the town, the German planes bombed haphazardly.

For those in shelters the noise was deafening. One neighbour shouted' let's all sing loudly and drown out the planes. Sarah was frightened and tried not to show it, so she got all the children together and they tried to drown out the adult voices. The most frightening thing for Sarah was the whistle of the bomb dropping then a few seconds of silence before the explosion. Mrs Russell hung onto Lizzie who was now nearly ready to give birth.

"Are you fine," she would ask the terrified Lizzie?

"I am great, don't worry." Lizzie lied. Everybody tried to keep everyone else's spirits high.

Once the All Clear sounded and they made their way up onto the street, the silence was overwhelming. Most doors and windows in the property had been blown in; the main thing was the property was still standing. The Warden told them the Sugarhouse had been hit and the East End of the town, and he reckoned that about fifty planes bombed Greenock that night. Most of the people who could went to see if they could help. Sarah filled her house with children and bedded them down anywhere she could so that others could help.

Much worse came the next night the 7th May, again they were all in the Shelters and bombing started after midnight and continued until after 3.am. Most of the East End was targeted. It was thought that the Germans were trying to bomb the shipyards.

When the All clear came and they left the Shelter it was unbelievable the destruction that they saw. Mrs Bell took Alison and other children and every-one went to see if they could help. Mrs Russell and Lizzie made tea and opened their house to most of the elderly neighbours.

Sarah could not believe what she saw. Everywhere she went properties were destroyed. Someone told her the Town Hall had been hit. As she went along the main street, she took along with her people whose home had been destroyed. They met others and made their way to the first church hall they could find. All the churches had turned their halls into temporary homes. Sarah helped others to make up beds and make hot food. She learned that the East End was the worst hit, but nowhere had escaped; over 250 planes had bombed Greenock that night. In the two nights over 250 people had been killed and hundreds had been injured. One of the distilleries had been bombed and the fire that followed lit up the East End of the town and people fleeing from the bombing were machine-gunned. The West End had been bombed; the South West of the town had been bombed as well. Two of the biggest churches in the town had taken direct hits, they were demolished, what the bomb did not do, the fire that raged afterwards burnt them out. The Distillers, the Docks, the Shipyards and the

Sugar House was bombed again. Everyone that came in for shelter had another bombing to tell off.

Sarah worked all night and then in the morning made her way to the Surgery. The doctors had been out all night with all the volunteer services. Dr Small told Sarah to go home at midday and to come back tomorrow if she could.

When Sarah returned home she found that Alison was with Lizzie, who had somehow or other got hold of man she knew and he had boarded up their windows and managed to repair the doors that had blown in. As Sarah was clearing up the broken glass, Lizzie who was sitting on the chair by the fire spoke quietly, "Alison, run and see if Mrs Bell is in and ask her to come here quickly."

Sarah turned and looked at Lizzie, who nodded her head. It had been agreed that when Lizzie was due to give birth, they would send for Mrs Bell to help out till the nurse came.

They looked at each other because they both knew that with the town being in turmoil from the bombing that had taken place; every emergency service was stretched to and beyond its limit. Sarah tried to reassure Lizzie.

"It will be fine, we will manage, don't panic."

At that moment Alison came hurrying back to say that Mrs Bell was not at home.

"Right Alison, go for Mrs Russell and get her in here, I will be back as soon as I can. When Mrs Russell is here go back and wait for Mrs Bell. Tell her Lizzie needs her."

"Is the baby coming Sarah?"

"Yes, I am going to try and get the nurse or the doctor"

The phone system in the town was out of order and girls and boys were delivering messages throughout the town to try and help. Sarah made her way to the Surgery as quick as she could and on the way watched for any one that could help.

She reached the Surgery as Dr. Small was leaving.

"What are you doing back her, have you had any sleep?"

Sara gasped out at him, "Lizzie has started."

"I am on my way to the hospital but I will come with you first."

They hurried to the car and as many roads were closed they had to detour to get back to East Shore Street. As they entered the house they both heard the cry of a new-born baby. Mrs Russell was so glad to see the doctor.

"The baby came so quickly, it has just been born."

"Let me take over."

Sarah ran quickly for towels and sheets that they had prepared for the birth. She was mesmerised as she watched the doctor. He handed Sarah the baby and told her to get him washed. Lizzie had given birth to a lovely baby boy. Mrs Russell helped Sarah and they wrapped the baby in a cot sheet and Mrs Russell sat with her Grandson until the doctor had dealt with Lizzie. When the Doctor had finished with the baby, they all smiled at each other.

"A fine son you have Lizzie, I will send a nurse in when I can find one, can you manage meantime," he looked at Sarah as he spoke.

"We will manage fine Doctor, I will help." Mrs Russell smiled at him.

As the Doctor left the house quickly he recalled that it was the first smile he had seen on Mrs Russell face since her son went missing

Alison and Mrs Bell came hurrying shortly after, Alison was desperate to hold the baby, and held him for a short while until Sarah and Mrs Bell had changed the bed for Lizzie.

"Are you fine Lizzie?" Sarah asked anxiously.

"Never better," laughed Lizzie, as they handed over her son to her.

"Well who was in a rush to be born then, now what are we going to call you?" she spoke softly at her son.

All eyes turned on Lizzie, waiting to hear what the baby would be called.

"I think we will have to call you David, what do you think of that name?"

"Oh Lizzi, would you call him David?" Mrs Russell eyes were brimming with tears as she spoke.

"That's it settled then, David it is."

They all toasted the baby's health with a cup of tea. It was now late in the evening but was still bright daylight outside, as double summertime had been brought in as a measure to help the war effort and also the farmers. People could work up until eleven o'clock in the evening in daylight. The children loved the long double summer nights as they could play nearby in daylight.

It was decided that Mrs Russell and Mrs Bell stay with Sarah that night. The schools had been closed until the Wardens said they were to be re-opened.

Sarah slept soundly all night, the baby wakened Mrs Bell and she helped Lizzie. The house was still so quiet, with everyone still asleep, when the banging of the door wakened them all. Sarah answered the knocking to find a Telegram boy on the doorstep. She stood and looked at him as he handed out the Telegram.

"Is Mrs Russell still staying next door?" he inquired.

"She is here," Sarah could hardly find her voice.

"Will you sign for it then?"

Sarah signed the receipt and turned and closed the door.

She walked into the kitchen and sat at the table. Lizzi sat up in the bed as the rest gathered round Sarah. Thy all waited.

"It is for you Mrs Russell."

"Open it Sarah."

"I can't."

Lizzie jumped out of the bed, "I will open it."

She tore open the envelope and slowly sat down at the table. She looked at Mrs Russell, the tears were pouring down her face and she was smiling.

"Dear God, thank you God, Davie is alive, and he is a prisoner." She read out the Telegram. "The War Office wishes to inform you that the Red Cross have listed Sergeant David Russell, The Royal Scottish Fusiliers, as a prisoner of war. No details available at present."

They were all laughing and crying and Alison was dancing around singing, Davie is safe, Davie is safe.

There was no more bombing for the rest of that week, still people were leaving their homes at night and going up in the hills above Greenock to sleep. It was not unusual to see a column of people heading up towards the hill, where they would sleep till morning and then come back and carry on as usual. The people in their close decided that they should all go but Sarah had said that between Lizzie with a new baby and Mrs Russell, it would be better if they stayed and took their chance in the close shelter. On that night Sarah prayed that she had made the right decision, however apart from a Siren warning the following week, which was followed closely by an All-clear siren, Greenock was spared another terrifying bombardment. Other towns and cities suffered all over the country and like Greenock everyone helped in every way. The war brought people closer together and most homes kept an open door to help anyone. If someone needed extra food because they had taken in people, the neighbours all rallied round. Food was very scarce at this time, Sarah's house was very fortunate for Lizzie could get anything that was needed and she always shared. Sarah would shake her head but she never refused the extra.

"How did you come by that Lizzie?"

"Don't you ask and your conscience will not bother you," Lizzie laughed

They were getting ready to go and see Jenny at Dunoon, and Lizzie was filling a basket with a few things. They wanted to take the baby so that Jenny could see him. Lizzie had even managed to get a second hand pram and they were going to walk to Princess Pier for the Ferry. They had to be there early and wait to see if they could get on. It was to be a quick trip because they did not want to leave Mrs Russell alone for long. Mrs Bell promised to look in on her.

Mrs Russell was pushing Lizzie to have the baby christened and Lizzie was trying to put her off. It was not that she did not want him christened but she had registered the baby as David Duncan. As she explained to Sarah and Mrs Russell her husband had never really done very much for her and this was one thing he could do.

She had her marriage certificate, and that was all the Registrar needed to register the baby, because she would explain that her husband was away in the war. She did not want to see 'Bastard' on the birth certificate and that was what would happen if she did not show a marriage certificate. If Davie had been at home, he could have registered the baby, as he was not, they could sort it out later. John Duncan would never know and she felt that she was harming no one. Now going to church and having the baby christened as David Duncan was really telling lies in The House of God and she did not want to do that. If the minister would come to the house and christen the baby she would be happy to go along with that.

There were times when Sarah never really understood Lizzie. Yes, she knew she went to church and did not often miss the Sunday service. At the same time Lizzie could get things from the 'Black Market' or where ever, and it did not seem to bother her. Now Sarah had a conscience about just everything and it worried her, maybe Lizzie was right. If it did not harm anyone and they always shared. Mrs Russell jokingly called her 'Mrs Robin Hood'. Sarah reproached herself for being so serious about everything, as Lizzie often said, "lighten up Sarah; you are frightened off the day you may never see."

Mrs Russell had taken on a new life with Davie's baby. No one had seen her laugh as much as she did lately. Although she seemed to have lost confidence in going outside, she was very happy to help look after the baby.

Lizzie returned to her work as soon as she could and went on back-shifts, so that Mrs Russell did not have the baby to look after for long. Alison was now eleven years old and was also helping when she came home from school. Life although difficult, was getting better again. If Sarah could just hear from the boys and they could get more news of Davie.

There had been letters now and again but not many. They wrote to Davie through the Red Cross and sent parcels. They never knew if he got them. Lizzie had written to tell him that he had a son; she had enclosed a photograph of his mother holding the baby and herself standing behind them. Time passed for them all very slowly. Like every other family throughout the country they worried about all the boys at war.

Alison was now nearly fourteen years old and David was now three years old and a smart little boy. His grandmother was so proud of him.

The war was nearly over, the Allies were in control of most of Europe and all the news was that the end of the war would come soon. As it was it took another year before victory in Europe was declared. Sarah was receiving a letter about every six weeks now mostly from Jimmy and Archie, fewer from Andrew, sometimes it was just a few words scribbled in a hurry. She hated these letters because she felt that wherever they were, they had no time. One letter from Archie just said, I am well, see you soon. It was all she needed to make her have a good day.

Alison had blossomed into a very pretty girl and the older she got; she looked more like Sarah than her mother. She had sat her Lower Examinations, and had been top girl in the Lower section. She would start studying for Higher Examinations after the summer holidays. She wanted to go to University and Sarah was determined that she would.

It was obvious that all being well they would need a much bigger house when the boys came home.

The school had organised a dance for the third year pupils and Sarah had made a dress for Alison out of one of her own dresses. Clothing coupons were still used to buy clothes and there were no extra coupons that could be used for party dresses. Alison was a very tall girl and needed women's clothes; only children sizes were free from coupons.

It was a warm afternoon and Sarah was sitting at the window sewing the dress when she realised that there was a commotion in the street. She leaned out of the window and as she did, she heard church bells ringing.

"The war in Europe is over, the war is over, and Germany has surrendered." People were dancing in the street. She hurried downstairs after knocking Mrs Russell door and telling her to go to the window. All the neighbours were out that could be, everybody was laughing. The lady in the bottom flat house opened her window high and brought her wireless over to the open window. They all listened, it was true, Victory in Europe, Victory in Europe. Sarah and her neighbours decided that they would have a street party and they planned it for the next day at night when everyone was finished their work.

Sarah managed to get Mrs Russell downstairs with Lizzie's help and everyone brought out tables and chairs. Tea was made, sandwiches were made, some had Spam on them and some had not, but it did not matter. One of the older men had an accordion and was playing all the favourite songs. Everyone was singing and dancing and suddenly it all stopped, slowly, and then there was silence. A Telegram boy was cycling up the street, nobody spoke.

"I am looking for a Mrs John Duncan of Dunoon; I have been given an address c/o a Mrs Bell, East Shore Street."

Lizzie stood up and walked forward, "Yes, that is me."

"I am sorry, I really am." He handed over the telegram and Lizzie signed for it.

Nobody spoke, Sarah signalled for Alison to take care of David and she took Lizzie upstairs. As they went up the stairs, Lizzie opened the envelope, the telegram read.

The war office regrets to inform you that Corporal John Duncan of the Argyll and Sutherland Light Infantry has been killed in active duty.

"I wanted free of him but I never wanted this, Sarah I never wanted this."

"I know, I know, come on upstairs."

"What will I do, this is dated last week? They must have been looking for me. He must have given my name as his next of kin. What did he have to go and get killed for; I don't want to feel sorry for him, what will I do Sarah?"

The tears were running down Lizzie's face.

"This is out of your control and you are not to blame. Do what has to be done, has he any family?"

"I don't think so, but I could put an announcement in the Dunoon weekly paper and leave my address should there be any family. I will have to go to the Police Office; they will tell me what to do."

They were standing in the kitchen when Sarah asked,

"Are you upset?"

"He always knew how to get me when I was enjoying myself."

"Lizzie don't say that."

"It's true though and I'm hungry, I was going to try and enjoy the party. I never wished him dead, I never even thought about him but it is sad. He was away fighting and nobody cared."

"Here eat this," Sarah handed her a sandwich that she had kept back for their supper.

"We will do right by him now though, I will help you. I suppose he will be buried wherever he was killed."

They both sat at the table and Sarah thought, yes it is so sad, nobody to care about you.

Next day they wrote to Jenny in Dunoon and asked her to put a request in the Dunoon Weekly Newspaper, that John Duncan had been killed in active duty. If anyone wished any further information, would they please get in touch with Lizzie? They went to the police office and were told to write to the headquarters of the Argyle and Sutherland Regiment. There was nothing else they could do.

VJ day, victory over Japan came in August 1945 and at last the war was over.

Chapter 13

1945

*S*arah waited for the boys to come home and each day started with her hoping she would hear today and every night hoping that she would hear tomorrow. She was also anxious about Mrs Russell who seemed to be failing again. She was hurrying home as she had been for their rations for them all and she was late for the meal. As she hurried up East Shore Street, there was a man in front of her walking very slowly, his suit hung of his shoulders and she noticed that he had on new shoes. He carried a brown paper parcel, it was not a big parcel but it must have been heavy. He gave the impression of being tired, but then everybody was tired, these days. As she past him she glanced back at him.

"Dear God Davie, oh Davie," Sarah took in the very gaunt figure. She could hardly recognise Davie.

"Sarah," was all he said. She took his parcel from him. He was so thin and gaunt.

"How is my mother?"

"Waiting for you, we thought they would have let us know when you were coming."

"I came into Liverpool and got the chance of a lift with a lorry driver to Glasgow. I should have waited and I would have got a travel warrant, I just had to get home."

They stared at each other; he was so thin and gaunt.

"Have you had a bad time?"

Davie just nodded," Are you fine? How about the boys and my mother, do you still see Lizzie, do you see Lizzie?"

"Oh Davie, have you not had any letters?"

"No, but I did get parcels through the Red Cross. They were always opened, never any letters though.

She took his arm and was appalled at how thin his arm was through the jacket.

"Come on Davie there are three people desperate to see you before the rest of us get all your news."

"How do you mean Sarah, is Lizzie still here?"

"Yes Davie she's been waiting for you."

They walked up the stairs together; she still carried his parcel, neither spoke. When they reached the landing of their houses, Alison was playing with David.

"Hello there you two," Sarah spoke softly. Neither looked up, they were too busy.

"I am showing David how to play marbles; Granny Russell thinks you have got lost tonight." As Alison said this she looked up. Her hand flew to her mouth, Sarah held up her finger to warn Alison not to speak.

"Alison just look at the height of you, look at her Sarah, I left a wee girl and she has grown into a woman."

Sarah left them smiling at each other and went for Mrs Russell.

"Come here quick, there is a surprise here for you."

Davie came in the door at that moment, "Mother."

"Oh Davie son, oh Davie," they were holding each other tight and everybody was crying except for David. He pulled Davie's jacket, "Are you my Daddy, my Daddy's called Davie."

He looked at them all through his tears, Sarah and Alison were laughing and his mother was nodding her head.

"Aye he is your Daddy and just wait till Mammy gets home. I never thought I would see this day."

Davie went down on his knees and looked at his son, he could not take it in and yet he knew that this boy was his. He had Lizzie laughing eyes,

"Are you going to give me a hug then?"

The boy put his arms round his neck, "Don't cry, Mammy will make it better when she comes home."

Sarah took Alison and they went into their own house, "Let's leave them on their own for a while."

The news had spread through the street that Davie was home from the Prisoner of War Camp. The close was busy with everybody coming to shake his hand and the men wanted to take him for a drink. Davie told them he would go with them another night, that he was going to meet Lizzie. Don't you worry he was told; we will get you a lift to the factory gates. It was like a party in the close. Someone shouted to Sarah 'no sign of the boys yet?' She shook her head and shouted back, "soon, I hope soon." Someone else wanted to know if Mrs Russell needed anything.

"No thanks, you don't need anything if you live with Lizzie." Everybody nodded in agreement for they all knew that without Lizzie, they would have all been short of a lot more. Lizzie always knew a man that knew a man and that man could get you anything and Lizzie never charged anybody. Someone shouted 'let's get Davie to the factory gates.'

"No, do not do that, because he could miss her coming out in the crowd. Take him to the bus stop, he can't miss her as she comes off the bus," someone else shouted.

The neighbour that played the accordion had turned up and they were all singing. Sarah had brought out a few chairs so that older people could sit. It was soon time for Davie to go with the men to the bus stop. They lifted him shoulder high and marched down the street to meet Lizzie.

Lizzie was tired tonight and a bit down, nothing had seemed to go right all day. She had been late and only got in because the Gateman on duty at the factory had turned a blind eye. The day had seemed longer than usual and she just wanted home. She piled onto the worker's bus for the journey home. She was cold and hungry; she could not even be bothered with the usual conversations on the road home. She was deep in thought, where was Davie, would she ever see him again. She waited every day to hear from him, but there was still no news. The news was that prisoners of war would be repatriated first and then they would bring the all the boys' home. Sarah and her had went to the picture hall to see if the Movietone News would give them anymore information but all that had done was to frighten them even more. The pictures of camps in Germany being liberated and the treatment of prisoners were unbelievable. Would David ever meet his father? Mrs Bell slid into the seat behind her and asked,

"Any word yet for you or Sarah?"

She shook her head and turned to look at her, "Have you any news yet?"

"No not really, other than what I told you, did you tell Sarah?"

Again she shook her head, shrugged her shoulders," what's the point, Sarah would only worry more for Andrew, anyway these things happen but I think maybe you should warn Sarah."

"Jean insists that they were only friends but I thought myself or maybe I took it for granted because they were always together. She tells me that when Ray goes back she will follow him and work in America. It seems so far away."

"You will miss her."

"She wants me to go out as well, but I can't do that. I will tell Sarah that she has met someone, who knows what will happen anyway, everything is so mixed up."

"Is it true what I heard about you and one of the Foremen?" Lizzie asked.

"Well we have been out a couple of times, who knows, I did enjoy myself though. I see him regularly in the factory but it was at the Victory Dance in the Battery Park, when I went to watch everybody enjoying themselves after work one night. I was leaning on the wall, when he came and spoke to me, then we walked up the road together. I went with him to the Town Hall Victory Concert. That's about it so far; if anybody had told me that I would be going out with somebody at my age I would have told them they were dreaming. Here I am nearly fifty years old," she stopped speaking then, and took a good look at Lizzie," You a bit down at the moment? It is not like you, hang in there, he could be home soon. Here we are our stop now."

They got off the bus together and started to cross the road to walk up their street. A crowd of men walking down the street had someone on their shoulders, it took them a moment to realise that they were chanting "Lizzie, Lizzie."

"Oh dear God" was all Lizzie could say and she stood still and stared across the road. The men had put Davie down and they all moved away from him, he seemed taller than she remembered and then she realised that he was so thin. All she could see were his eyes as she crossed over to him, they stared at each other and then they were hugging each other tight. Nobody spoke, the men all dispersed and Mrs Bell walked on ahead. They walked up the street to the close and up onto the top landing where his mother and Sarah were waiting for them. They went into the house, Sarah had taken Mrs Russell, David and Alison into Sarah's house to stay the night and leave Lizzie and Davie alone.

"Let me look at you, was it bad." All the time they clung to each other.

"We all had to get through it as best we could; when it was bad and I could not cope any longer I would relive our night together. I got parcels but never letters."

"I wrote to you."

"I know Sarah has told me, how did you manage, was it bad?"

"Sarah helped me through and we have all looked after each other. What do you think of our boy?"

"I couldn't take it in, I still can't, and nothing seems real. I keep waiting to be told what to do. We could do nothing unless we were told and you just survive as best you can. I wondered if you would still be here."

"Yes I waited for you, I have never been so lonely and yet I am always busy." They stood together still holding each other. The clock on the mantelpiece ticked out loudly, her heart was thudding in her chest. This was not how she had imagined his homecoming would be. She had imagined running to meet him and he would lift her off her feet and she would tell him about their son. The house was so silent as they stood holding each other. She realised that he was unsure what to do. She pushed him gently away from her and took off her coat; she slipped out of her work dress and sat at the fire in her underskirt. She poked the fire till it blazed in the kitchen and said to him.

"Do you remember that night?"

"Yes, oh yes," He took off his jacket as he spoke and sat down on the floor beside her.

"I don't know what to do Lizzie; I don't know if I can, I just don't feel anything but relief at being home.

"Well let me show you what to do and believe me you can. You leave everything to Lizzie." She unbuttoned his shirt as she spoke; she pulled him onto the floor beside her.

"Let's take up where we left off."

Later she realised that she was hungry and in the early hours of the morning she made them both a meal and they slept late the next morning.

It would be two more months before Archie came home followed shortly by Andrew. Letters from Jimmy were now arriving regularly, and he hoped to be home within a few months. The day Jimmy came home they held a street party for all the boys that had come home from the war and it doubled as a wedding party, for Lizzie and Davie were married the same day quietly in the Registrar's office.

As the war had brought many changes to Sarah's life the first few years after the war would bring more.

The house was now definitely far too small for them all but housing remained very difficult because of the homes lost in the bombing, and those bombed were considered first. Sarah was secretly relieved that she did not have to move to another home, she still feared the poverty that they had all experienced in their early years.

Sarah had been worried about how Andrew would take the news that Jean had met someone else. Andrew had taken her by surprise by telling her that he had met a Wren that had been posted to the same base as him before he went deep sea. They had corresponded all during the war and although she did not get many letters from him, they had agreed to meet up. He had been back to his place of business before the war and they were keen to have him back. He had been offered a place in a new office that the firm were opening up in |London. He had accepted the new position, as it would give him the opportunity to meet up with his new girlfriend, as she came from the London area and he wanted to be near her.

Archie brought his girlfriend home to meet them all, her name was Anne and she had corresponded with him while he had been away at the war. They wanted to be married as soon as possible, because of the time they had lost. In a very short time there was only Jimmy, Alison and herself still at home.

The years following the war were busy and National Health Service had been introduced and Sarah found herself Manager of a larger practice with six doctors, two nurses and six office workers.

Jimmy was back at the shipyard and had been offered a manager's position. There could be a possibility of a Company house in time to come. Alison was now sixteen years old and was a senior girl in the high school. This year she would sit her Higher Exams and all being well she was intending to study law at Glasgow University.

The country was returning to a more normal; way of life after the war, food rationing had stopped and there was still clothing rationing which was due to finish soon.

Sarah had enrolled at night school and was studying to try for qualifications that would lead her hopefully into University. She still hankered after education for herself.

At Archie and Anne's wedding she had spent time with the Minister who had also come to the Reception.

Now there was a saying 'three times a bridesmaid never a bride' and the Reverend wanted to change that for Sarah. When she was laughingly teased about being a bridesmaid for the third time, the Minister had jokingly replied on Sarah's behalf. That is one saying that will be proved wrong. Sarah was annoyed because it gave people the wrong impression. One night later as he walked her home he insisted in seeing her right to her door. As she turned to say goodnight, he pulled her towards him and gave her a long kiss, a rather wet kiss that did not please Sarah. That night she decided that men were out for her. Lizzie and Sarah always got together on a Friday night after their work was finished, they would catch up on what had happened that week.

"How is the Reverend these days?"

"Don't ask, I am not going to anymore socials or anything else with him."

"What happened?"

Sarah hesitated for a moment. "Well he walked me right up to the door and just as I was about to go in, he pulled me towards him and planted a long wet kiss right on my mouth"

"And?"

"It was ghastly, I hated it, and I don't think I really like men in that way, you know what I mean?"

"Come on Sarah, it couldn't have been that bad, I thought at long last there was something going on there."

"No Lizzie it is not for me, I am convinced of that, an old maid I am and an old maid I'll stay. I will stick with my books and I mean it. What's new with you?"

"Granny not so well, have you noticed?"

"Yes I have, mind you I did not think she would still be here, her heart is really bad."

"Yes, Dr Small has warned Davie, he told us that if she sleeps away, we are to be happy for her. The doctor has let Davie get back to work but I think he should wait yet. He still has bad nightmares and still will not tell me what happened to him. Has he told you anything?"

"No Lizzie, we talk to each other but we really do not tell each other anything, you know what I mean, don't you? Why don't you get Davie to keep that man on that looked after things for him when he was away? He would not have so much to do if he had him working with him."

"I will try, Davie wants me to stop working now but I don't want to. I don't fancy being a full time housewife and I know that is frowned on, but that's just me. He said I could work for him and not many married women work but that's all changing since the war. I will try and get him to keep the other man on. He was very honest you know, Davie came back to a notebook that he had kept of everything that he had done. Took his wages every week and banked the rest other than the petrol or any costs for the lorry. He is going to split the money with him, Davie feels that is only fair."

"Tell him to keep the money and keep the man on, maybe they could have two Lorries in time to come."

"We will see, now back to the Minister. Do you not want a man of your own and a home of your own? If Alison goes to University and Jimmy gets a house, what will you do?"

"I will not go with Jimmy," Lizzie shook her head as Sarah said this. "Listen Lizzie, what if Jimmy met someone what would I do then. This is my home and I have had my own home for years. Alison I am sure will move on and then I will try for University."

"You cannot cuddle up in a bed with a book; it does not keep you warm. Do you not want a child of your own?"

"I think I have left that a bit late, don't you, and getting back to the Minister, I will never cuddle up with him, I felt sick when he slobbered over me for that's what he done. No, if I ever marry it will be with someone who, as you have told me, 'will make the earth move'. You see Lizzie it is your entire fault."

They were laughing together over this, "I just want you to be happy and let's face it, I was a daft lassie."

"Yes but you told me and I quote, 'Davie is marvellous, if you know what I mean.' That is what I want; I will not settle for less, I will not marry because I feel lonely."

"Do you still feel lonely at times?"

"Yes, it is a kind of sadness or maybe I feel a bit depressed. I can't really explain it; I am living in the world and watching everybody else being happy. I am happy for them, I would like that special someone to make me feel that happy. I am older than I should be because I have had to be, I was never on the same level as lads of our own age. I should have had all the fun of my teenage years. Where was I then? Combing the beach looking for wood for the fire, and when they were in their beds sleeping, wondering how I was going to feed us all. Watering down two eggs to feed five of us, some days they went out near hungry. Dear God Lizzie it was awful and then it was washing, cleaning, working and worrying that someone might find out how young I was and take them all from me. Then later Mary died and there was Alison to raise. We have all been lucky, I used to pray to God, 'please let the boys come home from the war and I will take whatever you throw at me.' When they were young, I used to throw my eyes at the sky and ask, 'why me, why are you doing this to me.' Now I realise that I had to give up my youth and if I had to make that choice again, I would do the same thing. I now thank God that I managed to raise them all, that I kept well, that I had help and I had work."

"Well now that you have got that all of your chest, for God's sake give me a drink. The boys are right you know. They warned me that if I asked you anything I would get a sermon in the explanation and they are right."

"You are getting no alcohol here," they were both laughing, Sarah went and brought out a bottle of whisky that Jimmy kept and she poured a little into each tea cup. Lizzie took the bottle from her and poured more into her own. "If Jenny could see us now, drinking and talking about men, we will need to go and see them soon. I wonder if they ever guessed we took them black market goods."

"Talking of black market, how would you like a pair of nylons, cost you fifteen shillings mind?"

"Fifteen shillings for a pair of stockings, how do you come by nylons? Fifteen shillings, are you sure?"

"Sure as I'm sitting here, well the American ships have docked and those boys can get anything. Five ships are coming into Greenock and the place will be awash with sailors, and I have to be married, it is not fair. Davie says he will lock me up."

"You need locked up, you would not dream of looking at anyone else, would you?"

"Ah Sarah, the day I don't look at a nice looking man, you can lock me up and throw away the key. I will look but I will not buy. I would never do anything to hurt Davie. Do you want nylons, according to my friend of a friend; you have not lived until you have worn a pair of nylon stockings. I am having a pair and I am getting a pair for Alison for her birthday, so come on, dig deep."

"Are you never frightened you will get caught?"

"I never sell Sarah; I only buy; now you know that. I shared all during the war. Do you want the bloody nylons or not. I don't want a flaming sermon."

They were both laughing and giggling like two teenagers. Sarah poured more tea into the teacups and Lizzie poured more whisky into each of them.

They were still laughing when Alison came back from the Youth Club with the Minister.

He came into the kitchen, "Hello Sarah, are you?" He stopped short, looked at the bottle of whisky on the table, disgust was all over his face. Sarah twirled her finger at him.

"Now Reverend we don't want a bloody sermon, do we Lizzie?" The two of them burst out laughing again. The minister turned on his heels and walked out. Sarah and Lizzie were by now near hysterical with laughter.

"No more wet slobbers for you my girl, you have done yourself out of that pleasure."

Lizzie wagged her finger in Sarah's face.

"Are you two drunk?" Alison demanded. "I will never be able to go back to the Youth Club now. Mind you I only went because of you; you thought it would be good for me. So I will not go again." Alison was now laughing with them.

"I did not know what I was going to do about him, but I don't need to worry anymore.

One thing for sure, he will not move the earth for me."

Alison stood and looked at them, they were both holding their sides with laughter, and they laughed until the tears ran down their faces. She shook her head and wondered why the Minister should move the earth for Sarah and what exactly did she mean. She would ask her tomorrow for there would be no sense out of the pair of them tonight

The years that followed brought more changes for them all. Alison had finished at school and was now at University. She travelled to Glasgow daily and had become a lovely young woman, whose only interest at the moment was to become a lawyer. Jimmy had been promoted again and was now living in Gourock in one of the shipyard houses. All his pleading to get Sarah to move fell on stony ground. He kept telling her he was an unclaimed treasure and she replied that when he was claimed she did not want to play gooseberry. They visited each other often and would take long walks along Gourock promenade and front. Davie and Lizzie would encourage them to go to Cragburn, which was the popular place for dancing. They would sometimes go with them but not often.

Mrs Russell had slept away peacefully in her sleep. It had been expected for some time; nevertheless she left a huge gap in all of their lives. Sarah felt her loss acutely for Mrs Russell had taken on the role of Sarah's mother, guiding her through her early teen years and always hoping that she would have married Davie.

Davie was devastated by his mother's death, he reasoned that she had lived a good long life and she had seen her grandson. He knew that she liked Lizzie, but not the way she had loved Sarah.

Andrew had come home for the funeral and once again they were all together. He was trying to be transferred back to Glasgow as his girlfriend had finished their friendship. He told Sarah that he was not heartbroken because she wanted to be married and he did not. He just could not take the final step and because of this he reasoned that he did not love her enough. He did like London and his work satisfied him. There were so many opportunities for Architects because of the buildings that had been destroyed during the war. In time he hoped to come home.

Sarah and Lizzie still went over to Dunoon to see Jenny, who was now quite frail. Pierre had died just after the war had ended. Jenny told them she was grateful for the years they had shared. This time it was David who went with them. Now a strapping lad, nearly ten years of age, very like his father in looks and with the happy attitude of his mother. David could talk to anybody and charm them. Jenny was delighted to see them all, wanting all their news and so happy that they had all survived the war. Delighted to hear all their news and how well they were all were. Davie had now a thriving transport business with four Lorries now on the road. The three of them would sit and reminisce over all the years they had known each other. Life was getting better for them all.

Sarah was sitting at the window reading; she had a pile of papers in front of her. She had sat the Higher Examinations at the Night School and was waiting for results. It was her birthday and everybody had forgotten. Alison had gone out earlier for the evening and she went to see Lizzie but they were not at home. It was a Friday evening and the house seemed extra quiet. This was the time when loneliness would wash over her. She would remind herself that this is what she chose. All being well she would have qualifications to apply for a place at University. She had saved and was now financially ready. Still she hesitated, maybe next year, she would tell herself.

The door knocked and she hurried to answer it, she needed some company tonight. Lizzie came in with Davie and David.

"Happy birthday Auntie Sarah," David gave her a hug. Lizzie came in with a cake and Davie with a bottle of Port

"Am I not glad to see you, I haven't seen anybody all day. They have all forgotten my birthday except you." As she pulled out chairs, the door was knocked again.

Jimmy stood there with Jenny, "happy birthday Sarah," behind them came Archie and Anne, who had brought along Anne's parents. Sarah was delighted; Alison arrived last with a birthday cake. Food was produced from Lizzie's next door. Sarah had a party that night, Alison and Jimmy had organised it and had went over to Dunoon for Jenny. She was to stay with Jimmy for the night and he would take her back the next day.

"I thought you had all forgotten me," cried Sarah as the tears ran down her face.

"Here she goes again, she can cry at the drop of a hat, now Jenny and I can testify to that." Lizzie hugged Sarah as she spoke.

Sarah laughed all night and she was happy to see everyone. When everyone had gone and Alison had went with Jimmy to help with Jenny, Sarah was once again on her own, she had a lovely night and they had all been so kind but still the loneliness washed over her. Well this is my lot, she said to herself; count yourself lucky with a good family and friends. Loneliness is the life of an old maid.

Chapter 14

1950

*S*arah's results duly came and as it had been expected, she had excelled, she was delighted with herself and pleased that she could still study and learn. She had an interview with the Principal of the Evening School and he told her not to hesitate to apply for University. As far as he was concerned he could see no obstacles and with her excellent results there were many choices open to her. Still Sarah hesitated, she talked it over with Jimmy and he told her to go for it, he wanted her to move in with him so that she would have no money problems. Alison was due to Graduate soon and Sarah decided that she would wait till Alison was finished. An Edinburgh firm of Solicitors had interviewed Alison and she had been offered a two year training position if her results were as expected. Alison would move to Edinburgh and although Sarah knew she would miss her she was so proud of her. So Sarah decided to wait until Alison was settled and Jimmy had remarked that she was only putting of making a decision about herself and Sarah knew he was right.

The following months found her absorbed in her work at the Surgery as the larger Practice was growing and yet another Doctor was to join the Practice.

Lizzie and Sarah still enjoyed their Friday nights together and sometimes they would go to the Picture hall to see the latest film. Sarah's life was now good, the boys were all well and they were more or less settled. Andrew and Jimmy still had not married but she never commented on this because they would laugh and joke with her, and tell her they were waiting for her to get married first. So she avoided this conversation if she could, the only one she ever confided in about being lonely was Lizzie.

Sarah sat back in her seat; she was on her way to see Alison in Edinburgh. She was on holiday for two weeks and for once she had only herself to think about. As the train sped on she looked at her reflection in the window. I think I will get my haircut, she had the same style for years now but she did not need to worry anymore about being too young. No chance of that now she was approaching her fortieth birthday. She decided that she would have it cut and styled in Edinburgh. The girls in the office were always having it styled never cut, and she would do the same. I could buy a few new clothes, my skirt and jacket are a bit drab, and I will smarten myself up. She kept herself neat and tidy with the hair still drawn back. The boys were always telling her to be good to herself now that Alison was self-supporting.

She was so proud of her when she graduated. The boys had been there as well and for the first time in a while they were all together. Laughing and joking about how folk would have to watch out for them now with a lawyer in the family. She had been so proud that day. There they all were, Jimmy, a manager with the shipbuilding, Andrew, an architect working in London and Archie a painter and decorator, who was self-employed and was always busy. Yes she had been lucky, not one of them had been in trouble.

The train was nearing Edinburgh and she was really feeling excited. This was her first real holiday. Alison had paid her ticket and the boys had all given her money to treat the both of them. In two months' time she was going to London to see Andrew for another holiday. She was to have another two weeks holiday from the office because of all the extra hours that she had put in at the Surgery.

Lately she had been feeling lonely again, she remembered the times she would have been glad of a bit peace and quiet but now it was different. She could have married Davie; he had asked her a few times before the argument. We are so alike, we could be happy, he had said. She was tempted but she felt that she wanted something more; she did not know what though. They had long since made up and were friends again. They had settled the argument before his mother had died and she was glad of that. He would be glad now that she had never taken him up on his offer, he had Lizzie now and they were both so happy, she was glad for Lizzie and seeing them so happy sometimes made her feel lonely. They were both so proud of David, their son. All these thoughts were racing through her. The train was now approaching Edinburgh and she felt excited.

Alison was at Waverly Station waiting for her because it was Friday, and she finished early on a Friday.

They hugged each other, they were so happy to be together. Anyone passing would assume that they were mother and daughter, and they were so alike.

"Let me look at you, you are so smart."

Alison twirled round in front of her, "will I do?"

"Yes you will, and you will need to teach me how to dress better and while I am here I have decided to get my hair cut."

"I don't believe it; I'll only believe that when I see it. My boss gave me a lift to the station and he is going to take us back to the flat, that's him over there."

They walked over to where the car was parked. A very tall man was leaning against the car with his back to them, and he turned as Alison spoke. Sarah noticed that he was an extremely good-looking man; he had a presence about him. Sarah reckoned he must be well over six feet tall, dark brown hair and nice brown eyes, he oozed confidence and there was a look of amusement in his eyes. She took in every detail of him and she realised that he was doing the same of her.

"Mr. Ross here we are, this is my Aunt, Miss Shaw, Sarah this is Mr. Ross."

"How do you do Miss Shaw pleased to meet you."

As he lifted her case put it in the car boot he looked directly at her for the moment, their eyes met, then Sarah dropped her eyes. He smiled to himself; he was used to women admiring him.

These two women were very like each other; it was the first thing he noticed. According to office gossip they were mother and daughter, there was no doubt about this. The only difference being that the younger was modern and the older more staid, she wore old fashioned clothes, obviously no make-up and the hair was pulled back straight from her face, a bit dull really, but what beautiful eyes.

Once in the car, he adjusted his driving mirror, again their eyes met, he raised his one eyebrow, most people smiled when he raised the one eyebrow. She stared him out and then he dropped his eyes, then she smiled to herself. He looks a right pompous ass, she thought.

They were soon outside Alison's Flat, he got the case from the boot and came round as she was opening the car door.

"Allow me Miss Shaw," there was a hint of amusement in his voice.

"So kind of you, how kind of you." Again she thought, a bit over the top in smarm.

"Thank you for the lift Mr. Ross, enjoy your week-end."

"Thank you Alison and I hope you have a pleasant stay Miss Shaw." All the time his eyes were on her. She looked unblinking into his eyes and once again said,

"Thank you, how kind." She spoke so condescendingly.

He knew then that she was laughing at him and a hint of a challenge was born at that moment. He waited for space to move out into the flow of traffic, while he waited he watched them go up the few stairs. Sarah turned round and nodded.

"He is the most handsome man I have ever seen, so tall, so smart, is he married Alison.?

"No, he likes to play the field. "

They were now at the Flat door and as they went in Sarah exclaimed,

"Alison it is so huge."

"Take a look round, it has very old fashioned furniture, but yes I have plenty of room. Listen I have a surprise for you. I have tickets to the theatre tonight. We are going to the opera. As we have never been before I thought we should give it a try. I have also booked us in for a meal before the theatre."

"You should not have gone to all that expense Alison."

"Don't worry Sarah; the boys gave me money to treat you."

"They gave me money to treat you as well. I have looked forward to this. You know it is my first holiday."

"Yes I know, here," she handed Sarah a cup of tea.

"Drink this and then we will get ready, what do you think of the flat."

"It is great; it is so large, look at the size of this room, when you think of how we all lived on top of each other in a room and kitchen."

"We were all happy Sarah, thanks to you and don't you ever forget that."

I only done what any of you would have done had they been the eldest."

"Yes but you made sure we were all educated. Remember the rows with Jimmy and Archie, when you made them go to night-school."

"Yes but it has paid off now."

"What have you brought with you to wear, it's a bit of a dressy up for tonight."

"I have that black skirt and I bought a pair of black patent court shoes, I like them but they make me even taller. I only have plain blouses."

"I have a blouse that is nice with frills at the neck and sleeves that will do."

They started to get ready and Sarah loosened her hair to brush it.

"Let me put your hair up and it will give you an idea if you would like it cut."

After she had washed, Alison put make-up on her; this was something that Sarah rarely used. Then she piled her hair up on the top of her head.

"You look lovely like that; while you are here I will show you how to use cosmetics."

They were both ready to go and had a good look at themselves in the mirror."

"We are like peas in a pod, it is strange isn't it. More like mother and daughter than aunt and niece. I know people sometimes said that you were my mother, did it ever bother you?"

"No it never, we knew and that was all that mattered."

She did not tell Alison that it hurt when some people would shout at her for not being married, people who did not know them. In the nineteen thirties it still carried the disgrace of having a baby out of marriage.

They went downstairs and into the street. They strolled along Princess Street; it was a lovely evening and soon arrived at the restaurant. Alison spoke to the headwaiter and they were shown to their table. Heads turned as they walked in, they were a striking pair.

Alison wore a pale blue dress which showed of her dark hair, the colour suited her well, Sarah was more elegant than pretty.

The waiter arrived with the menu and they chose their meal, Alison also ordered two glasses of red wine, they toasted each other the way they used to with lemonade and they both laughed.

As Sarah glanced round the room at the other diners, Mr. Ross was looking straight at her. He raised his glass to her, and she nodded.

"Don't look now but your boss is over there, he has just raised his glass to me."

"Do not encourage him in any way, he is a womaniser. You should hear some of the stories that go round the office about him."

"He is extremely good looking but he seems so pompous, full of himself, what do you think."

"He is very clever and very well known as a Barrister but I am told that he likes women. You forget about him."

Alison could not tell Sarah that she would not worry because Sarah was a plain woman and Mr. Ross did not go in for plain or dull.

Their meal had arrived and they enjoyed it immensely, Sarah had not realised that she was so hungry. They were having their coffee when Sarah asked,

"Who is the woman with him?"

"What does she look like?"

"A very pale blonde, very slim."

"Yes that is one of his friends. I believe her name is Pamela. The story goes that she is hoping to catch him someday."

"I don't blame her, he is handsome."

"Listen you to me; the office gossip is that he has a brunette for breakfast, a redhead for lunch and a blonde for the evening."

"How I wish I was a blonde."

"Do not give him the slightest encouragement, you will regret it. "

They had their heads together laughing when Alison said,

"We had better go and take our seats at the theatre."

"Alison, he is coming over here."

Gordon Ross strolled over to them, "Good evening ladies, enjoying your night out?"

All the time he looked at Sarah,

"Yes thank you, we had a lovely meal."

He walked them out of the restaurant, the blonde was waiting at the door for him and she draped herself onto his arm and was looking up into his face.

Alison came then after she settled the bill, "Please excuse us we are in rather a hurry."

He held the door open for them as Sarah passed him he said,

"Enjoy your evening Miss Shaw."

"Thank you I always do."

"He has his eye on you; thank goodness we are going to the theatre, he starting to make me nervous."

"He can make me nervous any time he likes." Sarah laughed.

"Sarah I have never heard you talk like this."

"Don't worry it's the wine it always made me tipsy and silly, but it is a nice feeling being flirted with. He is pompous, though, isn't he? "

"Do you think he is doing that?"

"Well I think so, that's the way Dr Young used to carry on before he got married. Men like that are so sure of themselves, it irritates me really, pompous fools. Mind you I would be mad if I was the blonde, leaving her to speak to someone else."

They walked smartly to the theatre and were soon in their seats, as the lights started to dim, a hand came on Sarah's shoulder, and she turned round.

"We meet yet again Miss Shaw."

His face was so close she could feel her cheeks burning.

She nudged Alison, grateful that the lights were now out.

At the end of the first act he leaned over.

"Do you enjoy Bizet, Miss Shaw?"

"Yes amongst others." She could feel her face again. "Excuse us, she pulled Alison out of her seat and they went out into the foyer.

"What did he say, Sarah." she repeated the brief conversation.

"He is after you, try and ignore him." Alison was confused because she was sure Sarah would have been to plain for him. According to the others at the office, he went after women and when he got them, dropped them.

"Don't be silly, Lizzie would call you a spoil sport."

They returned to their seats and this time Alison went in first so she was sitting in front of him. As the lights dimmed she heard his voice clearly,

"Rather hot tonight, don't you think?"

She knew then that he had seen her blushing.

At the end of the evening as they were leaving he leaned over and spoke to Alison.

"Thank you no; we are meeting friends for supper."

"Get out as quickly as you can," she whispered to Sarah.

He was at the foyer door as they were leaving.

"Good night ladies."

"Goodnight Mr. Ross, did you enjoy Carmen?"

"Yes, did you?"

"Not one of my favourites but yes."

Alison nudged Sarah," Sarah, get out of here quick, you don't know anything about opera."

"I know but I'm a quick learner."

They were laughing as they crossed to a taxi. He watched them, she interested him, wondering why the big transformation from plain, no not plain, dowdy to attractiveness, she was really quite attractive, interesting, he smiled smugly to himself, and she would be easy. He turned to his companion and dazzled her with a smile.

"What would you like to do now Pamela," he teased.

"You are awful Gordon," she simpered up into his face, trying hard to smile, for she had noted his interest in the two women. She had tried and tried to make their friendship into more than friendship but it had not happened. She was always there for him, when he went from one affair to the other he always came back to her and that fact kept her hoping. Love did not come into it with Pamela, she wanted a good life and a Barrister could provide that.

Alison and Sarah were soon back at the flat and they were still laughing.

"I do not know how I will face him on Monday. Do not come anywhere near that office, Sarah I'm serious, you would only get hurt. Let's go to bed."

The next morning as they were leaving to go shopping they met a delivery boy coming up the stairs with flowers.

Alison stopped and thought, oh no. "Are these flowers for Miss Shaw?"

"Yes Miss Sarah Shaw."

"Thank you, they are for me."

They turned and went back into the flat and Alison found two vases to put them in.

The card with the flowers read 'Please have dinner with me, Alison has my number'

"This is bad news, he is after you. This is what he does; now you have to thank him and he will get speaking to you again. What are you going to do?"

"No he is playing with me that's all. We are going out to enjoy our day and I will think about it later."

They went shopping and then went to the park with a sandwich and a fruit drink. It was another lovely day. They sat and talked most of the afternoon and then went for their dinner to an Italian restaurant. Sarah had never enjoyed herself so much, she had bought a pair of trousers, something she had never worn and a long cardigan. She bought Alison a dress and Alison bought her some cosmetics. They had a good day and wandered back to the Apartment.

Alison had taken her record player and records with her when she had come to Edinburgh. It was her pride and joy and she had collected records over the past few years. Sarah had bought a bottle of red wine, so they had a glass of wine and listened to music.

They were tired after their day out and decided to have an early night.

"Before I go to bed I think I will phone him and thank him for the flowers, what do you think?"

"I don't think you should, he will talk you into going out with him another night. You could write a note and I will give it to him on Monday."

"No, I'll phone him."

"I'm telling you he is a womaniser. You will get burnt. You like him that's what this is all about, isn't it?"

"I will phone him and thank him, and leave it at that. He is playing with me and he will not ask me again, well not tonight. That will not be his way of doing things if you are right. Come on let me have a laugh, give me his phone number."

"I'm off to bed; it is nearly eleven o'clock, a bit late. You will find his phone number under office numbers, I listed all their home numbers and on your own head be it, Sarah."

She handed Sarah her phone book. Once she found the number, she then dialed his number, and the receiver was lifted quickly.

"Good evening."

"Good evening, could I speak to Mr. Ross please; I hope I am not too late?"

"Good evening Sarah, you don't mind if I call you Sarah?" Not waiting for an answer he continued," no you are not late."

"I would like to thank you for the flowers, we have been out all day and this is the first chance I have had to thank you Mr. Ross. As I am away very early in the morning I did not want to leave it any later to thank you."

"Please call me Gordon."

He is trying to soften me up, Sarah thought.

"The flowers are lovely Gordon, you are so very kind."

"Well let me take you out to dinner and you can thank me then."

"I'm sorry I can't at the moment, Alison has the next few days arranged and I can't disappoint her. Have you had a nice day Gordon?"

She is playing with me, she wants a chase, and I won't disappoint her, he thought

"Yes very nice, but if you had come out to dinner it would have been nicer. Did you enjoy Carmen? What do like best about Bizet, Sarah?"

He knows I don't know a thing about opera,

"To tell you the truth I don't know the difference between Bizet and a brass band."

He laughed then a deep throaty laugh.

"I knew it, I knew it, and you were trying to put me in my place, weren't you?"

"Yes you were so smarmy, so pompous; I wasn't going to let you know I had never been before."

"I am not pompous."

"Well I will take your word for that, but."

"But nothing, you will come to know that I am not pompous."

"Oooo dear me, if that's not pompous I do not know what is."

"Come out to dinner with me and you will realise that I am just like you."

They were now laughing together.

"Did your girlfriend enjoy the opera?"

"She was not my girlfriend Sarah. Did you want to know that?"

"Not really, I just thought as she was draped around you she must have been your girlfriend."

Once again the deep laugh.

"Oh come now, if you were out with me, would you not drape yourself round me?"

"No way," she was laughing again.

"What would you do if you were out with me?"

"Well that's something I don't think we will ever know, goodnight Gordon." she replaced the receiver.

She rose to go through to the bedroom and Alison appeared at the door, she was laughing.

"You are now playing him at his own game."

The telephone rang; they looked at each other and started to laugh. Sarah lifted the receiver.

"Hello Gordon." She laughed.

"You don't think I can let you away with that now, can I?" He was laughing.

"Come out to dinner and let us get to know each other, we are on the same wavelength."

"Heaven forbid Gordon Ross but if you are right, I think it is better we avoid each other, don't you."

"How long are you here for Sarah?"

"Just a few more days, I have rather as lot of commitments that I must attend to."

"Liar," he threw back at her.

"You are insulting me now, and that is rather strong language don't you think when I always tell the truth."

"Well tell it now and let me know why you will not come out to dinner?"

"I walked into that didn't I?"

Again the deep laugh, "tell you what, let's leave it there and I will phone you later in the week, would that do."

"Maybe, and then maybe not, I had better go it is getting late, goodnight."

"Don't go please, tell me about yourself. "

"I am five foot ten inches tall, a brunette, and ages with yourself."

"Oh so you found out my age, interesting that."

"I am going to my bed, goodnight Gordon."

They were both laughing together, as she replaced the receiver.

The next day was Sunday and they stayed in the apartment. Sarah had gone out earlier for the newspapers and they spent most of the day reading.

"What will you do tomorrow Sarah?"

"Do not worry about me, I will walk in the park, maybe shop some more or go to the Castle. I have a list of things I want to do and see, the Art Galleries, the Museums or just walk round Edinburgh.

"I could have a full day; I am working with him tomorrow. How I am supposed to keep a straight face I do not know. I could try and meet you for lunch in the Park about one o'clock. Then again I might not get out for lunch."

"I will see you when you come home at night and we will go out for our meal again. I have enjoyed eating out."

"Do you want to eat out tonight?"

"No I feel lazy, I will make us something. Do you think he will say anything to you?"

"He will want to know what you are doing, he is sure to ask something about you."

"Will I come and meet you at five o'clock, tell you what. Why don't I pull my hair back tight, no make-up at all, my flat shoes and that drab suit that I am

going to throw out soon? I am quite sure that will cool him down. Mind you I
think he will have forgotten all about us now."

"You wouldn't dare come like that would you?"

"Why not, I have dressed like that for years. I have a very strong urge
to change everything about myself now. Can you imagine it; he asked me
what I would do, if I were out with him, when I spoke about the 'Pamela'
draping herself round him. Think on it, old suit, flat shoes, and my hair in
a bun. Can you see his face; he would be so embarrassed even talking to an
old maid."

Alison was laughing; I would love to see his face."

"Well there you go then; I'll maybe even buy an old maid's hat

They were giggling now and it was not because of the wine."

"Sarah do not let him hurt you please. I do not mean to be unkind Sarah but
he goes for model types, you know what I mean"

"Forget all about him, he will have forgotten about us, but I will come and
meet you tomorrow night."

Have I hurt you?"

"No we are only having a bit fun; I know I am not modern, stop worrying."

"I finish around five o'clock."

"I'll make sure I'm there at quarter to five and I will wait at reception and I
think he will walk straight past me."

"You are playing with him now."

"What a lovely thought."

"You are getting worse in your old age."

"Cheeky monkey, you know I do feel different, happier somehow, I must say
I like Edinburgh. It has a wonderful atmosphere.

They were sitting at their meal when the telephone rang; they looked at
each other,

"Could be one of the boys and then again maybe not."

Sarah lifted the receiver,

"Hello there Gordon

"How did you know it was me?"

"Extra sensory perception."

He started to laugh. "Yes I am quite sure that could be it, I think you may be a bit of a witch."

"There is no doubt about it, I even have a broomstick."

"That I would like to see."

"Well hang around the rooftops and I might drop in."

"Why don't you, and I could take you out to dinner?"

"All tied up tomorrow, sorry."

"That's something else I would like to see."

"I will have you know that I am a good girl and nobody ties me up."

He was laughing.

"Are you challenging me?"

"No stating a fact, I am sorry but I must go, we have friends in for a meal, goodbye."

She replaced the telephone receiver.

The tears of laughter were rolling down Alison's face.

"How am I supposed to look at him tomorrow?"

When Sarah wakened in the morning, Alison had left for work. She made herself some breakfast, tidied the house and went and tried on the trousers that she had bought. They fitted perfectly; they were a deep blue in colour and the long cardigan matched. She was pleased with look of them but had she the nerve to wear trousers. She chose her pink blouse to wear under the cardigan and decided to walk to Princess Street bookshop that Alison had told her was nearby. She was looking for something else to read.

She left the apartment and it was a bright day with a slight wind. She strolled along slowly as she had on the court shoes and she was not used to them. Every now and again she would look in a shop window, to see her reflection, she was really not sure about the trousers, however they were very comfortable.

She went into the bookshop and started to browse, she was looking for something with some history of Edinburgh when she heard a conversation, the woman was speaking French and the assistant was struggling with the language. Sarah stepped forward and asked the assistant.

"Would you like some help?"

"Do you speak French, Could you help me please?"

The family from France was delighted and Sarah soon had it sorted out what was required. They went up to the cash desk to pay for their books, and again Sarah interpreted for them. As they were leaving they thanked her profusely. Sarah wished them a happy holiday and a good journey home. She had walked to the door with them and then turned to go back into the shop to select her own book when she saw him leaning against the wall. He had been watching her.

He had heard everything, how come she was so fluent in French. She was stunning in her smart trousers and jacket. Her hair was just pulled loosely back in a clasp, not so severe or old fashioned as when he had first met her. There was no way she looked dull today.

"Good morning Mr. Ross."

She carried on to where she had been browsing amongst the bookshelves. She was smiling to herself and was about to select a book when he joined her.

"Well you surely cannot refuse to have a morning coffee with me; there is a coffee shop two doors over."

"I have come in to buy a book and anyway, should you not be at your office? Skiving, that's what you are doing."

"No, I came in here for a newspaper it is my lunch break, honest. Come on, have a coffee."

She could not look at him as she was smiling and turned her head for the moment.

"I thought you were always such a busy person."

"Oh been making enquiries, have we?"

"Listen you," she turned to face him and started to laugh.

"That's better, come on, I can skive for half an hour."

She put her book back on the shelf and he tucked her arm through his and out they went.

He selected a table near the window and he held out her chair for her, and then sat down beside her. He ordered two coffees, the waitress obviously knew him,

"Right away Mr. Ross."

"I know I can depend on you."

"Certainly Mr. Ross, anytime."

Sarah shook her head, "Are you always this nice, or is it just to get your own way."

"Let's not waste time I only have half an hour. Please will you have dinner with me?"

"Why are you so anxious to take me to dinner?"

"I think we have a lot in common."

"That's silly, you do not know me and anyway I go home in two week's time."

"Ah, so we could have two weeks together, nice."

They were laughing again.

"Tell me about yourself, I know now that you are well educated but I don't know what you do."

"Guess." The waitress brought their coffee.

"Anything else Mr. Ross?"

"No thank you gorgeous."

"You're awful." She shook her head but she went away smiling.

"Were you born with a glib tongue or did it take a lot of studying."

"Do I detect a note of sarcasm there?"

"No, truth."

"Ah yes, you are a great one for the truth, so tell me truthfully, why won't you go out with me."

"I walked into that again."

She was stirring the coffee and looking into the cup.

"There are no tea leaves there to tell you how to get out of this, just say we can have dinner together, whenever it suits you."

She looked up at him and they looked at each other for a moment and then he took her hand. He did not know it but he had won. He turned her hand and looked at her palm.

"I see before you a wonderful time, a tall and of course handsome, intelligent, mature and understanding man coming into your life, in fact he could be in it right now. What do you say? Dinner?"

"Well maybe tall, intelligent, handsome is in the eye of the beholder, pompous and sure of yourself, certainly not mature. You can phone me towards the end of the week."

He checked his watch for the time.

"Promise me you will think about it."

"Are you worried about the time?"

"Yes I have a meeting, I am sorry but I must fly."

"Are you walking?"

"Yes."

"I will walk along with you then."

He was like one of the boys when they were small, he smiled and the smile lit up his eyes and the smile spread over his face.

They walked along Princess Street smartly and she left him at the far end. As he turned to go he waved, then walked away. She heard him call her name and she turned.

He hurried back to her, pulled her towards him and there right in the middle of Princess Street, kissed her softly on the cheek.

"I will phone you tonight."

She stood and looked after him with a smile on her face; he turned and waved, smiling. He hurried back to his office and it was only when he went in he realised that he was still smiling.

Sarah floated along Princess Street; well anyway, she never remembered walking.

Chapter 15

H e was still smiling as he entered the office, "They are all waiting for you Mr. Ross," his receptionist said.

He went into the office and his partners were there, three of them. There was still one more to join them.

"You looked pleased with yourself."

"Yes I am."

"Who is your latest conquest?"

"She is really wonderful but she will not come out with me. I am working on it though

"Will you win?"

"Of course I will win, do I not always. This should have been easy, but, "

"Oh yes, oh yes, showing a little resistance, is she? What happened to your charismatic charm, eh?" he was asked.

"Give me a few more hours, a few more hours is all I need."

"What happened to Pouting Pamela?"

"Now, you know me I do not tell on my women."

A burst of laughter followed this.

"Pamela is in the past and there she shall remain. I am a changed man this could be serious."

Another burst of laughter, "Laugh all you like, but I am a changed man."

"If she will not go out with you how can it be serious, tell you what. If you get her out with you by the weekend I'll put a fiver on it."

"No, this one is different."

"Coward, she will not go out with you, that's why you are backing down. Right a fiver, if you get her to go out and a tenner if you get her into bed."

The other two put their money on the table.

"You cover it if you lose."

"No problem, I hate taking your money."

Another burst of laughter.

The door opened and the senior partner came in, seeing the money on the table, he sat down and said,

"Gentlemen grow up, what poor girl is suffering now. It is not time you lot learned to be mature. Any of your nonsense rubs off on the firm I will not be pleased and from now on Office staff is out of bounds to all four of you. I understand that a girl ran out of this office in tears last week. This has not to happen again, do I make myself clear. You four were chosen for this firm to carry on a serious, reliable and important legal practice. As for you Gordon you are getting a bit past it for this nonsense. Now Gordon, take over the meeting and let's have your thoughts on tomorrow's case."

"Right Sir, can I just clear up the matter of the girl running out of the office in tears, it was nothing to do with any of us."

"No you cannot, no one should have to leave their work in tears and I do not care what the problem was. It should have been solved in this office behind closed doors, sympathetically and with consideration for our staff. You four are too frivolous for my liking and it makes me question my judgment, have I made myself clear, let's get on; I have a busy day ahead of me.

The rest of the meeting was held in a more serious atmosphere. Once the meeting was over Mr. Grant asked to speak to Gordon privately in his office. Gordon followed him through apprehensively.

Mr. Grant sat down at his desk and motioned for Gordon to sit down in the chair facing his desk. He stared at Gordon for a moment before speaking.

"I have decided to retire, well that was my original plan but if the behaviour of our prospective partners, and I include you in this, does not change, I will have to make drastic changes. I will not sit back and watch what I, and others before me, built into a fine professional legal practice become the laughing stock of the city." He paused and Gordon cut in.

"If you will let me explain."

"No I will not, not until you listen to me. I thought we had an agreement that you wanted to be senior partner, that you would guide the others. There are two silent partners and I wanted to join them. If not in full retirement I at least wanted partial retirement. It very much looks like I have made a mistake."

Mr. Grant sat back in his chair and watched Gordon squirm and Gordon was not pleased. He looked round the office that was nearly in his grasp, the prime office in the suite of offices. The oak paneling on the walls, the bookcases, the fine desk and chairs and also the excellent financial state he would be in when he became senior partner, he was speechless as he could see it slipping away. He was always so self-assured but not here, sitting in front of the man he admired so much in every way. His handling of cases, his excellent court procedures, Gordon had aspired to being as good as, if not better than his mentor in every way. A silence hung between them, and then Gordon tried again.

"If you would let me explain," he was not interrupted this time. "The girl in tears was a minor matter about her work procedure and the fact that she was not very well. When questioned about a work matter she broke down and in her embarrassment she ran out of the office. Nothing at all to do with any us, nothing at all. As to the money on the desk it was a joke at my expense, nothing at all to do with any other member of staff. If I may say so I take it hard sitting here being treated like a junior. Have I not proved myself and if not, I feel that I do not want to prove myself, not after the years I have spent here. I will not grovel for the position that I want and if I have not to become the senior partner as we previously discussed, and may I remind you, you agreed to my taking your position here. Maybe it is time for me to move on." He pushed the chair back, stood up and straightened his shoulders, and turned towards the door. He was furious that anyone should question him like this.

"Sit back down Gordon and do not be so pompous. I need to be assured that you can direct the others and run these offices. You damn well know the position is yours and the sooner we put our plans into action the better, but watch John Morgan, I am sure I made a mistake there."

Gordon smiled at the remark about him being pompous.

"This is not a laughing matter Gordon."

"No I know that, I am smiling at your pompous remark. Someone else said that to me recently. Now I am not pompous really, everyone knows that, don't they?"

They both laughed, "Someone important, Gordon?"

"Yes and I think she may become very important to me."

"Some woman getting the better of you at last? You know it is high time you married and settled down."

"Well I never really thought about it much, but recently, anyway why is that all you married men want all us single men married."

They laughed and joked with one another and when Gordon left office he was glad that they appeared to be back on friendly footing. Nevertheless he was annoyed at being questioned and this was a new experience for him. Forty years of age and being treated like a junior.

Gordon Ross had come into life in a privileged position, a mother and father who adored him and he had never disappointed them. His father had been an Architect until his retirement and had provided a good home and education for his only child. His mother had encouraged him in his education and he had exceeded all expectations. He was self-assured in every way and was not used to being questioned and resented it very much

He wanted the senior position, oh how he wanted the position. That was what he had worked hard at for years; all the nights that he took work home with him. The weekends that he worked at home studying past court cases, researching on his own. He knew that he had para legals to do the work for him but in researching, he had always found something that interested him. His ambition was not only to be senior partner; he wanted to be invited someday onto the Queen's Council. Yes he was ambitious, very ambitious, but this week the only homework he could think about was how to get Sarah to go out with him.

Sarah was waiting for Alison at reception at five o'clock. When Alison joined her she laughed,

"What happened to the great plan? You know the drab suit, the flat shoes, maybe a hat."

"You will never believe what happened." She went over the events of the morning and how she was dressed. "There was no point in the drab suit now. I have agreed to go to dinner with him."

"Sarah don't go, please you will get hurt and I am sorry to say this, but you have no experience of men."

"I like him and how could I have any experience?"

"I know, I know."

They were out in the street facing each other, when Gordon came out of the office door with his secretary.

"Now do you see what I mean?"

"Evening ladies." He put his hand on Sarah's shoulder, "I will phone later."

He had squeezed her shoulder. She was still facing Alison,

"Please, I want to. Let's go and have our dinner and I'll tell you what I have been up to."

They made their way to another restaurant that Alison used and made their way to a table. Once they had ordered Sarah said,

"Alison, he makes me laugh. He is full of himself I know, and maybe I will get hurt. What chance of experience do I have at my age? It is only dinner; you make it sound as if he was going to seduce me."

"He will try, that's what worries me."

"Well think of the shock, a virgin. He will not expect that. Please credit me with some sense. This could be my first lesson in experience and maybe my only one. You surely don't think that I am going to jump into bed with him."

"I worry about you. Davie wanted to marry you and you were good friends. You were so right for each other Sarah."

"Do you want to marry someone you don't love? Is that what you want for me?

I used to tell you to try things, don't be afraid of experience even if I was worried that it might go wrong for you. We laughed about this yesterday, what's so different now."

"You like him, that's what is different and the office gossip is terrible about him."

"Anything specific?."

Alison shrugged her shoulders," Well no, just that he has a different girl-friend all the time. I don't suppose anyone really knows."

"There you are then, stop worrying, please. I am enjoying myself for the first time. I am a big girl, if I get hurt and cry as I usually do, you can stand by with the tissues, promise."

Alison gave in," Fine, let's eat, here's our dinner."

They had a nice meal and afterwards they walked back through the Park towards the Apartment. As they went in the door the telephone was ringing.

"Don't answer it Alison, let it ring unless you are expecting a call."

"I don't understand the game you are playing."

"I am just having fun. Were you busy today?"

"Yes they have a case going to Court and that gives a lot of work that must be exact. There is a lot of checking to be done by the junior lawyers. I am working with a lad that has just joined the Firm like me, and we are doing the checking. They will go over it but Gordon Ross is a perfectionist when it comes to work and everything must be perfect. I still have a lot to learn and I could learn a lot from him. They say that he will be next senior partner when Mr. Grant retires."

"You are enjoying working with this firm."

"Yes it's great and I like Edinburgh. I love all the legal work and it breaks down into many aspects of the law. There is private law, family law, intestate succession, inheritance of title, executors, trusts, contracts and the one I would like to get my teeth into is primogeniture, that means preference of males, in the legal term"

Her face was aglow with her enjoyment of the work. Sarah smiled to see her so happy.

"I would just like to sort that one out," she laughed. "The lad that I am working with has asked me to go to the rugby with him at Murrayfield on Saturday. What do you think?"

"Go with him, I will be fine on my own, Do not put anything off for me, anyway if I play my cards right, I could be out with Gordon. I am so happy to see you so happy."

"I think you are as bad as him, have you been at the wine."

They were both laughing now and more at ease with each other. The telephone rang then; Alison looked upwards and made a face. Sarah lifted the receiver.

"Good evening."

"How are you Sarah?"

"Fine thank you, did you have a good day."

"Busy, busy after all that skiving. I am going to be busy over the next few days. Now about our dinner date."

"I did not know we had a date."

"I had hoped that we had settled that, had we not?"

"Well I have not been asked yet."

"Sarah, will you please have dinner with me on Friday evening?"

"Yes thank you I will Gordon"

"You are driving me crazy. I am a nervous wreck since I met you."

"You have not really met me yet, beware you might need counseling."

He laughed at that, they spent the next half-hour on the telephone joking with each other. One was trying to score a point over the other.

"I will call for you on Friday evening around seven o'clock, is there anything that you would like to do?"

"No I will leave myself in your capable hands."

"Is that a promise?"

"You know what I mean."

"Yes but do you know what I mean."

"Friday at seven, goodnight." she replaced the receiver

She was laughing and Alison was shaking her head.

"You are just as bad as he is."

Sarah spent most days walking and finding out about Edinburgh. She had bought a book on Edinburgh and chose somewhere different each day. She would meet Alison at night when she finished her work and they would eat out. They were both enjoying themselves. Sarah had bought a very smart cream linen dress and a pair of cream leather shoes. Gordon Ross phoned each evening and they spent about half an hour fencing words with each other. Sarah had never felt so good. This is what it is like to be free, she thought. Alison still worried but she could see Sarah was happy.

Friday evening arrived and Sarah wore the new dress and shoes. Alison had shown her how to put her hair up and she used a dress comb to secure it. For the first time she applied the cosmetics herself.

"You will knock him dead tonight, that dress is lovely on you and shows off your nice figure."

Alison had given her the use of a small cream clutch bag. At seven o'clock the doorbell rang. Alison answered the door.

"Hello there Alison I have come to collect Sarah."

"Come in Mr. Ross, she emphasised the 'Mr. Ross'

He could feel the tension between himself and Alison. Sarah came out of the bedroom and she was stunning. The week walking in Edinburgh had given her a slight tan, which the cream dress complimented.

"See you later Alison."

"Right you take care, have a nice evening." She could not look at Gordon Ross.

They went downstairs and helped her into the car. He got into the driver's seat. Once in the car he said,

"You look lovely this evening."

"Thank you," she could feel herself blushing and she was furious with herself. Nearly forty years of age and she felt like a teenager.

He drove out of Edinburgh and into the country; he pointed out different places and told her about them. They arrived at a lovely village and stopped at a small Inn

"I have booked a table here, the food is good, and I think you will enjoy it."

As they got out of the car, they were facing each other over the top of the car, and neither of them spoke. Sarah had never felt this emotion before.

"Do you want to eat just now or will we leave it till later."

"What about the booked table?"

"I will ask for a later booking, say in an hour or so." She nodded.

"I will be back in a moment." He left and was back very soon.

He opened the car door, helped her in then he went into the car. Neither spoke, she could not eat at the moment, nor did she know what to say. They drove off and they went out of the village. He parked the car at a small Park.

"Would you like to walk?"

"If you like, are you not hungry?

"You know at this moment in time neither of us is hungry. That is not why we are here, you feel the same as me, am I right?"

"I don't know and you are confusing me. All of a sudden you are so silent."

"Sarah look at me," as she looked at him, she was consumed by a passion she had never known. All sorts of feelings were rushing through her.

"Let's walk for a while."

They got out of the car and walked across the grass in the Park. There were picnic tables and benches laid out and a path that went round behind the park. As they got to the path he took her hand and that was all it took. She was in his arms and they were kissing passionately, she knew that this was what she wanted. They were breathless and when he let her go they started to laugh.

"I knew you felt the same about me, was I right?"

"Yes but I am very unsure of you and I so wanted to go out with you."

"Why so unsure?"

"I don't want to be one of your many girlfriends, I should not even say that and I have no right to say that, but I will not be."

He stopped her there by kissing her again, and again she was returning his kisses. The passion she felt overwhelmed her and frightened her. She pushed him away.

"What's wrong?"

"Nothing, maybe I am a bit nervous. You do not know me really and I really do not know you."

"Well tell me about yourself?"

"No, I am not the person you think I am and I do not want to talk about my past.

You have to understand I am not the educated person you think I am and I think that could matter to you."

"No, that's not true and I do not believe that you are not educated. I heard you having a conversation in French with people, when we were in the book shop."

Sarah looked at him, very quietly spoke, "Self-taught, I was denied an education, even when I won a bursary. I was taken out of school at thirteen. There I go talking about myself, please leave it. I also have no experience of men, now you know."

She walked away from him further along the path. He could not understand her. She obviously had a thing about education but this no experience of men, when she had a daughter. He did not care who Alison's father was, whoever he was obviously was way back in their past and he was happy to leave it there. He wanted to be with her, which was what mattered now.

He followed her but she was out of sight, where had she gone? Surely she had not left?

She was the most frustrating woman he had ever known.

Suddenly a voice in his ear said, "Come here often, with all your conquests?"

He turned round and caught her.

"Look I am only interested in you; I am not going to question you about your past. I don't care about what has gone before and I do not have a string of girlfriends, well not now that you have put your foot down."

They were laughing again and hugging each other.

"Where did you go anyway?"

"I doubled back through those trees over there."

"Were you going away?"

"No way, you promised me my dinner."

He laughed at that, "I am hungry now myself, let's go and eat and we will take up where we left off later."

"Promise?" Again they were laughing.

It was as he said the food was lovely and she was so hungry by then. After they had finished the meal, they had coffee.

"Would you like a drink, I cannot because I am driving, I know one won't harm me but I made this rule for myself because of my work."

"No thank you, I get silly with drink and giggle a lot. You see that is another thing I have no experience of."

They sat the rest of the evening and talked about everything, music, food, and life in general, not about her or him. He had his arm around her and she was leaning against him. She did not want to go.

"We should be on our way, it is getting late."

"Yes we should but I do not want to."

"Why?"

"Because I am," she searched for the right word, "comfortable."

"Is that the best you can do, comfortable?" he was so close looking into her eyes.

"You are fishing for compliments, comfortable will have to do."

"Well let's take up where we left off and see if I can do better than comfortable."

They looked at each other and both stood up together and laughed.

"I told you we are two of a kind."

They went into the car and he drove back to the park, she did not ask why they were there, she knew why they were there. They started kissing; they could not get enough of each other. His tongue entered her mouth and she was responding then his hand came round to her breast and she pulled away. They sat for a minute; there was silence between them.

"Look I am sorry. I don't know what to say but I am sorry."

"Do not worry; I am rushing you too much. It is just that you do feel the same, don't you?"

"Yes very much so," Sarah spoke very quietly.

He touched her cheek gently and said. "We shall leave it there."

The drove back to Edinburgh but it was not the same between them.

He could not understand her, he wanted her and she wanted him, what was the problem?

They were both adults, not teenagers, both experienced. He decided that he would play it her way

When they arrived back at the apartment, she turned to him,

"Thank you for the lovely evening and I am sorry."

She opened the door to go out of the car.

"Here just a minute, when will I see you again."

"Do you want to?"

"You know damn well that I do. Stop playing games, I thought we had sorted this out."

"Yes but I thought because of."

"Don't be silly," he was angry now. "Just what kind of person do you think I am? I will go along with whatever you want, this is ridiculous."

She got out of the car and went up the few stairs; he was at the door as soon as she was. The tears were spilling down her cheeks; he put his arms round her and held her.

"What am I going to do with you? Don't blame me for wanting you; it is not a problem that you don't want me."

"It is not that I don't want you."

"What is it then?"

"I am afraid; I think that is what is wrong with me."

"No need to be afraid of anything, certainly not of me."

"After all your other girlfriends I must be a bit of a shock."

"I am a nervous wreck with you, and where did you get the idea that I had such a lot of girlfriends. Let's change the subject, how would you like to go away for the weekend. My parents have a cottage at Northsands near North Berwick. We could go down tomorrow morning and come back on Sunday."

She looked at him, "a cottage by the sea, that sounds lovely, I don't know though."

"It has two bedrooms and I will put a lock on the door if you like."

"I feel bad enough, don't make me feel worse."

She was smiling again, and he was still holding her.

"Tomorrow then around eleven o'clock."

"Yes."

He ran down the stairs and into the car, he waved as he left, she was still standing at the door. The disappointment of there not being a goodnight kiss was awful.

Sarah let herself into the flat as quietly as she could, in case Alison was sleeping. She was curled up on the settee waiting for her.

"I was just about to go to bed. Did you have a good time?"

"Yes, the best. We went to a small inn, which seemed to more of a restaurant than anything else. I am sorry I am so late but we talked all night.

Alison he has asked me to go away for the week end, would you mind?"

"No not at all." All the time she was shaking her head. "I am going to the Rugby with Ian, and he has asked me out for a meal. They have been told, that is the junior male lawyers that there has to be no socialising with female members of staff. Ironic isn't"

"What will you do?"

"If any questions are asked, we will say we met there. They really can't do that, but, Mr. Grant, the senior partner has warned the other senior partners that it has to stop.

Apparently they were told to grow up and they have passed it on to the juniors."

"Alison are you angry at me going away for the weekend?"

"No, I really want you to have a good time, it is just him. Then if it had not been for me you would not have met him. I don't want to have any bad feeling between us. We never had it before and you are angry with me because I am worried about you."

"Anything that happens to me now, is my fault. Nobody else's and I do like him."

"Just like."

"How do I know? I have to find out for myself."

"I suppose maybe he could be settling down. I don't dislike him, I met so many at University that think it is great to have girls and I mean have them."

"Did it happen to you?"

"Well some tried it, but there was nobody that I really bothered about, we were more like pals, the boys I knew. There was one though that would not leave me alone. He took to waiting for me at the end of the day. This day, there he was, as we went down the stairs together he asked me to go for a coffee, I told him I had an appointment. We were at a lecture room door, as I thought, I said, I have an appointment in here. As I opened the door and went in, I was in the dark. The light went on after a moment, and I was standing in a broom cupboard. You have no idea the ribbing I took over that. He must have known it was a cupboard and it must have been him that put the light on.

The switch was outside the door and he must have told everybody."

They were laughing and more at ease with each other now.

"When are you going tomorrow?"

"Around eleven o'clock and I will be back on Sunday. Be happy for me Alison," pleaded Sarah

"I am, I want you to be happy. You looked after us all and we feel that we should now look after you."

"You lot are making me older than I am. I had thought that when I went home I would apply to College or University for next year."

"What would you study? Oh I know, French and Latin."

"Yes I would like to do that. How do you think I would be received being older?"

"They take mature students all the time. It would be a good idea. What will they say at the Surgery?"

"It is just a thought at the moment; we had better get to bed.

At eleven o'clock the next morning the doorbell rang, he was on time and Sarah was ready.

This time Alison was not so cool and told them both to have a lovely weekend.

They were soon in the car and on their way. The roads were busy in and out of Edinburgh and it was well after two o'clock when they reached Northsands. It was a bright and breezy day, with the wind whipping up the waves. When they arrived at the cottage Sarah was delighted to find it was right on the sea front.

"This is lovely, I love the sea."

"Do not expect too much of the cottage, it is pretty basic."

They went inside to a narrow hall. Two doors to the left and two to the right and one facing the front door, Sarah had a look through the cottage.

She was delighted, two bedrooms, a living room with kitchen off, a walk in cupboard and a bathroom. The curtains at all the windows were chintz. A small three-piece suite and a small dining room table with four dining chairs completed the living room. There were some lovely table lamps on small tables.

"It is lovely Gordon."

"It is pretty basic really; my mother will not do housework when she is here, so she keeps it simple.

"You do not know what basic means, this is sheer luxury to me you know." She stopped there and looked at him.

"Said too much about yourself, we can't have that." There was sarcasm in his voice

Sarah went outside and looked at the sea; she did not know how to handle him like this. Could it be that he was now sorry he had brought her.

Sarah was wearing the new trousers and long cardigan and she pulled the cardigan round herself tight. She crossed the road to the beach and started to walk, she did not know what else to do. He watched her from the window and wondered why he had spoken to her the way he did. Was she now sorry she had come?

Gordon went after her and caught up with her, put his arm across her waist and they walked on together. She eventually put her arm across his waist and they carried on in silence.

They had walked a good half-hour on the shore, climbing rocks to get to the next sandy beach, when it started to rain. They turned to walk back it was now raining heavily. They were getting soaked and they did not care. She took off her shoes and walked by the edge of the water.

"You are crazy,"

She kicked some water at him.

"Come on in for a paddle, I dare you."

He took off his shoes and socks, tied his laces together and hung his shoes round his neck. "You are in for it when I catch you."

They splashed water on each other and dodged back and forwards. They were wet right through by the time they reached the cottage.

He lit the fire and she changed into a robe that hung behind the bathroom door. She put her wet clothes on clothes dryer in the kitchen." Will I make a sandwich for us and some coffee?"

"Yes please I am changing, won't be a minute.

When she brought out the sandwiches and coffee he had the fire going well.

"Would you like to go to North Berwick for dinner tonight, it is not far away."

"Why don't I make you a meal, you have not experienced my cooking."

"If the sandwiches are anything to go by, yes we will stay in."

"That's what I am after."

"Good I would like to stay in with you. "He raised his eyebrow the way he had that first time they met.

She was sitting on the floor by the fire combing her hair out to dry it. She looked at him and laughed. The fire had warmed her cheeks, she was huddled in his old robe and she was beautiful. He stared at her.

"What's wrong?"

"Nothing, drink your coffee and get warm. If I take you back with a cold Alison will go for me and she is not very friendly towards me, is she?"

"No."

"Why."

"Alison thinks that I will get hurt."

"So this is where the story of all my girlfriends came from."

"No, it is a story that she has been told, after all she has not been there long."

"Sarah what do you think?"

"I am here because this is where I want to be."

He moved the settee over to the fire and sat on the floor with his back to the settee. She joined him there and they sat and toasted their bare feet. He touched her feet with his feet and she shifted over. He moved to beside her and he put his arm around her and they sat in silence. The rain was battering down outside and you could hear the waves lashing the shore.

"It is lovely here isn't it? I am so glad we came."

She was easily pleased, he thought. He had never brought anyone here before; anyone he knew would have been bored stiff here. He had never been very fond of the cottage before, but yes it was lovely.

"I'll put some clothes on now I'm dry."

"Yes please do, there is only so much I can stand."

She shook her head at him and her hair was tumbling down round her shoulders.

"I am getting this lot cut off next week."

"Don't you dare cut your hair, it is lovely."

"No, it is time I smartened myself up a bit."

"I will take it as a personal insult if you cut your hair."

Sarah laughed at him and went to dress herself. Once dressed she decided it was time to cook something for their dinner.

"What have you got to eat?"

"You'll find everything in the fridge and there is a small freezer in the top compartment. I did not bring any food I thought we would be eating out. Mother usually leaves something for the next time they are here."

Sarah went looking and found eggs, steak and crusty bread. She set to and made a fluffy omelette while the steak was grilling. She went through to ask how he liked his steak; he was fast asleep at the fire. As she sat and watched him she thought he does not look around forty, there was a boyish look to him. She realised then that she loved this man, this stranger for that was what he was. She had only known him a week now and yet she felt as if she had known him a long time. She set the table for their meal and when everything was ready, she gently shook him.

"I'm sorry I did not mean to sleep."

Sarah bent over and kissed him, a long lingering kiss. "Dinner is ready."

When they had eaten he complimented her on her cooking.

"Do you cook much?"

"Yes, a little." there was no point in telling him that she had cooked for years.

They washed up and moved back to the fire with their coffee. He put a little brandy in each coffee and the toasted each other with the coffee cups.

They talked well into the night. She told him that she ran the clerical side of a Doctor's Surgery. How she had started there years ago, she felt she was built in with the bricks.

How she wanted to go to College or University. How she had studied at night school.

He told her that he was a full partner in the law firm, all about his University days.

It was late when they went to bed. They walked to the bedroom door together and he opened both doors. Any room you like is yours. The beds are all fresh, mother was down last week and she always changes them before they leave.

She went into the first room and turned to say goodnight, he kissed her gently,

"Sleep well."

Sarah closed the door over and changed into her nightdress. She wanted to be with him, she reasoned with herself and lost, Gordon's bedroom door was opened slightly; he was standing looking out of the window. It was so dark outside she wondered what he was looking at.

He was staring out into the night not looking at anything; he did not know how to handle Sarah. He thought that if he made a move on her she would fly out of the door. She was a like a young deer, large eyes and terrified of anything that moved. One wrong move and she was off. She was acting a bit silly really, two grown adults and she was behaving like she was a teenager. He should never have brought her to the cottage, he was used to his woman friends being willing for him to set the pace and nobody had ever spurned him before. Trouble was he liked her in a different way, and he wanted to get to know her really well. Another thing was that she really had turned him on, and he could not even have a cold shower. The bathroom at the cottage did not have a shower; if he ever brought Sarah back here he had better get a shower fitted in that bathroom. He thought of the women he had known, not very many and had slept with only two. He knew he had a reputation for liking women and it had pleased his vanity to let the image continue. He turned from the window and there she stood. He walked towards her and put his hand out; in one quick stride she was in his arms.

232

"Gordon, I have never been with anyone before."

"I don't care who you have been with before but I want you now."

They made love and when he entered her she cried out in pain, and then let passion take over. Sarah went on a roller coaster that seemed to be, one moment on an edge of pain and the next moment on pleasure.

That was when he realised that she was still a virgin. He had taken her quickly and in haste, had given no consideration to the fact that she was a virgin. He never felt as bad before as he felt then.

"I am sorry I had no idea that you had never."

"I am fine, I did tell you."

"Yes I know, I thought Alison was your daughter."

"No, Alison is my sister's child; I brought her up after I brought up my brothers and sister."

She told him all about herself then, the beatings, the poverty, taking her brothers and sister out of the Poor House, what happened to Mary and how she was left with Alison.

He sat on the edge of the bed with his head in his hands,

"My God Sarah, I feel as if I have raped you, I feel terrible, are you alright?"

She then took him to bed and held him. She then made love to him and the second time was wonderful. She knew now what Lizzie had meant.

"Where did you learn to make love like that? He asked her gently.

"I told you I was an avid reader," she replied softly.

They laughed together arms round each other, and fell asleep.

When she wakened in the morning he was not beside her and she went to find him. He was making the fire up again and turned round looking at her.

"Are you fine? Get back to bed till I bring you in a coffee. It is not cold but the air seems damp. Are you sure you are fine?"

"Stop worrying I am wonderful."

"Yes I know that but are you sure you are feeling well."

"Oh I feel a bit feint, could you help me to bed." She grabbed the back of the chair for support.

He went to her quickly and helped her back to bed; she pulled him back in beside her,

"Got you and I am cold, so warm me up."

"You are absolutely crazy, behave yourself."

"No I will not I need some mouth to mouth resuscitation."

"You are impossible," but he did oblige and she never got that coffee.

They lay in bed for a while and then had a late breakfast. It was still raining gently.

"Let's walk on the beach."

"It is raining, woman, raining, we will get wet."

She had seen a golf umbrella somewhere in the hall and she went looking and found it behind the back porch door.

She came in brandishing the umbrella as if she was fencing.

"Out of that chair now and take me a walk on the beach now."

He made a dive for her but she was out of the door before he reached her. He caught up with her and in the rain they walked the beach, Sarah was bursting with happiness. Gordon Ross had never been so happy; she had lost her nervousness and was back very confident again.

The weekend was a great success and they drove home late evening, on the way he asked her,

"Have you had many boyfriends?"

She started to laugh, "With my lot, no I don't think so, there was a doctor and then a Minister," at this she started to laugh again.

"What's so funny?"

"I was not nice to the Minister." She told him then about Lizzie and her giving the poor man a bad time. How he had slobbered a kiss over her and she did not like it. I had to find a way to put him off gently. She related the incident and then he started to laugh. He pulled the car in off the road and stopped.

"What about the doctor?"

"Oh he was nice but that was all and anyway I really did not have the time to go out nights or week-ends. My spare time was spent with washing, ironing and cleaning and when I did go out I carried a shopping bag not a handbag. I always thought that maybe I was cold. I did not like people touching me and I never sought the company of men other than Davie and my brothers.

"Take my word for it you are not cold, you are a very loving person." They were now kissing again. "I am glad you waited for me."

"How many girlfriends have you had?"

"Well according to my staff hundreds, but that is not the case. I had a steady girl through the University and yes we slept with each other. We went our separate ways when we graduated; I am not going to lie to you. I have had three girlfriends and yes I have slept with two of them. I have never lived with anyone, surely that will stand in my favour. You and I start from this week end."

It was a statement rather than a question, he started the car and they carried on with their journey. He was quiet as they travelled, she wondered what he was thinking, and at this moment she did not know whether to break the silence or not, she did not feel so confident now and she did not know why.

When they arrived at Alison's apartment they sat in the car, neither of them wanted to go, he leaned back in the seat and looked at her.

"When do you have to go back?"

"Friday, I must go then, I have to let two of my girls go on holiday, so it will be hectic at the Surgery with two off."

"I am in Court this week, but we must sort something out."

He wanted to say more to her, he felt that she would expect some kind of commitment; I'll leave it till later, he decided.

"Did you enjoy the weekend and are you sure you will be alright. I am sorry if I offended you by think that Alison was your daughter."

"No you did not offend me, but I had told you earlier, anyway it does not matter. It used to bother me when I was younger and neighbours, who did not know the situation, would shout after me. It was a disgrace to have a child before marriage and it mattered a lot where I came from but I never made them any the wiser. I had enough problems at home without worrying what people thought of me."

"Could you not have moved your home?"

"People in my position are glad of the roof over their head, you don't take chances.

Alison and I are so alike it is no wonder people thought she was mine. They have all done so well, I am so proud of her and my boys, there I go again, and no wonder people think they are mine

Davie was always there to help, he would sort out any problems that we had or I could talk over things with him."

"Was he a boyfriend?"

"Well I suppose you could say that. He did ask me to marry him three different times.

We were great friends and could talk to each other about anything. That was before the row and things are not the same anymore."

"What happened?"

"Well I found out that there was a possibility, that Davie's father could also be Alison's father. Davie hid this from me and I have never forgiven him for that."

"If you were such good friends should you not be able to forgive him, if he helped you so much before, it is a pity to lose that friendship. Weigh one up against all the other kindness that he has shown you. You should not be so serious about things Sarah or so hard on yourself."

"You do not understand, how could you? I raised the boys and Mary, just when life was getting better for us all. Alison is born and Mary died. Davie tried to get me to have Alison adopted. He suspected his father; I told him I suspected the school janitor and he let me believe that. Knowing that he thought it could have been his father. I felt so betrayed, he was my friend and the only other one I had apart from Lizzie."

"No you are right, I am not criticising you but you must have liked him a great deal. Stay away from him now though."

"Why."

"I don't want him asking you to marry him again."

"That will not happen; he is married now to my best friend. We are on speaking terms again but not like it was."

"Sort it out Sarah, it is bothering you.

"I had better get in, it is late."

"I don't want you to go."

"I don't want to go either, I have never been able to talk about myself before with anyone, you are not anyone though, are you?"

"Definitely not and you are special."

They kissed good night and he helped her out of the car and up to the door, he kissed her again.

"Sarah we have to sort something out, I can't stand this."

Sarah did not know how to answer him.

As she went inside, he drove off, telling himself, you should have said more.

The house was in darkness and Alison was sleeping, as Sarah lay in bed, she thought what a wonderful time they had. Something was niggling at her, though. He had never once said he loved her or for that matter that he even cared, she felt he somehow danced around it, in case he was saying too much. He had told her she was crazy, not exactly words of endearment, but the way he said made all the difference. She was lovely; well he was exaggerating there. She knew she could look good if she was all dressed up and with make-up on, but lovely, no. What a good cook she was, there again loads of experience. Nice to be with, was another of his compliments, how he had never enjoyed a weekend like it before, she was special. Which made her wonder just how many other women he had at the cottage? Let's face it he had left her a bit off-hand; maybe he was not happy when she asked about his girlfriends. Then again he had started that conversation and he was very quiet after that. Then again he was not curt, but yes, he was casual. She loved him she was sure, and she had never told him either. There you go she scolded herself. You want him to say the word love but you will not. One thing for sure, Lizzie was right, sex with the right person did make the earth move. She slept well all nigh

Chapter 16

When she wakened in the morning Alison had left for work. She had a bath and then some breakfast. The phone rang then and Sarah rushed to the phone, it would be Gordon.

"Good Morning Gordon."

"Listen Sarah, do not go out this morning, I will be home at lunch or quicker if I can."

"What's wrong Alison?"

"Nothing is wrong but I have something that I need to discuss with you, must dash."

She wondered what that was all about, time will tell. She spent some time tidying up and she vacuumed the few carpets, with an ancient electric cleaner. By the time she was finished she heard Alison's key in the door and then she came in. Sarah knew immediately that something was wrong.

"What is wrong Alison you look really tense."

"God Sarah, what a morning I have had, I am sick. I don't even know how to handle it. I have been fighting with myself, should I tell you or should I not. Ian said I should tell you."

"Will I make a sandwich and coffee, are you hungry?"

"No, I will have a coffee before I go."

They sat down on the settee facing each other.

"I don't know how to tell you this and I am not telling you because," Alison stopped there, tears were in her eyes, "I am so sorry."

"Is something wrong with one of the boys?"

"No no, it is him, look I will tell you what I have heard, how you deal with it, I don't know.

"There was a lot of laughter from the senior partners this morning; well three of them and two are real clowns. Ian was asking the receptionist what all the hilarity was about; she told him that they had a 'Bet' on, on what he had asked? Some woman that Gordon Ross had been trying to date and he had managed to get her to go out with him. When he went into his office with files that he needed, there was a ten-pound note on his desk. As Ian left, he heard them arranging to spend it in the Bar after work, the bar they sometimes have a drink in."

They stared at each other; the impact on Sarah was in her face, her eyes. She covered her face with her hands,

"Dear God no, oh my God I was a 'Bet' No, he wouldn't."

They sat together holding each other, never once did Alison say 'I told you so', she held her tight. Sarah cried her heart out at how cruel he was. She was a joke nothing but a joke, she had been a joke. What a poor sense of fun he had, it was sick.

"Sarah."

"I am fine," the tears were still flowing, "he left me last night and I felt that there was something he wanted to say or something he did not want to say. We had or I thought we had a wonderful weekend, my God. I'm a joke, well it deserves me right and you warned me and warned me well. She was crying uncontrollably, Alison became very concerned about her.

"Listen to me Sarah, we have not got all the facts, and we do not know what was said in that office. They could have been laughing about anything."

"You are defending him now, why?"

"Men think differently from women Sarah, it might not be as bad as it seems. I do not want you so upset; do not let it get to you. If anything laugh it off."

"No, I will not laugh it off, you don't understand, I told him things about myself that I have never told anyone. I feel like a prostitute, mind you with the weekend he had, ten pounds was a bargain."

"You don't mean."

"Oh yes I do. I am a fool; at my age I should have known better. He played me so well and I quote 'I won't hurry you, it is up to you,' I was only too eager.

Mind you when he realised I was a virgin, he was very upset. I thought it was consideration for me; still maybe they will give him a bonus for that. "

Sarah's voice had now changed and Alison knew that she was furious; from experience she knew that there was no way she would let him off lightly. Anyone who deliberately hurt or annoyed any of them suffered with her tongue and she could leave them standing in shock.

"Maybe you should get his side of the story first. Maybe it is not really as bad as it sounds. What was I to do? Not tell you."

"No this is not your fault; I should have stayed in Greenock, look at the problem this could cause you at your work."

"No, if I have any repercussions on this regarding my work I will take it to Mr. Grant. He is the most senior partner and then it's 'him'. The other two are only working their way into the partnership. Believe you me; they should not have got involved in anything because I heard Mr. Grant has warned them to grow up."

"Where is this Bar?"

"Don't go near it Sarah, do not let them see that they have got the better of you."

"Yes they have got the better of me but better to fight back than run away. Where is the Bar?"

"Off Princess Street, just up a few doors from the book shop, Sarah don't go near them."

"When do you think they will be there?"

"He is at Court today but always comes back to the office, I think around 5 'o'clock."

"Right you go back to the office and do not go anywhere near the Bar, I will see you when I come in."

"What are you going to do?"

"I am going to face them and him in particular. I will take the feet from them. I will plan it that way."

The crying had stopped, she was hurt, humiliated and she was ashamed of herself. She was so disappointed; it was hard to take in just how he had set a trap for her.

Alison brought mugs of coffee and they sat and sipped the coffee, neither could eat.

"You know I made it so easy for him," she laughed a very dry laugh, "I was so willing, no fool like an old fool and you warned me well. I have let you and myself down. He will know what I think, because I will tell him straight to his face and I don't care where he is when I do it."

"Are you sure you want to handle it this way, look leave it till tonight, I might hear something else."

"Heaven forbid Alison. No the sooner this is dealt with the better."

"What will you do?"

I don't know but as sure as hell's burning, I will do something. You go back to the office and stay out of this; I will see you back here afterwards."

Alison left, and Sarah sat drinking her coffee, she could not take it in, how could he, and no wonder he never said he even liked her. She loved him that was what was worse about the whole situation. She had trusted him, and the tears were flowing again. She was furious at him and yet she wanted him. She had been stupid enough to think that he was going to suggest she came to Edinburgh or they even kept in touch.

She washed her face and put on a little make-up, as she was combing her hair she laughed at herself remembering his words. 'If you cut that lovely hair I will take it as an insult'. Right that's what she would do, she wanted it cut anyway, easier to handle if I should be able to go to college. When I go back next week I will try and get into college or University, I could try for a grant. This was a very bad experience but then she had survived worse than this. Really this was nothing, He was despicable and she had been so easy, so willing. They must have had a good laugh, so be it, nevertheless she would face them.

She put on the cream dress and shoes and borrowed Allison's cream handbag and out she went. It took three hairdressing shops before she could get an appointment to have her hair cut and styled. She could be taken in fifteen minutes, so she waited.

When she was seated in the chair the Hairdresser, a man, it would have to be, wouldn't it, she thought wryly?

"What would you like done with your hair."

"I want a short hairstyle please."

"Do you not think shoulder length should be your first step? You may find that you do not like it short. You have beautiful hair, he was running his fingers through her hair and he was annoying her.

"I am sorry and I don't mean to be rude but I came in here for a haircut so please cut my hair."

"Very good, the girl will shampoo your hair first and then I will style it."

He brought her a book showing different hairstyles.

"Maybe there is something here you may like."

She chose a very short hairstyle that was called an Urchin Cut. When he was finished and had towelled it dry and curled it slightly. He stood back, examining his work.

"Well I must say you had lovely hair, but you are now beautiful and you do suit that hairstyle. Why your eyes are enormous now and I do believe it suits the shape of your face. Going somewhere nice?"

She could hardly talk to the man, well he was a man and that was enough to annoy her today. Flattery that's all they think about, think they can get away with anything with a few kind words, she was mad again.

"Thank you very much and yes I do like it."

Keep your head it is not the hairdresser's fault she reminded herself. She paid and left.

She checked her watch it was now nearly four o'clock. She decided to go and have a something to eat maybe another coffee and sandwich. She went into one of the big stores that had a tearoom. As she went in she noticed a dress in the window that was a lovely colour of deep lavender. I would love a dress like that she thought, why not, there was only herself to take care of now and she made up her mind to take care of herself very well. She went into the dress department and asked to see the dress. When the assistant brought it and she tried it on, she loved it.

"That dress is just for you and you suit the colour so well."

"Thank you I will take it."

"If you don't mind me suggesting this, you should wear navy or black shoes with it."

"Thank you. That is what I will do."

She went for a coffee and a sandwich, but still could not eat much. She bought herself a pair of navy blue shoes, slightly higher than she had ever used and a navy blue clutch bag. On her way out she went over to the cosmetic counter and asked if there was anyone who would do make-up for her. The girl told her that they employed beauticians and yes she could have it done now.

When the girl was finished with her Sarah could hardly believe the difference. She felt good, well as good as she could feel at the moment. She went to the Ladies Room and changed her dress, shoes and handbag for the new one she had just bought. Yes she did suit the dress and she looked good. She went back to the dress department to ask if she could leave her carrier bag,

"I told you that was your dress, didn't I," the assistant was admiring her.

"Yes you did, could I leave this carrier bag with you, maybe until the morning."

"I will need to check with the supervisor, I won't be a minute."

A very smart woman came to speak to Sarah,

"I believe that you would like to leave a carrier with us until the morning, it is not our policy but I understand that you have just purchased here today, so we will look after it for you."

"Thank you, I am going to a special occasion and I saw this dress and had to have it. I want to wear it now and I don't want to carry the bag with me."

"Have a lovely evening then, and Miss, you will knock them dead."

"I certainly hope so."

She was glad she looked good, she wanted him to see her looking good and she would really try not to cry. Why she cried so much she never understood. All her life she had cried easily, tears flowed easily. No not this time, she would keep what little dignity she had left, for he had robbed her even of that.

She checked her watch and it had just left five o'clock, time to go and have it out with him. She followed Alison's directions and found the Bar easily. She checked inside quickly and saw that they were sitting right in the middle of the tables. She went over to the bar and asked the waitress

"Would bring two separate pints of beer over to the centre table when I give you a sign, it is a surprise for my friends, and I will pay for it now, could I have it in beer mugs please."

"Yes fine, but there are three over there."

"Two will do, it is a kind of a joke between us."

The three of them were sitting at the table and Gordon was checking his watch. There was a bit of laughter between them.

"Not go so well then your week-end."

"No, she is a very proper lady and I have to admit to the fact that I want to get to know her better. So boys this is my last time with you lot on the prowl. I am happy to pay for these drinks but that's it I am afraid. I have been well and truly hooked."

There was more laughter between them as Sarah approached them slowly.

"I would not mind a bit of this coming over, have a look at this, my God, she's lovely", one of them muttered.

It took a moment for Gordon Ross to realise that it was Sarah. She was stunning but she had cut her hair, he stood up,

"Sarah."

"Don't you Sarah me," her eyes were blazing.

"What have you been up to Gordon," one of the wimps said.

"You shut up; I will deal with you later."

"Sarah."

"Enjoying your drink boys, mind you I thought I was worth more than ten pounds, not much of a wager." Looking straight at him, "You despicable apology for a man, you are a cheat and a liar. You are obnoxious; you are a coward, what a poor life you have when this is how you get your fun."

"Sarah it was not like that, I am paying for the drinks because I lost."

"So that makes it alright does it, you made the 'Bet' in the first place."

"No it wasn't like that, please Sarah." He put his hand out to her.

"Don't you touch me; you are a rotter, a despicable rotter." She had raised her voice and although she was not aware of it, those in the Bar were watching.

"As for your trashy friends, you are nothing but low, look at you all, God's gift to the rubbish dump. Do you think you are all so special? You may be lawyers but somewhere in your education you all fell in the gutter and no matter how you try to climb out, you will not be able to, for that is where you belong.

By the way boys this liar and cheat lied to you as well. If he told you that he had lost because he wanted to be a gentleman, not that he ever will be." She leaned closer, and lowered her voice to a whisper.

"Let me tell you that he did not have me once, he had me three times, so you did not lose, and do you know what the cherry was on the top of his cake, I was a virgin."

The other wimp stood up, she pushed him none to gently back into his seat.

"Oh please do not go, have another drink on me."

She had signed to the waitress, who had come over,

The waitress was mesmerised, she had been watching. As Sarah thanked her she said sweetly,

"Enjoy your drink boys."

She threw the contents of the two pints over the three of them; they were absolutely dripping with the beer.

There was a gasp all round, nobody moved. Gordon sat with his head in his hands. She leaned forward and put her hand under his chin and lifted his head, they were staring at each other.

"Did I spoil your little party darling?" The beer was still dripping down his face; the tears were running down her cheeks. She turned and walked away.

She hurried as quickly as she could but he had run after her and caught up with her on Princess Street.

"Sarah please, you were not a bet, and it was not like that."

"I will tell you what it was like, will I? You made a fool of me, you humiliated me, and you have now made me feel dirty. I feel like a prostitute because you sold me for a joke. You are sick, you pompous fool, and that's what you are. A high and mighty lawyer looking down on me and I matter so little that I can be a 'Bet'. Well let me tell you this, where I come from we leave people with their dignity, we may be poor and uneducated on my side of town but we do not treat each other the way you have treated me."

"Sarah please?"

"Do not interrupt me I am not finished. You have taken my dignity from me, and you have left me like this."

The tears were running down her face and she was sobbing. People were passing and turning to look at them.

"How could you? How could you? Am I such a sick joke?"

There in the middle of Princess Street she asked him again, only this time quietly,

"Why?"

"Sarah please, it was not like that, please."

Then she turned and walked away, and she never looked back. She walked as quickly as the high heels allowed her and hurried into the flat.

When Alison came in she found her sobbing and she cried most of the night. The telephone rang often. Alison answered it the first time it rang,

"Hello, I will see. It is Gordon Ross, Sarah; he would like to speak to you."

She shook her head, and left the room.

"No, she will not speak to you."

"It was not how it looks, could I come round?"

"No, she is distraught. If you wanted to upset her you should know you have succeeded. She has cried since we heard what you have done."

"Please Alison, it is not what happened."

"Goodnight," she replaced the receiver. They never answered the telephone again that night.

Alison tried to cheer her up by telling how nice her hair was, how she suited it, how nice her dress was even though it was now beer stained, that was only time she smiled.

Sarah never slept and Alison made her go back to bed in the morning,

"Have a long lie. We will go out tonight when I come home; I will phone you later on."

She went back to bed but could not settle. She had a long leisurely bath and started to feel better. She also felt hungry and made some scrambled egg with toast, made a pot of coffee, which she never drank.

The telephone rang; Alison had said she would phone her later on in the morning it would be Alison.

" Hello."

"Sarah let me come round." She replaced the receiver.

Alison came home early. "I said I had a headache, nobody questioned me."

"Did you see him?"

"Yes he wants to see you. Speak with him Sarah."

"No."

"Let me tell you what he said. He said that when he went in this morning, he threw ten pounds on the table and told them that he had lost. He told them that he would not be drinking with them anymore as he was well and truly hooked."

"Don't you see, he must have made the 'Bet' with them in the first place? All the telephone calls, they were all done for a 'Bet'."

"No, he says will you think back to the time you went for a coffee, the first time, it was only after that the other two had asked him what he was going to do at the weekend. He told them he was trying to get you to go out with him. They put the 'Bet', not him. He said that he thought if he paid as a loser that would be the end of it. He asked me to assure you that everything between you both is very confidential."

"It is not now, because I told all in the Bar."

"You never, Oh Sarah you never"

"I did, you would have been proud of me; it was one of my better moments." Sarah started to cry again. "Look at me, nearly forty years of age and a dithering wreck. Did he tell you that I threw two pints of beer over him, and the other two wimps?"

"Sarah you should not have done that, he has a position to maintain in the city, you really should not have done that. What are we going to do Sarah, and you will make yourself ill. If it's any consolation he looks worse than you."

"That's fair enough it is his entire fault and if he has a position to maintain he should stop acting like a, like a, I don't know, yes I do, a bloody rotter."

"Look we are going out, you must stop crying. Remember what you used to say to me, 'where is the sunshine polish' and you pretended to shine up my face, so shine up that face."

"I can't go out with these eyes."

"Yes you can, get make up on and be ready in half an hour, wear a pair of sunglasses if it makes you feel better, but we are going out."

They walked through Princess Street with the late shoppers and found a new restaurant and went in for a meal.

They sat for ages and talked, and they made a pact not to talk about him.

"I can hardly believe that I go home on Friday. It was a very quick first week, and I like Edinburgh and all the buzz. Greenock will be quiet and dull after this."

"You miss us all don't you?"

"Yes but life changes and we must change with it. I have decided to try for the University or college. I will try for a Government Grant and my savings will see me through"

"Why don't you come and live with me here, you could go to University or College here."

"I will go home and let things settle down and then see what I will do. I really feel I should change my life. I am now free, nobody needs me."

"We all need you Sarah, never forget that. Jimmy told me that he asked you to go and live with him."

"If Jimmy ever marries and he could, where would I be then? No I need my own place but I do not want to stay at East Shore Street any longer. I don't feel I belong there anymore. When you think of the times I would not move because I was frightened of being poor, it is just not the same anymore. I also feel that I should even change my work, I will stay at the surgery until I find out about college, they might not take me and then again I don't think I want that anymore."

"What do you want to do?"

"I wanted him to ask me to come to Edinburgh but that won't happen now."

"It maybe could Sarah, if you give him a chance."

"Imagine how I feel, I bared my soul to him, I told him things I never told anyone. I slept with him. It is the idea that he would take me on as a 'Bet'. I always tried to keep my dignity, even when I did not know how we would eat or how I could keep us warm. There were days when I did not know how I would get through them, we had nothing but I kept my dignity. He has robbed me of that; he has made me feel dirty."

"I know I warned you about him, I am sure he played the field but I don't think you were a 'Bet'. I am not taking his side against you but I feel that you are being just too hard on him. He made a mistake with his choice of friends, and then again I don't think they were really friends' just colleagues. There was some atmosphere in the office today, the Wimps were hardly to be seen and he's at Court. Everything is not black or white Sarah. You used to teach me that, anyway we are not talking about him anymore. Stay over the week end and go home when you feel better."

"No, I have two girls off on holiday, I cannot let them down. I will go back on Friday and I do not feel just as bad now, obviously my pride is hurt, it is not hurt it has been cremated."

They left and wandered back to the apartment, they went to bed early to read. Alison checked on her later and was pleased that she had at last gone to sleep.

Next morning when Sarah wakened she was surprised that she had slept late. Alison had long gone to the office as it was well after nine o'clock. She had some breakfast and washed, then decided to go to the shops for a wander and she was still to pick up the carrier bag she had left at the shop. As she was leaving the apartment the telephone rang.

"Good Morning."

"Would you meet me for lunch?"

She replaced the receiver, the tears started again and she was not able to go out until she calmed down. The telephone rang three times while she was in but she never answered.

She left for the shops before lunch and just wandered. She felt that the sooner she was on the train home the better. She could go today but she did not want to upset Alison. She bought some chocolate and sweets for the office and wandered down Princess Street, then crossed to the Park. She sat in the Park for most of the afternoon, she was miserable and lonely so decided to go back. As she went in the door the telephone was ringing again.

She lifted the receiver,

"Hello."

"Get your glad rags on we are going out for a girl's night out. We are going for our dinner and then on somewhere for a few drinks and a laugh."

"Alison I do not feel up to it."

"Sarah be ready and at the office for five o'clock."

"He could be there."

"So, are you going to hide for something you did not do? Anyway none of the girls are speaking to any of them unless it is about work. They got no reply to their usual 'good morning ladies' and they got cold coffee."

"Why."

"I told them what they had done. The opinion is that it was not before time for the Wimps, but that he is not as bad as the Wimps. The general feeling is 'good for you' so we are celebrating."

"Alison, how much do they know?"

"Just enough and no more, right. See you at five o'clock."

She did not feel up to this but she knew that Alison was trying to cheer her up. She went over to the office but stayed outside until they came out. Alison introduced her to everyone and off they went.

They were a boisterous noisy lot but nice to her. They were all much younger and she felt out of it. She laughed at the right time and enjoyed the meal and had a few drinks. She was glad when they decided to leave and they headed back to the apartment.

She slept that night again, as she seemed to be very tired; then again she was not used to having wine and maybe it made her sleepy.

On Thursday she spent time getting her things ready for going home. The phone rang twice, and as before, she did not answer it. She made a meal for Alison coming home and they spent the last night together.

"Will you get a taxi in the morning to the station and I will try and get down to see you away."

"Look do not worry, I will phone you from the phone box at the corner tomorrow night and despite everything I have enjoyed my visit and it is not a long journey. I will go whenever I am ready."

Alison watched her; she was worried about her now, as she seemed a bit depressed. She decided to phone Jimmy tomorrow and get him to keep his eye on her.

They said good-bye to each other in the morning before Alison left for work.

As soon as she had gone Sarah left, she could not get on the train quick enough. There was no hold ups on her journey and she was back home late afternoon.

Chapter 17

The house was quieter than usual and she felt more lost than she had in a long time. Lizzie knocked the door after seven o'clock to see how she had enjoyed herself. They talked about things in general. Sarah told her how she liked Edinburgh, about the lovely Princess Street Park, the Castle, how majestic it was, and how she felt as if the castle watched over city and how safe she had felt there. Also about the shops and restaurants that Alison had taken her to. For the first time ever she did not confide in Lizzie, she was so ashamed of herself and the knowledge was choking her. He had treated her like a prostitute, she had been so easy, a good meal and a weekend that was what he had paid for her and she felt dirty, no filthy. She asked herself over and over again, how could you behave like that, and to have thrown the beer over him, to lower herself to his standards. She was disgusted with herself and took no comfort in it. She walked down to the phone box after tea and rang Alison.

"Hello Alison, it's me. I am home safe and sound."

"He went looking for you at the station, Sarah he is in a state; I do not know how he worked today. He wants your address, what will I do?"

"Do nothing and let the dust settle. I will come back for a weekend soon. I do not think I can stay here anymore. It is as if I don't belong here now. I wish I had never met him. I was quite contented before. I don't think I am wrong or that I over reacted. How could I believe anything that he says? He took the 'Bet' end of story. I will phone you soon, bye."

Sarah returned to work on the Monday and was busy all day. Everyone was so surprised at her hairstyle, all agreed that it suited her better and made her look years younger.

The next few weeks were busy at the Surgery and she worked extra hours to keep herself busy. She had phoned Alison a few times to let her know she was fine. Jimmy came over at the weekend and they had their dinner together on Sunday. He did not comment but she looked very pale.

"Are you keeping well? You don't want to be working to many hours Sarah."

"I am fine but I do seem a bit tired, more than usual. I will speak to the doctor next week."

As he left he asked her again to think about sharing his house with him. They joked about it. How he only wanted a housekeeper and what if he married.

"Nobody will have me Sarah, I am an unclaimed treasure."

"Get away with you, I lost count of the girlfriends you have had. Away home and leave me in peace."

She walked him down to the bus stop and waved him off.

She kept herself busy over the next few weeks and two letters had come from Alison with a letter from Gordon in each of them.

He asked to be able to explain everything to her, how he missed her. Alison had told him that she was coming for a weekend soon. Would she please meet him? If she liked he would come through to Greenock or they could meet in Glasgow. She did not reply, she was now not very well and the tiredness was getting her down.

Next morning when she got out of bed, she had to hold on to a chair, the room was turning and she felt so dizzy. All at once she felt so sick and had to go back to bed for a while. She could not go to her work; she dragged herself down to the phone box and phoned the Surgery to tell them that she was not well.

The next day the dizziness had settled, but she still was sick after rising, she thought that she must have a virus and then reality hit her. She had morning sickness, dear God she was pregnant. What was she going to do? No maybe, it must be a virus. She was letting her imagination run away with her. No, she must be pregnant.

She went to work the next day and stayed late to speak to the Doctor.

"Can I have a word with you when you are finished?"

"Come through now, what is wrong Sarah; you have not been your usual self lately."

"There is no point in me not being truthful with you. I think I may be pregnant."

The doctor was taken aback. Sarah was a very dependable and sensible woman, and then love makes fools of us all he thought.

"Right we will need a test, you know the routine. Let me examine you and we will take it from there".

After he had examined her, and only when she was sitting back down in the chair facing the doctor across the desk, he spoke.

"Yes Sarah, I think you could be pregnant but we will have to wait a week for the results of the test. We will not discuss it until we know for sure. He advised her about how to cope with the sickness and suggested that she took sick leave until she felt better.

"I would rather work if you don't mind."

"Fine but take it easy."

She went home her mind in turmoil. The next week was a very long week and the test results were positive."

"What will you do Sarah," the doctor asked, "You are on your own "

"Yes I am but I have family, I will discuss things with them."

"Do not panic, there is no problem that cannot be solved. I am here to help you, come to me at any time."

"I will take that sick leave now if I could, at least for a week."

"Right I will get the girls to do extra hours to cover you, don't worry." He could see that she was distraught but was very calm.

"Thank you Doctor, I will keep in touch.

Before she left the Surgery she phoned Alison, she was not at home. She phoned the office and found her there.

"Can I come to you tonight please?"

"Yes, what's wrong?"

"I will tell you later, I will phone you from Glasgow and let you know what train I am on."

Alison replaced the telephone back in its cradle, and sat thinking for a moment, when she lifted her head; Gordon Ross was standing at the door of her office.

"Was that Sarah, Alison?" She nodded. "Is she still as angry?"

Alison did not answer him she just asked, "If you do not need me I would like to go, there is something wrong.

She left the office and hurried home, something was far wrong with Sarah. She had made herself ill over the affair. She was far too serious about everything. It was time she put herself and him out of their misery. Maybe it was because they were older but they were carrying on like children, really.

Sarah phoned from Glasgow and Alison met her of the last train at Waverly Station, she had one small case with her.

"Are you ill, you are so pale? You have lost a lot of weight. Let's go, there is a taxi stand just outside the station. Once in the taxi Sarah sat back in the seat and closed her eyes

"Dear God what a mess, I panicked and had to see you."

"Did you let any of the boys know you were coming here?"

"No, I panicked."

"Wait till we are home then we will sort it out."

"This cannot be sorted out Alison," Sarah buried her head in her hands. "I am so sorry Alison, what a mess."

Alison put her arm round her, "it will be fine, wait till we are in the Flat."

Once they got into Alison's apartment Sarah threw herself down onto the settee and started crying.

"Sarah. What is wrong?"

"I am pregnant."

There was a stunned silence between them, and then Alison spoke," My God Sarah, you will have to speak to him now."

"I just needed to talk with someone I can trust."

"You do not look well, how have you really been?"

"So sick and so alone."

"I have made up your bed, why don't you go to bed and we will talk tomorrow."

"Alison I am sorry to give you this."

"Where else would you come but to me. If you had went anywhere else I would have been annoyed. What did Lizzie say?"

"I could not even tell Lizzie, I am so ashamed of myself. The doctor told me not to panic and that is exactly what I have done."

Sarah wakened through the night feeling very sick, she managed to get to the bathroom, and Alison wakened and came to her. She was on the floor and she was bleeding. Alison phoned the doctor and explained what was happening. He came very quickly; once he had seen her he decided that she would go into hospital right away. The ambulance came and Alison sat the rest of the night in the Casualty Dept. It was at seven o'clock that morning when a doctor came to Alison.

"Did you bring in Sarah Shaw to casualty?"

"Yes, I am Alison Shaw; I am her next of kin."

"Come through to the ward office, I am sure you could do with a cup of tea, I know I could."

Once they were seated he explained that Sarah was threatening a miscarriage, she was bleeding rather badly but had not lost the baby. She is very early on in the pregnancy. The bleeding has stopped and it is a case of wait and see. She must stay here, we have to take into consideration her age, and she is not a young mother. I would be very surprised if she manages to keep this baby. However nature has a mind of its own and could prove me wrong.

A nurse brought tea and Alison drank it gladly, as the doctor drank his tea, Alison asked,

"Is she in any danger?"

"No, she is comfortable; once you have seen her we will help her to settle for a sleep. She does not want to stay in hospital, but she needs twenty-four hour care right now. This is where she will get it. I need your help to make her stay in hospital."

"Yes she will stay, I will see to it."

The doctor took her upstairs and through a ward until they came to a single room.

Sarah was propped up in bed and looked so pale. Alison held her hand,

"Listen Sarah, you have to stay in hospital or you could lose the baby. You have to be as well as you can, this is where you should be."

The doctor sat on the edge of the bed.

"I cannot guarantee that you will not lose the baby if you stay in hospital but your chances are better if you stay. If you are rested, the baby's chances are better."

"How long will I be in hospital?"

"I cannot say at the moment, as I told you before it is a case of wait and see."

Sarah looked at Alison and the Doctor, "very well, I will stay here and do as you say."

"Good, I will leave you and I will check on you regularly." He nodded to Alison as he left.

"Sarah I am going to go home, and I will come back tomorrow, I will take care of everything. I will let the boys know tomorrow."

"Alison, please do not let him know just now, I will sort it out myself when I know how things are. I did not want this baby and now I don't want to lose it."

"Right we have a deal, you stay here and I will do as you want."

As Alison was leaving the doctor was waiting for her.

"Could I have a word with you? Her chances of keeping this baby are slim, so she must be kept as calm as possible. As an unmarried mother will she have any immediate problems, if there are I could arrange a talk with a social worker?"

"No, there are no problems; I will take care of everything for her."

"Very good, would you leave your telephone number in case of an emergency? She will be fine, we will take care of her and she really needs a lot of rest just now. Limit the visitors please."

"Yes I will see to it, thank you Doctor."

Alison returned to her apartment and phoned into the office to let them know that she did not feel very well and would have to take the day off.

She went to bed and slept and when she wakened she returned to the hospital with the things that Sarah would need. She telephoned Jimmy at his work and told him that Sarah is with me, will you telephone after nine o'clock tonight, I will explain then.

When she returned to the hospital Sarah was looking better and seemed to be more relaxed.

"I have brought you some goodies and a dressing gown and nighties. There are some magazines there but I just grabbed a few. How are you now?"

"I have seen a Consultant and he wants me to stay in hospital indefinitely."

"How do you feel about that?"

"What else can I do? I need you to help me Alison."

"You know I will, look we do not need to let anybody know you are in hospital at the moment. We will talk later on how we handle this. I have left word with Jimmy to phone me tonight and we will all help you. Try not to worry."

Alison returned home and decided that she had better get organised. She was going to be busy working, hospital visiting and dealing with things in general. There would be a lot to see to but Jimmy and Archie would help. Andrew was in London so there was little he could do.

Next morning as she went into the office she met Gordon Ross.

"I believe you were not well yesterday, are you feeling better now?"

"Yes thank you, "she could hardly look at him. She could not tell him and yet she thought he should know.

"Is Sarah coming to Edinburgh at any time Alison? I really need to sort things out for both of us. If I could see her, if she will talk to me, I am sure we could," he stopped speaking then.

"Could I ask you a favour, without you asking me why?"

"Yes."

"Leave things alone for the present, I am sure that given time everything will sort itself out, and you could be pleased. I must go and catch up for yesterday."

When she left him she thought, surprised, was maybe a better word than, pleased.

He watched her walk into her office and thought, what a strange thing to say.

He had been miserable over the whole affair. He had handled it badly. If he had even said how he felt when they came back from the cottage, but he never. It was not unreasonable that she had lost her temper. He could not have believed that she would have done what she did. Her hurt, her sarcasm had been hard to bear. That she had believed he would have behaved like that. She must have thought he discussed what happened at the cottage. This had to be what she thought. He missed her so much; she must know that he loved her. If he did not have her he would never have anyone else in her place. He was as low as he had ever been and he found it difficult in every way.

Sarah wakened to find that she had slept all night, and it was daylight outside. A cheery woman popped her head round the open door of the single room,

"Cup of tea, love, milk and sugar, good, there you go then, sleep well?"

"Thank you, yes."

She sipped the tea and it was good. At the moment she did not feel sick, the first time in days. She was staring out of the window thinking, some mess I am in. When she thought of all the times she had warned the boys about getting girls into trouble, how they could not just walk away. Respect girls and be known as nice boys. To remember always that some girls were only out to catch a man. They used to tease her, because when they were going out to a dance or social, they had to listen to a ''Sarah Sermon'. Then when it became Alison's turn, she would get the same lecture and be told, watch out for these boys, some of them are only after one thing. Here she was in a mess, and the author of the 'Sarah Sermon' had ignored all warnings. She was even surprised that she was pregnant. She had changed her brains for marbles, they had never bothered about protection, what did she expect?

"Good morning, how are you today? I am Sister Brodie. I believe you have come to visit us for a wee while." The Sister perched herself on the edge of the bed and took Sarah's hand.

"Feeling a bit lost at the moment."

Sarah nodded, her eyes filled with tears.

The Sister closed the door over and handed Sarah some tissues,

"Listen to me Sarah, you will be well looked after here. We must get you well and that will help the baby."

"The doctor thinks I may lose the baby."

"Well you do as we tell you and you just might keep your baby. I have seen girls come in here with really bad 'threatened miscarriages' and go out with bouncing babies. You could be one of them. Now we will take your temperature and blood pressure, then you will have a wash. You will feel better after that. Then some breakfast."

"I would like to go to the bathroom."

"Sarah you have not to get out of that bed. The more rest you get the better the chances are. We will see to all your needs. Do you see that door over there, well you leave your modesty at that door and you pick it up when you leave. Do not feel embarrassed just remember we all have backsides, every one of us including even the Consultants."

Sarah was smiling at her now.

The door opened and in came two nurses,

"Good morning, good morning good morning, we are the wash and wipe brigade."

"You two are far too cheery in the morning; they get on my nerves Sarah. I have to listen to their dawn chorus every day. I will be back to see you soon, keep that chin up."

The nurses worked with Sarah and chatted about the hospital talent, complaining that there was a great lack of good-looking available doctors at the moment.

"Have you got any brothers you could put our way, mind you we are not fussy? As long as they have good looks and a good job, were not mean, no mothers, no, mothers could be a problem. Nothing worse, than some man quoting, how wonderful his mother was. They preferred orphans, the richer the better.

Sarah was laughing by now and when the nurses left she was washed, changed and sitting up in bed combing her hair, and feeling much better.

The day passed with more blood pressure and temperature checks. The same cheery woman popped in to see her regularly with tea. The blinds were drawn in her room and this was a rest period. You were expected to be very quiet; you could read if you wanted to. Sarah slept again and was wakened at four o'clock, again with tea.

Sister Brodie came to see her before she went off duty.

"Right I will see you tomorrow, I have a long shift tomorrow, I am on all day until eight o'clock at night, and we will get a natter then. Remember to keep that chin up."

Sarah waved as she left, she was a lovely person, they had struck up a friendship somehow, or maybe that was the way nurses were.

Alison arrived at seven o'clock for the night visit. She brought more night-dresses, more books and toiletries.

"How are you Sarah, feeling a bit better?"

"The doctor told me that I must have complete bed rest, they are very good to me and the Sister is very kind. What's new?"

"I phoned Jimmy and told him, he will let Archie know. I phoned Andrew and told him, they are all making arrangements to visit at the weekend. Andrew is hoping for a flight up. They are all asking for you and send their love."

She did not tell her that she had spoken with the doctor and that he had told Alison that it was most unlikely that she would have this baby.

The boys all thought, maybe it was for the better. It would let her get a life of her own at last and who was this rotter anyway? They could not believe the news but none of them criticised her.

"Where will they all stay Alison?"

"They can stay with me, we will squeeze in, and it will be like old times. So they are all staying for the weekend. I am sorry this has happened but we will all be together for a while. I think that's what you need right now."

"Have you seen him?"

"No, I have been avoiding him; I still think he should be told."

"Let me wait and see what happens. I should have spoken to him but time is passing and it is not so easy now. What if he has another girlfriend, think of the position he could be in."

"You are impossible; even now you are trying to protect him"

"Alison I cannot use him when I would not speak to him. I promise when we know for sure how things are with me I will write to him. Then it will be his choice not because he has to because of the baby. What do the boys think of me?"

Alison could see that she was worried about the boys and what they would think of her.

"Jimmy says that you obviously met someone; fell in love, that's life. Andrew says that you must have forgotten the,' Sarah Sermon.' He was not being unkind. We will all look after you of course, Archie is going to bash his brains in and Anne said that this only happens to good people. She says bad people don't get caught, anyway Archie stopped speaking to me, to ask Anne, what did she know about bad people and she shouted back at him, I married you didn't I. How they ever married each other I will never know. He said to tell you that he would be here at the weekend."

"They have a good marriage and I think the shouting is all about hiding how they really feel. Remember the fights he got into."

They both started laughing, Archie was the smallest of the boys, and was always looking after the other two who were much taller than he was.

The bell for the visitors to leave had just sounded and a nurse came in to see that all visitors kept to the rules.

"I will see you tomorrow night."

"No, Alison I do not want you coming every night, you will wear yourself out, please. Try coming every other night, if I need you I could phone you. If you could bring writing paper and envelopes I will write to Lizzie and fill her in."

"I wrote and told her that you had decided to stay with me a bit longer and that you would write yourself soon. I also phoned the Surgery to let them know that as you were not well, you would not be in. Leave it like that meantime."

"I have made a right mess of things, haven't I?"

"Other people survive and we will as well, I will get away I will see you soon." She hugged Sarah and went away.

Sarah soon settled into hospital routine and as promised the boys came on Saturday.

Sister Brodie was on duty and she said that they could all get in together as they had come a long way.

"The patient must not be upset." She ordered them, as she left.

"Would not like to get in her bad books," Archie warned.

"Nice looking girl, did you see that figure," Jimmy remarked.

They all looked at him; this was something new, from the brother that never bothered about women.

"Me thinks he has been smitten," Andrew laughed.

"I thought you lot came to see me, you are all the same."

They all looked at Sarah, wondering what to say,

"I will help you all out; I have made a mess of my life. I always wanted time to myself, and when I get it, I go and do something stupid. I am a fool to have made such a mistake. I am sorry."

She looked round the three of them, and Alison joined them at that moment,

"Right what have I missed? How are you today Sarah? I let them come ahead because they were all desperate to see you; cat got all your tongues."

"You were always too quick for the rest of us."

"Ah well, I am much younger than the rest of you." Nobody knew what to say. "Cheer up the lot of you."

They all started talking at once and then burst out laughing.

Sister Brodie made a quick entrance,

"Did I or did I not say that the patient was to be kept quiet."

She marched back out at that.

"Ya mein General," Archie saluted.

Back Sister Brodie came, "right you lot out, and I am surprised at you," she spoke directly to Jimmy. "Come on, two at a bed."

"Please let us stay, please, please," Andrew implored, all six foot three of him.

"Right last chance, and you, keep this lot in order," again she spoke to Jimmy.

As the Sister left the room, they all looked at Jimmy.

"Whose the favourite then, you been giving her the eye" Archie wanted to know.

"No she just knows by looking at me that I am the sensible one, I would not mind a night out with her, and she's lovely."

"Bet you a fiver she would not go out with you and anyway she could be married." Andrew retorted.

"Leave it to me boys, the women can't resist me, a fiver it is then."

Alison looked at Sarah and shrugged her shoulders, "they are all the same."

"I cannot believe you lot. Have you any idea how demoralising it is for a women to be treated like this."

"Lighten up Sarah it is only a bit of fun," Andrew replied.

"I don't see it that way; she is a lovely person not a joke."

They realised that she seemed really upset,

"Come on Sarah, don't give us a row, and give us a hug instead. We had better go before the menace comes back," Jimmy ordered them.

They all left together with a see you tomorrow, as they left the ward.

Sister Brodie came to see that Sarah was fine and stayed for a little while.

"Fine looking brothers, you have got, they are all so tall, who's the one that was beside you sitting in the chair."

"That's Jimmy, the eldest of the boys, he is six feet, two inches tall, Andrew is the tallest at six feet three inches and Archie, he is the smallest, and just under six feet, and he is married."

"Fine looking men, every one of them," she was tidying the bed as she spoke.

"Jimmy not married then."

"No and he's not engaged or got a girlfriend either," Sarah laughed.

"An unclaimed treasure, just like me."

"You watch out, they have a 'Bet' on that you would not go out with Jimmy."

"Much am I worth."

"A fiver, they say."

"Well you and I will need to see that Jimmy does not lose any money, won't we, what does Jimmy work at Sarah?"

"He is a manager for the Shipbuilding Yard."

"Well that clinches it Sarah, he can't lose his money."

The Sister realised that something was wrong; Sarah eyes were full of tears." Come on, tell me about it?"

"That is why I am so upset, I was a 'Bet' but when I discovered it, I lost the place. I called him awful names and I would not speak to him. He tried but I did not give him a chance. She told the sister all about Gordon, how he did not know about the baby and that now she could not tell him."

Taking Sarah's hand the Sister asked her" Why not? "

"It would look as if I only wanted him to get me out of this pickle I am in."

"If he loves you he would want to help."

"If I lose the baby, I would always wonder if he came only out of duty."

"Right then, wait to see how things go, every day that passes your chances are better. If all goes well, then write to him and let him know you would like to speak to him. He will either come to see you or you will not hear. You will then know where you are.

I should not be advising you, it is not my job. Do not take life so serious Sarah. It will all work out in the end, it always does. I think you could do with some company. What if I asked to have you put in with the long-term patients? These women are in for most of their pregnancies, and the noise that comes from that ward is unbelievable. They all have different reasons for being in for a few months, they get to know each other, and maybe you could do with some company."

"Surely I will get out if all goes well."

"The doctor is the one who knows, I do not. Do not go against advice Sarah if you want the baby."

"When I knew I was pregnant I thought I would have the baby adopted and then when I knew I could lose the baby, I now want to keep it. I want the baby whether I am on my own or not."

"You are all upset, you are lucky you have a great family. You will never be on your own."

"I know I am lucky but I still feel so alone, I have always felt lonely. I watch other people being happy and wish it was me."

"I know what you mean; I feel that kind of loneliness sometimes. I work in a busy hospital and have made friends with many of my colleagues. Sometimes when I go home at night and shut the door that is when I feel the loneliness. I have waited for Mr. Right but he does not seem to be around but you never know. Now about this 'Bet', let's you and I put our heads together. If he asks me out I will make him work for his fiver. How long are they staying?"

"They all go back tomorrow night."

"Well we will wait and see what time brings."

"How are you so free and not worried?"

"In my work Sarah, a date is not a worry, lighten up for your own sake, be calmer, and take life as it comes. I am going to tuck you up and you will get a good sleep. I will see you tomorrow."

The boys came back on Sunday as boisterous as always, one look from Sister Brodie and they all calmed down.

"What a night I have had, sleeping with Andrew, ever shared your bed with a Giant. His feet were everywhere."

"You should have taken the settee Jimmy."

"Archie grabbed it first; anyway I am only one inch taller than you, so less of the giant."

"Excuse me please, would you all leave while I attend to Miss Shaw."

They all turned from the bed, a young doctor was standing at the door, a lovely girl.

"I do not feel well doctor," Andrew said.

"Well I tell you what, you wait outside and I will have a male nurse help you out."

"Coward, I thought women wanted equality and here you are trying to shelve your responsibility. Would I not be experience for you?"

"Not the kind you have in mind, I eat little boys like you for my tea. Shove off Lothario.

My patient's blood pressure will be up. "

"I don't think we are worried about your patient's blood pressure, are we?"

The three brothers all burst out laughing Andrew's remark.

The doctor walked to the door and called "Sister Brodie"

The three of them walked smartly out of the room.

Sarah was helpless laughing; she had never seen her brothers in action.

"Who is that cheeky monkey?"

"My brother, well one of them, he came up from London to see me."

"Good looking isn't he? Do not tell him I said that, he's trouble that one. Mind you a bit of trouble like that would not go amiss. We could all do with a bit trouble like that now and again, couldn't we?

Let me examine you and then we will let that lot in."

After she examined Sarah she told her,

"Everything looks fine today, good, I will see you later.

The boys were allowed to return to see Sarah.

"You lot behave yourself or I will get thrown out of here."

They all left later to go back home, telling her not to worry and to keep an eye on that Sister and Doctor.

The next day Sarah saw the Consultant who told her that he was pleased and if they had another week the same it looked as if they could be more hopeful.

"Will I have to be in another week?"

"I think you should prepare yourself for a long stay. I would like to keep you in until the baby is born; this is your baby's best chance. Sister Brodie has suggested that you move into another ward. It would maybe better for you. I will speak to you again later on in the week."

Sarah was desolate; she was to be in hospital for all of the pregnancy. The Sister came and had her moved that morning. She went into a ward with five other women. In this ward Sarah learned to laugh at life and laugh a lot she did, six women and all from different walks of life. One woman wore her poverty like a medal, proud that she could manage on so little. So unlike Sarah, who had always been ashamed of her poverty, she learned that she did not cause it, she coped with it. The woman who had everything but the baby she and her husband so wanted. The teenager, whose parents, had such great hopes for her future, and now having to cope with a baby. The other two women expecting twins, and like Sarah because they were older needed rest. It surprised Sarah that such a mix of women could live together and never a cross word between them. They were all there for each other with every little crisis that came their way. As time passed she came to know them all very well and she was surprised at how the time passed.

She had written to Lizzie, and she and Davie came to see her, Lizzie gave her a hug and said,

"You should have told me, I would help you, and you should have known that.

"Oh Lizzie, I know you would have but I was all mixed up, and so ashamed."

"Don't worry Sarah, it will all work out, the way it did for me. Does he know?"

Sarah shook her head, "No not yet but when I am sure I will let him know and we will see what happens then."

"Is he nice, and leaning forward whispered in her ear, "did the earth move?"

"No, it bloody well exploded." They both laughed till the tears were running down both faces.

"You two behave yourselves, David wants to see you, he's waiting outside."

"Let him come in, he is such a lovely boy, I am so happy for you both, you know that, don't you."

"I know Sarah, what will you do now. Are you coming back to Greenock?"

"No, the boys are going to clear out the house and hand in the keys. I have also resigned from the Surgery, and in time I will work and stay in Edinburgh. I will write to Dr. Small, He has been so very good to me over the years; I will just have to see how it all works out. It looks as if I might have this baby after all. Alison is looking for a place for me but it is a bit early to make definite plans. I will be going to see Jimmy from time to time so we will still be in touch."

They left and promised to come and see her again.

Alison came that evening; she was visiting every other day. She found Sarah to be so much better of being in a ward with company. There was always some tale to tell about life in hospital. Sarah was resigned now to the fact that she would stay in hospital till the baby was born.

"I think it is time I wrote to Gordon and we will leave it up to him."

"You write a letter saying that you would like to see him. I will put the letter on his desk and we then know that he received it."

She wrote, Dear Gordon, I would like to see you to clear up any misunderstanding, if you would like to see me, please speak to Alison. Love Sarah.

Alison took the letter away with her and when she went to the office the next morning she left the letter on his desk. She waited for him to speak to her but he never did.

Sarah was devastated when she realised that he would not be coming to see her. This time she accepted it was over. She often wished she had spoken earlier but it was too late. She herself was to blame.

Chapter 18

Christmas and New Year came and went. The boys were regular visitors, coming to see her every month. Jimmy came very often, as he was very interested in Sister Brodie who he now called Nancy. They had been out together a few times after he had visited Sarah.

January and February eventually passed and Sarah found herself in March awaiting the birth of her baby.

Alison had found a small flat in Leith Walk. It was very small but near the shops and the Princess Street Park was nearby. Archie had decorated the flat, and Anne came through for a week to help Alison with finding furniture. Anne also loved Edinburgh and she told Sarah that they would be constant visitors. Andrew came unexpectedly one day; he was in Edinburgh on business for his firm. He told her that Nancy had introduced him to 'the doctor', you remember her, and they had been out for a drink. I think you will be seeing a bit more of me than you thought. How it was Sarah, who had brought them all together. He had left money with Alison for a pram and a cot for the baby whenever she was ready. The boys and Alison had decided, if Sarah agreed, that the four of them would be the baby's godparents and they would all help bring up her baby.

After he had left Sarah felt so lonely, it was working out for them all and she was glad but somehow it made her own loneliness more hurtful.

The ward Sister wakened Alison, through the night in late March, asking her to come to the hospital as Sarah had gone into Labour.

When Alison arrived she was taken into the office by the doctor and told that they had to operate and deliver the baby by caesarean section. There was a problem when the baby was delivered, with bleeding. Sarah was not at all well and they felt that the family should know. The baby a boy was very well and healthy.

Next morning found the four of them waiting in the hospital; they had all arrived as soon as possible.

"I am going to kill him. He has never even shown any consideration. I am going to see him." Archie was adamant.

"This is not all his fault, he took a 'Bet' to get her to go out and she can't forgive him for it. You have done the same thing yourself." Alison shouted.

"Keep calm, this is not helping Sarah." Jimmy was walking back and forward.

Andrew was silent with his head in his hands.

Early afternoon the Surgeon came and spoke to them.

"Your sister has had a very bad time, to stop the bleeding I have had to operate; I am as confidant as I can be that she will now recover."

From somewhere Sarah floated back, she felt so relaxed,

"Sarah, come on Sarah, she heard the nurse call her name. She struggled to open her eyes and she smiled at them all and then drifted off to sleep again.

Later on that day Sarah fully wakened and the nurse brought her son to her. She was so happy, as she looked at her son she promised him, 'I will take good care of you."

"Nine pound baby boy, didn't you do well. Your family is all here and will be back soon. I have sent them all for a cup of tea."

They all came to see her and to see the baby.

"You all look dreadful, have you not had any sleep, what are you all here for today?"

She had no idea she had been so ill.

Sarah recovered well and was ready to go home two weeks later.

Alison had come with Nancy, who was not on duty. They took Sarah to her flat and helped her to get settled. A new flat, a new baby, a new life, it was all organised for her and she was grateful to them all. The flat was very small but very nice. Archie and Anne had worked hard. Alison decided that she would stay with Sarah for two weeks to help her. Alison's year in the firm's flat was now over and Alison would need to find another flat soon. She had been told that there was no urgency at the moment and to take her time over finding somewhere else to stay.

Sarah felt so strange after being in the hospital for so long and a bit lost in what to do next.

Nancy was a regular visitor and seemed to be coming one of the family, as she had become Jimmy's girlfriend and Jimmy was a regular weekend visitor to Edinburgh.

"I think you should have a rest it must seem all so strange. I will stay with you, as Alison has to go back to the office, I will see to the baby. Right what are you going to call him?

You cannot hedge this any longer, and we cannot call him baby. Come on spill the beans."

"His name is Gordon Ross Shaw, I did not want to name him in the hospital but Alison has registered the birth for me."

"He has his father's name then, do you think you should call him that?"

"It is all he will ever have of his father and he will be known as Gordon Shaw. Nobody will connect the name I am sure. He lives in a different world."

"I never thought it would come to this Sarah, I was so sure he would have been here for you. I can hardly look at him. When my two years is over with the firm I will move on. I will not stay and work for him. "Alison said dejectedly

"Do not jeopardise your career, I do not have any bad feeling now. I must take more than half of the blame; nobody knows that better than you. I do not feel bad about myself being a single mother now. The Fat Clan taught me that."

"They were some crowd that, I do not know why these babies were not all born laughing. Their mothers were something else. At midnight we were telling them all to stop talking and go to sleep. Every baby a boy, did you know that?"

"Yes we are all going to meet up once a month when the babies are three months old. I have made good friends and I have a great family. In time I will look for work and will support my son and myself. I am looking forward now to my life."

"How do you feel about not getting to University or College now?" Alison wanted to know.

"I obviously was never meant to get there, it does not seem important now."

"We have decided that we will all meet up in two weeks' time, the boys want to see you regularly and we will make arrangements to keep in touch. Now you off to bed and Alison off to work."

Sarah and Alison laughed; Sister Brodie was back on duty.

Sarah regained her health and her figure very quickly and the baby was doing very well. The flat was lovely but when the pram and cot came in it was even smaller. It did not matter Sarah loved it. Life had settled down and she started to take the baby out, through the baby she met her neighbours who had the same flat as herself on the top floor.

The flats were over shops and had been modernised inside, outside the building had been kept the same, for tradition. The flat was so convenient for the shops and the Park, which Sarah was never out of. She pushed baby's pram through the park on a daily walk unless it was very wet or windy. Summer was coming and she looked forward to that. Alison was a very regular visitor as was Nancy. Sarah did not visit Alison often, as she stayed away from that end of the City. There was no point in looking back now.

Sarah and Alison had a 'Bet' on how long it would take Jimmy to propose, if Nancy would leave her career and marry him or would he come to Edinburgh. They often laughed at the 'Bet' now.

"Do you remember how affronted I was? I was a silly fool."

"No, you just were not wise with men. You are feeling better about it now. Would you change anything if you could?"

"Yes I would change myself, never my son or the time I spent with Gordon. I am not concerned now about being so lonely. I know I have all of you but you know what I mean, how about you and Ian?"

"Oh he's just like one of my brothers. You know I think we are marked because of them. Think on it, we know all the football teams, all the slang words. We see jokes from a male point of view. I remember being disappointed when I discovered that I was not a boy, do you remember that."

"Yes you screamed, you said I never told you, you were such a tomboy Alison. Every time I looked out of the window at you, if you were not walking on your hands you were hanging upside down or playing football."

"That's what I mean we missed out on not being cute. Knowing how to bat your eyes, how to sigh at the right time and how to pout. If I were to do any of these when I am out with Ian, he would tell me to take keeping the tablets till I was better. By the way, Pouting Pamela has been around and he seems to be dodging her."

As soon as she said it Alison wished she had not, a look came over Sarah's face.

"Maybe he is better with someone like her, someone who does not think for themselves."

Alison knew then that all the talk of being free of him was all a mask. Many times Alison wished that she had never warned Sarah about Gordon, maybe it would have ended differently and then again, he showed his true self when he did not reply to her letter. He very seldom spoke to Alison now, only over work, and even then she always tried to avoid him.

She had made up her mind to move after her two years were over. Deep down she blamed herself for how badly everything had turned out. If she had never said anything it maybe would be all so different and then again she had to remember that, he never answered the letter that she had left on his desk.

Sarah was pushing the pram along Princess Street and she was in a hurry, she was making for the bookshop. She did not like to be around Princess Street at lunchtime or five o'clock. These were the times that she had met him before, it was now four o'clock and she wanted to buy a book for Andrew's birthday. She had taken the baby to the park and because it was a lovely day had stayed longer. The baby was lying on his back trying to catch his foot. He was a lovely child, his hair was very dark like his mother and he was going to be tall like his father, if the length of his legs were anything to go by. She was so proud of him, they had both settled down after a few restless weeks and he now slept most of the night. This was Sarah's time, when she would knit, sew or read, it was also the lonely time, and she never allowed herself to dwell on the lonely time.

The family had been so good to her that they had to know that she was happy.

She had arrived at the bookshop and she left the baby in his pram outside the shop and quickly bought her book. When she went to pay for the book, the girl remembered her from the time that she had helped her with the French people.

"How are you, I have not seen you for a while."

"No, I have been in hospital for a long time."

"Are you well now?"

"Yes thank you, I am fine now."

I would like to speak to you, have you time just now."

"I have left the baby outside in his pram."

"Bring the pram in, come through to the back; I would really like to speak to you."

Sarah went and brought the pram into the shop, wondering what the girl wanted.

"Through here, the baby is lovely, how old is he?"

"Over four months now, he is why I was in hospital so long."

"We are going to take on another assistant part-time only at the moment. I was telling the manager how you helped me out with the French tourists. He thinks it would be a good idea to have someone that can speak another language. Would you be interested in a part-time position?"

"Yes I would love it but the baby is still too young to leave with a stranger, if he was a year old I would jump at the chance and try and find a baby sitter, thanks anyway for asking me. It makes me feel good to think that I will be able to get work later on."

"You leave it with me and I will let the manager know, there could be something when you are ready."

As she pushed the pram along the busy street trying to avoid people, she was stopped suddenly.

"Hello Sarah, how are you?"

She turned and as she turned, she knew it was him.

"Hello Gordon, I am fine, thank you, and you?"

She was shaking but she would face him, this had to happen one day.

"Fine thanks, here on holiday again?"

"No, I am living here now; I never really went back other than to close up my home. I am sorry but I must go. I have to get the baby back as they will be waiting for him."

"Are you baby-sitting then?"

"Oh you know how it is Gordon, you oblige someone, and before you know where you are, you are being used. Then that's just me, and no one knows that better than you, must dash, bye."

He watched her as she hurried away and thought, he felt as if she had slapped him, for that was what it had felt like, no, more a kick. He could not believe that she had been living here all this time and he had never known.

Where did she work? How did she pass her time? Did she have someone else in her life now? She looked very pale, looked thinner too. Was she looking after herself? One thing was sure she was still mad at him; did that mean she still cared?

She pushed the pram away as fast as she could because her legs were shaking. She was so sure she could handle meeting him again, but she could not. Why did she say such a stupid thing to him, why did she behave like that? She knew why, she had not got over him and she wondered if she ever would get over him? He was looking a bit gaunt and thinner than she remembered. She hoped he was well; he did look a bit down.

She was glad she was nearly home because she wanted to phone Alison at her office. There was a phone box that she used at the corner of her street, she got through very quickly.

"Hello Alison sorry to bother you at the office. Could you find out if anyone knows of a nursery, where I could leave Gordon, for three afternoons a week? I have been offered work at the Bookshop. They are looking for someone who can speak another language. I would love it, it would get me into other company and the money would be great."

"Are you okay? You sound excited, I will ask around the office. The girls here know of so many things in Edinburgh."

"Thanks Alison, it would be good if I could get something and it is in the Bookshop that I use, so it is near to home. I was thinking of walking over to see you some night, when will you be in?"

"I have no nights out planned this week at all, why not walk over on Friday evening and we will have something to eat together."

"Sounds great, thanks, I won't keep you any longer, see you soon."

"Are you sure you are fine Sarah. How is Gordon, sleeping any better? That's great, you take care now, see you soon."

When Alison replaced the receiver and swung round in her chair, back to her desk, it was to find Gordon Ross standing there at her door.

"Do you have the file ready for 'Black versus Black 'please?"

"Yes, I should have left it on your desk, sorry."

Alison wondered if he had heard her, no, she did not think so.

Gordon Ross had heard most of the conversation. Who was Gordon, she was obviously speaking to Sarah. Whoever he was it appeared to be good that he was sleeping better. As he walked through to his office he was still wondering about the conversation. He was still upset by Sarah's remarks from earlier on. He could not get her out of his head at all. He started to work and still she came back to him, it might be over for her but it was not over for him and he did not think it ever would be. He suddenly realised who Gordon might be. The baby, could that be it? Surely the baby wasn't hers, if it was why Gordon? The realisation that the baby could be his dawned on him very slowly and he called himself a stupid fool. You might have a legal brain but you are so slow at times.

Now what was the conversation again? 'Walk over on Friday night and we will have something to eat together. Well I will just have to bump into her again. Friday evening found him walking back and forward near Alison's flat.

Sarah fed her son before she walked over to Alison's and settled him on his pram. This was the first time she had gone to Alison's, as she was afraid that she could meet him. It did not matter now if she did, she could not hide forever. He probably did not even think about her now anyway.

It was a lovely night and she enjoyed being out even for a short time. As she came near to where Alison's flat was she heard her name being called, she turned to find Gordon hurrying after her.

"Hello again, I thought it was you. Babysitting again, my you are a glutton for punishment."

"I enjoy walking the baby for my friend."

"I am going this way, I will walk with you, I assume you are going to see Alison."

"What makes you think I want to walk with you?" Sarah retorted.

"Why would you not want to walk with me, can we not be friends even for old times' sake. What is the baby called?"

"Helen."

"Helen, I thought it was a boy."

"What made you think that?"

"Looks like a boy but then what do I know about babies?"

"All babies look the same when they are sleeping."

"How old is Helen?"

"Must be coming up for nine months now, not really sure."

"Don't you know the baby's age?"

"Why are you questioning me, I will ask the mother to let you know, would that please you?"

"It would please me if you would let me explain about the 'Bet'"

Sarah looked at him, really looked at him. As she stared into his eyes she felt herself shaking again.

"What is the point of us going down that road again when you never even answered," she was interrupted by Alison calling on her.

"Sarah, you are walking past the door, here let me help." Alison did not speak to Gordon Ross, just nodded.

"Sorry I had to bring the baby but I was asked to watch her at short notice." Turning to Gordon she said.

"Goodnight then."

They left him standing on the pavement watching them.

When they were in the flat Alison asked,

"How did you meet him, Sarah?"

"He caught up with me, that is the second time I have met him this week. He wanted to know what the baby was called, I told him Helen."

"I wondered why you said that you were asked to watch her. He should know Sarah that he has a son, I have always said that."

"I know, I know that, but he did not want anything to do with me then and it is too late now. I am not up to playing his games anymore."

"Are you still so tired?"

"Yes I am still tired but I feel better and not so depressed since I was asked about the work at the Bookshop."

"I may have a solution for you. One of the typist's aunts is looking for a small job, just a few hours a week. She would maybe be prepared to baby-sit for you. She has given me her address and if you are interested she will arrange a meeting for you both. What bothers me is, are you well enough to work?"

"It would be like a hobby to me, you know how I like books and it is only three hours in the afternoons. I would enjoy the company as well. Some days are very long and lonely. I would enjoy the work but only if the lady is dependable. Yes, arrange a meeting and we will take it from there."

Gordon Ross had watched them as they went into the flat; once they were inside he turned and went back to where he had left his car.

He did not believe that the baby was a girl. He was sure the last time he spoke to Sarah the baby was referred to as a boy, maybe he had made a mistake. He did not know what to do next; if the baby was nine months old then it could not be his child. He wondered about what she was going to say, what answer was she looking for? He was miserable, there was no other way he could describe his life since he had lost her.

He worked harder now than he had ever worked. He put all his energy into the firm. He now did not care about being the Senior Partner. Nothing was the same since he had lost her. He had only known her two weeks and yet he felt as if he had known her all his life. At weekends he would visit his mother and father, something they could not understand, as he had never been such a constant visitor before. He would drop in every week for a quick visit but he was now spending most weekends with them. A night out with any of the girls was of no interest any more. Even less was a night out with his colleagues. He had kept hoping they could get back to where they were, but she would never forgive him. He took all of the blame. He had wanted to be one of the lads, and had never really enjoyed the role. It was only after he met her that he realised what he wanted. He was clever, yes he knew that, but only in his work, he had been a fool everywhere else. He was forty-two years old now and going nowhere, all he could do was pretend he was happy. He wondered if she was living at Alison's.

Next morning at the office he made a point of speaking to Alison. It was obvious that she did not want to speak to him about anything other than work.

"Good morning Alison, I bumped into Sarah the other day, she seems well."

He did not expect what came next. She drew him one scathing look,

"Don't you even try to go down that road with me, have you not done enough damage. Bored with your life at the moment, looking for another little bit of excitement."

They had an audience from other members of the staff; he turned and went into his office.

"Cool it Alison," Ian advised, remember who he is."

"I don't care; I won't be staying round long."

"What do you mean?"

She turned and went into her office. He followed her and closed the door behind him.

"What did you mean?"

"I will not work here after my two years are up."

"Were you not going to tell me? I hoped we would be working together. I hoped that we would both be offered a position here, with a possible partnership in the future. I thought we had a future."

"Well if you thought that, you never discussed it with me. Good old Alison, one of the boys, that is how you see me."

"You are impossible when you are in this mood. The sooner you live your own life, the better, and let Sarah sort her own problems out."

He turned and left her office, what on earth did she mean. They enjoyed working together, they went out together, she liked the rugby and going to the pub afterwards. She bought tickets for the football, what on earth did she mean. This affair of her aunt's with the boss, to which he was sworn to secrecy, seemed to be the only interest she had other than the rugby or football, women, who understands them, certainly not me, he thought.

He was working with Gordon Ross this morning and not looking forward to it. You had to be on your toes with him, he stood no nonsense if you had not done your work to his expectations. He knocked the door before he went in to find Gordon Ross staring into space. They worked together for nearly three hours and when they were finished, he gathered up his files and as he left the office he said,

"I never said this, but she is in the Park most afternoons with the boy."

The door closed and Gordon Ross sat staring at it, what a strange thing to say and then he realised what he meant, he meant Sarah. Sarah was in the Park most afternoons with the boy. She must look after that baby and take it to the park. So, it was a boy.

He went out into Ian's office, but he was not there. He saw him standing at the reception and when he looked at him, he nodded back, as if to indicate, yes I did say that.

It took into the middle of August for Gordon Ross to hit the right time, to see Sarah in the Park. He changed his lunch hour if he was not at Court and took to walking in the Park.

If the weather was nice she seemed to take the baby onto the grass by the Bandstand. She would be sitting on the grass playing with the baby. Other days she would be sitting on a bench on the path. He wondered about the baby, no, it could not be hers. Why not, he reasoned with himself. She could have met someone else. He watched her lying, face down on the grass and the baby was trying to crawl to her. How she laughed. She lifted the baby and held it close. He decided she was not baby-sitting, no, this baby could be hers. Could this baby be his, no, not if it was nine months old? She could have met someone else. She must have met someone else. She did not waste any time then after him. How old was the baby? He guessed maybe five or six months old, looked similar in size to one of the Firm's secretary's babies. He could not cope with his emotions, because he thought that this baby could be his. He felt sick, he felt elated and he had to know. He crossed over the grass to where she was. She must have seen him coming because she lifted the baby and was putting the baby in the pram when he reached her.

"Hello there I thought it was you, how are you. Baby-sitting again?"

"Yes I am, just for a few hours, helping out. I must hurry I am always late."
She started to push the pram over the grass and it was slow to move.

"Here let me help you till you get to the path."

"This is a sight you better not let your friends see." She spoke sarcastically.

"Only helping a lady in distress," he replied quickly.

"Let me assure you I am not in distress."

Back came is quick reply, "No you would never be, you are never wrong, a great one for the truth, but you do not want to hear the truth."

They had reached the path; she walked away very quickly and did not look back.

He was angry with himself, why did he say these things to her. He wanted to shake her, he wanted to love her and he wanted her back. Leave the baby out of it, it could be that she was babysitting but the seed he had sown in his mind would not go away.

Chapter 19

The weekend found him back at his parent's home, his parents were sitting in the garden reading, and it was a lovely afternoon. His father turned to his mother, "Has he said anything to you yet? I mean he always talked you."

"No, but something is wrong and has been for well over a year now. He is not happy, where is he just now?"

"Cutting back that hedge for me, at the bottom of the garden, it's a surprise that he suddenly likes gardening"

"Will you not ask him what's wrong?"

"No, he will tell us if he wants to. Time he was married anyway."

"What do you mean; he has not got a girlfriend just now."

"No but it is time he was married, let's face it, he has been happy long enough."

"Is that what you think then, have you been miserable for the past forty seven years."

"Yes absolutely miserable, I don't know how I survive."

"Anymore talk like that and you won't survive much longer, why don't you talk to him, kind of man to man, he might tell you what's wrong. "

"You know that he will talk to you sooner than me."

"That is just an excuse and you are only shelving your responsibilities as a father."

"Look, Gordon will wonder what is wrong with me, do you remember the conversation when he was a teenager, going with his school to France. When you made me speak to him about women, do you remember? I told him, your mother wants me to speak with you about sex and girls and he asked me, well Dad, what would you like to know?"

"I'm going to talk to him, he is so unhappy."

"Make some coffee first would you?"

"No, not after you insulting me", she threw back at him." She went and made coffee anyway and gave him a cup, and took two cups down to where her son was working.

"Would you like some coffee, Gordon?"

"Thanks, yes. They sat side by side on the wooden bench.

"How is your work these days, still as busy as ever?"

"Yes, it's fine but."

"But what?"

"I am not so interested in it anymore, I like it but I have lost my ambition or drive, I just don't know. Nothing is right at the moment, nothing to do with work though."

"Girlfriend trouble, are you still seeing that girl called Pamela?"

"No, you would not want to know the mess I have made of things."

"Try me."

He looked at his mother and then looked away. After a while Gordon spoke.

"I met this girl, well this woman, she is ages with myself, must be well over a year ago now.

It was a bit of a joke to begin with but we got on so well. It was hard work chasing her and for the first time I was the one doing all the running. We had such a good time trying to get one over on the other. I only knew her for two weeks, we had a coffee together then a dinner and then I took her to the cottage."

"Our cottage, but you don't like it there Gordon!"

"I do now. We had a great weekend, I did not realise it at the time but I really love her." His voice broke at this point."

"Does she not love you; is this, what is wrong?"

"No, I think she did love me, but," he paused here, "I got involved with a 'Bet' over taking her out and she found out. She will not forgive me."

"Talk to her, make her listen."

"She does not belong to Edinburgh, she comes from Greenock and I thought she had returned to Greenock, I think she might be living here now, I have met her again. She will not give me a chance. It is not really as bad as it sounds; I made a date with her before the 'Bet' came into it. I did not ask her out for a 'Bet'"

"Stop making excuses for yourself Gordon, I told you all this running about would trip you up one day. Find her, try and start again, you could not be any more miserable than you are at present. You have nothing to lose, if you love her, swallow your pride."

"I don't know what to do, she has a baby, well I'm sure it is hers and," he looked straight at his mother, "I think the baby is mine."

"What! Do you mean to tell me that this girl has had a baby, where were you during her pregnancy? No wonder she will not talk to you."

"I have written to her, I phoned her, well that was over a year ago now, she would not speak to me then. I have practically been stalking her for a couple of weeks now, when I realised that she must be back. She does not even want to pass the time of day with me. You know she threw a pint of beer over me when she discovered that there was a 'Bet'

There I was sitting with beer running down my face, everyone looking at us."

"What do you mean 'us'?"

"I was with the boys from the office and she got us all with two mugs of beer, 'have a drink on me boys' she said as she threw it over the three of us. Have you any idea how I felt. If Mr. Grant had heard about any of this I could have lost the senior position. Fortunately he obviously had not heard. How could she, there I was sitting with my colleagues, how could she do that to me?"

"Good for her, I would have thrown a barrel at you."

"I went after her and tried to explain that she had got it all wrong, but no, she would not listen. She told me in no uncertain way what she thought of me, and it was not at all complimentary. I felt as if she had slapped my face, right in the middle of Princess Street."

His mother looked at him, "Good, you needed it. Let me get this right, you took her to the cottage and I take it you seduced her."

"No it was a mutual, it was two consenting adults," he paused again.

"Well," his mother demanded.

"She had never been with anyone before, and this is something you do not discuss with your mother, is it?"

"Too late Gordon, have you any idea how this girl feels, she goes with you for a weekend, she trusted you and then she discovered that it was all a joke among the boys"

"I lost the 'Bet', I told them she would have nothing to do with me. I bought the drinks because I lost. Why do you and Sarah believe that I would treat someone like that?"

"It is how it looks Gordon. Where did you see her last?"

"She takes the baby to the Park most afternoons."

"How do you know this?"

"One of my junior lawyers is friendly with her niece and he told me. Her niece works for me."

"Dear God Gordon, it is getting worse by the minute."

"I know, I know, I met her through her niece." He buried his head in his hands, "I have lost her and maybe my son as well."

"What does she look like, this girl?"

"She is very tall, maybe five foot ten or so, lovely dark hair, she keeps it short now, just because I said I liked it long, everything she does is to get back at me."

"Don't be silly, no woman does their hair to suit a man. Go on."

"Well she has the most beautiful eyes and she has a lovely voice, she speaks as if she has been very well educated. Why do you want to know what she looks like?"

"I will try and speak to her."

"No, No, do not do that."

"I cannot possibly make it any worse than you have and if you are right I want to see my grandchild, is it a Grandson or Granddaughter?"

"I think, in fact I am sure it is a boy, about five months old."

"Leave it like this and let me see what I can do. Give me a few days, I cannot just walk up and say, 'Hello, I'm Gordon's mother'. Give me some time, I will be very careful. Why don't you stay here tonight, you are all stressed out?"

"Please do not interfere, I am a grown man, I cannot have my mother intervene on my behalf."

"Oh come on, take off your barrister robes and do not be so pompous, stay here tonight."

"Now that is what she called me pompous, me pompous. I cannot believe that you both think I am pompous. No, I cannot stay, I keep hoping she might phone, I tried to speak to Alison, she bit my head off, and so I cannot approach her again.

It was Wednesday before Grace Ross spoke to Sarah. She had spotted her on Monday afternoon and smiled as she passed. Yes she was a lovely girl but surely must be a lot younger than Gordon had said. On Tuesday Sarah was sitting on the grass at the Bandstand playing with the baby, she sauntered over and as she approached her she smiled.

"I see you like this Park as much as I do."

"Yes, I love it here, it is a lovely day now, I thought earlier that it might rain and maybe we would not get out today."

"You enjoy it all you can then, I see you have got your hands full."

"Yes he's a rascal, aren't you," The baby giggled at her.

"Cheerio then I will get my walk in."

"Bye, wave bye bye, to the lady, she held up the baby's hand.

On Wednesday she could not see her and sat on a park bench just on the path. She was just about to give up when she came along pushing the pram." Hello again."

Sarah stopped, "oh hello."

Grace lifted her book and moved over on the bench; Sarah hesitated, and then sat down.

"I am late today; the baby did not sleep last night, now he is sleeping all day. I think he is teething, but he is only five months, I think it is a bit early for teething."

Grace looked at the sleeping child; he was lying on his back with his hands stretched out at each side of his head. She could not speak, he had to be Gordon's child and it brought memories flooding back.

"He is lovely, he is a credit to you, how old did you say?"

"Over five months now. I don't know what to do, should I waken him or not. If I waken him he will be cross, if I don't neither him nor I will sleep tonight." She laughed as she said this.

"I would let him sleep for a while and then waken him, keep him up a bit later tonight and maybe, just maybe you will both sleep. I used to try everything and anything; sometimes I would walk my pram round the neighbor-hood at night, because I felt that made him sleep. You are possibly right; he is just at that right age for teething. Speak nicely to your husband and maybe he will take over for tonight."

"I am on my own, I have a great family but they do not live in Edinburgh. I have a niece here, who has been a great help to me but she works and I really want to manage myself. I feel that I must not depend on my family so much."

"I admire you coping on your own; did you want it that way?"

"Not really, but it is a long story, and most of it is my fault."

"Can you not put it right?"

"He does not want to know" Sarah spoke dejectedly, "I should have realised, never once did he say he loved me."

"Are you sure, what makes you think that? A lovely girl like you and a beautiful baby, any father would be proud of you both."

"I am sure, I wrote to him and he did not answer." Her eyes filled up with tears.

"I am sorry my dear I do not wish to upset you but maybe he did not get the letter."

"No, he got it; I had it put on his desk at work that is how I know he got it."

The tears were running down her face now, Grace felt dreadful.

"Would you like to walk, let me come with you and we will just walk."

"Yes please, I am sorry about this, you must be embarrassed. Don't worry about me I cry easily. I must apologise for giving you my problems. I am alone and sometimes when I have not spoken to anyone for a time, I just feel lonely and sorry for myself. I should be more grateful, my family has been very supportive but I cannot talk to them about him, as I have said, I cry easily."

They walked in silence for a while,

"Are you feeling better now?"

"Yes, thank you for listening to me for I have no one to talk to about him."

They sat down on another park bench at the end of the Park.

"Has he tried to get in touch with you since the baby was born?"

No, you see I was in hospital for all of the nine months, I threatened a miscarriage and I was well over three months before they would say that I could possibly have the baby."

"What hospital were you in?"

"The Edinburgh Maternity, they were so very good to me there. I wrote to him before the baby was born and asked him to speak to me, my niece works for him and she could have told him where I was. I never heard from him. He does not know about the baby, I feel I am wrong there, he should know he has a lovely son, but it would look as if I was trying to trap him. He does not want me now or he would have answered my letter. I have met him twice recently but he thinks I am babysitting for someone else, I tried to give him that impression."

"Do not worry your head anymore about this, do you know something, you have met your fairy godmother today."

"If only, how I wish, oh how I wish. Sarah sat staring at her hands then she shrugged her shoulders. "I have a great family but."

"You want him more; you must love him very much."

Again Sarah stared at her hands, this time she nodded.

"Everything will work out soon, you mark my words. I had better get home, I have a grouchy husband at home who appears to need watered and fed at regular intervals. Cannot make a cup of tea for himself. Sometimes when I look at him it is hard to remember that we had a passionate love affair."

Sarah laughed out loud, "I am so glad I met you and I am sorry about giving you my problems, I don't speak to many people, I am sorry." Sarah spread her hands out to emphasise, "this is one of my bad days, sorry."

"Now do not worry so much, I will see you very soon."

She could not get to Gordon quick enough.

Sarah watched her walk away and thought it must be nice to have a mother like that. She wakened her son and as she suspected he cried all the way home.

Grace Ross took the bus to her son's house and put a note through the door, 'come over as soon as you can, Mum'.

Gordon arrived at nine o'clock that night and found his father in the Lounge, reading.

"You are late tonight visiting Gordon, everything fine."

"Yes, I got a note from Mum, she wants to see me, where is she?"

"About somewhere, maybe she is in the garden, she likes to sit there at night for a while.

As he went out to the garden his mother was coming in.

"You got my note then?"

"Yes, can I have something to eat; I have not had any dinner."

"Sit down and I will get you something. I will tell you all about it in a minute.

She made coffee and found some baked ham and salad for him, cut fresh bread,

"Eat that, you will make yourself ill not eating properly." She poured two coffees and sat opposite him.

"Well I have met your Sarah and she is lovely. I am sure the child is yours, he is so very like you but his hair is much darker.

"We got talking and after much coaxing she told me a bit about herself. How she was on her own with the baby, because its father did not want to know."

"That's not true."

"Eat and do not interrupt. She wrote a letter to the baby's father before the baby was born and had the letter put on his desk at work. She said in the letter that she would like to speak to him and to get in touch through her niece. She was in," and his mother hesitated here, to emphasize her next words, "Edinburgh Maternity Hospital for over nine months, have you any idea what that girl has been through."

"I never got a letter, that means that she had never left Edinburgh. I will get to the bottom of this, I am going to see her now, and do you know where she lives?"

"Do not go tonight, it is too late, the baby is not sleeping and she is hoping they both sleep tonight. Get to the bottom of why you did not get the letter. From what I know of her, and I have only just met her, she seems a very honest person. She must have written a letter. You can then go and see her, maybe now the niece will help you. This girl is so low that she could do with some romancing; you know something over the top, something to make her feel better about herself. You have stripped her off her dignity and her self-confidence; well that is how she sees it. Put her straight and do not give up until she knows the truth, because she does love you"

"Does she? How do you know?"

"She told me that she loves the baby's father, that's how I know."

She watched the relief wash over her son's face, "sort it Gordon tomorrow before it is too late."

Gordon Ross was furious, where was the letter?

He barged into the office late because he could not sleep and then when he did sleep, he overslept.

He stopped at Reception.

"Can I see you in my office now?"

He barged through to his office and threw himself down in his chair and scowled at the Receptionist.

"Tell me about the mail procedure in here, what happens to it?"

"I sort out all the mail and then give it to the relevant people."

"Ask Alison Shaw if she would come into my office, now."

He waited for her and when she came in, she stood and looked at him.

"Did you ever put a personal letter from Sarah on this desk?"

"Yes, I did."

"Sit down, Alison when was that, can you remember when that was."

"Yes very clearly, it was the first week in December."

"Ask Christine to come in here, you please stay."

She left and returned with his secretary,

"Sit down Christine, I want you to tell me if you ever got a personal letter for me, it was left on my desk, it was early December."

There was silence and she appeared flustered.

"Think about it and tell me about it, if you value your position in this office, tell me the truth."

"There was a letter one morning, but I left it for you with John Morgan. I brought the mail in as usual to your office. I sit here and open it all. I put the mail on top of the letter and started to go through them. I was opening them when he came in, and he was clowning about, asking me to go out, well you know what like he is. Anyway I did not realise that it was personal, but it was marked personal. I only realised this after I had opened the letter. I was worried about how you would react when you discovered that I had opened your letter. It was a mistake; I did not mean to open it. John Morgan saw I was upset and told me not to worry, he took the letter and he said that he would explain it to you. He felt it was a much his fault as mine. I was really worried about it because you have been so," she hesitated here.

"Well," he demanded.

"Very difficult of late, it was a long time ago now."

"Yes Christine, it was over nine months ago and you have made my life sheer hell because of it. You are my secretary, supposed to be looking after everything for me. I don't care how difficult I appeared to be. You should have come to me yourself."

His secretary was now crying,

"I am sorry Mr. Ross; I really thought that John Morgan would have given you the letter."

"Right, that's all just now."

She left the office and there was still silence, Alison said nothing, she sat and watched him.

"Will you now put in a good word for me and see if Sarah will speak to me. Or better still will you give me her address."

He left Alison sitting there and went to find John Morgan. He was sitting in his office,

"I have a bit of news I would like to share with you, see me in the Store room, will you?"

"What have you been up to," he laughed.

They both strode through to the Store room at the back of the office. As soon as they were inside, Gordon Ross grabbed him by his shirt and asked him,

"What the hell do you think you are doing interfering with my personal mail?"

"What are you talking about?"

They were now shouting at each other.

"The letter that you took from my secretary to give to me months ago."

"That letter, the one from that bitch, I tore it up, it was payback time for her."

All they heard in the outer office was a crash; Gordon Ross came out and shouted,

"Somebody get me a coffee."

When he sat down, Alison had left Sarah's address on his desk

Sarah wakened to the door being knocked very hard; she looked at her son who was happily talking to the cot bars. She heard the door again and shouted.

"Coming, coming." Who could it be?

Alison stood there, face beaming all over.

"Have I got news for you?"

"What's wrong Alison, should you not be at your office?"

"I have been at the office and Gordon Ross has left the Wimp with a black eye. He never got the letter that I left on his desk. The one you wrote to him asking him to speak to you.

"What happened?"

"That apology for a man John Morgan took it, and never gave to him. There has been one awful to do. I am not sure but I think he has hit him and he has your address."

"How did he get it?"

"I gave it to him; he will possibly see you soon. I do not know if he is in Court today, but I am in no doubt that he will be knocking at your door."

"What will I do?"

"Listen to him Sarah, and stop pretending that you are so happy. He has a right to know his child. Sort it out, please."

Sarah made two coffees, the baby was happy playing in the cot, and so she decided to leave him.

"Drink this, you looked all stressed out. How is Ian?"

"I don't know," she answered exasperated," he has been working at one of the other offices last week. I have not seen him today. I am just one of the boys to him; I am fed up right now."

"Do you like him?"

"Yes, but how would I really know, his romantic evening is, 'what did you think of that goal?' or did you read about this sportsman? He is making me miserable."

Sarah put her arms around her, and gave her a hug,

"You need some tender loving care. Don't we all."

They laughed at each other.

"I had better get back to the office, I am supposed to be at work, I skipped out because I had to see you."

"I will let you know what happens."

The baby started crying at this point, they went and lifted him out of his cot, and played with him for a minute.

After Alison left Sarah washed the baby and fed him, dressed him and left him strapped in his pram. She had a bath and washed her hair. Decided what to wear, tidied up the house and waited. He had not come by lunchtime, so she took her son to the Park.

It was a dull day with the sun trying to come through the clouds, she kept walking and then she went to the shops for some groceries. She had brought the baby's feed with her and went back into the park and sat till she had fed him. He drifted off into his afternoon nap and she sat reading, but she could not concentrate on her book

Would he come to see her? What would she do if he didn't come? How did he not get her letter? She did not know whether to go home and wait or just let him find her. Why should she make it easy for him now? No, she decided, she would not make it easy for him. It had started to rain so she took shelter under a tree near the bandstand and pulled the pram in beside her. Pulled the hood up and put on the apron, the baby had only started to sit up by himself and was happily playing with splashes on the pram apron. She would wait till the rain stopped and then go home. It started to rain much heavier and as the rain was now dripping through the tree, she decided to wait a little longer, one way or another she would be wet right through. She did not know what to do, should she go back and patiently wait for him; she decided to shelter a little longer. If the rain did not ease off she would just walk home through the rain. What if he had been? What should she do? After all she had been through; he could just come and find her and then, what if he did not come. She dithered between one decision and the other meanwhile the rain had stopped and a blink of sunshine was coming through the clouds, so she decided to walk home.

Chapter 20

Gordon Ross could not get through his day quickly enough. He had a lot to do and it was four o'clock before he was free. He went and bought a bouquet of roses and then went looking for a toyshop and bought a Teddy Bear. He was feeling nervous and yet excited, he had tried to see Alison before he left the office, and no one could find her. He made his way to the address that Alison had left on his desk; there was no one at home. He waited for over an hour and then decided to try the Park. He left the bouquet and Teddy Bear at the door and made his way along to the Park.

As he went into the Park it started to rain, he could not see anyone other than those hurrying out of the rain. It had now turned into heavy rain and he was getting really wet. It made him remember the day at the beach when they had got really soaked, and they had gone into the sea with their bare feet. If he could get back to that day and change things he would, but he could not. There was no sign of anyone with a pram and he turned to walk back along the path when he saw her under the tree near the bandstand. He was sure it was Sarah and started to walk across the grass towards her. She seemed to look towards him and then turned the pram round; surely she was not going to walk away again. He then realised that she had turned the baby round to see him coming. She started walking towards him and he hurried towards her. She stopped suddenly and looked back at the baby and then turned to look at him. They were staring at each other and as he stepped forward, his foot slipped on the wet grass. He tried to get his balance but he slithered on and ended up, flat on his back, she ran towards him.

"Have you hurt yourself?"

He shook his head." Why is it that every time I am with you I am soaking wet?"

She had her hand over her mouth and all he could see was the laughter in her eyes.

"Let me help you up."

"I am not getting off my back until you listen to me."

She looked down on him; the laughter had gone from her eyes." I am sorry, I should have listened."

"Yes you should have, you should have also let me know about my son."

"I tried to, now you know I tried. You must know I tried."

"Yes, but there is one other thing that has to be cleared up Sarah and I am not getting up until you listen."

"Please get up, please get up."

"No I will not get up until you promise to marry me."

"You have never asked me."

He was stretched out on the grass, both arms flung out, still lying there he said,

"Please Sarah will you marry me?"

"Why?"

"Why? Because we love each other and we need each other, everything else will work out if we are together."

"What makes you think I love you?"

He lay there on the grass and was now shouting at her. "Are you saying you do not love me?"

"Do not shout at me, you," she floundered for an insult but none came.

He sprung up from where he had fallen, "Do not even think of calling me pompous."

"To near the truth for you, is it?"

He turned and started to walk away, then turned back and faced her.

"I love you and I want to marry you, the next move has to be yours."

He turned and started walking away from her, all the time praying, please God let her call me back.

She screamed at his back, "Yes."

He turned "Yes what?"

"Yes I will marry you and yes I do love you." She shouted back at him.

He turned and walked back to her as she threw herself at him and then they ran back to the baby and sheltered under the tree.

He put his hands out as if to explain, "Listen to me Sarah, please let me explain."

She would not let him, because she pulled him to her and they kissed there under the tree and clung to each other.

"I never knew, believe me, I never knew that you wrote to me."

She would not let him speak, she reached up and drew his head down and she was kissing him. They were breathless and laughing all at once.

"Let's get out of here we are soaking and by the looks of the baby he must be soaking as well."

He reached down into the pram and touched the baby gently on the cheek, "And what did you call our son?"

"Gordon Ross Shaw."

"Thank you,"

When she looked at him the tears were running down his cheeks, he could not speak but drew her close to him. They were now soaked through.

"Let's go to my place it is nearer."

They had to lift the pram between them because it would not run smoothly on the wet grass until they got to the path. They hurried along with one hand on the pram and the other arm round each other. Before they left the Park he kissed her again.

They never stopped until they were at the flat. Sarah lifted the baby out and Gordon carried the pram upstairs. As they turned the bend in the stair Sarah saw the flowers and the Teddy Bear.

"You were here then?"

"Yes I waited for about an hour and when you did not come, I went looking for you."

"I waited for you and then decided that maybe you would not be."

"I have been in court for most of the day."

She opened the door of the flat and they went in.

"I will have to see to your son first and get him dried. You will find trousers and a sweater of Archie's which will let you out of these wet clothes."

The baby was attended to and he watched her as she stripped him and then dressed him in dry clothes. Then she fed him and gave him to Gordon to give him his bottle.

He clung onto one of his father's fingers all the while that he sucked at the bottle. Gordon kept looking at Sarah and smiling. It was the most wonderful feeling and the tears were running down his face again. Sarah left them and changed into dry clothes.

Then she took the baby and settled him in his cot. All of a sudden she felt nervous again and went into the small living room and stood at the door.

They were staring at each other again. Which one moved first they never knew nor did they care? They were kissing each other with a fierceness that left them breathless. They held each other so tight that they could feel every part of the others body. He pushed her away and looked into her eyes.

"There is only one place for you and me right now."

"Where?"

"Where do you think, bed and the sooner the better."

They were hungry for each other and they went to bed. Later on he asked her,

"Did I ever tell you that I love you?"

"No, that was one of the problems, you did not and neither did I tell you.

When did you realise that you loved me?"

"That night when you sat at the fire drying your hair, remember we had got soaked at the beach. Seems to be a habit of ours, you wore that old bath robe, do you remember that."

"Oh yes Gordon, that night is burned in my brain, I will never forget that night. I was so frightened of you and yet I wanted to be with you."

"If I could go back and change things I would but you must believe me, you were never a 'Bet'. I had pursued you before the 'Bet' was made. The 'Bet' was first mentioned after we had coffee together

"Why was it made then?"

"I came back from having the coffee with you and they wanted to know what I had been up to when I was so happy. I told them that I had met someone who would not go out with me but I was trying hard. I told them that day that I was well and truly hooked. I told them that you were a lady and would not go out with me but I was working on it. That is the truth. Then they 'Bet' me a Fiver if I got you to go out with me, and a Tenner if I got you into bed."

"Why did you pursue me the way that you did?"

"Because you challenged me."

"I never did."

"Oh yes you did, you stared me out in the mirror the first night I met you, remember. When I dropped my eyes you smiled to yourself, because I looked back into the mirror. That was a challenge Sarah. When you went into the house you looked back at me."

"Yes you are right, I was hooked that night, well no, it was a bit of fun till I met you at the Bookshop and we went for a coffee. I walked you back to your office remember, that was it for me, remember you came back and kissed me on the cheek. Well that was it for me. I am hungry; we must get some dinner on."

"I will just have another helping of you."

"You will not, well not till I am fed."

The baby stirred in his cot and they went into the kitchen quietly.

He was astonished at how small it was and how homely it was. She moved the pram into the bedroom.

"I have to keep everything in its place to give me room." She realised that he was eyeing it critically.

"It has been a haven for me, my brothers bought it for me and Alison furnished it for me. The pram and cot were an extra gift from Andrew. I was in hospital nine months; it was the loneliest place to be. The boys and Alison were wonderful and they visited regularly but it was not them I wanted. Does that sound dreadful? "

"No I should have been there for you; you should have let me know. I did not make a 'Bet' in taking you out. You would not let me even speak to you. I should have persisted in trying to tell you that you were not a 'Bet'.

You should have let me know, I had a right to know, and if I was truthful I am furious with you for trying to cheat me. I have been miserable without you, nobody has ever meant so much to me, and we can go round in circles with this."

"I am sorry I really am, I should have lightened up, I take everything so seriously and when I did not get a reply to the letter, I tried so hard to put you out of my mind, but it was no use. I told you I had no experience of men but I really had no experience of growing up. I never learned how to flirt, how to have a laugh with the girls, maybe if I had I would not be so serious about everything. If it had not been for Lizzie," she smiled then.

"Why the smile, is Lizzie so special."

"Yes, Lizzie told me that I would know when I met that special person; she said the earth would move. When she asked me if the earth moved, I told her it exploded, I never knew you and yet the time I spent with you matters more than," she could not go on.

"Let's sort things out now. The first thing I had better do is make something to eat for us. What have you got in the cupboard?"

He opened the cupboard door and looked along the shelves, Baby food, baby cereal, baby drinks, there was plenty for the baby and very little for her. It suddenly struck him that there was a very obvious shortage of money. Once again he felt so guilty; he should have been there for her.

"I tell you what; let's settle things before we do anything else."

She nodded and kept looking at him. He put out his hand towards her and she took his hand that was all it took. She rose into his arms right away and they were kissing, they were breathless and laughing again.

"That's better isn't it?"

She nodded

"I will apply for a special license for us to be married, the sooner the better. You will marry me? You promised me."

She nodded again.

"Why don't we move into my flat until we get a house with a garden, would you like a house with a garden?"

"It's a dream."

"Well, you can have that dream. You are needing a good rest and well looked after."

"The boys and Alison have done their best; I cannot call on them all the time. I will feel better given time."

"Where would you and I be without the boys and Alison, I am not criticising them.

Will you leave everything to me and let me deal with everything until you are better?"

"Yes, I get tired easily but the doctor said that I will get my strength back soon."

"Right, let's stay here tonight and we can make plans and we will move tomorrow. Now off you go for a bath and I will get us a nice meal.

Once the baby was settled for the night, he left her going for a bath. He left and went to his favourite restaurant and explained that he needed an appetising meal for an invalid.

They made him up a tray of a variety of meals and he bought a bottle of wine. He set the small table and had everything ready when she came to the table.

"This is lovely and thank you for the roses." He served the meal and poured the wine.

"This will make me silly and giggly, remember the Minister," she laughed

"Drink it; I don't believe you are ever silly."

"I soon will be." Again she laughed.

He thought that she was still very nervous and decided that he must take this very easy. He noticed that she ate very slowly as if savouring every mouthful. When they were finished he leaned forward and took her hand.

"Is there anything bothering you now?"

"Yes two things, first I would like to say sorry for how I behaved when you were with your colleagues. Alison was appalled at how I behaved."

"Yes you did behave badly, I could not believe it, but nevertheless it did not put me off you. I did try to make up with you and maybe I did not try hard enough. That is all behind us and that is where it should stay. We have moved on and we will not go back there."

"Did I really hurt you badly?

"Of course you did, I will have you know that barristers are not used to people throwing beer over them. I tried to get a taxi home and the driver would not let me in his taxi. One smell of me was enough; he was of the opinion that I was drunk. You also left me a dithering wreck, and also with the knowledge that I was a pompous ass, which did not help my image at all." The tone of his voice changed and became angry.

"How could you believe that I would act like that, how could you? You thought I was a liar and a cheat. I would never treat anyone like that, I never have and especially you, how could you Sarah believe that of me?

"I am truly sorry Gordon, I was just trying to defend myself, I am truly sorry.

"So you should be but I will make you pay for that"

He was smiling again," what else is worrying you?

"Yes there is something, I had a difficult birth and they could not stop the bleeding I had to have cesarean section because the baby was becoming distressed. The bleeding would not stop and I had to go back to the theatre. They had to operate and, I can never have another child."

"Do you want more children?"

"You have to understand, I have brought up two families. I get the first lot up to teenagers and then my sister dies and I am left with Alison, who I put up for adoption. Once they placed her in my arms I could not let her go, so I have to start again and I love her so much. I love my baby so very much. I was having my baby adopted till I threatened a miscarriage and then I could not, I wanted my baby. On your own is such a lonely place to be. You have no idea how alone I was. I could be very content with one child now but could you?"

"The baby is a bonus to me, did I ever want children? I never really thought about it, till I started to realise that your baby could be mine. I felt pleased with myself, angry with you for not letting me know. Then you told me the baby was a girl, remember, around nine months old you thought. That wiped the smile of my face I can tell you. Yes I want my son but I do know that I want you more. Did you think that not having any more children would change my mind about marrying you? Do you think that would put me off? Do you know what I really want more than anything else?"

What?"

"I want to go to sleep with you every night, I want to wake up every morning with you beside me, I never wanted this with anyone else, just with you. When you speak about being lonely I know what you mean. I was so alone without you, I was busy with my work, I would talk and laugh with other people and yet I never felt so alone, as if I was on the outside looking in at other people's lives. I never felt like that with anyone else, if they did not want to be with me, I just shrugged it off and thought to myself 'their loss', but with you it was all my loss. I could not believe that I knew you for a week or so and yet I feel as if I knew you forever. Oh yes I know what being lonely is like, you taught me that, among other things."

"What else could I possibly teach you," she smiled as she said this.

"You taught me how to love and be loved, I never experienced that before."

He reached across the table and touched her cheek; she laid her cheek on his hand and put her own hand on top of his.

"Would you like me to show you how sorry I am about how I behaved."

"Yes you have to suffer so I think we could do with an early night."

He arched his eyebrow as he spoke and she started to laugh.

"Are you feeling better about everything now, tell me, how do you really feel?"

"I love you and our son so much, I am so happy and of course comfortable. I never thought happiness was for me, I always felt trapped in my parents' life and then my sister's, there never seemed to be a life of my own."

He laughed then, "Oh you are well and truly trapped now and I will spend my life making you comfortable, cheeky monkey, am I not a bit better than comfortable? Do you remember the night you told me you were comfortable. I was affronted, all these girlfriends you were told I had, always described me as wonderful."

"I remember well, you will just have to try and improve on comfortable."

They were laughing together and now relaxed with each other.

They went to bed and he held her close, "now show me how sorry you are."

He went into the office next morning; he had a busy day ahead.

"Good morning everyone, Christine my office, please."

His secretary was dreading this morning, she did not know if she still had a job.

"Right Christine, we are going to be very busy today, I need your help. Find out about a special license for getting married. Find me someone, who will move some things for me, I would need a small van. Get my mother on the phone for me shortly."

"Mr. Ross I am sorry about,"

"Let's leave it there, it was not all your fault, you were used, is he in, by the way."

"Yes nursing a black eye."

"Good."

He went through to Alison's office and knocked the door before opening it,

"Hello there, Sarah will phone you later on today and I will fill you in at lunch time."

"Is everything fine?"

"Yes, great, we are going to be married by special license; Sarah will fill you in when she speaks to you."

"I am so glad; the pair of you have made me a nervous wreck. I have been worrying all night."

"I don't think Sarah is really well yet, what do you think?

"No, I would agree but she nearly died, did you know."

"My God I never knew this; she only told me that she had a bad time."

"We were called to the hospital through the night, the boys came as well. It was a long night I can tell you. My mother died because the bleeding would not stop. We all thought that Sarah was going to be the same."

"What do you all think of me?"

"Oh Archie is going to bash your brains in, make no mistake about that. By the looks of John Morgan this morning I don't think you will be too worried."

"Is it bad?"

"Yes it is a smasher and he had it coming. By the way what do you think of my little cousin?"

"You mean my son, that's makes us related, how do you feel about that?"

"Don't ask," Alison laughed." I am glad for you both, let's face it has been a traumatic year for us all.

The day was over before they all knew it, Sarah met Alison and Gordon for lunch and they were all going to meet Gordon's mother and father for dinner. Sarah phoned Jimmy and Andrew. Jimmy assured her that he would let Archie know.

After lunch Sarah returned to the flat and a removal van and two men came to help her. She only needed to move at the moment the baby's cot, pram, high chair and all their clothes. She left her small flat neat and clean, as she turned at the door to look back at what had been her haven in a very difficult time. She felt just for a moment afraid to take the next step. She closed the door and decided that they would all discuss what they should now do with the flat.

Gordon's flat was massive compared to hers. There was plenty of room there and the most wonderful kitchen that she had ever seen. Two very large bedrooms and a large sitting room. The bathroom was also large and it had a shower, something that Sarah had never experienced before. Everything was very plain; it was not at all homely. For the first time in ages Sarah became interested. Once the cot was assembled, she put the baby down for his afternoon nap and she lay down on the bed for a rest.

The doorbell rang and she went and answered it, it was a delivery from a florist or so she thought. When she opened the box up there was one red rose and round the stem a small square box was attached. When she opened the box it was a solitaire diamond ring. At that moment the telephone rang,

"Hello."

"How are you, are you both well."

"Gordon the ring is beautiful and so is the rose, thank you very much."

"Don't worry of it does not fit, the jeweller will sort that out later for you. If you would prefer some other ring that is not a problem, I just wanted to surprise you."

"It is a perfect fit, it really is too much."

"Please let me spoil you, it helps me, please."

"Hurry home Gordon please."

She lay down on the bed just to rest while the baby slept.

The baby wakened her just in time to get ready to go to meet Gordon's parents. She wondered what they would think of her, would it be difficult and how would they feel about their Grandson

They arrived at Gordon's parent's home and Sarah was so glad Alison was there. As they got out of the car they looked at each other. Alison squeezed her arm as if to say everything will be fine.

Gordon carried his child into meet his mother and father and as he opened the door he shouted,

"We are here."

An elderly couple came to meet them, Sarah could not believe her eyes, and her friend from the Park was his mother.

"Don't be annoyed Sarah, somebody had to get you two together."

"I am not annoyed I am delighted."

Introductions were made all, Gordon's father took the baby,

"Well now Gordon Ross, the third, let me get a good look at you, yes Sarah, you have done well, fine grandson."

The ice was broken and they all sat down to a meal.

"Well now what are the wedding arrangements?"

"Mother don't start, we are being married as soon as possible and quietly with just our families, right. I told you Sarah, we have to watch her or she will be organising us all our life."

"Well if you are having just the families, have it here and let me arrange things for you, I am sure Sarah would like that."

They were all laughing and talking at once.

"Yes I would like that, Grace you go ahead."

"Right, paper and pencil," and off she dashed and came back with a notebook.

"Dad do something, stop her."

"If I could have done anything do you not think I would have done it years ago?"

Everyone laughed. They were all relaxed and happy and the evening went very well.

They talked about the coming wedding and when her brothers would arrive. Alison was to be bridesmaid and Gordon was going to ask Ian if he would be his best man.

"That would suit you Alison, wouldn't it?"

"You please yourself Gordon but he will expect me to turn up in rugby gear or have a football under my arm, he would not know a woman if he met one, him."

They all looked at each other, the outburst was unexpected. Gordon looked at Sarah and Sarah shrugged her shoulders.

"Is he giving you a hard time Alison?"

"No, I would not allow him to give me a hard time; anyway I am not bothered about him. He just wants his pals and that's just what he now has."

"Would you rather I did not ask him."

"No you must choose who you want, he will not bother me, I couldn't care less about Ian."

Everyone there knew that was not what she meant.

They left shortly afterwards because of the baby and they took Alison back to her apartment. Sarah promised to phone her tomorrow.

"What brought that outburst on, have you any idea."

"According to Alison he does not treat her like a woman, only like one of his pals.

Women don't like to be treated like 'one of the boys.'

"Is that a warning for me?"

She smiled at him then, she did now seem more relaxed.

The days prior to the wedding were busy and Grace had organised everyone and everything in sight.

Sarah went back to the flat for the rest of her clothes one night with Gordon. Alison had agreed to baby-sit. There was some mail and amongst it, was a note from the Bookshop.

It was to let Sarah know that they now had a vacancy.

"What's wrong Sarah, you look worried."

"No, I am not worried, the Bookshop have offered me some part time work."

"No, No Sarah I am not having that."

Sarah looked at him in disbelief.

"You are not having that; you are not even going to discuss it."

"No you are not working anymore. I am going to take care of you from now on."

"Oh are you? Well remember this, only if I let you. "

"On this Sarah I will have my way."

"Not with me you will not. You are not going to be my spokesman without consulting me. You are not going to bully me."

"Do not dramatise this Sarah, do not make an issue out of this. I only want to take care of you."

"No you want to control me, well sorry, no one will control me."

There was a heavy silence, neither spoke.

Sarah walked to the window, folded her arms across her chest.

"I was only thirteen years old, the last time I was bullied. I promised myself that I would not allow this to happen to my family or me again. I will not tolerate this. It is just as well I have not given up this small flat, isn't it?"

She turned to face him then, her eyes full of tears.

"I thought I was your family now, obviously not. You may not tolerate bullying, well I will not tolerate blackmail."

"Who is blackmailing you?"

"You are, must be your way or you will not marry me."

"I never said that."

"That is what you meant when you said; 'it is just as well I have not given up this small flat' is it not?"

"No, well yes, oh I don't know, you are twisting my words. Do not use your Barrister's tone with me; we are having our first quarrel."

"I thought we had plenty of those."

"Not since we settled things."

"I thought we had settled things between us, I thought we wanted to be together and that should come first, everything else must fit round that. So what is it going to be?"

He walked over to her and pinned her against the wall by the shoulders. She pushed him away but he caught her hands and held them against the wall. He started kissing her, and she turned her head from one side to the other to stop him. Then she stopped, and he kept kissing her and she would not respond. He stopped and started kissing her neck and then down to her breast.

"You really know how to fight dirty Gordon Ross."

"Don't I just, and remember I am trained to win."

He pulled her down onto the floor and she thought, what the heck does it matter, he can bully me like this anytime he likes.

"Sarah I would like to discuss with you the possibility that you will not work, that it would please me, if you would let me look after you."

He was unbuttoning her blouse as he said this.

"Liar, you just want to seduce me."

"Can I?"

"Yes, on condition that any decisions will be made by us both, and both of us agree that I should not work. Agreed?"

"Agreed."

They were now helpless laughing.

Alison wondered what kept them so long.

The boys all arrived the night before the wedding and they all came to Gordon's flat.

Andrew arrived first and with him, the young doctor that had nursed Sarah, her name was Claire.

"You kept this quiet," she laughed at him.

"Early days yet but I am on the right track."

Andrew and Gordon, from the minute they met became firm friends.

Then Jimmy arrived with Nancy, who was flashing an engagement ring round for all to see.

Sarah hugged her.

"Well we thought we might as well have a double celebration."

Archie arrived with Anne, they gave Sarah a hug, and then Archie said,

"Well where is he? I have promised myself I am going to bash his brains in, so get him in here."

"Everybody shouted "Archie."

"You step out of line boy and you are dead, I warned you," Anne ordered.

Gordon came into the room,

"Well here I am, might as well get it over with?"

Archie stretched out his hand and shook Gordon's hand.

"Well look, I didn't realise you were so tall, so, look after her and I settle for some food instead."

Everyone was laughing and the baby was being passed round when Alison arrived.

"Here comes trouble." Andrew said, as they all hugged her.

Gordon watched them all; they were so relaxed with each other. Sarah may have brought up two families and it must have been hard. The results were well worth all her efforts.

They squeezed in round the table for a meal and Sarah was the happiest he had seen her in a long time.

Alison was to stay with Sarah; Gordon was going to his parents. Lizzie, Davie and their son David were all to stay with them as well. The rest of them were staying at Alison's flat and Sarah's small flat. Nancy was coming to take the baby early in the morning and she would look after him all day. When they had all left, Alison cleared up after the meal and left Gordon and Sarah on their own for a while.

"Looking forward to tomorrow?"

"Yes but I have done nothing to help."

"You have to take it easy; don't worry your head about anything. I do not want you worried about anything. I will take care of everything."

They said goodnight, he kissed her on the cheek, Sarah felt it would have been better had they shook hands because it looked as if they were settling some business arrangement.

After he had left Sarah and Alison sat and talked for some time.

"Are you really happy Sarah?"

"I am really happy, but this attitude that I have to sit back and have everything done for me is making me angry. He is so bossy about it at times, I feel that I should salute him and carry out my orders, I suppose it is his work that makes him so, well, and bossy."

"You have to be sure about this."

"I want to marry him, I love him, and he loves me. I told him about the operation, and how I cannot have any more children. I just wanted to warn him, I felt that he had a right to know. I told him I was tired and I think he thinks I am tired all the time. I have to take it easy. I am not used to taking it easy.

He said it did not matter. He has wrapped me up in cotton wool and I am bored stiff with myself and with him at the moment."

Maybe you will have to learn to let Gordon make decisions for you. Think about it, you have always made most decisions for the family. What do you want? To make decisions about everything or would you not rather be with Gordon, it looks to me as if you may also have to learn to be happy, you have been unhappy lately. Everything will be fine after tomorrow; he is taking care of you. Learn that other people can be right as well as you Sarah."

"Am I getting a lecture?"

"Yes and you taught me to listen, so listen to me Sarah. Go and be happy, I wish someone would spoil me."

"I want this to be right; I will work hard at it. Let's get to bed before I go all melancholy.

Next morning Nancy arrived to take the baby away. Sarah and Alison went to the hairdressers and then came back to change. They were ready for Jimmy coming to take them to the church. They were admiring each other's dresses when the doorbell rang.

"That will be Jimmy." Alison said as she opened the door.

It was the florist with one red rose in a box tied with satin ribbon. Look what has come for you. Sarah opened the box and read the card. It was not for her it was for Alison.

"Here this is for you."

"For me, who sent that to me?" She read the card, 'to Alison, love Ian'

"Well what do you think of that, what I am supposed to make of this? What do you think?"

"I think he has been missing you, and you have been missing him, admit it."

"I will admit nothing on the grounds that it may incriminate me, it is a lovely rose."

"They laughed together and the doorbell went again. It was Jimmy this time with their bouquets.

"Ready ladies, you both look lovely and how is the happy bride?"

"Happy Jimmy, I really am very happy."

They arrived at the church and everyone was there. Both families and friends of Gordon's parents were already seated in the church. Lizzie and Davie were there with their son. As Mrs. Barr was now very frail, she had decided not to make the journey; Sarah had promised that they would visit her soon. Most of the office staff was there and people that Sarah was still to meet. Grace had organised everything.

The music started and Jimmy led Sarah down the aisle to Gordon who was waiting with Ian.

Sarah was to remark afterwards that she wished she could do a re-run in case she had missed anything it was all over so quickly. The Register was duly signed and amid congratulations Gordon said to Sarah.

"Well Mrs. Ross shall we lead everyone to the reception."

It was a lovely wedding and Grace had excelled herself. The baby was passed from one person to another and seemed to enjoy it all. They stayed and saw everyone off at night. Sarah went and spoke to Davie when he was standing on his own. She went over and put her arm through his,

"Now Davie, do you believe Lizzie about the earth moving."

He hugged her tight and said,

"Yes Sarah, she was right wasn't she. Am I forgiven now Sarah?"

"Yes Davie I was wrong, I was young but I have grown up now. I want you back as my friend."

"I was never away Sarah, Are you happy?"

"Yes I am and I know you are as well. We will still see each other, won't we?"

"Lizzie is trying to tell me that I could run my business from Edinburgh just as easily as Greenock and maybe it is time I made the break."

"Davie that would be wonderful, one way or another we will get together later."

Everyone was watching them and they all laughed together.

They were unable to have a honeymoon, as Gordon could not get a holiday because of Court work. The baby was staying with his grandparents to let Sarah and Gordon have the weekend to themselves.

Sarah went upstairs to tuck the baby in before they left, Grace came with her.

"Everything fine Sarah, are you happy?"

"Yes I am happy, I really am, but Gordon will not let me do anything, I am not used to being this idle."

"Everything will settle down, he is just trying to make up for what you both have lost. Learn to let him think he is having his own way, how do you think I have managed all these years." They laughed together over this.

"I tell you what, I will look after your son and you look after mine tonight."

They left shortly after everyone else and drove back to their home.

As they went along the road Sarah noticed that they had not turned to go back to the flat.

"Gordon, where are we going?"

"We are going to Northsands to the cottage; I thought you would like that."

"I would love that, do you remember our last time there?"

"I will never forget it. I was a nervous wreck with you, and no walking in the rain this time. Mother has put a box of groceries in the car boot for us."

Sarah never answered, she was thinking over the last time they had been to the cottage.

"Are you happy?"

"Yes, I was thinking of our last time at the cottage. How afraid I was and how happy I was. How can you be afraid and happy at the same time?"

"You were not afraid you were nervous; do not ever be afraid of me Sarah, please."

"You know what I mean, don't you."

"Yes, we will have a re-run, what do you think?"

"Yes please, a complete re-run. They both started laughing.

It was dark when they arrived at the cottage; the moon was full and reflected on the water, it was quiet and very peaceful. They went up the front path together arms across each other's waist. They turned and looked out over the water.

"You know Gordon I lived with this memory night after night and I thought it was lost to me. I was never as happy as I was with you that weekend. I never dreamed that it would all turn out so right." The tears were streaming down her face.

"I know what you mean, when I was down and I was so often down, I would relive our week-end. I wanted to bring you back here and we will come often with our son, he will love it here. This is special to us, I hate to admit it but I never brought any other girlfriends here, you are the only one I brought here. Now let's see if I can improve on 'comfortable.' "

They closed the door behind them as their laughter rang through the cottage

THE END.

Printed in Great Britain
by Amazon.co.uk, Ltd.,
Marston Gate.